This special signed edition is limited to 1000 copies.

Stories from the Plague Years

Michael Marano

Stories from the Plague Years

Michael Marano

Introduction
by John Shirley

Illustrations
by Gabrielle Faust

CEMETERY DANCE PUBLICATIONS

Baltimore
❖ 2011 ❖

FIRST EDITION
ISBN-10: 1-58767-218-9
ISBN-13: 978-1-58767-218-7
Cemetery Dance Publications Edition 2011

Stories from the Plague Years
Copyright © 2011 by Michael Marano
Introduction copyright © 2011 by John Shirley
Artwork copyright © 2011 by Gabrielle Faust
Typesetting and book design by Robert Morrish
All rights reserved. Manufactured in the United States of America

This book is a work of fiction. Names, characters, places, and incidents are either a product of the author's imagination or are used fictitiously. Any resemblance to actual events, locales, or persons, living or dead, is entirely coincidental.

Cemetery Dance Publications
132-B Industry Lane, Unit 7
Forest Hill, MD 21050
Email: info@cemeterydance.com
www.cemeterydance.com

"Displacement" appears here for the first time.
"Little Round Head" originally appeared on Gothic.Net, July 2001 issue.
"Changeling" originally appeared in *Last Pentacle Of The Sun: Writings In Support Of The West Memphis Three* (Arsenal Pulp Press, 2004).
"The Siege" originally appeared in *Queer Fear*, ed. Michael Rowe (Arsenal Pulp Press, 2000).
"Burden" originally published on Gothic.Net, March 1999 issue. Reprinted, *The Mammoth Book of Best New Horror 11* (Carroll & Graf, 2000).
"…And The Damage Done" originally appeared in *Outsiders: 22 All-New Stories From the Edge*, edited by Nancy Holder and Nancy Kilpatrick (Roc, 2005)
"Exit Wound" originally appeared in *Queer Fear II* (Arsenal Pulp Press, 2002). Reprinted on Gothic.Net, January 2003 issue.
"Winter Requiem" originally appeared in a shorter version in *Peter S. Beagle's Immortal Unicorn*, ed. Beagle and Janet Berliner (Harper/Prism, 1995). This novelette was serialized on Gothic.Net, October 1999 and November 1999 issues.
"Shibboleth" appears here for the first time.

Contents

Introduction: Michael Marano and the Forbidden
by John Shirley   9

Days of Rage
Displacement   15
Little Round Head   93
Changeling   107

Prayers for Dead Cities
The Siege   117
Burden   131

Two for Marian
...And The Damage Done   147
Exit Wound   163

Winter Tales
Winter Requiem   179
Shibboleth   203

Afterword & Story Notes   235

"Laura, illustre per le proprie virtù, e lungamente celebrata ne' miei versi, apparve la prima volta agli occhi miei, nel primo tempo della mia giovanezza, l'anno del Signore 1327, il giorno sesto di aprile, nell'ora mattutina, nella chiesa di Santa Chiara in Avignone; e in quella stessa città, nello stesso mese di aprile, nello stesso giorno, nell'ora medesima, l'anno 1348, quella luce fu tolta dal mondo, essendo io allora in Verona, ignaro ahimè! della mia sciagura."

–note scribbled by Petrarch in a copy of Virgil

For my Nanitchka, and for Bill…

Introduction
Michael Marano and the Forbidden

John Shirley

This is an age of sound bites, of the internet, of words flickering by on Twitter, of headlines scrolling by under talking heads; of videogames, youtube, and the little chat-room boxes people in which people hopelessly try to express themselves with something more than claustrophobic superficiality. This is not the age of long thoughts.

Michael Marano may be close to finding a bridge that could span the static-crackling void between the age of literature and the age of the internet. But if he is indeed trying to build that bridge—he's doing the forbidden. It's not really allowed.

It's not allowed, now, especially in writing that is rooted in genre, to have long thoughts, to explore visual descriptions with any depth. Basically what many people do now—sometimes some quite talented writers do this—is they make up their books (and films) out of Legos, out of prefab blocks and connectors, pre-existing tropes and premises and images, bits of their favorite movies and old books, and they click them together in "fresh" ways, form them into "new" shapes. I just saw an enjoyable, high-quality animated movie based on a book by a (very good) respected writer, which did just that. I had a good time watching that picture but, despite its pleasing gothiness, let's not pretend the writer and filmmaker were reaching for truly original imagery. I see the same in urban fantasy novels—perhaps in works of my own! And Lord Knows that's what the great spreading red puddle of the vampire genre is about—parasitism, ironically, on earlier writers.

Well. It's hard to be original. I wrote a very clever story recently—so I thought, but the editor I submitted it to claimed it was too much like a story from the 1970s by one EC Tubb. I may indeed have read that story, and forgotten it, and disgorged it, whole, in new terms. I don't know. But I do know, that's part of the struggle of being a writer, a search for originality—we're all products of our influences, our reading.

But writers like Marano transcend influences by merging their absorptions with honest impressions of the world around them; they're reflecting it, refracting it, through a theme darkly, and their observation, their distinctive interpretation, however surreal the form might seem, is what gives it verisimilitude, the satisfying quality of imagery impregnated by real life; this capacity for observation, this attempt to formulate an existential ballad in fiction, is what can save us from being in lifeless league with whichever "Octomom" of genre-writing is currently spewing books.

Marano really goes for it. He plunges in; he dives fearlessly down. And I'm telling you that, commercially speaking, at least in the *conventional* wisdom, this is usually not allowed.

But the conventional wisdom is often wrong—because it doesn't take into account talent and originality of vision; it doesn't take into account personal experience, lived and projected through the lens of art.

Marano is well aware of the ironies and underlying psychology of book publishing itself. He writes:

...doubt bowed in reverence to my new certainty as I tranced to the window display of a chain bookstore that doubled as a corporate coffee shop...I looked at the high-end hardbacks and paperbacks laid in a carefully posed jumble. There was no stated theme to the display, beyond the fact that all the novels had been released in the past week. Yet the cover of each book is a prayer. An idolatry to fear and sainted worry. Fear that the sacred home, and all the home implies and the goods it contains, might be violated, might be depreciated by the stigma of a bloody bootprint on its white carpets. The razor-wielding apes and speckled bands swollen with poison that stalked the sitting rooms of more than a century ago are reborn as diabolical killers, Dark and Shadowy Men given new expression as fiends suitable for defeat by Sandra Bullock, Ashley Judd or Angelina Jolie in the inevitable film adaptations...

We see a number of characteristics on display here—one is Marano's being steeped in popular culture, old and new. This is one end of the bridge I mentioned. Another is the ironic tone, however grim, and the quick intensity of the imagery, which is very modern: the other half of the bridge.

We also hear *voice*. This is the mark of a writer coming into his power—he shows a capability for immersion in voice, in the merging of point of view and narrative. It is apparent when he writes, much later in this book,

The smoke was beautiful the way that only things that herald death can be, haloed by swirls of crows we were thankful we couldn't hear.

Or, this, voice about voice:

A mirror of steel is silent, as are the ghosts I still feel each day as I walk streets that plague has emptied. Ghosts, like reflections in steel, have only the voices we give them, even though what they speak is theirs alone.

None of this is allowed, of course. It's not permissible to think elaborately, to look for real poetry in nightmare. Horror is only to shock—not to express. You're trying to be *expressive* with horror? Shocking!

Nor is it encouraged to write frankly about drug users, and street people, as if they were, in fact, the people right down the street that you pass every day. The lost people all around you. Marano dares to do it, as if Hubert Selby were working in dark fantasy. And in breaking the rules, he engages in a synthesis that may just get him notice, may make his work stand out in the pounding surf of genre literature, like one of those luminous, gelatinous creatures that scared Lovecraft as he stared aghast at a New England oceanside.

So let this gaping beast of a book consume you.

You'll find yourself looking out of its eyes, as you swim through subterranean depths. And suddenly find yourself back on the midnight streets of your hometown.

Displacement

I didn't decapitate Catherine.

I liberated her from her body, trespassing on her self-inflicted inner wound… doing her the favor of pulling it to the tangible. She hated her body with the spite a mother saves for an unwanted child—because her body, in its arrogance, never fit the carefully purchased fiction of her life. She punished herself for being fat, though she was translucent-thin from a lifetime of shifting physical hunger to trinkets she could buy and people she could control.

With one thankful stroke (*thankful*, in that only one stroke was needed), I rewrote the fiction she'd so foolishly bought. New, red words defaced the *Sex and the City* calendar that hung in tribal-mask adoration over the Norwegian pine table in her breakfast nook, blurring calligrapher-precise notes made in peacock blue fountain pen. Rude, thick words, darkening, rewrote the still-life tableau of the lone espresso she'd made for herself just before my arrival, marked the perfect twist of lemon rind resting beside it on Italian porcelain that she'd first shown me years ago, when she'd theatrically unpacked the set to which it belonged. Cooling ink blotted the covers of the book she'd placed beside the espresso, so she could preach to me the marketed Truths the book asserted. All that stayed legible of the back cover copy was the idolatrous bold type prayer: "*She seemed to have it all…*"

I stood in the lifetime of half-seconds, in the muted *between* that vista'ed from one beat of her Pilates-strengthened heart to the next, taking in the entirety of her kitchen, her home into which she invited me in the way that legend says one should *never* invite the un-living. And I saw that Catherine had nothing, that she was owned by all she thought she owned.

So it was a *good* thing I did for her. A benediction wholesome as St. Francis's forsaking his life of comfort to wash the sores of lepers.

True, it was good for me as well—maybe the most intense moment of mutual gratification we'd shared. As her frail and spurting prison fell, *I* was liberated, too. Liberated from the rage I'd just felt and the stone-heavy hatred for her that had pressed inside me for years. Both rage and hate dissipated like smoke, and at last I knew without distraction the good things my heart held for her. I felt light as the avatar I'd become, ghost-dense as those in trances are said to feel as they let divine spirits speak through them.

I needed Catherine to understand I was helping her, to understand the baroque theater she'd invoked by inviting me here. So while her eyes dimmed, I held her by her delicate jawline (and not by her strawberry blonde hair perfumed with the conditioner and shampoo she'd used since before we were lovers), and showed her the still-breathing mass that had been distasteful to her for so long.

In my dusk-trance, in my *becoming* her longed-for demon of the vindictive ex-lover, I held her level to the catharsis of my sight, freeing her from her vanity. I shared my view from my apotheosis as myth and let her see her own painfully distant thinness. I let her see that she'd exceeded the fäery-slightness she'd always thought beyond her reach. The body she rejected lay where it had fallen beneath hanging expensive cookware she never used. For the first time, she saw herself outside the tyrannical, mirror-defined view of her life that had held her hostage, saw that her starved flesh was worthy of forgiveness.

I turned her face to mine. Her eyes, clear and blue, were losing their glimmer as beads do when they become scuffed and dusty. I smiled, letting her know in those desperate seconds that all was forgiven. And that I still loved her.

Her lips moved, sweetly, trying to speak. I thought of carpenter ants I used to catch, how their jaws flexed as I hurled them into a spider's web or steadied them for the Truth of the sun focused through a magnifying lens.

And that was when, as I was fixed by her lorelei gaze, the police charged and ground me against the refrigerator, which wasn't necessary, as I'm not a violent person.

Tackled from transcendence, shoved back into earthly, bruising flesh, I cried out as I was pinned against cold white metal. I cried out at the injustice that my final instant with Catherine should be violated—that the last thing she'd feel would be pain—because the rough blow of the policemen had made me drop her to the wet linoleum floor.

Through streaked vision, I saw pictures Catherine had taped to the refrigerator of models from the Victoria's Secret catalogue: motivational reminders for her to stay away from food, to own her body the way she wished to own it.

And she'd been thinner than those models were.

Nightsticks came out.

Soon I was unconscious.

Displacement

—You're very sick, Dean.

As he spoke, the gaze of the mirror touched us: a fourth wall blinding us to our audience as would stage lights. In blinding us, it took the place of our audience. My twin, my hypocrite brother, lurked behind the mirror and the whirring lens that watched just past the mirror's dead, silvered gaze.

—You shouldn't make judgments like that. It's not conducive to good patient/therapist dialogue.

Doctor Johansson was my court-appointed psychiatrist. His statement about my health (said without preamble) raised the curtain on this, the Second Act of our one-room drama. This was when I'd midwife things forward. When I'd make palimpsests of our First Act for those who'd have access to records of our exchanges only from this moment on, due to the red tape thickets of court bureaucracy. By now, Johansson was used to my hijacking his professional rhetoric (even, at times, setting his own rhetoric aside). He struck me as a nice person who knew to not take my *Doctor Phil*-flavored parries personally. He wore on his tweed sleeve his rich liberal's need to help people like me. His voice was soothing and unsettling, like HAL's in *2001*. (—*I really think you should you take a stress pill and think this over, Dave.*) Thoughtful sessions of white wine and NPR programming no doubt filled his evenings, and World Music no doubt filled his CD collection, stacked alphabetically on a teak rack from Pier One. Past his Brahmin demeanor glowed a warmth incongruous as the big, Mr.-Potter-from-*It's-a-Wonderful-Life* wooden desk he sat behind in this sterile, fluorescent-lit room. By his desk squatted a dishwasher-sized air filter that seemed placed to pull smoke from the grandfatherly pipe he never lit, but always held.

—I have your medical records here, Dean.

—You spoke to Doctor Baker, back home? How's he doing? I said, for the benefit of the polite mirror that, unlike any other audience, wouldn't cough or shift chairs. And for the benefit of the underpaid hacks and interns at CourtTV who'd never get access to the files Doctor Johansson held, but who should know the name and location of Doctor Baker for the sake of a supplementary interview or two.

—I didn't speak to Doctor Baker. The records were faxed last night by your lawyer.

—I…left instructions they should be made available if I were arrested.

I shifted noisily in my as-yet-to-grow-warm metal chair and smiled; my chest twinged, as if I were waterlogged from a day of swimming. Things dimmed, the way they do when you step into the shadow of a great church on a sunny day. Seated, I crossed thresholds again…perhaps this time, not alone.

Doctor Johansson chewed his lip that clearly craved the stem of his pipe.

—You planned? For your arrest? We'd thought it was your lawyer's idea to send the records…

—No. Mr. Seltzer followed my instructions. I try not to do anything slipshod.

The lighting of our little one-room drama continued to dusk in my sight as I inflected my role, and floated my lawyer's name to our silver-eyed audience… my public defender's name was in the papers. The mirror is a hungry audience, even when a camera doesn't lurk behind it. Its gaze is a prison that never blinks. And it's ever-greedy to see and to inflict wounds. Torn bodies. Torn psyches. The mirror savors both. So does the lens, and the mirror-dulled eyes the lens summons.

—*Slipshod?*

—You have my records. I'll be dead by spring. No time for subpoenas and all that Paul Drake stuff.

—Ahh…Paul Drake?

—He's the detective Perry Mason hired to do leg work.

—I see. About your cancer…

—I feel fine. Thank you. My digestion's okay. But I should be on a bland diet. Then it's weeks before my stomach, pancreas and liver give out.

—And you know, he said, running his thumb along the folder holding my medical records as if testing the keen of a razor, —that there's no way to get your case to trial before you die.

I'd known Doctor Johansson was no fool before I'd met him, and had researched who'd likely be assigned my case, should I be arrested in the jurisdiction in which I had been. His few publications were quite good, and his dissertation was better than the limp-dicked work of his graduate advisor. He understood, though not the way I did, that the Second Act curtain had been raised. It was time for our interaction to change as would that of two smoking-jacketed characters in an Ibsen play. So he stated the obvious, referring to the figurative pistols we'd placed on the mantel in our First Act. He knew he had to be bluntly certain of the implications of what we were saying, and to gauge how to adjust his interaction. As would any actor, for whom *listening* is the most vital skill, I followed his cue.

—Doctor, I knew that before I started to…

There was a sound behind me, like the swift *click-click* of dog claws. I whipped my head back and, as always, saw nothing… and as always, scolded myself for looking when I knew I'd see nothing. I'd not even caught a shadow-glimpse in the silvered eye that framed our modest stage; the mirror disdained reflecting even the change of light that shaded my vision. I turned back to Doctor Johansson and said, —I may not be dead by then. But I'll be too sick to stand trial.

—Dean, what were you looking for just now? Behind you?

He spoke the way a Dad would to a confused child. A final sip of the vintage Rogerian therapy exchanges we'd shared throughout our First Act in this glorified closet of dirty-chalkboard-colored cinderblock and linoleum, begun when I'd first been delivered here in my orange and silver raiment as Doctor Johansson stood like a gentleman to greet me from behind his mahogany stockbroker's desk.

—Thought I heard something. Sounded like a dog. Maybe a guard dog. Sorry. I'm kinda jittery here.

All I told him was true, though I didn't tell him the dog in question sounded to be walking on two feet.

—Ah. I see. Dean?

—Yes?

—Why did you kill those people?

—They killed me first.

He jolted, like a man awakened on a subway to find he's gone past his stop. He'd asked me that question many times, with many inflections, over the past week. Each time I gave no answer. I think he'd been ready to give up, and had re-asked the question just now as the same kind of farewell we'd just given to our Rogerian interaction, of a kind once quaintly cherished by gin and valium-fogged '60s housewives. In answering, I'd taken off my mask of recalcitrance, and had put on another mask that was much older, and potent.

He collected himself, re-took his own priestly mask of the cool clinician and asked, —*How* did they kill you first?

—They gave me cancer.

—How…did they give you cancer?

I drank a deep breath and carefully chose my words, knowing he expected a rant about microwave towers and tin-foil hats. The feeling of being waterlogged left me. The jig of dead shadows in my sight stilled.

—By making me miserable for so long. By filling me with self-loathing for years. By denying me so much sleep, peace and well being that my body devoured itself.

I sighed, as if a splinter had been pulled from my psyche.

Tension, poison crowding my chest and throat like wet black fur. Quiet violence steeping my heart—thoughts of the arguments I should have had, the things I'd been coerced and manipulated to do.

The end of a typical day for me: the world grown large and me overwhelmed like a child within it. With no outlet or recourse save that which I had cut from my self in order to despise it for my weaknesses.

Pathetic. Useless. Helpless.

I gag on these feelings now, and the feelings of dread that washed over me each time I cracked my eyes to a new day, still tired from the riot of dreams that had bludgeoned my sleep, my jaw and teeth sore from the endless grinding I suffered through the night.

—The people you killed...*stressed* you, so that you developed cancer?

—Stress causes disease. What they did to me was...*is* murder.

Doctor Johansson reached for a lighter that was not on his desk, closed fingers on air, rubbed his thumb against his index finger as if to strike the flint. The thumb of his left hand pressed nothing into the bowl of his pipe. The prop that gave him an air of authority may not have been prop, but relic. The air filter by his desk, with an intake vent the color of old teeth, hinted that he once smoked here in defiance of state ordinance.

—You shouldn't smoke near someone as sick as I am, I said helpfully.

—From what you tell me, it shouldn't matter if I smoke or not.

Touché, I thought, as he placed the pipe between his teeth, and after a moment, removed it.

—You killed ten people to avenge your own death ahead of time?

—I can't set things right *after* my death. I don't believe in ghosts, not the Dickens kind that get things done. And what I did wasn't revenge. It was balancing the scales.

—Then why did you kill in the ways you did? Why were you so...
—Creative?
—Extravagant.
—There had to be meaning to their deaths. If their deaths had no meaning, my death would have no meaning. Then my life would have no meaning.
—Revenge for the cancer isn't meaningful enough?

There was no judgment in his voice: a true professional, so rare in this world.

—No. Even children have a sense of revenge. It's a basic instinct. But *Justice* requires a sense of art. Like art, Justice has to challenge. It has to intrude on preconceived notions.
—I don't follow.

My words fell from my mouth as would stones.

—I killed those people in ways that reflected how they'd killed me, or ways that reflected fundamental Truths...Truths from On High or from deep within those I killed... that could cut through their senses of comfort. That would let me reclaim the hijacked power they'd asserted over me. I had to challenge what they'd imagined to be safe for them, because they'd challenged and warped my sense of being safe in my own body.
—I...very much...need an example. Please.

His judgment-less request *obliged* me to speak of how I'd passed Judgment. My throat clotted. This was much harder than I'd thought it would be, no matter how many times I'd prepared to cross this threshold, when I would have to make known and then cast aside the turmoil that had driven me to reap lives. Strong emotions *hurt* as they are released. Even emotions like love hurt. Yet unless I purged what was inside me, I'd never be free of it. It would latch to me beyond my pine-coffin escape in Potter's Field. If I escaped still burdened, I'd not truly be free.

Doctor Johansson wished to understand my trespasses... the mask I wore, the avatar I'd become. Invading the senses of safety of others is unsafe for the trespasser as well. To explain all would lead Doctor Johansson into these unsafe places with me. Did I have the right to do this, to a man who held no ill will toward me?

I choked down the blood-warn scree in my throat.

—All right, Doctor. I'll give you an example. Professor Molino was a two-faced son of a bitch. He was a liar and a fraud and he could have better served us both by telling the truth. But because he was such a manipulative, shifty-eyed snake he ruined two years of my life. Just took them away from me, for *nothing*. Nothing but his own niche in that Political Science department he thought he ruled.

Sickness, outrage, as Molino greased me with that half-living gaze of his, his left eye never fixing on me, but afloat, drifting in the welling of clear gel that congealed under his lids. His one dead eye was less animated than were the smooth, stone and metal eyes of the Great Western Thinkers whose busts adorned the shelves of his office along with gimcrack Doric column bookends of plaster.

"I'm recommending you be dropped from the program, Dean." Each word is like a blow. Not random, like the blows I'd landed on a face more like my own than that of any child I might father. But precise as those of a martial artist.

"*Dean.*" How fucking dare he use my first name now? As a weapon? For two years it's been "Mr. Garrison," and now as he brings down the axe, he wants to be a friend? All his reassurances amounting to a mouthful of shit, the scalding flood of memories of his "grooming me" to be one of his prized students making me loathe myself for being so gullible. Molino is throned before me, sitting in complete comfort into his own paunch. Even his face sits.

"*Why?*" The word is a choked whisper. As a choked whisper spoken by another, the word would haunt me in a way that would rewrite this moment.

"You're not qualified to be a student here, certainly not in the graduate program. It's doubtful you'd be qualified to be an undergraduate at this university. For two years, you've been conning this department into thinking you're a competent scholar. But competence is beyond you. You demonstrated that when you first came here."

I stand in this arena of career execution, the rules of this terminal game unknown to me. Livy and Lorenzo Valla look down in disdain from their perches behind Molino. With his affected Noel Coward diction, Molino refers to the grades of my first semester, when I'd come to this university exhausted, having had a full class load throughout the summer while working forty hours a week. For a year and a half, he's told me these grades would have no bearing on my career. Now he's done with me, and this ace comes into play.

I'd been given warning letters to improve my performance, which I had. But now, according to the head of the Graduate Division, these improvements weren't enough…despite Molino's hand-on-my-shoulder assurances that he'd gone to bat for me at the academic review sessions.

Displacement

I know he's betrayed me, and I feel like cackling. The man's academic specialty is Machiavelli, whose bust presides over the infamous overstuffed leather sofa that dominates the wall to my left. It's the sofa on which a number of female grad students and undergrads had come to deeper personal and intellectual understandings with Molino. It's the sofa on which desperate prospective new faculty members were invited to sit during campus interviews; once the candidate had sunk deeply into the cushions, Molino would invite the paschal lamb to help himself or herself to coffee from the porcelain service baited across the room. Molino and the other Inquisitor faculty would judge the suitability of the candidate based on how gracefully he or she could rise from the sofa.

It's too sick to acknowledge, this man's nature and his field of study. But why am I worth the effort of crushing *now*?

"This department does not have any more time to waste on you. You are a distraction and a liability."

My mind screams: "THEN WHY HAVE YOU TOLD ME THAT I'M YOUR GOLDEN BOY?! WHY THE FUCK HAVE YOU STARTED GUNNING FOR ME AT EVERY OPPORTUNITY?"

I instead bow to the totemic power of this office. This chapel. I genuflect to the Great Tomes on his shelves. The staid Ivy League mustiness of the carpet. Even the yellowing rolls of thick newsprint he's placed among his books to suggest Roman scrolls. He wears the place as a cloak of earthly and spiritual power the way that Borgia popes wore their robes.

My voice defies my screaming mind and whispers: "I think I understand, sir."

"I'm glad of that. There's no reason to protract this unfortunate situation. It should not be more complicated than it need be."

His upper lip does not move as he speaks words of cutting emptiness; his still lip and shaggy moustache make him look vaguely like a rabbit. His dripping eyes float with his gaze, and I realize I hate his eyes. Poe's "Tell Tale Heart" murmurs to me of how an unsightly eye can drive someone to murder. With that thought, the fine wood clock in the corner beside Petrarch ticks in my awareness with the rhythm of water dripping in a pan.

"Will I be awarded the master's degree?"

"You've earned the master's. In theory. It's reflected on your transcript. In spring, you'll have it as a consolation prize."

The clock's metronome dirge continued as I turned and passed under the guard of Dante by the door.

I signed for a letter the next week informing me I'd not be awarded the master's degree. I was numb as I read it, too dazed to feel Molino's *coup de grace*.

Later, in the kind of sympathetic exchange tinged with gloating that is the jellied backbone of academia, I was told by one of the younger faculty members that at the last meeting of the year, Molino had urged I not be granted the master's, that to award it to me would invalidate the credibility of the department and the university. The young faculty member, in his tenure-track largesse, paid for the coffee at the end of our meeting. I stared at the brown rings dried in my cup long after he left.

To compound the humiliation, I couldn't pack up and leave; I had to linger through the exam period to come away with credits for the courses I'd paid for. I dangled. Inert as the Hanged Man in a Tarot deck.

I was deadwood in Molino's reign. Disowned. Errant. Over my last weeks at the department, I figured out, through asking the right questions and eavesdropping at the right moments, that Molino had big plans: he'd petitioned the University to hire away from Harvard a Professor Herliman, a grad school friend of his who'd become a luminary in Early Modern political theory. News of Herliman's move virus'ed through academia, and sterling applications to the Political Science department flooded in.

Molino would lap up Herliman's overflow. Therefore I, and his other chaff-students doing unorthodox research at his behest, had to be jettisoned in favor of the new crop. Each of us he cast aside were unable to secure the letters of recommendation needed to go on.

Two years of my life made ash in a graduate program with nothing to show for it. Two years of my life exiled in a shithole college town with nothing to show for it, all for a petty tyrant's inflated ego. A man who'd lied to me, knowing I was expendable, that if the research I did proved unfashionable, he could be rid of me. But if it turned out well, he could cry to the world how he'd fostered my brilliant young mind.

A man who knew I could be flushed when better prospects to jack his reputation came along.

I carry defeat like lead beside my liver.

—And when you killed Molino, you reflected his two-faced nature?

No trace of tension in his voice. In his position, I don't know that I could be so calm.

—*Brought forth* might be more accurate than *reflect*.

Displacement

—By taking a machete and giving him two faces, literally?

He spoke as one would ask, *May I come in*? I granted him entry to my trespasses.

—No. Splitting his face gave him two halves of a face. What I'd tried to do was fit a two-sided mirror in the wound, so each half-face would find a whole in the reflections. But I couldn't get the mirror to stay in the bloody groove.

After hours near the campus, on an errand in the college town I hated. It was twilight: a time not defined by the setting of the sun, but by the shift from the vespers-shuffle of students bearing spine-curving book bags to the chugging of fortress-like SUVs, their rear windows reflecting the flicker-glow of backseat DVD players sedating trophy kids just picked up like laundry parcels from daycare.

I walk familiar streets unburdened by thick tomes, just a small valise. I worry I'll be recognized. But though I see people I've taken classes with, I'm unnoticed. The face of one tossed out of grad school is a sight resented by other grad students. Bit by bit, the offending sight is pushed into invisibility, much like the long-vacant house of a suicide on a sunny street.

Sandwich shops I used to frequent are now grooming salons for men and women. Massage and aroma-therapy suites have replaced a used bookstore. The wheeled suburban homes that are minivans thin out as I catalogue the changes to the town. I babble to my cancer, muttering things like, "*Soon I'll have some payback for you*," and "*I'm going to set right the reason you exist, yes indeedy*," to distract myself, to keep from backing out. I walk the streets, full of the deep-gnawing uncertainty that has caused my very cells to shark my flesh. I half hope that I might get lost in my thoughts and miss Molino in his office, and thus recuse myself from vengeance.

I carry the doubt in my marrow, until I come to a reliquary of that which will keep me safe throughout my crusade of Justice and righting of Karmic wrongs. Over the span of a breath, doubt bowed in reverence to my new certainty as I tranced to the window display of a chain bookstore that doubled as a corporate coffee shop, a place like one in which I'd worked as a humiliated puppet in another life, when a future with options still seemed to stretch before me. I looked at the high-end hardbacks and paperbacks laid in a carefully posed jumble. There was no stated theme to the display, beyond the fact that all the novels had been released in the past week. Yet the cover of each book is a prayer. An idolatry to fear and sainted worry. Fear that the sacred home, and all the home implies and the goods it contains, might be violated, might be depreciated by the stigma of a bloody bootprint on its white carpets. The razor-wielding apes and speckled bands swollen with poison that stalked the sitting rooms of more than a century ago are reborn as diabolical killers, Dark and Shadowy Men given new expression as fiends suitable to for defeat by Sandra Bullock, Ashley Judd or Angelina Jolie in the inevitable film adaptations. These killers don't merely kill. Mere killing is *vulgar*, suitable for dank bars that are shown on the evening news to be full of lowlifes who might deserve to die. These mythic killers disrupt. They crack foundations. Their power to induce sweat-sweetened worry is as primordial as their capacity to induce delight. The books in the window are a sacred pandemonium. A wallow of bourgeois trinkets intended to be taken home and ultimately reaffirm the home's safety and sanctity. But only after an investment of anxiety is offered, like the church testimonial of a hypocrite, to the shadowy figures on the books' covers…ominous as the silhouettes on Neighborhood Crime Watch signs. Lush homes with single lights left on in attic windows adorn several covers, hinting of victims inside awaiting the arrival of the Mythic Killer the same way a lascivious old aunt in an Edwardian melodrama would await her lothario. Other covers show family photos with the glass of their frames cracked, dashed to lovely hardwood floors cluttered with the remnants of violence. A bloody handprint on the window of a country cabin. A young woman whose frightened eyes are held in the sliver of light that strikes the ornately molded closet door behind which she peers.

The stimuli of the covers are Pavlovian as the glowing, gaunt-cheeked faces on magazine covers that beam next to article teaser-lines like "Pathogens in Your Handbag?" The books nurture a loving blend of envy and worry: envy for their comfortable settings and the lifestyles of their protagonists, and worry that those settings and lifestyles might be invaded. The delicious treat awaiting the buyer is the re-assertion of normalcy after the Shadowy Men have accepted the adulterous invitation to trespass. The books are narcotics, as carefully marketed and tested as the soothing greens of the carpets between the bookstore shelves and the opiate greens on the logo of the coffee mugs sold in the adjoining cafe.

The sight of the books, totems of what I would channel, crystallized a kind of armor around me. I felt safe—a walking vessel of potential. Where doubt had been, the dark angel of our times now entered, much in the way New Age charlatans are said to take their Atlantean and Alien "Walk-Ins."

I turned from the reliquary, and saw with a quiet laugh that a theatrically fine rain had begun to fall. The town I hated acknowledged my return in a way no former colleague on these streets could. I cloaked myself as a shadowy figure, a Dark Man backlit by halogen street lamps as I entered the walled campus. My shadow was long and looming on the beaded grass as I looked up and saw that the light was still on in Molino's office.

I used my old key to enter the department, and climbed the gorgeous oak staircase, leaving damp footprints with secondhand shoes bought that afternoon from a vintage store. Portraits of former department chairs looked at me with contempt. I was an excised tumor returning to their sacred body. I expected a rush of memories as I walked to Molino's door. But I had tunnel vision, focused only on the task ahead.

I knocked, unsure if the ache in my stomach was a last twitch of nerves or the cancer that nursed on my guts.

"Come in."

The room had changed. Molino had changed.

His new wife, a former student less than half his age, had made her loving Electra mark. I'd expected to walk towards Molino's desk under the eyes of intellectual Patriarchs, not under eaves of ferns hanging rain forest-like from the ceiling. Gone were the oak-browns, blacks and greys. The colors of sand and deep-forest moss dominated the room. Through surgery or exercise or both, Molino had less of a paunch to sit into. His bottom-feeder face had become even less expressive. His mustache was trimmed. When his awful gaze focused on my face clumsily, the way an infant's gaze finds the eyes of a stranger standing above its crib, it was as if it was a struggle for his face to express the disdain he wished it to.

"Mr. Garrison," he said, his voice accentuated by the gurgle of the tranquility fountain by his desk, "I think you should leave."

I don't know why he said that. Perhaps others he'd screwed over had confronted him at night. Maybe scenes like this were something a crawling shit like him got used to.

I dropped my shoulders, gave him the body language of submission, the posture of a whelp backing from a grey alpha wolf, in this, his forest-themed office.

I reached in my overcoat, closed my fingers around the damp wood handle.

I've no memory of bringing down the machete, only of the blow's shuddering up my wrist and the twinge it cracked in my elbow. There was connection between us, a *current* passing through the blade that tingled in the brass rivets of the handle.

His eyes still had their air of authority, though his right brow arched, as if some aspect of him were offended by the awful Truth that he was not a Prince, infallible in his reign, offended that he was nothing more than a fuck whose time had come. The death rattle seeping from his split mouth sounded like an objection, a refusal to accept the situation. The trickle of his expiring incontinence made harmony with his tranquility fountain. His face at last found its desired expressiveness as his severed, botox-soothed muscles contracted and relaxed.

At last, with his wandering left eye separated from its twin by a steel blade, his gaze didn't offend me.

—There was nothing about a mirror in the police report.
—Pardon?
My body had gifted me with the memory of how it had felt to glide to Molino's desk, to move like a breeze with ecstatic, ballet precision, and kill by way of symbol *as* a symbol. I knew as I crafted his wound that many people walk away with injuries more dire than what I inflicted. Molino was hurt, thought not as hurt as he'd be by a windshield striking him at sixty miles per hour. He *could have* lived. He *could have* required another blow from my blade. But I'd become aware of myself as we were joined by the machete. I was aware of how I would look from the campus lawn below: a shadowy, irresistibly dark figure framed in the window of a comfortable space on a rainy night. *That* was the instant I'd felt Molino die, the instant that the vibration of the handle soothed with his surrender to the symbol of his wound, to the flattery of the wound's baroque iconography. It was the instant his flesh accepted as fatal that which his Id-deep imagination had dreaded and welcomed, as if his body were a fetish doll I'd stabbed with pins.

—The police report on Molino's death mentioned nothing about a mirror.

His hand rested on a file at the far left of his desk; I guessed it was the file holding the report. It was as if Doctor Johansson tested the reality of the file as its contents were proving to be untrue or incomplete. How disconcerting it must be, to face the fallibility of what on cop shows provides irrefutable plot points and exposition.

I smiled as my arm twinged an echo of what it had felt through the handle of the machete.

—That's no surprise. The cops in that town never have to deal with anything worse than a co-ed getting her purse snatched. Place makes Stepford look like Fort Apache. Before I left Molino's office, I spread fake evidence… cigarette butts with lipstick on the filters, a surgical glove, photocopies from the *Satanic Verses* for the sake of old-fashioned, pre-9/11 paranoia. I left the mirror in Molino's office closet. Probably still there.

—It could be.

He lifted his hand from the offending file, put the cold, smokeless pipe back in his mouth and rubbed his palms. The lens that would allow my hypocrite brother to watch our Second Act recorded all that we said from behind the one-way glass that dominated the east wall. It will be the one-day foundation of my twin's perhaps Stanislavsky-based performance. Even with such a complete record, transcribed from videotape by an intern from the Psychology department of the nearby state college, all the information I just presented to Doctor Johansson would have to be sorted and analyzed in new reports he'd have to file in triplicate. I'd just increased Doctor Johansson's investment in our drama. My hypocrite twin will use the drama of this one-room setting to craft further drama. Aristotle taught us that drama cleanses. But at a price: participation. Investment. I craved, I *earned*, the full catharsis of this theater. I needed such cleansing to complete my pauper's grave escape. I increased my investment to match that of Johansson's.

—It's from Dante, I told him…in hard and shadowed words.

The air trembled in the gel of my eyes, as if from the heat of a furnace.

—Pardon me?

I found, even as the shaking air took the aura of a late summer field about to know a hail-bringing storm, that I felt a certain loneliness. Doctor Johansson's judgment-free questions, so short and uninvolved, made me miss his more active conversation. The catharsis of this theater brought a kind of isolation. I might isolate myself further as I added detail to the mask I wore.

—My ideas about Justice and how it needs to be poetic. In *The Inferno*, the punishments of the damned fit their crimes. Gluttons wallow like pigs, tyrants boil in rivers of blood. Dante struck me when I read him. His vision of Justice is very profound. Beautiful.

My words further changed the space of our drama the way aromatic woods burned as offerings change a place of worship. The words, unlikely by virtue of their dramatic force, made themselves more likely by my speaking them.

—I've never read Dante, he said. But I've meant to. Could you explain more?

How would my twin nurture his own work when he viewed the tape of this exchange? I wonder if he, through his craft, could feel or express the river-ice fragility of the reality I knew… the reality I crafted that allowed me to speak as I did without sounding mad.

—I killed through myth. I killed *as* myth. I used myth to become as invisible and deadly as the bogeymen that stalk our culture. Dean, *me*, the dying schmuck without health insurance, couldn't do what I've done. I set aside Dean and became myth. Part of the mythology of one who kills is an obsession with myth. Paintings by Blake. Poems. Hogarth illustrations. Dante. Milton. The Old Testament. Look at late night cable TV for my mythic forebears. My templates. Just graze on through the channels. To kill mythically, you have to tap the mythology of the killer. And you have to tap all the myths that such a mythic killer taps. It seems all airy and ethereal, I know. But the clothes and shiny jewelry I wear now are an iconic part of that mythology, too, and they're real enough to chafe me. Ideas like the ones I just talked about are part of the myth too, and they're real enough for you to hear them.

Could I know, as I spoke from my twilight of the real and the unreal, whether I changed the day-lit realm in which Doctor Johansson heard me? Could I know if I were to view the tape of what I'd just said?

—Why the myth of Dante? Or…the myth…the myth of the killer who uses Dante? Is that…more correct?

His words were now like stones, cast tentatively into the wind and shadow I breathed. Like stones, they tested depth. If he hadn't read *The Comedy*, he couldn't understand Dante's *hard and shadowed words*, the graven letters over the Gate to Hell that had made metaphor tangible the moment Dante and Virgil passed through the Gate into the unreality of the Afterlife. If he'd not read *The Comedy*, I couldn't in good conscience further damage the day-lit world he occupied. Even while my own faint echo of those *hard and shadowed words* inflected the play we enacted, he wouldn't understand. I couldn't be an adequate guide to this Underworld. I'm no Virgil. He seemed the sort who'd done drama club in college. I threw him the tether of another myth.

—You've read *Hamlet*? I asked.

—Yes. I've read *Hamlet*.

—One your favorites?

Displacement

As if a little embarrassed by my insight, he half-smiled as he said,
—Yes.
—I borrowed from the myth of *Hamlet*, too.

A certain relief touched his face. Wind and shadow became more dense, now that Doctor Johansson chose to follow my voice into their realm.

—There's nothing in the reports about poisoned wine.
—No.

I smiled at his small goading, so unlike anything *his* mythic counterpart, the Profiler-Clinician, would be expected to do. I liked that he could surprise me. The atmosphere in the room steadied. It clicked, the way a log shifts and settles in a fireplace. I felt less alone under my hail-burdened sky.

—Though poisoned wine's a lovely idea, in the right context. I killed Evan with poison poured in his ear. I took a page from Claudius, because Evan tried to kill me to get a woman he coveted. I killed Evan the way Claudius killed the king. Evan was so good at pouring poison in people's ears, he deserved a squirt of his own piss, on that count.

Evan, the All-American boy. He looked like a skinny farm kid, fresh as wind-blown Iowa corn, even though he'd grown up in Chicago.

I fell for his farm-boy charm, his goofy smile, and his bullshit "aw-shucks" demeanor. He was my age, but I still wanted to treat him like a kid brother. He seemed John-Boy Walton come to life—the Four-H kid ideal, stepped forward in the flesh, with the residue of the imaginary clinging to him like droplets. The kind of kid so many of us felt we *should* have been, based on what TV had so helpfully instructed us of the world. Evan's clothes were ten years out of date, down to his canvas sneakers with deftly crafted holes where his big toes poked through, furthering the impression that he was a wholesome rerun made real.

He told me a wonderful story the second time we met about his Uncle Nicholas, a simple man of the soil who bought a TV in the late fifties against the wishes of the leader of the local Brethren. Later, when his uncle was trapped in a bad marriage, the Brethren blamed his sorry state on the ideas the TV had put in his head.

Evan, figment of my own TV-fed imagination, told the story so well. But one year later I found out how much better the story could be told by

Garrison Keillor when I chanced on a repeat of *A Prairie Home Companion* one night while studying.

—Who was this woman Evan wanted so badly?
Those were his words. His meaning was, *Who was your Ophelia?*
—Karen. She was a friend. We weren't lovers. She needed someone to look after her, and I needed to feel needed and worthwhile. We had a dysfunctional friendship, if there is such a thing. I forced her, with her permission, into the delicate flower role. She cast me as her protector from all the ills of the world. With my permission. We clung to each other in a way that dehumanized us both. The roles we needed each other to play were so important to our senses of self we made objects of each other.

The Moment.
The Moment that froze me so my bones felt they'd crack, that scoured my eyes as I saw in a brutal mirror how vain and stupid I'd been, how I'd derided myself into a darkness blind to my place in the world.
I met Karen in a teacher certification program. I thought I could salvage my exile from graduate school by transferring credits to another school…and perhaps do some good by teaching America's youth. I was, of course, an idiot to think that.
Yet the program was good for me. I was among recent college grads, happy in their part-time jobs and night classes. Around them, I felt young as I was, free from the diatribes, the strained professionalism of seminars and the academic hoop-jumping that had so filthed the last school I'd been to.
The Moment came as I sat in Karen's apartment, drinking bad wine and talking of our friendship. We spoke of our friendship often, a way to make it more real than the plaything it was. Our relationship matched the décor of her place, which was cobbled from goods unearthed at thrift stores, giving the place the illusion of lived-in comfort and durability. Karen sat on the threadbare couch that had been clawed by a now long-dead cat, near the beaten case holding the violin she'd not played since sixth grade. On the carpet by her bare feet were wax drippings from a prior late night of earnest talks we'd had by candlelight. Beside the wax

was a Lord Dunsany paperback from the '70s, a reed-like bookmark of sandalwood poking between its pages.

"I'm really glad we found each other," I said.

And I'd meant it.

"I'm really glad, too," she said with a smile. Her cream complexion glowed in the soft reflected red of her flannel shirt. "But if I hadn't found you, I know God would send someone else to take care of me."

And in that Moment, I knew that my friendship was just commodity. That I was capable of profound self-delusion, that maybe all the friendships I'd ever known had been hollow charade.

How many other roles I'd played were just delusion? To what extent had I only lived for the sake of others? What life did I have of my own?

—If you and Karen were just friends, why did Evan have to steal her from you?

His words had the quality of being spoken near a lake of whitecapped water. The wind and shadow that cloaked my perceptions and the hail-burdened sky all changed his voice. If this was due to how he spoke or how I heard him, I can't say.

—Because I was there. Evan saw me as Karen's protector. That was the mantle I'd taken, sure. But he saw me as a bad protector. A Svengali. Or maybe he coveted my role as protector, or wanted to become a Svengali himself. Karen and I moved ourselves like ritualized puppets. Like the ones in Indonesian shadow plays. We were afraid of who we might really be and made ourselves into tropes. Evan didn't want just a lover, but someone to make him feel more than the skinny goofball he was. Karen *the trope* could be that for him. So Evan vilified me. Or he made the trope I was into a villain. He convinced Karen, her family, her friends, *everyone* we knew that I was a monster, a control freak playing mind games with poor Karen. He was so good at twisting half-truths that within weeks I was alienated and adrift. That cut me, because I'd felt safe for the first time since Molino booted me. And I lost a friendship that could've become a thing to treasure. All because Evan looked on Karen as a trophy to be snatched from me.

I moved away from Karen after the Moment, terrified of what she wanted me to be and what I needed her to be. She could have become a permanent emotional crutch for me, and I'd become at once best friend, brother and father to her. So I dropped the trope I'd been, freeing her and me from the role I played.

I tried not to hurt her as I put distance between us, giving her the standard excuses of needing space, more time to study and all the rubbish so convincing in a life full of youth-tainted melodramatic rubbish. Karen wasn't stupid, and saw there was more to my absence than what I'd said.

There was a lesser moment that inflected the legacy of *the* Moment. It happened while Karen spoke through my ancient answering machine. Her voice sounded lost through the static as I watched the cassette spindles turn. "You there, Dean?" The sigh she exhaled into the receiver made a deeper whisper of itself under the cotton-wool sounds of the dust-furred speaker. "Call me. Please?" The *click* of her hanging up made a sharp echo in the vestibule of my one-room apartment.

I had faith things would work out. That in a month or so, she and I would pass through the crucible better friends than we'd been. In the meantime, I had fun with my newly rediscovered youth: drinking with friends from the program, going to live music shows. I savored those ember-moments of my early twenties, eager to have a rich life despite Molino's dismissal. These were times of playful debates about serious topics, conducted late at night over cheese fries and coffee in the student union.

Then Evan chose to strike.

No. "Strike" implies the honest swiftness of a cobra. More like a boa, Evan dropped and slowly squeezed. I found out what lies he'd used to entrap and degrade me, when I'd wished him no harm, and held him no malice.

"*Dean never thought of you as just a friend, Karen. You know that, don't you? If you heard the ways he talked about you, you'd know…*

"*Maybe Dean isn't spending time with you because your relationship wasn't going the way he wanted it to…*

"*Look. We know Dean is a dishonest person. Was he honest with you about his feelings for you? How do you really know he's not angry with you? You know what kind of a temper he has…*

There was sudden belligerence between Karen and me I couldn't fathom. A resentment that filled me with a heavy guilt that I'd dismissed her unfairly, without explanation. The melancholy of her echoed sigh in my vestibule metastasized in my thoughts.

Rejection withers the soul. I'd choked on it when I was young and had been banished from the love of my parents. I'd choked on it as I backed away from my parents' table, my dinner half-finished, as they told me with silent stares I wasn't welcome in their sight while they ate. Hungry, I'd spend hours in my room, staring at patterns in the cracked paint of the ceiling, wondering why I was so wretched that my parents shut me out of their lives. Karen deserved better. But I wasn't certain how to explain myself to her. I went to Evan for advice. Who else could I turn to, but the most unspoiled farm boy I'd ever known?

Evan was more Iago than Claudius. I realize that now, though I'm no tragic figure great as Othello. Evan was a scrawny little man who had to conquer me, a *nobody*, so he could feel a great and tawny lion. I confided with him over beer what had been happening. He seemed aware I was out of sorts, a good and smiling pal to talk to while the chips were down. God. When I think of the triumph he must've felt while we talked in that dark bar...triumph over a guy who wasn't his enemy. Now that he's dead, I can stand to remember that night clearly. While he lived, whenever I thought of his good buddy advice, the memory warped to a bank of fog-grey, and a roar of shame crowded my hearing. Only details like the glint in his eyes would resolve into tangible recollection. Even so small a crumb of memory as that twisted my guts with fury at my own stupidity and his shit-soaked guile.

"Dean," he said, shaking his head and smiling after a manly gulp of the Lite Beer he was so fond of. He looked around at the pub that was "our place," even though generations of college kids had claimed it as "their" place before us, as would generations yet to come. He breathed in the "authenticity" of the pub, generated by the Manchester United soccer paraphernalia on the walls and the "vintage" Guinness ads from the '40s and '50s that bore copyright notices from just the year before. "It's obvious what you've got to do," he said. "You've got to be honest with Karen. Tell her why you're in the state you're in. Sure, things're rough. But you're friends. Nothing can change that."

He changed that. Oh, how I wanted to make my friendship with Karen a healthy thing, not a waltz of mutual dependence. I sipped the poisoned cup of his advice, spoke to Karen. It was a meeting he'd been grooming her for with sensitive-guy pep talks. It was a meeting he'd lured me to with a happy-go-lucky turn of voice and a wink.

Karen admitted me to her apartment, backing from the door as I entered, eyes wide and fearful.

An hour after my arrival, we were screaming at each other.

An hour after that, it seemed impossible we'd speak to each other again.

When I got home, I shoved aside my shirts and coats and tested the heavy dowel in my closet, to see if it would support the strain of my belt looped around my neck.

—Evan couldn't spread such vicious rumors about you without slipping up. There must have been things he said that people knew weren't true.

The lake-echoed, wind-tossed quality of his voice may not have come from how he spoke, or how I heard him…the *mirror* may have changed his words. The thought that our silver-eyed audience could so intrude frightened me for reasons I can't name.

—After a while, not everyone believed him, especially after he remade Karen into what his ego needed her to be. He wrote me into a tool with which he could rewrite Karen. Karen was hollowed. She used to have such a sureness about her place in the world, thanks to her good Lutheran upbringing, but Evan manipulates people so skillfully, he…

I paused, wondering how Doctor Johansson could listen so intently with that horrible scratching being made low by the leg of his desk like the teeth of a rodent on untreated pine. The world warped, as it does in my sight when I'm enraged, and know life in the blood-tones and blacks that is called "seeing red". The sound was *near*, untouched by the heath-winds that enfolded his words. Obviously, he couldn't hear the scratching or see the rage-light, and if that was the case, I shouldn't bring them up. He needed to believe every word I said, for my sake…and for his, since he'd chosen to follow me into this place of red-tinged shadow.

…so skillfully, he dismantled her certainty that the world is a benevolent place. Evan's lies made a new reality, and she waded into it. Eventually everyone saw what he did, and thought about from whom they'd heard those terrible things about me. Gossip redeemed me, a little. But the damage was done to my dignity and to Karen's mind.

—But you felt no resentment toward Karen.

—I don't blame victims. Karen was wounded by me. Evan wounded her further. There was no need to hurt her more than she was.

—Was your killing Evan retribution as much for Karen as it was for yourself? A rectifying of what she suffered?

—I'd never kill for someone else's sake. That presumes too much karma on the person not doing the killing.

The rage-dusk in my sight deepened.

—That's very responsible of you.

His voice was steady, still without judgment. The scratching and chewing was steady as well, yet though it was wordless, it still bore a kind of judgment.

—Thank you.

—What happened to Karen?

—Evan desiccated her after six months. He moved on to the next woman: Tina, I think. A beatnik type who dabbled in Wicca…pretty sure she got her pentagram necklace from Hot Topic. He did the sensitive artist routine with her. Called himself a misunderstood poet, smeared himself with patchouli and lugged around books he didn't read. Karen moved back to Michigan. I got Christmas cards from her for a while. Manger scenes on all of them. She got knocked up, married and divorced in the span of a year. Last I heard, she and her kid live with her parents, now.

—Excuse me, please.

Doctor Johansson glanced down, and I thought for a heartbeat he did so because of the teeth crunching by his feet. Instead, he put his pipe aside and opened a file on his desk by his left hand. I'm certain the scattering of files on his desk wasn't haphazard, that he had a sort of system.

The scratching and chewing fell quiet as he closed the file, and the blood-tinge in my sight itself bled away. I was glad of that. The sounds and red shadows could still get to me, despite the fact I knew the little thing, heralded by the light, that made the sounds better than I knew my own face. How many more reflections could the mirror, our witness, our audience and our stage, endure? With this drama, I wished to relieve my pain, and not recall a relic of punishment from my wounded past.

Doctor Johansson looked up from the file, picked up his pipe.

—You didn't use *poison* on Evan.

—Metaphorically, it was poison. And it's metaphor that counts. Especially if you act as a metaphor, if you use the full power of that metaphor to do more than just end a life. Besides, I don't know toxicology. I couldn't have known what substances poured in his ear would've been fatal, no matter how many hours I spent in the library.

—And Dranō in saline solution would be incredibly painful.

—Yes, Doctor. That's why I used it.

The last trace of redness in my vision faded, and a trembling I'd not been aware of in my hands fell still.

Slipping into Evan's building was easy. I pantomimed a search for keys while a tenant, smiling, let me in as he left. Yet I didn't feel the same grace and confidence I'd felt while using a machete to purge the rage with which Molino had poisoned me. I felt fleshy, mortal, afraid. I had a gym bag of clothes bought from the Salvation Army; the nylon handle was damp with palm sweat. I found the building's basement laundry by guessing its location from the dryer vents outside and washed the clothes. I sat in the far corner, where the floor was littered with balls of dryer lint, and opened a college geology text bought from a used bookstore. I underlined passages randomly. The being I wished to be, the fiendish master of deception whose élan I tried to invoke, knew that the best way to hide is in plain sight. Even when you don't want to hide.

Under water-stained plaster walls, I waved and said hello to people as they came to use the other machines. They wore stress-lines on their faces like tribal scars as they slid down the social ladder: middle-class exiles who wondered if living in this low-rent neighborhood and student slum was just a rough patch, or the start of a permanent decline. Evan lived in a very friendly building—the downwardly mobile are always prone to kindness. I wondered what mischief Evan wrought here, what lies he'd used on his neighbors. Maybe he manipulated the manager to get special favors. Who knew?

I washed my load of ratty clothes over and over, hearing Evan's neighbors chat about how rough things were. Near midnight, I left the clothes in the dryer and walked to the first floor, where Evan's apartment was. I knew he'd be asleep. His ex-roommates used to complain about what an early riser he was: the one glimmer of truth to the farm-boy myth he'd crafted for himself.

I walked to his apartment along a hallway carpet that'd once been plush, fear cramped my mid-section, as if rubber hands twisted my guts. I stood before Evan's door, next to an incinerator chute welded shut years ago. Lines of dust on the door's molding sat at my eye level. I had a lock jimmy, the thing thieves use. But I didn't know if it'd work on Evan's door. It'd barely worked on my door when I practiced at home, and had made a small racket. Even if I jimmied the lock, what could I do if Evan kept the chain on?

I was afraid... if I couldn't kill him tonight, I'd never summon the courage to try again. I owed killing him not only to myself, but to Justice. Yet the power of that higher cause had abandoned me. I couldn't find within me the poetry I inflicted on Molino, unable to *become* the metaphor I was driven to inflict. My sick flesh couldn't cloak itself as the Dark and Shadowy Man, the diabolical figure of such awesome power. Such power had as its basis, and as its foil, the imagined power of the victim: the *vanity* that can be sundered along with the victim's sense of security in the fortress of the bourgeois home, made all the more potent in the arrogantly false homespace of Molino's office. Here, in this rickety building, there was no such vanity. There was no smug security that could grant me strength through the act of my trespassing upon it.

People were awake in the apartments nearby. I heard shuffling feet, a shower, a late-night talk show host telling jokes, a Jerry Springer-like crowd chanting, the almost alien screech of a dial-up modem as someone reached through the ether for what he couldn't find in reality.

A stink like wet dog fur wafted from me as I crouched by Evan's lock: the stench that leaks from my pores when I'm under duress, when my hands twitch and my stomach digests itself. I swallowed down the panic, took the jimmy out of my denim jacket and raised it to the brass lock. I heard something scuttle on the other side of the door, like the bolting of a cat on a wooden floor, quick, and low to the ground. It had to be a cat. What else would it be? I didn't care, so long as it didn't bark.

The jimmy waved in my grip like the prong of a tuning fork. It had been so much easier with Molino…

I was too nervous to use the jimmy. I'd have to give this up. Stop with Evan. There was no point going on, naked, with no raiment of otherworldly power. I stood to leave.

And a ridiculous thought occurred to me.

I turned the brass knob.

As the door swung open, I clothed myself in the guise of the killer I needed to be within *these* shabby halls: a figure of urban nightmare, who can sap will and action, who can forge a microcosm of suffering within the isolation of a city crowd. I moulted the need to be the Dark Man and became the lethal being of *this* place. My senses buzzed and sang—aware of everything, the beat of my heart, the drip of a sink in the bathroom, traffic on the main street nearby, the taste of fresh air coming through opened windows and the smell of cheap strawberry incense burned hours before. I shut the door and threw the bolt that should have been thrown to thwart my Coming. Reaching for the chain, I noticed it swung slightly. I must have brushed it when I came in. Its dangling reminded me of a noose.

I fastened the chain and searched the living room with a penlight. Evan's CDs were stacked by the stereo. I put them in my gym bag, careful to turn on the player and take the disc inside. I left the player open, a flag for lazy cops: a sign that a crack addict or dust-head had done this, come to lift easily fenced goods. I clicked off the penlight and walked to the bedroom, in silence that was not mine, dreading I'd step on the cat, make it screech and wake Evan.

Moonlight striped the bedroom, filtering through Venetian blinds that rocked in the cool breeze. Evan slept in a fetal ball on his futon, a pillow hugged to his crotch and chest. He looked like the innocent, fair-haired boy he pretended to be. His eyes darted under his lids…thus did a being of TV cliché dreams lay dreaming before me. My last trace of fear quieted. My hands steadied, like those of a surgeon. For I knew this shit had to die tonight. Now. It was *right* that this sham innocent be expunged from this mortal coil.

With the glass syringe in my left hand and my right on the light switch above him, I woke Evan to the moment of his death.

He howled and bolted upright, jabbering like one possessed or speaking in tongues. In an instant, he was on the futon, whirling. He saw me, spouting debased language as he covered his wounded ear, reddish froth leaking between his fingers. His pathetic body contorted with the pain that whispered into the fleshiness of his mind. The autistic stamp of his feet snapped the the futon frame under the mattress. I wanted to explain his death to him, to tell this howling man why I dissolved his life as he fell to his knees in the depression that had been his bed.

I was about to walk away when Evan grabbed my shirt, rose from his knees and screamed the last words of his shitty life: "DEAN!! MAKE IT STOP!! PLEEEEEASE!!"

I felt my eyes crack wide with his shouting my name and pummeled him four, five, six times in the throat, crushed his larynx. As he fell in a gurgling lump onto his bed, I pulled a small canister from my jacket and maced him, thankful I'd thought to bring the spray.

And I enjoyed using it. Like spraying a cockroach.

As I watched him thrash, the reddish froth turned a deeper red, and the rest of the room, the rest of the world, dropped in shadow. As if a spotlight focused on his agony, and nothing else existed. It was the sort of concentration I knew when I stared at the death throes of a legless spider or beheaded ant. Time walked differently in that sweet dome of light—sound and vision became viscous as oil. This was the urban space of suffering, the cupped silence in which Kitty Genovese was butchered, the quiet that smothers the voice of Munch's *Scream*.

His pain opera over, Evan wheezed among the coiled, bloody blankets as the rest of the world faded back into existence, as if afraid to intrude. I pitied him, still longing to explain his death and give it meaning to him. I thought to fetch a knife from his kitchen to give him a tracheotomy, so he might live long enough for me to fully enjoy his death.

Displacement

But time and sight and hearing flowed rudely as they had before. Evan's neighbors were pounding, shouting at the door. Soon they'd get the manager with his passkey.

I shut off the light, went to the window.

It wouldn't open more than three inches.

Nor would the next window.

Evan had put screws into the window frames, so they could open wide enough to let in air, but not wide enough for a thief to get in, not wide enough to admit the figure of urban nightmare I no longer was.

The pounding at the door grew louder, there were more shouts from neighbors called away from TVs and the lonely quest for cyber-porn. I couldn't break through the window, not as the mere man I now was. I'd get lacerated, there'd be questions at the hospital, my blood on the broken glass.

Concerted blows thudded against the door.

There was nothing heavy in the bedroom to break the windows…the only furniture besides the futon a beanbag chair in the corner piled with dirty laundry. I could use Evan to break the glass, hurl him through…

A sound…a clatter…like a plastic bottle on tile. I heard it between thuds against the door. It came from the bathroom.

Clarity. Sudden epiphany.

The cat.

The cat had bolted, and knocked something over in the midst of this commotion to get out.

To get out. For the span of a breath, I thought I saw through the creature's eyes as it escaped: a flash of darkness, and a flight through weeds under the ugly glow of halogen. In the bathroom I saw the shower curtain billowing, and behind it, the horizontally sliding aluminum window above the tub half-opened, the piss-light of streetlamps glinting off the frosted glass.

I tried opening it. A block of wood had been set into the window slot to keep it from opening all the way. I took it and slid the window open as I heard the hall door splinter. I dropped to the soft dirt, made myself lost in the lot behind the building. I was three blocks away before I heard sirens.

Home, I stripped the clothes I'd worn just for tonight, the purple tie-dyed T-shirt with "Bad Trip" stenciled in black marker, now stained with blood (and perhaps with traces of the brain that had plotted the assassination of my character) where Evan had grabbed me, the John Lennon spectacles with plain lenses I'd found in a head shop for two dollars, the bicycling gloves…all the accessories people would remember before they'd remember the face of that young man in the laundry room.

I shoved them in a plastic bag and heaved them into the Dumpster behind my apartment. Evan's CDs were tossed out, too, as was the geology text. Before I slept, I scraped the three days' growth of beard I'd raised for tonight, and washed the blond frost from my hair.

The next day, a composite of someone who looked nothing like me flashed on the six o'clock news, just after a piece on how some people are genetically pre-disposed to not like green vegetables, and a report on counties in California competing to host the Scott Peterson trial.

I wept with relief.

—I have to tell you something, Dean.

Doctor Johansson's voice changed. This was dialogue he'd planned, a pre-determined line he'd waited to deliver. His voice rang clear enough for those in the back row to hear. In following me into shadow, this was his tether back to his world of controlled outcomes, to where his voice wouldn't sound as it would near a troubled lake. I've read that the first true profiler of criminals and killers was Stanislavsky. The thought gave me comfort as I answered his practiced line.

—What's that, Doctor?

—You didn't use enough of your poison on Evan to kill him.

Greasy illness trickled the lining of my guts, as I remembered the endings of so many novels in which the supposed murder victim was really still…

—Evan isn't alive, is he?

—No. You killed him when you broke his windpipe.

—Thank God.

The words were flung from me as I embraced the knowledge that Evan had not attained a totemic mask of his own: the maimed-yet-resurrected victim who accuses his thwarted killer.

—Why are you relieved? Isn't his death now contrary to your vision of Justice?

His lines performed, his expected results gathered, his tone returned to what it had been, as if we spoke under a sky that would drown out our voices with sudden storm.

—I killed him by taking his voice, the tool he used to ruin lives. The Justice is still there. Just not the original Justice I'd envisioned. It's the same with Molino. There's still Justice in his death, even without the mirror. And I'm relieved Evan's dead because no one, not even him, deserves to suffer as much as he would have after what I'd done.

—You're sympathetic.

—Shouldn't I be?

—You're the one who killed him.

—Because I take people's lives doesn't mean I want them to suffer more than they need to.

Doctor Johansson leaned forward, elbows on the desk and chin set on his knuckles.

—You'd think that about Molino? You seem to have truly hated him.

—Passionately. Until after I'd killed him. And as I killed Evan, my resentment toward him drifted away, like morning fog. After I killed Evan I started feeling better about my…well *victims* is such an ugly word, but let's use it for now.

And it is an inaccurate word, since over a lifetime of victimizing, I've had only one true victim.

—How did you feel better about them?

—I started forgiving them. As I killed them, I saw the frailties that made them make me miserable. It was a lack of personal power that drove them to seek power over me. I also started forgiving myself, because as I saw their weaknesses, I saw clearly my own weaknesses, what allowed them to cause me so much unhappiness. I'd *given* these people power over me, and by killing them, I took that power back.

—But you kept killing, after Evan and Molino. Why weren't you content with the power you'd gained back from them?

—The power I'd given the people I killed was essentially portions of my life, parts of my being. I want all my life back before I die. I'm entitled to it.

—What about your victims' weaknesses? Wouldn't it have been fair for them to regain the parts of *their* lives lost to weakness?

—In this context, my killing them was their own weaknesses killing them in the end. Tragic flaws collecting their due.

—You're shirking responsibility for their deaths, blaming the victim.

No judgment in his voice, only in his statement. Even in this realm of wind and shadows and a coming storm, there was catharsis to speak of catharsis, to speak of the sweet obliteration I'd felt while obliterating the lives of others.

—No, Doctor. I killed these people out of a sense of responsibility, to myself and to Justice. We were just speaking in a particular context, not addressing the totality.

—Could your victims see their deaths the way you did? Were they aware of the Justice you dispensed, or know why you killed them? If they didn't know the ideals you served, then your tasks would remain half-complete.

—The people I killed knew there was...friction between themselves and me. That I was correcting wrongs done to me.

—None of them had a sense of your Justice?

I smiled slightly.

—Maybe Brian understood the Justice of his death.

—Brian Williams? he asked, with a glance to a file to his right.

—Not Williams. My former boss at the bookstore. Keene. He approved of how I killed him. He was drunk when he died, and that gave him insight.

Doctor Johansson's hands touched down on another file he quickly opened and scanned. I wish I knew what his system was. He spoke as his eyes darted.

—You killed him with a bottle because he was an alcoholic?

—There's more to it than that. His drinking ruined his life. His wife had left him, and he alienated most of his family and friends. The only control he had was in that bookstore. So he made his control supreme. In the end, I controlled the bottle and him.

"Hey, Dean. Where'd you learn this interesting alphabet you're using?"

My first month on the job in this chain bookstore. The pay's shit, but I have to keep busy while I decided what to do with my life. I wasn't sure I wanted to teach. Instead of a place of learning, I work in a temple that holds anxiety the way the tight skin over a wasp bite holds venom. The store is an ant-swarming palace that comforts those who believe they are entitled to never worry... yet who thrill to worry that such entitlement might be taken away. I hawk medical thrillers to face-lifted suburbanites terrified of bodily decay. Political thrillers about men in positions of power to square-jawed yuppies who are as fascinated by the power exerted over them in office hierarchies as they are by the fake tits on the cover of *Maxim*. I hawk novels to bird-twitchingly nervous professional women about "liberated women" who flee freedom by running into the arms of fit, wealthy men too perfect to exist save as caricatures played by Richard Gere. These women have the same hungry hurt in their eyes as do the wounded orphans of reality who stare wistfully at the dragons adorning the fantasy novels they buy in stacks each week. I watch worry and comfort waltz in this place, where in the attached café I saw a yoga-mat-bearing mother approvingly stroke the head of her little girl for refusing a pastry because she felt she was "too fat."

Keene's question took a moment to register; the latice of worry-soured gazes in the store slurs human syntax. I crouched low, unpacking boxes of books. Keene loomed over me, a man in his late forties with a great paunch. His grey, iron-stiff hair is pulled back in a tail. I smell liquor on him, and piss-tinged sweat. Customers, junkie-anxious for comfort, turn their consumer-dead gazes to me, longing for the opiate assurance that a hierarchy is about to be re-affirmed. Their gazes trespass... and nest like asps behind my breastbone.

I felt like a child cowering under the shadow of my father, when he'd stand over me as I played on the floor and he'd look at me as if I'd chosen a spot for the sole purpose of being in his way. Pops of sweat bead my brow. A cold trickle runs from the pit of my arm to where Christ was lanced.

My pulse drums my neck. A learned response from when I would tense, awaiting my father's kick. Like a shark, Keene bites down for the humiliating kill.

"I told you to stack those books alphabetically," he says with great fluster as he kneels to my level and re-shuffles the piles I've made.

"They are alphabetical by author," I say softly, refusing as best I could to contribute to the scene he crafts. But more gazes from the attached café drift over and strike me with another jolt of unease, shaking my resolve and making me hunch my shoulders as tightness grips my chest. I'm pushed further into the role of a child. My parents brought their wrath upon me for breaking a myriad *rules* they never bothered to explain. At any moment, I was uncertain if I'd be punished for breaking some unstated law; powerlessness and fear were my watching angels. A situation that made me a tyrant in the fantasy world of play, that made me lash out against the few things weaker than myself.

Keene's smile slides over nicotine-dyed teeth as he looks in my eyes and sips strength from my fear.

"In *your* special little alphabet, yes. But not in the alphabet we use here. Not in the alphabet our *customers* use." The booze on his breath plashes my face, making me feel faint.

It was the *Star Trek* books he was bitching about. They were to have gone in a separate pile stacked by author, not by the number of each book in the series. That was all he had to say. But instead, he staged this splendid show for the whole store to see and feed upon, which took five minutes to enact under his taut direction, as opposed to the one minute it would have taken me to correct the mistake if he'd simply told me what to do.

At least one wound-incident like this is inflicted each day, not just on me, but on every employee in the store. Like Typhoid Mary, Keene spreads his shit like contagion. As each day grinds on, and as he slips more covert drinks in the back room, his attacks become more personal and abusive.

My nerves fray, my hands shake regularly. I forgo breakfast, because the dread of going to work has forced me to start the day bent over the kitchen sink with dry heaves. When I come home, I have to wash the oily sweat from under my arms that reeks of the tension I've packed within myself. Soon, I'm unable to eat during the day, my innards are so twisted I can only keep down coffee and the odd pastry.

I hate Keene. I hate the job. Yet I never summoned the courage to quit.

Until I was fired.

—*How* did Keene understand your killing him?

—I'm not certain he understood that I was killing him, or that the bottle was. You know, *The* Bottle. All I know is he thought it was funny.

In the storm-heavy space in which I spoke, the thought occurred to me that, as a thing of myth, did I use the poetry of the Bottle for Justice, or did *it* use *me*? The possibility seemed to make a traveling patch of sun through the cloud-dimmed ether.

Hard-packed ice sheeted the mall parking lot, making it a sham frozen lake. Toward the corners of the lot were mounds of plowed snow, scarred with ice-chunks like boulders on steep hills. I hid behind one of these mounds, close to where I'd watched Keene park his car that morning. I wore thick clothes and thermal underwear to make my long wait possible, yet I wore something beneath my skin that kept me warmer than any outdoor gear could. Through *will*, I became what I needed to be. I didn't wait for the spirit, the avatar I needed, to enter me. I summoned and tamed it, the way Faust would a demon…breaking it to suit my needs.

From habit, Keene parked at the far ends of the lot, away from the mall entrance where it was crowded, so he could pull out quickly at the end of the day. On Fridays he forgot about leaving at six and got drunk at what had been in the '80s a yuppie pick-up place by the South entrance, where he got a deal as a mall manager on mixed drinks. The place was a relic, with Reagan-era décor that was a vile collision of *The Big Chill* and Planet Hollywood. It had been a matter of time before he parked by one of the snowbanks, far from where the cars of the bar patrons clustered.

At 9:30, I saw him stagger across the ice, looking in his besotted state like a trapper from a Jack London story, trying to reach an outpost in the middle of a long Arctic night as wolves bayed in the distance. Tonight, a different sort of wolf would take him. One with glass teeth.

At his car, he fumbled with his keys, crunching open the rusted door with a maximum of fuss, grunting as he eased his bulk in the driver's seat. The car's spent shocks tilted. There was freedom in my so observing him that made me feel lifted from above like a marionette, that let me run over the ice with a sure-footed lack of weight that I knew would not let me waiver as I closed on his car and slipped through the passenger door I'd unlocked with a coat hanger.

His head snapped right, his booze-fogged eyes fixed on me, and with the awareness only fools and drunks have, he knew that I was going to kill him…that I *could* kill him. That I embodied the Rambo-esque specter that stalked the tough-guy fairy tales he peddled to men who embraced Darwinian cruelty as they read books gripped in hands slathered with spa-bought moisturizers.

He jerked up his arm. Booze and his heavy coat slowed him. It was as if a living, twisting weight clung to his wrist. With my left arm, I pinned his shoulder to the seat. With my right, I broke the whiskey bottle I'd brought against the steering wheel and drove it into his neck, where the blood pulses closest to the skin. There was a sound like tearing sandpaper. The Velcro I'd taped to glove and bottleneck let me go deep, to scrape loose the vocal cords that had cut me so many times.

Arterial spray painted the windshield; steam from his sundered throat filled the car with summer-moist humidity. I nearly retched with the sweet-copper stink of blood and the booze on his breath. Yet I felt a strength, a satisfaction that I at last had power over him, as I'd once gained power through violence as a kid so long ago. Keene made noises like a pig makes as the butcher's knife slides. I thought he tried to speak, then realized what bubbled from his sauna-warm throat was laughter. This pleased me. Irony unshared can be flat and lifeless.

In a few moments, the flow of steam from his split double-chins stopped. But I thought I still heard laughter, like the soft giggle of a child.

I took his billfold, careful to rip the buttons of his coat as I groped into his suit jacket. I took his watch, careful to mark its passing with scratches on his wrist. I broke his ring finger, where his thick gold wedding band was. I don't know why he wore it. He did nothing but call his ex-wife a cunt.

Then I got out of there. I took off the thin vinyl jacket, like a raincoat, that I wore over my parka. I'd bought the jacket at a hardware store out of town…it was what some companies require workers to wear when they spray pesticides. Keene's blood had dribbled off it in streaks. I let it drop to the ground, then took a plastic garbage bag from under my coat and wrapped it.

I rubbed out my prints in the snow, invisible to the ice-caked security cameras mounted on the lampposts, invisible to any who might see me, blending into shadow as a wilderness-hardened killer, the kind invoked in banal myth-novels by the short-hand "crazy vet" or "rogue agent"—a creature forged of cultural guilt for the betrayal of ex-soldiers. The power of that figure didn't let my cancer-riddled body know thirst in the cold, dry air, didn't allow me to shiver, or feel weak. I threw the bag in a trashcan by a Burger King, took a bus home.

No one gave me a second glance.

—Did you think Keene's death was funny?

Doctor Johansson's voice took a clarity from inside the patch of light that seemed to have become still within the bank of cloud-dark shade.

—No, Doctor. I don't think death is funny.

Doctor Johansson set down his pipe, leaned back, hands behind his head. It was a position I'd have taken myself, if it weren't for my shackled arms and legs; the metal links were silver-shiny against the orange jumpsuit I wore. The jumpsuit had no belts, buckles, laces. Silly precaution. I wouldn't hurt anybody. Yet, like the hunter's costume I wore the night Keene died, my vestments had iconic value I welcomed, despite my aching shoulders. The metal chair the links looped through was very uncomfortable, too. Yet if this throne were meant to accompany the ceremonial robes I wore, so be it.

—And you were able to forgive Keene?

—There's something tragic about a drunk. Maybe that's why so many clowns look like tramps. Keene never looked so pathetic as he did when he bled.

—How did this allow you to forgive yourself?

—I realized I pitied this boozer whose life had turned to shit. And that's why I took his abuse. On some level, I knew he couldn't help it.

—But you don't regret killing him.

—If I hadn't killed him, I wouldn't have this insight, and he wouldn't be at peace. Forgiveness is part of the Justice I sought. Justice comes from art, and art works on many levels. The forgiveness of the deaths, for the victims and for me, is just one level of this art.

—Art is subjective. So is Justice. And in this context, so is forgiveness. If each of those you kill can't understand what you've done, then your service to Justice is one-sided.

I admired his lifting my rhetoric, to throw it back to me. I'd like to see what a linguist would think of the transcript of this day's session, because it seemed that Doctor Johansson was, consciously or not, stealing my speech patterns. Did I pick up his? As part of the fabled *degree absolute*, from the days when psychology was less science than it was medicine show? Since I'd taken my cold steel throne today, the Second Act of our play had shifted from interaction like fencing to something like shadow boxing. On our stage defined by our reflections, his voice was itself a mirror…which would be a great tool if the point of our sessions were therapeutic.

—Forgiveness can be undertaken by one person without the knowledge or participation of the one being forgiven. Death, Justice, art and forgiveness…they're facets of the same thing.

—And how did you…realize that? How did you come to that notion?

The shadowed and wind-swept reality trespassing on my nerves tore. A clarity pealed through my hearing and my sight, taking the light of mundane spectra. In an act of contrition, to myself, to him, to the Justice to which I'd devoted myself, I offered him the truth I wasn't certain I wished to offer.

—It was Catherine who taught me. Forgiving her was especially sweet.

—Because you loved her?

—I love her now.

—What about when she was alive?
—I loved her. Maybe. But I didn't know it at the time.
—If there was love between you, how did she hurt you to the point you needed to kill her?
—Catherine hated herself. Everyone near her suffered for it, because she had to alienate herself to prove she wasn't worthy of human company. She wounded me so many times, I couldn't see the pain she was in.
—Could she see the pain you suffered?
—She saw that very well.

Dinner with Catherine is ritual. The place mats, wine glasses, napkins all must be laid out perfectly. The meal must be eaten slowly, while the classical music station plays in the background. Catherine never comes to my place. All must be done in her domain, lined as it is by shelves of the self-help books, biographies and novels that nurture the traumas and scars she uses to define herself. I'm comfortable in this place of ritual. Because as with my parents, I don't understand what rules I'm to follow, nor am I permitted to be certain. Catherine, I think, doesn't understand the rules she lays down either, and uncertainty shared is doubly comforting.

A sip of wine, the glass held daintily in her long narrow hands. Faint lipstick traces on the rim of the glass. Candlelight touches the prints of her fingertips above the stem.

"Claire told me I should sort out my relationships."

Claire is Catherine's psychologist.

"What did she say?"

Catherine never speaks directly about herself. All must be channeled through the divine authority of Claire. Catherine's sessions with Claire are a purchased commodity, brought forth to be admired along with the pinewood-themed décor of her home. I think of her expensive coffee and espresso set, and how she called me on the day it was delivered and told me to come witness her unpacking it.

"Claire said I have to re-focus how I stand in relation to the important people in my life. I have to see myself in a stronger position in relation to my father, and my mother. And she said I should sort out my feelings about Steve."

Steve is her ex-boyfriend who used to treat her like shit. He thinks himself a writer, and his way to be a writer is to drink a lot and pretend to be Hemingway. He grew a beard and left town some months ago to rent a cabin in Maine and finish the Great Novel he's been working on for five years. As far as I can tell, the man's gotten nothing but form rejections. Like the meal we've just eaten, Catherine has taken Steve into herself. Like all she ingests, she regurgitates him from time to time, so her forced definition of her earthly existence can be maintained.

"What else did she say?"
"We didn't talk about much else."
"I see."
"We didn't talk about you."
"Uh-huh."
"Do you want to watch TV tonight?"
"Sure."
"Are you upset at me?"
"No."
"I just sense a lot of bad vibes from you."
"Had a bad day."

This is one of her favorite tactics. Belittling me indirectly, making me not important enough to discuss, a nonentity, our relationship only worth mentioning as a thing not worth mentioning to her shrink. I see this now with hindsight. At the time I didn't know why I was suddenly so upset, and why I found being upset comforting as wrapping myself in a treasured old quilt.

"Well, what happened today that was so bad?"
"Nothing."

No words, as Schumann plays behind us a moment. She speaks again, touching the stem of her glass.

"Dean, you really hurt me when you exclude me from your life."
"I'm sorry."

—Why didn't you break up with her?

Clarity made our stage a world made of glass. The *hard and shadowed words*, that defined our journey into the realm where the poetry of Justice is sharp enough to cut the flesh of ghosts, folded themselves into the hidden sheen of that glass.

—I gave her all the power in the relationship. I let her own me. I had nothing…no real job, not in school. I needed someone to show myself that I could have something, a relationship, anything. But the relationship belonged to her.

I felt naked now that the *hard and shadowed words* slept, or had perhaps bowed in reverence to Catherine, the Beatrice of my descent into the realm those words so cruelly defined.
—What did Catherine get from the relationship?
—She had a victim.

A great fluster as Catherine gets her coat, checks her brittle, protein-starved hair that, like her body, won't bow to her magazine-ad-defined will. I wait on the limbo of her couch, jacket on my lap like a sick and needy cat. The ferns by the window she's just watered cry droplets to the hardwood floor.
"Don't," she says.
"What?"
"Don't rush me."
"I'm not." I leaf through *Cosmopolitan*. It occurs to me, against my wishes, that Catherine's apartment is a figment out of old catalogues. Once upon a decade, a photograph of this place would have shilled an offer for a Windham Hill CD, free with the purchase of the coffee table. I am sadly un-handsome enough to fit the retro-yuppie tableau in which I'm placed, sadly under-dressed, and my jaw not nearly square enough. It's twenty minutes until the movie starts. Catherine didn't start getting ready until five minutes ago, complaining from the bathroom that she can't get her blush right. Though she is beholden to her impossible standards, our departure time is hers to own, and I'm a squatter within it.
"I wish you'd stop breathing down my neck," she says from the closet, amid the click of cedar hangers.
"I'm trying not to," I say as I skim an article on flirting and office politics. She sighs loudly. A woman of infinite patience, she, to tolerate an ill-shod fool like me. She reminds me of this. Often. With rolls of her eyes and expulsions of breath from her aerobics-toned lungs. I open my mouth, but say nothing, a sliver of my awareness touching the memory of a great black-armored ant, its fierce jaws opening and clamping in silent protest, as it died under circumstances its hundred-million years of adapted perfection couldn't understand.
We enter the revival house late, but don't miss the beginning of *Casablanca*. We come in during the old Warner Brothers cartoon. It's one I've loved since I was a kid, in which Bugs Bunny has to return a lost penguin to Antarctica. I laugh out loud, as does the entire audience. Except

for Catherine. She gives me looks, as if my braying embarrasses her at a refined garden party. When the cartoon ends, everyone in the theater applauds. As does Catherine.

During the movie, she becomes a little girl, swept away by the story. She talks out loud, pointing at the screen, remarking how beautiful Ingrid Bergman was, loudly as if we were in her living room, watching one of the shows about dashing professionals she loves so much that feature the kind of handsome, rich lawyers and doctors she knows it's her WASP birthright and duty to marry.

As she chatters, *I'm* embarrassed. Eyes drift to us in the cataract-grey reflected from the screen. I ask her to be quiet, once, twice, three times, giving whispered voice to the silent stares thrown toward us. At each request, she looks at me as if I've slapped her for no reason. The world narrows, changed by the fiction on the screen, moving couples around us to lean together, to rest heads on each other's shoulders, to place arms around each other. During a romantic scene in which Bogart and Bergman drink champagne as Nazis march on Paris, Catherine takes my hand, a gesture of empathy, I pray, with the doomed and phantom-colored lovers on the screen. She squeezes my hand tighter as the music swells and the scene bleeds to that drenched train station where Bogart becomes a man forever exiled from his own heart. And Catherine squeezes my hand tighter. And tighter.

And tighter still as the scene shifts from Paris to Morocco, her nails biting between my knuckles. I'm being punished. But this can't be… Catherine is a mature woman…she reminds me of this. At every opportunity. She wouldn't vent anger at me this way. Not even subconsciously. No. By telling her to be quiet, I've stifled her cathexis, her empathy with the characters on the screen. The only outlet for her is to grip my hand. I'm in the sweet homeland of knowing pain for an unfathomable transgression, yet deny myself the comfort of homecoming, of acknowledging the punishment. I nest the pain beside others I've collected. To squeeze her hand back in retaliation would the basest of immaturities. To ask her to stop would be petty and ridiculous. And it would let her know she's hurting me. That's something I can never let her know, for reasons I can't understand myself.

The movie ends and our hands part, slick from the oily sweat of our palms. She snatches her coat and is up the aisle before I get my jacket on.

Outside the theater, she maintains her lead, looking over her shoulder, encouraging me to hurry with that expectant gaze of hers, to be by her side as a real lover should. I slip on my jacket and jog next to her.

"So what did you think of the movie?" There's an edge in her voice, as if she asks how a difficult meeting went. She knows *Casablanca* is one of my favorites. It was my idea we come tonight. What she truly asks is: "*What did you think of seeing a favorite movie with me?*"

"I loved it."

"Hmmph."

"Did *you* like it?"

"Seen it before."

We walk half a block in silence. She still leads me with that tireless quickstep of hers, under lights that paint the city the color of an old man's fingernails. A pain creaks where my jaw hinges the skull. I'm grinding my teeth. I relax my jaw as best I can. Catherine has told me she doesn't like the sound. She speaks, mostly to the sidewalk before her.

"There's a lot in that movie I don't understand."

I'm relieved. We can talk without her becoming more upset with me.

"Me too."

"I don't know why that policeman acted the way he did."

"Well, he was a figurehead. A symbol for the Vichy government. He's really not a character, just a stand-in."

"Hmmph. Just a stand-in. I see."

She casts her gaze further downward and then to her right toward shopfronts we pass, looking at things that she would just *have* without even the bother of purchasing them, if the world were fair.

I risk speaking.

"What I didn't understand was what a refugee Czech resistance fighter and his wife were doing with all those expensive clothes. I don't think too many guys in the underground were drinking champagne cocktails in white dinner jackets, back then."

She stops and stamps her foot…makes a sound like someone who has crushed a leech with a bare hand.

"Goddamnit, Dean! Why are you so fucking cynical?"

"I wasn't being cynical. I was mentioning something that didn't make sense."

"You're too cynical to let a beautiful movie like that be beautiful."

She looks at me as if I'd wrung the neck of a child's pet for the pleasure of hearing the child scream.

"Barbara was right," she says in a harsh whisper, and snaps to her quick march again. I take long strides to catch up.

"What're you talking about?"

"Barbara Jameson. *Remember her?*"

Displacement

Barbara is a friend of Catherine's. She proclaims herself a poet, but lives off the interest of her trust fund. Barbara doesn't like me, and makes plain her feelings at every opportunity. Catherine has told Claire that Barbara thinks I'm the classic abusive boyfriend, that I isolate Catherine from her true friends so I can control her. I felt touched to be mentioned to Claire at all.

"I remember Barbara."

"She says you're too bitter and cynical. That you have a lot of hostility in you. She's right." Catherine speaks as if this is something she's told me many times before, the way one would explain something to an idiot. I assume she has. Why else would she take that tone?

"I'm sorry if I'm cynical. It's just the way I am."

"Hmmph."

"I'm sorry."

"You wouldn't be cynical if you didn't want to be."

This rings as a maxim Catherine has purchased from Claire, spoken as an invocation of infallible authority. The air around Catherine seems to tremble, as if it waits to be changed by the act of Catherine crossing herself.

We reach the bus stop. Cold wind surges here. Catherine assigns me blame for this with a glance, and then, like a child coming to her mother's skirts, presses her body against mine, both her arms hugging my right arm, her head nestled on my shoulder. Another couple stands here, young and very much in love. Things must be perfect between us when other couples are near…at parties we seem the happiest lovers in the world. My hand still aches from the happiness we shared in the theater, though I'm thankful for the charade. At least now I can touch her.

A woman approaches, just as Catherine lifts her head from my shoulder as if to kiss me in imitation of the other couple's intimacy. The woman is in her fifties and wears only jeans and a purple T-shirt. A garbage bag is slung over one shoulder and autumn's dead leaves swirl at her feet. The woman reminds me of someone…a friend from high school's mother, or maybe a neighbor from long ago. Her features look sunken in the dim light. She speaks to Catherine and me, standing some five feet away, not wanting to invade our space with her less worthy presence, not wanting to interrupt the kissing of the other couple.

"What bus goes to Washington Terrace?"

"The sixty-three," I say.

Catherine hugs my arm tighter, afraid of this possession-less specter of a woman, of the effrontery of her poverty and perhaps her age. The woman drifts her gaze to the edifice of the bank we stand before. The bank clock flashes that it is 10:09, and forty-eight degrees Fahrenheit. The wind churns more leaves our way that whisper-flow over the sidewalk.

"I'm not going to make it," she says, her voice like cracking stone.

"What?"

Catherine shakes my arm, the way someone kicks another person under the table who's making a terrible *faux pas*.

"I'm not going to make it to the shelter. They close the doors at 10:30." The woman turned her head about, as if trying to gauge by sound which alley nearby would be most sheltered from the wind. I wonder how old she really is. Living on the street ages people. She might not yet be forty. Worry and sorrow have slackened her face. Her hair is clean. Her clothes are clean. She's trying to live with dignity.

I free my arm from Catherine's grip, and hear a small gasp from her. I reach into my pocket and pull out twenty dollars.

"Take a cab," I say to the woman, and hand her the money. "There's a taxi stand around the corner."

I don't hear what the woman says. It could be "Thank you." All I'm aware of is her eyes, because they're suddenly empty of despair. The change in her eyes makes me feel warm and human as she turns and walks away.

When I meet Catherine's eyes, they brim with fury I've never seen before.

Our bus comes, stinking of soot, the brakes making an asthmatic grunt as it pulls to the curb. She boards without paying, takes a seat in the rear. I pay for us both and join her.

Her gaze is fixed on the inky view of the window. I look at the back of her head as the bus pulls out and the other couple at the stop is left behind, fading to shadow.

"You want an Oscar, or something?" she says to the glass, her words misting the window with each syllable.

I say nothing.

"For your theatrics."

"I wasn't being theatrical."

"Don't you be condescending to me…don't you dare!"

She turns to me. The soft blues of her mascara run in streaks down her face.

"You did that to embarrass me. Did you enjoy embarrassing me? I hope it was worth it."

"No."

"Then why did you do it?"

"Do what?"

Displacement

"Give that woman money for a cab? While we take the *bus*? Was it because of what I'd said about your cynicism? You had to do something nice and humane to show me wrong, didn't you? Well that's the most cynical fucking thing you could have ever done, you fucking misanthrope!"

In her apartment, in the prison of her possessions, in the Victorian four-poster bed that had been a graduation gift from her grandmother, to the tune of the sound machine mimicking the fauna of an endangered rainforest, we lie naked and distant from each other, invisible barriers raised against each other's touch.

I feel awful, and wonder what I can do to make amends.

—Catherine had a victim in you, but you've had victims yourself.

With the sudden absence of the dusk-world I'd been defining with *harsh and shadowed words*, the room seemed naked as I felt. Our stage hollowed itself to the brutally minimalist.

—I've taken eyes for eyes and teeth for teeth.

The echo of my voice returned from a greater, emptier distance than it had before, a distance void of props. My hypocrite twin, sheltered by his curtain of silvered glass, felt further away as well. He was our audience, who himself had yet to be cast in the role I now played.

—You've victimized people to feel better about yourself. You and Catherine are the same.

To deny what he says would lead to a too-deep and detailed reiteration of the chess games of our First Act. I needed to push forward our drama, and so surrendered a pawn to him. I had no interest in his insights to make me well. How was there any possibility for the years of therapy it would take to make me well by his standards? Why bother? Life's too short.

—How they victimized me was more insidious than what I've done. They each betrayed a trust, abused power I'd given them. I just killed them.

Doctor Johansson leaned back. I envied his ability to move that way, to make leather cushions creak and groan. His eyes narrowed. He was drawing something into focus, as would a good actor playing Sherlock Holmes, weaving strands into a solution for the crime. Was this a *new* role he played? Or a new layer to the role he'd been playing?

—Dean, I have to be direct. Everyone deals with abuses of power and trust. But not everyone does what you have. I need specifics. Contexts.

The D.A. wants a preliminary hearing in the next two weeks. So I have to ask, Were you an abused child?

His asking this long-expected question was invasive, despite his decorum and the shift in his demeanor that told me he was about to ask that very question. *Of course* I'd been abused. Even if I hadn't been, the enchanted cloak in which I'd mantled myself would require me to say I was. Parthenogenesis of monsters without human fault diminishes their power. Doctor Johansson held the question of my abuse over me as he would the crown at my coronation as an archetype.

Yet I didn't want to split open the old and bone-deep scars, and in so taking the crown, feel the stigmata of my past bead through my skin. I've been afraid of this question, of its potency. But I decided to answer for the sake of my epitaph, the wizard's glyph that will free me from my self-devouring body, and for the sake of my twin's craft.

—I…I was a neglected child. My parents didn't want me, so they didn't acknowledge me as a living thing.

—Neglect is a form of abuse.

—Then I was abused.

—Do you want to tell me about it?

How do you articulate a void? How do you speak absence?

—My parents wanted a baby, but not a child of school age or older. Then a kid isn't cute and helpless, like a pet. It's a responsibility. I was only wanted as a plaything. So I became an object they grew to hate, because it wouldn't be owned the way they wanted it to be. Despite the neglect, they prodded me, to keep me in line. And they punished me, too, for things I was expected to know, but was never told. At any moment, I was punished for doing something I wasn't allowed to do…something simple as making a cup of hot chocolate. Fear of being punished kept me…paralyzed. I didn't dare do anything.

I'd never mentioned this to anyone before. Nor consciously articulated it to myself in thought, though I've known it to be true. I've held this Truth close, keeping it as a secret engine I could harness to become what I have. The grammar of what I'd just said was a string of incantations too potent to utter before this moment, like the revelation of a secret Name. The mythic killer needs a mythically wretched childhood, just as surely as Tricksters must be youngest sons. Loki is my brother; cloaked, we inflict mischief on the worlds our parents made.

—Did they hit you?

—I hope no more than most kids are hit.

—Did they lock you up?

—They ignored me. Put me in a figurative closet, I guess.

Displacement

—That made you angry?

—Only later. Back then, I'd rot in my room wondering why I was such a horrible kid that my parents hated me. They knew I wanted their approval, and they used it as a weapon to make me follow their unspoken laws and not be a problem.

…And in not being a problem, in not *being anything*, I lived in a dead world from which I resurrected myself. So many tales of childhood tell of kids who wander through portals to other worlds of magic and wonder. I found magic and wonder, but not the kind of Nursery Magic that would whisk me to Narnia, or bring stuffed animals to life. I trod an undiscovered country in which I found the strength to make metaphor real, to give poetry flesh I could twist and hurt, so that later, I could twist and hurt flesh through the poetry of Justice.

—Did you avoid your parents?

—As much as I could.

—Did you leave the house, to get away?

A pressure clenched my throat. The room was now so clear in its glassy translucency, my eyes hurt, as they do just before they brim.

—I couldn't leave the house, or the yard. It was a prison for most of my life. For all their impatience with me, they were over-protective. If they gave me independence, they'd have to worry about me skinning my knee, or just being a kid. They locked me in their realm to minimize their responsibility for me. They hated unknown quantities, and by keeping me mousey and afraid of the outside world, they controlled me as a variable, compensated for me not being an…not being an infant.

My voice cracked. My eyes pooled their first betraying hint of blurring, and a cold grey cloud turned in my chest. The specter of the child I'd been was folded within that cloud, speaking its un-fleshed rage and hurt.

Please, God. Don't let me cry. Not now, while the videotape runs and my hands are shackled and I can't wipe the tears. Please spare me that humiliation.

I swallowed down my grief, quieted the child I'd been through suppressive will. The twin inside me fell still, while my *future* twin, who will take up my standard in his role, answered my plea for strength as a saint would answer the plea of a black-shrouded grandmother.

—Did you understand all this about your parents at the time?

—No. Later. I was a teenager. I was walking with a girl I liked when we ran into her mother on the street. Her mother was happy to see her and walked up to her and kissed her. They smiled at each other. I was shocked. Parents could love their children? It wasn't TV myth? It was like meeting a blue fairy or a troll on the street.

 I paused, tasting the silence unbroken by the gnawing and scratching I expected. Though my eyes still hurt, they welcomed the absence of the red dusk that heralded those sounds.

 —And later in college, I saw a film in Education class about the plight of the neglected child. What teachers can do to spot one and report the neglect. That fifteen-minute movie could have been taken from my life. It showed a kid of about six waking up in a dirty room and putting on dirty clothes lying by his bed. The kid had no toothbrush, and didn't wash before going to school. He had a glass of Coke for breakfast, because there was no food in the house. And that was...*me,* God-damnit! That was my life as a kid. The realization...

 I couldn't say any more, of this canted Truth I'd learned of while netted within an audience, beholding the performance of a child who played what I'd been. My first hypocrite twin. The strength granted by my saint faltered, became bitter as the air of a church thick with the cigars-and-old-lady-perfume stink of its dying parishioners.

 —And you became angry with your parents then.
 —Bitterly.
 —Why didn't you kill them?
 —They were honest when I confronted them. They offered no apologies. No crocodile tears. I let them live.
 —How would you have killed them?
 —Air pushed into their hearts with a hypo. I liked the idea of a hollowness in their hearts stopping them from beating.

 Doctor Johansson struck a pose like Rodin's *The Thinker,* still holding his pipe. Over his hand, he asked, —How did you feel when your father died?

 The ghost of the clean smell of the newsprint as my court-appointed lawyer set the paper detailing my father's death before me rose up. The smell was more visceral and real than the sight of the paper, and what was printed on it.

 —I pitied him. His son, such as he understood the term, being a monster was too much of a variable in his life. I was shocked he had the gumption to off himself. Maybe he was mortally insulted by my being individuated from him.

 Exhaustion flooded me, as if I were an urn submerged in a cold pool. The emotions I rode on this small stage were taking their toll. My illness was part of that exhaustion. There have been times recently that I've walked to the corner shop, and my ruined stamina would fold when I got home, and I'd sleep for two hours. How long had it been since this Second Act began? It had been around ten when I was ushered in here, my chains clanking like some Victorian apparition's. To judge by the gilded October glow leaking through the small windows, it was now mid-afternoon. Despite the sword-sharp danger of the theater we enacted, I felt safe in his office, away from the gibbering lunatics, the sewer smells, the shrieks and cold bars of the rest of the facility, which seemed as cruel in its Bedlam-legacy as I had been powerful as the embodiment of a myth. This office was an island of sanity, maybe made safe by the incongruity of the grand wooden desk separating me from my Confessor.

A look walked through Doctor Johansson's eyes, like that of a watchmaker restoring an antique.

—Does it bother you that you can't resolve things with your father? By killing him, or talking to him?

—I knew after I confronted my parents I'd never see or speak to them again. I'd get killed or caught. They'd never visit their son in a place like this.

—Can your resentment toward them ever be resolved?

A pressure on my shackled feet, a living weight. As if something heavy rested on them, with flesh like the brow of a feverish child. The thing squirmed as if to get comfortable. The hairs on my legs rose, and chills coursed under my skin like spilled mercury. My heart felt full of spun glass, and my genitals drew up inside me. The thing across my feet breathed with a shifting of its weight, as if its lungs didn't draw air, but thick fluid.

—What's wrong, Dean?

—Just a bad feeling, like someone walking over my grave.

A little laugh. Like a bark. (Can't he hear it?) And the weight heaved itself off my feet. I can relax now. But it has never *touched* me before; it has never been real to me, save in the blood-lit world that had retreated from our stage.

Doctor Johansson frowned, sensing, because he's no fool, I lied to him.

—How did you deal with your anger when you were young?

—Before I started killing people?

—Yes.

—I killed things.

In his furrowed brow, I read where his thoughts traveled. I was angry with myself for goading him by accident, for letting that which had dared to touch me fluster me so that I set his clinical alarms ringing.

—I killed *insects*, Doctor. Just bugs. I never hurt anything higher on the evolutionary scale than a spider.

The glassy-clear reality that had burned away the dusk-red shadows...I sensed now what it was: the hard light of my fellow actor's clinical training imposing itself on the poetry that had given me strength, power, and the will to use them. I spoke, as if to crack that reality, to free myself from its oppression, lest it take all trace of that power from me.

—I never killed *vertebrates*. And I didn't wet the bed or start fires, as the literature says all serial killers must. I could never enjoy killing animals.

Oh, but I *did* taste rapture killing insects. I enjoyed compensating for powerlessness. And hopelessness. I still savor the child's thrill of hurling a black beetle atop a hill of red ants, watching them churn like angry breakers over the larger beast, rending past the thing's armor. Its huge jaws clamped, unable to close on the small foes that so efficiently killed it. And there were the centipedes I poured hot candle wax over, entombing them, force-feeding them the paralysis and claustrophobia that had been life in my parents' house.

But what I loved to kill most were the great, black carpenter ants. They were tough bastards, true warriors. It pleased me that despite their strength and fury, I could kill them without a thought.

Though I did *think* about killing them, always writing new scenarios, new premises, with which to punish them for being so insolently strong and pure. I thought of needles to drive through their heads (there was such pleasure when the point pressed against their chitinous shells, and the shells *yielded* with a faint pop as the metal shaft went through...they lived through that, for a while). I thought of matches, vivisections to be done with the scissors of my pocketknife, and drops of fine motor oil that suffocated them so very quickly.

What I especially loved were the Games, the gladiatorial contests I arranged that so beautifully expressed the feelings that defined my little life. The Games were fictions for which I was creator and audience, a semi-divine reaper of lives who found peace in witnessing death. I took up Godlike power, because God didn't bother to do the job, having abandoned the world in which I'd been abandoned.

Behind my house near the rear porch, I'd draw a chalk circle on the summer-hot concrete. Two carpenter ants from different colonies would be thrown into this ring. If they did not notice each other, I grabbed one in each hand, their powerful jaws would snap in silent rage, dripping formic acid that smelled so slightly of maple. Then I'd bring them together in an awful embrace, their jaws clamping down on each other.

Then I'd set them in the chalk arena, with the Rule in mind that if either one disengaged and left the Circle, I would crush it with my thumb. If their struggle took them out of the Circle, I'd knock them back in. The battles could last hours. And it pleased me no end that they fought and were in pain for reasons they couldn't understand, under laws they couldn't understand. Sometimes, when the struggle went too long, I'd change the odds by ripping off a leg or snipping an antenna.

And if one ant proved itself worthy, if one ant followed my unknowable laws and killed the other, I crushed it anyway, happy to make another entity suffer as I'd known helplessness, following the oppressive rules of my parents, and receiving for it no love or acceptance or freedom or power.

It was good to kill the victor. I'd walk away from the chalk circle feeling wonderfully clean, and no longer angry.

Doctor Johansson packed his pipe with another bowlful of tobacco as fictional as the dreams I'd used as weapons.

—Would you describe yourself a serial killer if it would help your defense? To cop an insanity plea?

No, I am an avatar.

—I wouldn't. Besides, I'm not going to see the inside of a courthouse. I'll see the inside of a cheap coffin, first.

He began puffing, and my mind saw the bowl glow red. A blue-grey fog formed around him like a halo.

—There must have been times when killing insects wasn't enough. What did you do then? Or when there were no bugs around, in the winter?

I was transfixed by the blue-orange will-'o-wisp glow of his pipe. I didn't want to answer his question, even as my body answered it, with memories of blossoming pain echoing beneath my skin.

I'm seven years old. I've locked myself in a bathroom, and I'm punching myself. There's joy to venting anger and frustration, joy in damaging my self, making real and feel-able the rage that stabs me from within with ghost-blades too dishonest to draw blood, or to leave scars that offer the consolation of watching them heal. I can't remember why I'm so enraged...some comment from my father has roiled me into this frenzy, or some accusation of my mother's has bewitched me with a fury that must be released somehow, even against myself. All I can recall is the passionate need to hit and hurt and *punish* someone, anyone, anything. Saints have known this pain through hair-shirt self-martyrdoms that let them feel the love of the Divine Father and see the Light of Heaven, not through rage that stains shadows the color of dying scabs.

In my ecstasy of loathing, amid the blows I smashed against my brow and the back of my head, I looked up and saw my red, wrath-twisted face in the mirror...my little boy's mouth fixed in a grimace, veins bulging at my temples, and bruises spreading like wine spilled on satin.

I stood there, my small fists stopped in mid-blow, panting like a wolf over a steaming kill, thinking perhaps I could reach through the mirror and kill the boy who inspired such pity and contempt in me, hoping to travel through the Looking Glass to the fantasy world where a weak little boy could die by my hand as he deserved to.

Instead of reaching through the unyielding and cruelly solid glass, I reached instead into my child's mind and pulled forth a screaming, pleading surrogate: a thing to punish besides my own face, yet that still bore my face.

After several minutes of pantomimed blows against another, non-existent thing that cowered in the corner where two sheets of ugly vinyl wallpaper met, my rage subsided.

In the mirror, it seemed as if my bruises—for which I was often rewarded with extra food at dinner for sparing my parents the bother of inflicting them—faded. I washed my throbbing face with cold water and left the room with a soothing emptiness in my chest, knowing that what I had done was a ritual that offered me salvation.

I decided to tell him.

—Most children have imaginary playmates. I had an imaginary victim.

—I...don't understa...

Displacement

—I didn't *play* with my imaginary friend. I beat the shit out of it. It was smaller than me and weaker and I could pummel it and bully it. I made it pay for the unspoken crimes I committed. It was my little pal. My coping mechanism.
—It?
—Yes. It.
—It wasn't a child, then? Another boy or girl?

I know where the little shit came from, now. I've witnessed his birth twice. When I was older, just going to college, I'd sprained my knee. For two weeks, I walked using an elastic brace. Late one night, while getting ice water, I was too tired to put on the brace. My knee buckled. My arms flailed as I grabbed hold of a chair.

And I saw myself ghosted in the night-black glass of the window over the sink, a mass of palsied movements, jerking limbs, reflected as on a pool of oil. A ridiculous caricature of who I am. The distorting glass made me look squat and twisted, like pictures I'd seen of the hunchback in Poe's "Hop Frog."

What happened next was more than memory. It was a snapping of my mind through time that drowned my senses. Years collapsed, cracking into the moment in which I now stood on a burst knee, my arms trembling to support my weight.

I'm five years old again. My body remembers its weakness, its smallness. Even my mouth recalls the old set of my jaws before the loss of my milk teeth. I'm running through melting snow in my parents' back yard. It's warm for a winter's day, spring-like. Despite this, my mother has packed me into a snowsuit too large for me, filling the space my body does not with layers of sweaters and pajama bottoms. Because it's still winter out, no matter how warm and sunny and bright it is, no matter that the snow melts and drops from the branches… and to go to the yard in winter is how little shitty ungrateful boys catch cold and die, and that is how they show they don't love their mothers, because their mothers have to worry all the time and if little boys really loved their mothers….

So I wear the snowsuit and the layers and I'm miserably hot, because I also wear a hat and scarf. The drawstring of the hood is knotted to press against the underside of my chin: punishment tied by my mother's sharp-nailed and rose-scented fingers for my wanting to step out into the air. I feel stupid and silly and angry. My movements are weighted, as if the air were thick as stale honey. The outfit is a prison I've been forced to wear, a prison like the loveless home I live in. I'm enraged that my body is co-opted as part of my prison. That I'm forced to be as weak and useless as my parents wish me to be.

I try to run, as any child would, through the snow that glistens brilliantly, the only way I can: by holding my arms out almost to their sides and throwing my legs in front of me one at a time. I look up and see myself reflected against the windows of the house. They warp me like fun-house mirrors. I look like a twisted fat little goblin in a story book, a troll creeping from under a bridge. Something rips inside me, tearing away like a strip of skin. The pain offers a kind of relief from the oppressive heat.

That had been the first moment of self-contempt I'd ever felt that I understood to be self-contempt. The first time I'd been consciously sickened by my own image, the first splitting of the first cancerous cell that would devour my psyche. I realized this as I leaned against the table, recalling how I'd leaned that day against the swing set from which my father had removed the swings, lest I fall. My knee ached as I tasted the gorge that the Truth had pushed into my throat, through its revelation that my little scapegoat who'd helped me cope with my childhood had been *me* at that specific moment. A visualization of everything I'd hated about myself *before* I'd shattered myself in front of the bathroom mirror and pulled forth my victim: weak, whining (oh, how it used to whine so for mercy while I imagined torturing it), and pathetic.

Thirst forgotten, I limped to bed.

But wondering if this small totem of self-hate had been with me since birth, I didn't sleep that night.

Nor the next.

—No. It was an *it*. Not human. Like a gremlin.

—Did you imagine it to be not human so it would be easier to hurt?

I watched the bank of phantom pipe smoke float between me and Doctor Johansson. The sun, creaking to the west, came from behind a cloud, and shadows from the thick window bars bled onto the smoke like slashes. I wondered if the yellowed air filter in the corner could draw the smoke that was not there.

—I don't think I'd have been as fond of hurting it, if it had been easy to hurt.

—Did it have a name?

The shadow bars faded. I don't know how long I must have been silent for the clouds to hide the sun again. How much of this day had I spent in fugue-like silence? I was afraid to answer, to speak the Name I had never spoken, and invoke whatever hidden power might be knotted within that Name.

—I gave it a stupid sort of kid's name: Piggy.

Nothing changed with the invocation of the Name. I watched Doctor Johansson's eyes, to make sure he didn't think the name funny. Or trite. It would embarrass me if he did.

—Why did he have that name?

—I think I gave it to him because he was kind of baby-pink, like a pig, or a puppy's belly. It seemed to fit. I'd never heard the name before I gave it to him. Maybe the name floated in the ether as the name of victim, and I picked it up. I'd never heard of any victim character named Piggy until high school.

The phantom smoke dulled the glass-hard reality before my eyes. The effect was soothing, yet I still felt a dread between my shoulder blades, that the Name so long unspoken might still reveal a potential that had been dormant.

—What did you do when you ah…punished Piggy?

—Most often, I'd shut myself away and throw punches at it. Before that there had to be the chase, where I'd look all over the room to see where it was hiding. Then I'd drag it from the hiding place by the roots of its hair. And then I'd start beating it.

—And this was like imaginary play?

— I'd swing and kick at where I imagined Piggy to be. I'd get something like a sugar high during the punishment. My vision would get grey and buzzing. I'd be spent afterward.

—Did you talk to it?

—Sometimes I'd speak to it, to re-enforce the punishment. Things I'd learned from my father. Things like, *Come out and take your medicine, you little shit!*

—Did Piggy say anything?

—Mostly it just begged not to be hit. Sometimes I'd imagine it screaming.

—You never had conversations with it? Like most kids do with imaginary friends?

—We weren't on speaking terms.

—Sort of like you and your parents.

His insight struck me like a heavy boot. The tumors nestled in me felt as if they shifted, like waking things.

—Yes. Like me and my parents.

—In fact, you were its parent. At least as you understood parents to be.

Realization is the crash of a thing you didn't know. What turned my guts to clay was not realization, but the stripping away of a *refusal* to know that the proportions of the creature, as I'd first imagined it, were he same as I had been proportioned to my father.

—I suppose I was.

—How old were you when you gave up Piggy?

—About eleven or twelve.

That wasn't entirely true. The last time I'd used Piggy was about a year ago, the day I was diagnosed, the day all the nagging fears bloomed to awful fruition, when the worries about the bloody stools, cramps and fatigue boulder-crashed upon me and shattered whatever hope for a life I'd ever had.

The world had chewed me and spat me out. I drunk-stumbled home from the doctor's, wanting to vomit, wanting to take a knife and cut out the cancer myself, to make bloody and visible the inner maulings I'd suffered. My jaw locked, my fists felt fused solid, immobile as blocks of wood. Blood trickled from where I'd bitten through my lip, and I was afraid of my own blood, of the toxins it held that I could be ingesting back into me. *Blind rage* is a half-truth. Rage doesn't blind. It inflicts more clarity than you can bear to see.

The pain of vision searing me, I upended the table, threw dishes against the walls, embedding fragments into cheap sheetrock. I pummeled a wooden door until it splintered. My gaze, vicious as desert sun, fell on a shelf of shiny new paperbacks. I was cheated of the time to read them, so I destroyed them, cracking their spines and ripping them as strong men rip phone books. I kicked apart the bookshelf; a jutting nail sank deep behind my Achilles' tendon. My raging sight burned away the pain of it. I moved on my wounded foot like a wind, not walking to the things I destroyed, but surging, like a swarm of leaves.

I grabbed the phone from the wall. It was high-impact plastic, and would take a good long violent while to break. I hammered the receiver against the wall, watching lovely clouds of dust rise from the craters I punched into the plaster, watching each mote turn with the grace of malignantly indifferent planets.

Displacement

I smashed my thumb against the wall, crushing it between receiver and plaster.

I howled as clarity burned itself to onyx. Evil thoughts packed themselves tight into my head, like a million blind maggots, a million demons all lusting for blood crammed inside my skull.

I could have murdered all that lived in that second.

In that darkness, in that mass of pitch that boiled itself from spectra that had been so unbearably bright, I remembered my little surrogate, my little scapegoat. I reached into my mind and dug up the mind I'd had as a child. In there, cowering, I found Piggy.

Forcing my mind to be that of a child, I ripped away my blindness and found the little shit standing in front of me.

I bellowed and launched myself at it.

It was sweet—like when I knew the immortality of youth—to have it suffer and beg and plead and to hear with my mind's ear the splintering of its bones and its screams and suddenly…bedded within the music of its screams I heard words, not the pleading excuses I'd been used to, but one syllable, uttered over and over beneath my imaginary blows like sobs.

"Why?"

I stopped and saw the bloody little face, so much like mine, the lips and cheeks hanging in shreds.

The little being faded from my mind's eye, and I wondered, Why should I punish the thing that had helped me cope? The thing that helped me survive?

It was time to punish the ones who had hurt me, who had taken my life.

I crawled over the rubble of my apartment, trailing blood from my left ankle. I hobbled to bed and slept a death-like sleep for almost a full day.

When I awoke, with the sheet snaked around my feet clotted with dead brown blood, my mind felt wonderfully focused, clearer than I ever remembered.

I planned the rest of my severed life with a new sense of purpose.

—Why did you give up Piggy at that age?

—Maybe I outgrew it. Maybe I re-focused my anger into other channels, like all adolescents do. Not sure.

—Do you think at some point, you would have given up killing, if you hadn't been caught?

—I think I would have *finished* my killings, or gotten tired of the planning and execution of them. Or died.

—Did you ever want to stop?

—I'd thought about it.

—Did you want to be caught?

—*Oh please, stop me before I kill again?* That's so melodramatic. No. I expected to be caught, but I didn't want to be.

—Whom would you have killed after Catherine?

—I thought about killing Sarah, another ex-girlfriend. But I thought about what she was like, and realized she must have been screwed up in the head, only I didn't realize it when we were together. Too young. There was a lot bad in our relationship, but it was…*human.* Not cruel. Not malignant. I got in touch with her, just to see what she was like, now.

—And?

—We had a nice talk. She's been in therapy. She had a pretty rough life I didn't know about. I couldn't hold her responsible for the crap she'd given me. The poor kid was scrambled. We had a quiet dinner date, for old times' sake. It was all very nice.

—There was no way you could have reconciled with Catherine?

—No. We could only have peace after she was dead.

Catherine knew my voice when I called her. I could taste the Tom's-of-Maine-scented huff she blew into the receiver, the same expulsion she made whenever I asked for a crumb of help, even when I asked for coins with which to make a phone call. Still, she asked (with the same high-pitched pain in her voice that I once heard in the yelp of a stray kitten I found as the vet drew its blood), "Who *is* this?"

"It's Dean."

"Dean?"

"Dean Garrison, Catherine." *Jesus Christ! You could* pretend *to remember the people you've pumped fluids with, you toxic, skeletal bitch.*

"Oh…Dean." She let out a different flustered sigh, like someone called about back taxes. She had a wide vocabulary of sighs, complex and subtle enough to compose Haiku with.

"I need to see you, Catherine."

Displacement

"I don't think that's a good idea." She spoke as a teacher would to a bad third grader, voice thick with finality. Yet there was a reflexive quality to what she said, the same with which a shopgirl would mutter "Have a nice day."

I know her too well for her games to stab me now. I've read the fictions and the lies that are her life, to write myself into it as its coda. I know she's had many lovers, a mass of half-remembered names and limbs and cocks she has puppeted not with strings, but words. I've choked on her gnawing hunger for control, and I know many of her lovers have come back to her, desperate for the opiate freedom of her manipulation, and for the woolen-soft comfort of her abuse. I've seen her pick up the phone when ex-lovers call and vivisect them with her scalpel-precise tongue, only to tell me afterward that she was meeting them for coffee.

But none of them have played the card I held, the totemic charm I'd now utter.

"I'm dying, Catherine."

"What?!" She gasped, perhaps taken off guard while on the phone with a man for the first time.

"I'm dying."

"*How?!*"

Through the phone lines, I felt the air around her tingle with her worry that her psychotic love life has risen, like a chain-draped ghost, to haunt her...that I gave her AIDS or she gave it to me. Since she was the greatest AIDS risk I've ever run, I let her sweat. I choked crocodile tears, took deep breaths.

"I have cancer."

"Oh." A new sigh, rich with poetry I've never heard before: a fucking *sigh of relief*.

"I want to talk. I want to make sure everything is squared away between us. It would mean a lot to me."

At no point during our exchange did I tell a single lie.

The walk to Catherine's apartment was pleasant. The wonderful smells of crisp October night thickened to a delicious liquor; the stars were bright as angels' eyes, not faded by the glowing rot of the city. I hungered to drop my anger toward Catherine: a burden I'd carried too long. It was a near sexual need, a quasi-tantric state that trembled beneath my muscles deep near the bone. The desire, its silent, healing passion, told me along my very nerves that there had to be something decent at the core of my relationship with Catherine, otherwise we'd have never gotten together. Otherwise, we wouldn't have stayed together as long as we did, and let our relationship twist into the knotted web that it became, something that grew like a cancer and sundered what was healthy between us. Tonight I'd cut that cancer away.

I stopped below Catherine's building, palms damp, heart fluttering, as if I wore another body, like a coat, over the one full of tantric expectation: another body that I formed through the act of looking *at* and *through* her home. I leaned against a tree and unslung my book-bag, the final emblem of my youth, for I'd die at the age when I was expected to start carrying a briefcase. The bag clattered from the shiny metal instruments inside that I'd purloined from an undertakers' supply house—the keen blades that would help Catherine and me fix our relationship better than any couples' councilor could.

I lit a cigarette to kill time as I watched her place and collected myself…as I collected *more* than myself into myself. The cigarette was an icon, potent as the caduceus of a healing god: a symbol of danger, the smoke of which I drank into my lungs to steady the nerves of the secondary body surrounding me, so that it could take the power I'd need to intrude on Catherine's home with my presence before I intruded on her body with a blade of near-impossible fineness.

I don't smoke, of course. But I had to try as many new things as possible in the weeks I had left. It made the ritual act of *watching* richer, gave the flavors of October air a new depth, like the essence of heat-aged cedar. The iconic danger of the cigarette rose up to dance with the breath of a time of reaping, when sheltering darkness gives its grace to those who are blessed to walk within it.

October has always been like a mistress to me. I love the new sublimity of the weather, the first frost, the painted sunsets, the decorations for Halloween. Everything becomes a mystery.

To stand and *watch*, during a season when masks and all their terrible power are themselves masked as child's play, made the deep-water shadows on the street seem like velvet, made the stone fences and oaks more solid. The neighborhood was a tomb to the dead middle classes that had lived here. The disappearance of the people that had defined the place made it seem haunted, like land that had belonged to mound-building Native Americans. *Absence* made the reality here worn as the sole of a cracked boot. I could walk more easily through fiction and myth tonight than I could on any other night on which I've killed. The geometry of the street (with its once-sturdy single-family homes and duplexes cut into condos and high-end apartments with fire-code ugly stairways of steel) was made fragile as a light-sleeper's dream by what October whispered upon it.

I was going to miss October.

Displacement

I heard the shuffle of feet through leaves.

No one was there. October air changes sound. It was a kid on a side street, or a cat chasing mice through mist-damp piles of yard cuttings. Let it stalk. For that was what I now did, enrobing my form as the summoned demon of the vindictive ex-lover, the dangerous Phantom who possesses women, who is the monster lurking within facile love songs about "making you mine", the stalker who terrifies through his harnessing the Deadly Sin of *vanity*. A different vanity than that which makes homes sanctuaries that Dark and Shadowy Men can violate. It is a deeper vanity than that, and much more potent.

As I finished the cigarette, ceremoniously throwing it in the gutter, I scanned Catherine's five-unit building that had been a two-family duplex, making sure my escape routes were viable as I remembered them should Catherine have time to scream. It would be easy to swing from her balcony to the fire escape grafted to the side of the once house-like house. Depending on the situation, I could go down to the street or up to the slanting roof. From the roof, I could jump to the next building. If I missed the jump, what did I lose? Six months? A year of medical bills I couldn't afford?

I went to the front door and rang her apartment. She buzzed me in. Like old times. Only now, I didn't enter with a bird's-nest lump of dread in my craw.

She lived on the top floor. The foot of the stairwell touched a unit in which I heard people yelling and crying with the deep, rich pain of loss. Their pain *hurt* to hear. But in a way that shamed me, I knew their cries would create distraction, should I need it. On the second floor I went to the apartment just below Catherine's and touched my ear to the door.

Absolute quiet. No newscasters. No laugh tracks to the misadventures of Chandler, Phoebe, Ross and Joey. No talk radio. Just the shade-still heartbeat of a vacant living space.

I'd cased Catherine's building over these last few months of my existence, waiting for the people below her to go on vacation before calling her. It wouldn't do for the *thud* of her body and what it would leak through floor and ceiling to alarm anybody. Evan's death taught me how troublesome neighbors can be.

I took it as divine providence when the people below moved out, letting the turn of events melt on my tongue as a Catholic would a Communion wafer. I made an appointment with the building manager to view the apartment while Catherine was at work, and asked for an application to fill out in private. While he was gone, I unlocked the window closest to the drainpipe that ran down the southeast corner of the building. If

73

Catherine made an aria of our reunion, I could shimmy down the pipe outside her window and hide in the vacant apartment, assuming I didn't shatter my limbs on the alley below trying to get in, and so let floating bits of marrow join my tumors in their revolt against my body.

    I climbed the stairs, drawn by Catherine's siren-call she didn't know was hers, because its notes were so deeply buried in the self-love at the core of her being—the self-love that punished her body for its disobedience in not bending to her focus-group-defined will. The tantric urgency in my flesh was changed by her song as I became the killer she sought: the stalking lover, the thing of myth that drew its strength from the voyeurism and narcissism of women such as Catherine, who make pretty and vicarious myths of empowerment and melodrama out of the plight of women who truly are stalked. Women such as Catherine...who longingly see victimhood as an opportunity for personal growth, to shine through adversity, and so perhaps meet a smoky-dark and handsome cop/protector. Victimhood wormed in their imagination as a chance, like multiple sclerosis or cancer or spinal injury or any other dramatically severe illness worthy of a made-for-TV movie, to *will* yourself to become better than you were, to not let adversity beat you, and so spit in the face of the truly stricken and afflicted.

    I reached Catherine's door. I knocked on the barrier that my passage through would finalize the bestowment of power, the vindictive actualization, I had begun by *watching*.

    "Who is it?"

    "It's Dean." *Who else?*

    I heard the rattle, the clank, the rumble of locks being undone. Catherine's protective barrier against all evil in the world. The throwing of locks was precise as the *noh*-play rigid dinners and conversations and lovemaking we'd shared, for the *door* was not the barrier that made her feel safe, but her control over it, her mastery of it through the manipulation of locks and bolts from one state to another.

    She opened the door, relinquishing her control, admitting me to the imaginary safe space of her home as a mythic being that, like monsters out of folklore, can only harm upon being invited in.

    When I saw her, my resolve to kill her faltered. She smiled the way people smile only for dear friends. She kissed my cheek, and it felt so very nice. I thought of Sarah, how we'd reconciled. Maybe Catherine and I could end on good terms. My mythic state, coursing within me, flowed into a warmth I could share with her, that could call from our hearts what had been good between us and save it, like a small thing pulled from a burning home. Maybe with understanding, not blood, we could quell my deep anger for her.

She blew her chance.

As she locked the door, controlling it and the entire world beyond by turning three throw-bolts and setting the New York T-bar that braced the door, she asked, "Are you okay?"

"For now."

"You look okay."

A long moment as I took off my jacket and dropped my bag carefully, so as to not make a clatter. The silence stood by intrusively, counting the seconds of its own duration.

She blurted, "Do you want coffee?" As soon as she asked, I saw the same flash of regret that darted behind her eyes when she asked me one night to light the red candle she liked lit when making love. As I struck the match, I saw that the candle had been melted down much farther than it had been two nights before, when I'd last been to her place. I felt her gaze on my back as I lit the candle, wondering whom she'd fucked the night before. I *felt* her hunger to start a fight or slight me, so she could control the moment and deflect any chance of discussion. I heard the flap of her turning down the sheets. She said matter-of-factly, while I stared at the new flame cupped in the diminished candle: *Barbara thinks I should break up with you."*

Though how *coffee* could inspire the same flash of regret in her gaze, I couldn't fathom.

"Tea's fine."

She spun and walked her nervous springing step through the realm of her possessions and the two-decades-old "elegance" she treasured to the kitchen, past the uncomfortable couch where she made me wait on so many occasions. She's lost weight since I've last seen her. She looks like a ghost, or a fault in the negative of the lifeless catalogue photo her home resembled. Her hatred of her body has grown more passionate.

I rested my book-bag by the fortified door, opened the top zipper a fraction of an inch, followed her to the kitchen as I heard the faucet shut off.

"I wanted to call you earlier," she said as she set the kettle on the stove.

"Why?" I asked, when what I wanted to ask was, "*Why didn't you? And why bring it up, now?*"

"I wanted to see if you wanted dinner tonight."

"I have to watch what I eat."

"Oh."

A pause of a second or two as I smelled fresh coffee, turned and saw the lone espresso she'd made for herself, the still-life with demitasse, book, and lemon rind she'd placed on her fine table to *show* me that I was not worthy of her making a second cup. I glanced to her espresso maker. It had been cleaned and wiped and shoved into the corner by the fridge where she stored it; the coffee grinder was not to be seen, and the counter was still damp and streaked from the sponge that had erased any trace of spilled grounds. Even the paring knife used to cut the lemon rind rested washed and shiny in the drainer by the sink. Her offer of coffee had been a mistake, a loss of her sacred control to fill the silence by the entryway, just as her asking me to light the candle had been a blurted loss of control. I stared at the espresso, at the demitasse that bore no mark of her lip on the rim, the perfect twist of rind that would be the envy of any barista, the book that had been so carefully placed. I felt Catherine's eyes on me, touching my back as they had while I stared at the melted red candle.

I waited for her slight.

"I crossed out your number in my book. That's why I couldn't call."

"I'm *listed*, Catherine."

"Oh, yeah."

I turned as she laughed a pretty little laugh, her almost translucent hand covering her mouth like a geisha's. "I hadn't thought of that."

Before, this coffee tableau and verbal exchange would have set my teeth grinding and flurried my guts into self-digestion. Her little attack, her reduction of me to nothing more than an inky smear in her address book…a new and living ink, changing color as the red cells within lost oxygen, would be a justified blot to give in return.

We spoke blithering small talk a few moments as the kettle heated, then, in mid-sentence, she walked toward me and took my hand… her fingers gently, sensually, caressing my palm. She kissed my lips. Her left hand touched my cheek as she said, "It's really nice to see you again, Dean."

"It's nice to see you, too."

And then she went to her cupboard, to take down the vacuum-sealed bags of tea.

I know her too well.

This whiff of erotic interlude is bait. I smell it. She wants me to want to sleep with her. She wants me in the whining role of the ex-lover, back for one last meaningful night, so she can have the control of saying, 'No, Dean. We shouldn't ruin this.' While we were lovers, she'd told me about the others she'd turned away like that. It would be her way of having the last word. Before I die.

I know her too well.

Her teakettle is glass. With a rubber fixture on top like a stopper. A hole in the fixture whistles when the water boils.

The water started to boil, a corona of bubbles forming where flame kissed the glass.

It was time. I became what I had to be in that moment. I let it glow out from my bones, with the taste of the cigarette painting my mouth, and the taste of her kiss on my lips.

"Catherine, I have medications in my bag I should be taking now. I need to go get them."

She smiled sweetly. "All right."

I went to the door and fetched my clanking book-bag, which smelled of formaldehyde from the place I'd gotten its contents. As I walked to the kitchen, my path knifing through the lies of her home, I pulled the shades of her living room windows. People from the building opposite could see into the kitchen at an angle if a flash of metal or spray of red caught their eyes.

I went to the kitchen doorway and unzipped the bag.

The kettle started to whistle.

Now, God-dammit, *now*, while she faced the stove to turn down the heat.

The rest you know.

—Dean, I believe that just as you outgrew Piggy, you outgrew the need to murder. We should consider the possibility that you didn't kill Sarah because your need to kill was weakened.

So did he begin to end our Second Act, with a revelation he thought would have a profound impact, the sort of shift intended to make audience members eager to get back to the Third Act after lavatory breaks and smokes under the marquee. A new iteration of *Stop me, before I kill again*. He insulted me by saying my *choice* to kill was a gauche and animalistic *need*.

—If that's your professional opinion, it should help my lawyer. Will you be paid a stipend, by the way? I'd hate to think you'd waste a day in court for nothing.

—Dean, part of you wanted to be caught.

I had this coming…cloaking myself as an archetype, I subjected myself to clichés culled from the fictions that shaped the myths I used. *Part *of me wanted to get caught?* A way to give me, a monster, a dusting of pathos. Too bad no beautiful and pure-hearted girl who could have been my salvation had been in my life at the time of my capture, to give my tale a hand-wringing whiff of the tragic. Even if such a Tess Trueheart had been in my life, the hard little stones of rogue cells in my testicles would have made our requisite night of tenderness awkward. And painful.

—Which part wanted to be caught? The part with cancer, or the healthy part?

—The part that orchestrated your capture.

There are moments in theater, like that in which Macduff states that he was from his mother's womb untimely ripped, when a wave of silence spreads from the stage over the audience. Such a moment should have washed over my senses in that moment. Instead, I glimpsed a silence in my sight, as all traces of Doctor Johansson's phantom pipe smoke refracted out of visibility.

—Have *you* considered therapy, Doctor?

—You ensured you'd be seen killing Catherine, and that the police could to get to you.

I had a violent insight to what Keene must have felt as broken glass arced into his neck: the imposition of a fiction that I didn't write over my reality.

Doctor Johansson read the doubt in my face, reached for a file, opened it. If he did so for the sake of having another prop to hold along with his pipe, I can't say.

—It's here, Dean. About the cat and the dog you killed, the window you…

—*What* cat and *what* dog?! *I'd never kill an animal!*

I'd crashed back down when the inches of slack on my chains pulled taught before I realized I'd shot up my chair. The glass-sharp geometry of Doctor Johansson's clinical reality snapped, and the room took an iron solidity, so harsh and unyielding that my sight cracked on it.

Doctor Johansson went on, looking to the police file…the talisman of papal infallibility, of unimpeachable expositional fact that challenged me to throw my sanity against it.

—There are the shades you left up so you'd be seen killing Catherine, the door you cracked open so the police could get in easily. I can use all this to your advantage, Dean, if you'll admit doing these things.

My twin's gaze pressed on me, as if I stood on stage (playing the role that would one day be his) and had forgotten my lines. The urge to ask him for prompts from the wings twitched in my throat, even as the lens that was his surrogate eye fed on me.

Displacement

—I've admitted *murder* to you. What I've told you will get me lethal injections in most states. If what you say made any sense, I'd admit it.

—The police were in the building when you killed Catherine. You brought them there by killing the pets of the couple in apartment 103. You left a kitchen knife with your prints on it....

My lungs felt full of wet sand.

—Why would I waltz into a building to kill someone while there's a cop car in front?

—You wanted to be caught. And even if the sight of the car would have driven you away, the car could have, should have, pulled up while you were in Catherine's apartment. The police were a few blocks behind you. You timed it that way. You knew when that couple would come home and find their pets. You knew their routine. The building manager recognized your mug shots. He's certain you'd been casing the building.

—That's not what happened. Not that way.

My simple statement was like a small verse in a whirlwind. I've been telling the truth to this man and now he tries to entrap me? With a facile twist on the good cop/bad cop treatment? Or was I mad? Were the *fictions* that defined Doctor Johansson's world corrupting my existence and my mind? In their training, forensic shrinks and profilers such as he use novels and drek thrillers as textbooks. Men who look for the *leakage* of sadistic fantasies in the behavior of those whom they hunt and treat themselves have intellects shaped by fantasy. Were Doctor Johansson's fantasies, the ways in which he read them, the ways in which they sculpted his mind, crushing the reality I'd crafted out of the same stone?

—It's the only way you could have been caught. Police in three states had no idea that one person had done what you've done. You surrendered yourself. You knew you'd be seen with Catherine through the window. You knew once the call to the police was made, the dispatcher would put the officers in 103 in direct contact with the person making the call.

—I made sure the door was bolted, that the shades were drawn. I had three escape routes worked out, I had...

No...this will stop, now. To control a fiction, one can stop reading it. I'm not going to act crazy, prodded like an ant in one of my chalk-circle arenas to participate in its own destruction. I won't deny these things like a character in a horror comic, blithering to his shrink: *But, ya gotta BELIEVE ME, Doc!* I willed my body slack, took a deep breath, forced clean air where wet sand had been. The gaze of my twin (whose face I'd never see, even as he lifted a mask of my face to his own in order to play me) watched me with sight that had changed over the span of the last few heartbeats. It felt cold as winter runoff in a gutter.

—I have no recollection of the things you say I've done. What you're saying is fantastic to me. I don't believe the circumstances of my arrest were as you say they were.

He wasn't buying it. I wouldn't have, either.

—I believe that's what you believe.

—That's all I can ask of you. You've given me something to talk over with my lawyer.

—How?

—If he thought me in control of my faculties, he'd have told me what you have just now. That disappoints me. I thought he and I had an understanding.

—Would you kill him for such a betrayal?

—No. It was a professional decision on his part, I'm sure. There was no malice behind it. And his betrayal could only have occurred after my getting cancer. He couldn't have contributed to my death if I was already dying. You can take that as a diminishment of my need to kill if you wish, Doctor.

I sighed, glanced to the barred window high on the western wall. I saw a bird fly past the beginnings of an October sunset, and ached to be outside, walking the countryside near the facility, feeling leaves crunch underfoot, sipping autumn air. I was aware of a weight behind me, as if I sat near a great spur of granite. All that had been a *stage* in my perceptions dimmed to shadow cloaked by shadow. My twin left us. The biting gaze of the lens numbed itself. This Second Act wound down yet further to blackout. I suddenly missed my twin…he who would one day place me into the mythology I'd tapped by playing me on film. His companionship had blunted what I'd felt rising like floodwater behind me…the madness of this institution.

—Do you want to stop, Dean?

Lord, I'm so very tired, exorcising a lifetime of demons…

My mind felt like a sore muscle, from the strain of carrying so long and brutal a performance this day, and from bearing the level of erudition Doctor Johansson had foisted upon me. My catharsis was a labor for me, as an actor and as an audience. Doctor Johansson had entered my fictions, and in so doing, had set aside his professional decorum at the threshold of my realm the same way that knights had once set down their weapons on the thresholds of cathedrals. I had determined the determining course of his questions. He'd placed on my shoulders the task of being the sophisticated killer, since monsters such as I must be dark and fascinating mirrors. It is that dark otherness that flatters those to whom I speak.

Displacement

Because who wishes to speak to a common killer? To a thug with a tire iron, or a semi-literate shit with a gun? Or a bastard who beats his wife? To be an adequate mirror, even for a bureaucratically commissioned shrink, I had to be brilliant in the way that Doctor Johansson wished me to be, even if he was unaware of that wish. The wish is born of the same vanity that drove him to steer our sessions the informal way they have gone, and it is the same vanity of which my victims partook. I flattered them in death, and thus did they participate in their murders. Only a person of great worth and importance can be killed in such Gothic ways by a brilliant fiend such as I have become…such as they conscripted me to be. Vanity has been my prime weapon, more lethal than any machete or gun. I completed their desired reflected images of grandeur by killing them. The strain of being a mythic thing of brilliant darkness for a man as intelligent as Doctor Johansson has left me hollow. To be a mirror requires a kind of silence past speech that is exhausting to maintain. Yet the catharsis of our theater was so very worth this exhaustion.

—I would very much like to stop, please.

Doctor Johansson pressed a button on his desk intercom. After a moment I heard the door behind me open. He collected his files into one stack, drawing our curtain closed and drawing his mind closed, making it pedestrian and small before my eyes with visible relief. This day had been hard for him, too. The mask of the clinician/priest can be heavy as a crown.

—Will we continue tomorrow, Doctor?

The guards, some subset of County Deputies, to be precise, tended to the padlocks on the chains that hung off me. Doctor Johansson and I paid them no mind, as we would bus boys clearing salad plates.

—Tomorrow I'd like you to have a physical. The judge will want to know what your medical needs are.

My chair was surrounded by walls of flesh in grey and blue uniforms. My feet and hands were still chained in an X formation, bound by another chain around my waist. It amused me, the precautions they took. As if I were some kind of transcendently superhuman fiend. Dangerous for them to think so. Maybe their belief in my monstrosity would allow me to snap the chains and overpower them.

I groaned as I stood up, icy pinpoints boiled in my legs, and a charley horse clenched my left hip.

As the Deputies positioned themselves to herd me to my cell, I asked, —Doctor, in light of all I've told you, and the grief I've spared the taxpayers by being up front, would it be possible for me to have a bath tonight? Not a shower, but a long soak?

—I'll see what I can do.

—Thank you.

I turned and let the Deputies usher me offstage. The mirror did not applaud, which may have been rude, or reverently polite. It was disorienting to walk again, as if I'd just snapped from a troubling dream. Fog pressed the corners of my vision.

A draft eddied around me as I clanked to the hall, whispering against the base of my skull, the exposed parts of my wrists, even my ankles. I realized I'd worked up a clammy sweat in Doctor Johansson's office. Maybe the cold was the absent gaze of my twin, which, like the warmth of a hand placed on a wrist for a long while, leaves its ghost wrought under the skin.

The steps of the Deputies were soothing on the linoleum floor. Their silence was a testimonial to their fear of me, more than were the chains. They joke with others as they shuffle them to their cells, so they'll be well thought of in the event of a hostage taking. Killers they find vile they are overly civil with, like the finest of British butlers: a way to mask their urge to kill them as they would mad dogs. I think they said nothing to me out of fear I'd walk into their minds and wreak havoc there.

The quiet, defining itself by my escorts' heavy treads, made what screamed in my mind seem all the louder: the inverse of an echo. A ghost of a sound that strengthened to become what had first been echoed. It built to something like the shriek of a pavement saw. Yet layered, verbalizing the gibberish of shattered minds, taking knotted cadences as my escorts walked me through checkpoints of steel mesh and sliding iron doors. I've tread the deepest dreams of my victims; the clawing thoughts of madmen are audible to me. I feel how they can make their own invisible yet unyielding walls. They press against the walls of this prison, as if trying to crack the cinderblock from within.

From the final checkpoint we entered the purest expression of Hell I'd ever know, beyond the imaginings of Goya or Bosch, because it was so mundane. We entered a world of unspeakable ugliness (unspeakable, in that it does not allow itself to be expressed, like the desperation in the eyes of people on city streets) where footsteps on concrete thunder through the corridors, where the fear-scented shouts of the damned and the criminally insane hang like smoke from a fire of damp leaves and coat your mouth with the stink of zoo animals and of psycho-pharmaceuticals sweated through the pores of lunatics. These are men enslaved by their fantasies, too cowed by them to master and use them. These are men twice-maddened: upon being locked here, they snap again for want of a

Displacement

way out such as I carried in me, a malignant key that grew more cells by the hour.

The hallway of cells that do not liberate is long and very tall, a lamp-pon of a cathedral in industrial drab.

My fellow inmates are psychopaths who've taken axes to families as they slept, child molesters who've taken rusty knives to their victims' genitals, compulsive cop killers and other throwbacks whose minds have never risen above the reptilian. I enter their fever-wakened dreams as I walk the corridors with my escorts.

Some men hoot and call from their cells, not out of malice toward or even interest in me, but to make desperate sounds of defiance, to shake the world awake from the dreams that have made them brutal. Theirs is the brutality many can smugly glimpse through psychology texts, the reports of social workers watered down in newspapers, and in grainy films shown in the grey-shadowed altars of sociology seminars.

Many here resent me. Media coverage has made me a celebrity. They know I'll leave a mark on the fictions I have harnessed. Killers based on me, invented by writers I'll never meet, will be my sons for years to come. My fellow inmates will leave no such legacy.

They yell, their voices booming then fading as I pass.

—HEY! Garrison!!

—Hey!! We got a *super*star, here!

—Say, Dean old buddy!! Can I play you when they make a TV docudrama aboutcha?

I feel oddly close to my father as I hear them. For they, barking their derisions at me, whistle up from the dust the derisions of their own parents, who had so lovingly crafted the sadisms that defined the crimes of their sons.

They're crazy fucks. Every one of them. Animals. Even the ones who don't shout still yell with their deadly silences. Their voices are quiet, yet their eyes are glassy with fury so deep and black your own mind can become lost in their shattered gazes.

I've read about psychologists posing as patients in places like this, to find out what conditions were like. They often went crazy themselves. Madness is deadly because it's so tempting to touch, the way fire is to a child.

The idea of going mad terrifies me, because as one who has lived and killed as an idea, my madness would be complete. Especially in this Godforsaken place. Here, where the winds blow constantly, whistling through the corridors of cement and steel…here I wouldn't just lose my mind. My spirit would die. It would wither in a depression that could never be broken. Ennui would devour me a nibble at a time, breaking my soul with the slowness of an earwig biting the tissues of my brain. I have offered myself to this danger. In becoming a spirit, I've made myself permeable, as vulnerable as a shaman in a deep trance.

Not with a bang, but with a whimper.

Yet for me there's light at the end of the tunnel, an earthen darkness comforting in its finality.

Soon I'll be shipped to another facility. This place can't care for me, not while a rosary of tumors stalks up my innards like ivy crawling up a trellis. Soon I'll be taken to the security wing of a hospital. Cuffed to a comfortable bed, with decent food and quiet. To not provide me with adequate care would be cruel and unusual.

Despite the awful pain I'll be in at the time, I look forward to my last breath.

In my dream, I was aware of October. I can't remember the substance of the dream, and I know there is a mercy to that. But I recall the impression of standing beneath a fantastically big sky, under trees so tall, they loomed in my sight as they'd seem to a toddler. I breathed air full of the smokeless burning of leaves rotting into the rich soil they blanketed. October died in my dream, made dim by those unbreathing shadows unique to corners of grey cinderblock. Still sleeping, I knew on some deep level that this was Halloween morning, just as I once could know before waking that snow had fallen in the night.

My sleep was ripped like the skin of Keene's throat, by a scream that woke me and threw me from my cot with the violence of a seizure.

Tuttle, in the cell opposite, crouched atop the steel sink in his cell. He screamed with all the strength of his lungs, all the volume of his barrel chest. His features twisted, as if his grimace would pull the corners of his mouth below his jaw. His powder-blue eyes bulged, and when my gaze touched his through the bars, the man wailed like an infant as he dropped to the cement floor with a sickening thud, more lifeless when he struck than was Catherine's body.

The attendants rushed to Tuttle in less than a minute, along with the head psychiatric nurse, an ex-Marine named Richard who weighed two-hundred and eighty pounds. One held a straightjacket, another had a hypo at the ready. But as they neared him, Tuttle rolled on the floor like an autistic child on the verge of exhaustion, mumbling or praying in a language of his own.

Tuttle's monstrosity is unique, even here. Six foot three, with arms like logs, an IQ of about fifty, and the inability to come unless he snaps the neck of the prostitute he fucks. He had been a bogeyman of my youth, a monster culled out of newspapers into schoolyard folklore. A bogeyman I'd feared as a kid now lived close enough for me to smell the stink of his morning shit.

They had Tuttle upright now. The nightmare being of my youth was still bawling, pointing toward the door of his cell and saying, *Kitty, kitty*. Or maybe it was *Kiddie*, I couldn't tell. His face was the color of turned wine and his mouth spilled frothy spit that mixed with the tears that leaked from his idiot child's eyes.

Madness collects here, as if in a great battery or dynamo, and it arcs now and then in the minds of people like Tuttle. The bars hum with the threat of a discharge.

The wind surges. Over Tuttle's quieting sobs, I hear dead leaves flying against the outside wall through the slot-like window of my cell. And although the window can't be opened, I feel a draft coalesce around me and drift like river fog out of my cell. The tumors in my lower guts twitch like hatchlings.

Tuttle screams again, and covers his face with his blanket.

Three hours later, I sit in Doctor Johansson' office, chained to my usual seat. For days now, in short sessions of less than an hour, we've gone over the particulars of my ten avengings…details that won't help my twin in his portrait of me as a fascinating monster, but that will help the police, and perhaps the Anne Rule wannabes who'll make meager advances dashing off my story for paperback houses.

Doctor Johansson has his files placed before him. I think I've partly figured out his system. The placement of files is like a series of Japanese fans, spread in semi-circles, slightly overlapping. His mind operates on many levels. He's not the sort to impose phenomena into the linear formations that are the delight of the arrogant and stupid. He's not afraid to use a maze-like model, or a model like a house of cards. I wish I had time to know him better.

He looks at a new file, not like the others: it's stapled and has several differently colored pages, white, pink, goldenrod, and blue. The folder seems unstable in my sight, as if made of television static.

—How do you feel, Dean? he asked, puffing on his cold and empty pipe.

—Fine. For the time being.

The draft came again, making me uneasy, bringing thoughts of Tuttle and his shrieking tirade. The eyes of my twin from behind the silvered glass seemed a fleshy, oppressive presence. The light of the last October morning I'll ever see streamed from the window. Dust motes didn't churn in the light, but seemed to stay almost suspended, despite the draft.

—From the time you killed Molino to the time you killed Catherine, how had you been handling stress?

He massaged his right temple as he spoke, the pipe nearly touching his wrist. Had it been lit, it would have burned him. Looking at the bowl, I felt the *anticipation* of it burning him, the involuntary flinch of seeing someone about to suffer pain. My spine compressed, my shoulders hunched, until a *pulling* changed the tilt of my vertebrae, so that the cartilage between them felt packed with shaved ice.

—What do you mean?

—Were you having sweats? Grinding your teeth? Stomachaches? Shaky hands?

—Not as much as before.

The *anticipation* of seeing him burned personified itself, brought itself into being.

—And you felt better about the people you killed?

I tried to not to pay heed to the *tugging* I felt on the chain around my waist, like a child trying to get my attention. It was very hard to stay focused.

—I've told you that.

The tugging stopped, and I heard the quick *click-click* like dog's paws on the tile by my feet, receding as if the paws walked toward the door.

My shoulders fell.

—And better about yourself, too?

The paws ran towards my back, wide long steps like a high jumper going towards his mark. A weight thudded against my shoulders and a wet mouth pressed to the nape of my neck. Fever-hot hands gripped my collarbones. The warmth of moist palms bled through my jumpsuit.

Don't scream. Don't scream. Don't…

—Yes, I felt better about myself.

I trembled like a man freezing from blood loss.

Displacement

Ignore it. Ignore the little shit. He's nothing without attention. Ignore him...

—Your cancer has gone into remission, Dean. Whatever internalized stress that fueled it is gone. The cancer has stopped.

Within a heartbeat, all I'd ever been and felt and tasted and done crowded through the doors of my consciousness. Blinders of perception ripped, awareness of everything sluiced into my mind, the inverse of what I'd felt as Evan died: an *inward* awareness, abrasive, wounding. Each thread and seam of my clothing itched. I smelled the oily links of my chains, the dust baking atop the buzzing fluorescent lights, the residue of nicotine in the long-dormant air filter. I felt the vibrations of the heating pipes, each nail of the fingers digging into my flesh, each tooth of the mouth, each nodule of the sliding tongue, each crease of the lips.

I heard the timber-creak of Doctor Johansson closing the cardboard file and the tumble of motes.

And like a crease of lightning against a pitch-black void, I felt my mind cracking and folding and crushing under its own weight as the gift of my mortality dropped from my grasp.

Because I knew then, and understood.

Doctor Johansson's mouth cracked open, and the words he spoke struck my chest with a force that could snap my ribs.

—The court recommended you stay here...

I knew and understood.

...under our care...

I knew and understood.

...unfit to stand trial...

I knew and understood.

...incompetent...

I was going to stay here.

...medication...

And I was going to go mad.

...intensive therapy...

No way out.

The tiny mouth detached from my neck and the spot where it had been felt cold and wet. Little feet scraped against my back and I heard faint laughter and felt the warmth of breath against my ear, felt the noose of flesh that had never lived tighten around my neck as little arms hugged my throat.

I screamed.

Doctor Johansson flew back from his desk.

—YOU LITTLE SHIT!!! YOU BROUGHT ME HERE!!! YOU *PLANNED* THIS!!

My throat ripped within as I yelled and jerked in the rattling chair, trying to detach the little fuck from my back. I felt it drop off, then heard it run to the door. Like the hands of a diabetic going into shock, my mind grasped and clenched and groped as what I had wrought shived itself into the core of my awareness.

The little being ran towards me again and its hand grabbed my hair. The thing *hung* off my scalp, dangling, jerking my neck to the sides, and Oh, God, why couldn't I see it, like before? Why was it hiding behind the air, now? Why was it laughing like a happy child?

The door opened, I heard it over the hollow and hoarse sounds my torn throat made in lieu of screams, and suddenly Richard stood over me with three attendants.

—Get it off me, Richard. Please.

But my voice was too mutilated to be heard.

Richard had a hypo in his hand.

Oh God, no.

I started crying.

A prick on my shoulder and a grey cloudy void.

I'm going mad.

I know this, for I have written this poem, and have only now discovered its last stanza.

It's as if I'm going senile, parts of my mind strobe out, leaving holes in my consciousness. I'm aware of the hollow spaces left behind, like the soft sockets that mark where a tooth has been pulled.

The bars hum deafeningly with the madness of this place, and the barn-stench of psychotherapeutic drugs taints my own sweat now. The chemicals paint my mouth with a taste like burnt tin foil. I rewrote myself as myth, and all myths are defined by their endings. Warrior kings become great because of the final battles that await them. Killing avatars such as I, Grendels of this day, who invade the white-carpeted halls of those we kill, are defined by the normality that is restored by our capture and our deaths. By the catharsis those who drink of our fictions feel as they close the book or watch end credits roll. By our being invaded by the dybbyks that are our downfalls, as we are tormented by our suppressed selves. By our Others. The fiction demands it. I made myself a Trickster,

Displacement

and in so doing, I've been tricked. I am not Loki. In becoming an archetype, I am ruined by my own Trickster son whom I exiled…just as I, an exiled son, have ruined my father.

Why has my little victim done this to me? I try hard not to use its name, anymore. Because there's a power, a magic, to Names that can make things real…imaginary things. Specters can accost you in the broad light of day if you give them the right Name, even if you've made yourself an accosting specter.

That's the real question. *How* could he have done this to me? He's a goblin. *The Velveteen Rabbit* told how things can attain the gift of life through nursery magic. The Velveteen Rabbit was given life for helping a little boy cope with sickness. My little twin, my Other, was brought to life through nursery magic, the same magic that turned me into a god over the smaller things I tormented. Maybe my little victim was given life for helping me endure my tortured childhood.

Torture.

That's the issue, isn't it?

I tortured him, and this is his payback. His trick, as the dispossessed child of a dispossessed child. But he's unfair. I'd let him go. I'd freed him long ago, and he won't let me out of this place, won't give me the peace of death.

When I'd come out from under Richard's needle, I tried to cut my way out of here, a way cut out through myself. The one legacy from my father: the easy way out.

It was dark, and I was chained with my arms crossed when I came to. But it was simple enough to slide the links down to expose my wrists. I should inflict upon myself a Gothic end, poetic. What else should be expected of me, who, invoking the poetry of fiction, inflicted Gothic ends on others? I thought of Filippo Argenti, Dante's enemy who, in Hell, went mad with anger and turned his teeth against himself.

I followed his example, and felt hot blood bubble into my mouth.

I spat out the skin of my wrists and sat on the bed and bled onto my blankets, so the sound of blood streaming on the floor wouldn't bring the attendants.

Minutes later I heard a crash against the bars of Tuttle's cell. (Could the little monster get through the bars of my cell?) Tuttle woke and started screaming again, blanket thrown over his face. Could Tuttle see it because he was a Fool? A Child? A Monster? Did all three masks he wore give him such Sight?

I was too weak to move when the attendants came into the hallway to check on Tuttle. Despite their coming, I knew I had a good chance of dying. But before they could return with the med kit, I felt pressure on my forearms, a small hand on each choking off the blood-flow to my chewed wrists.

The attendants saved my life. God damn them.

My aching wrists were then separated from the reach of my mouth by the thick canvass of a straitjacket. Undaunted, upon my return from the infirmary, I took another lesson from my poetic mentor, whose myths defined the killers' myths I have used to define me. Dante wrote of Per della Vigne, who, after a running start, smashed in his own head against the walls of his prison.

When I tried, a soft body placed itself between the wall and my head, clinging, perhaps, like a spider.

I'm sure my little victim didn't mind the impact. He's suffered worse under my rage.

I fell backward to the floor, as if pushed by a schoolyard bully.

My second attempt made quite a racket. The attendants came and bound me to the cot with restraints that look like seat belts. They took no chances, and left me in the canvass jacket.

And so tonight, I swallowed my tongue.

My victim opened my mouth and pulled my tongue from my throat. I tried biting the fingers, but my teeth passed through them as if they were clay.

My only hope is the cancer.

But that's a vain hope.

Because I think my little victim is my cancer, displaced in some ethereal way outside my body.

My miserable life when I was young gave birth to Piggy. Later, my miserable life gave birth to my cancer. They're the same thing, products of my mind under like circumstances. And when I faced death born of my own pent-up rage, I created a third set of circumstances. He prompted me to seek the catharsis that would free him with a single whispered word: *Why?*

As I have been taking my life back by taking lives, Piggy has been taking back the lives I have stolen from him. Maybe that's how he got a life of his own.

And a will of his own.

Oh, my. I've been using his Name, haven't I?

I couldn't not use it forever, could I?

So this is Piggy's revenge, as all Tricksters have their revenge. Or his Justice, perhaps. His hunger for the Justice of seeing me imprisoned and broken, as I had kept him imprisoned and broken in my mind.

Displacement

At least I hope he's done this out of Justice, or revenge, or rage.

I hear him now, my exiled twin, the click of his feet on the hallway floor. He passes through the bars like a whisper. He runs a few steps and jumps atop my chest, where my raw and aching wrists press over each other in their canvas sleeves.

I can see him, this twisted little creature taken from my mirror image. His ugly goblin's face is like my own when I was a child, and like a child, I cry when I see him.

Because I *am* a child again. I have no freedom, I waste here in neglect. The straitjacket is so much like the restricting snowsuit from so long ago, an embodiment of my prison I wear as a garment.

Just like old times.

I am a child again, and Piggy is smiling warmly at me, like an old friend. And grinding my stitched wrists as he does so, he rocks back and forth, as a toddler would, expecting to hear again a much-loved story.

I hope he has done this to me out of rage or revenge.

Because I couldn't bear to think he has done this to me out of Love.

Little Round Head

Mother found me in the sun today and "*woosh!*" out she came on her fast legs when there were clouds and took me inside.

She wasn't mad, but she held me against her fur and her tears fell, *drip! drip!*, on me and I started crying too because I was bad and didn't want to make her cry. When she saw me cry too she kissed me and rocked me back and forth and she said my name, "Little Round Head! Little Round Head! What am I to do with my Little Round Head?" And then she sang me one of the songs I like so much and cleaned off the tears with her tongue. Later, Father came with food from down deep and he and Mother and me cleaned each other before we ate and I slept between them and felt safe.

I didn't want to be bad.

Father and Mother played a game with me with sticks and bones. It was fun and there were songs to sing with the game and Mother and Father said the game was very old and the songs were from the Old Times. One of the bones was a head bone, and it was round and funny looking like my head and I picked it up and kissed it like Mother and Father kiss my head and called the bone "Little Round Head" like how they call me and I held it close like it was my baby.

Mother and Father thought that was funny and laughed, "Ha-Ha!" They held me close and ran their hands over my skin that doesn't have fur like theirs to pick off bugs.

It is nice to be loved.

Father brought home a paper box with milk in it. When he comes home down the big pipe he shakes the paper box "*wusha-wusha*" so I can hear that there's milk inside that he is bringing. He makes sound because I can't see down the big pipes like he and Mother do.

Sometimes the paper box is covered with the sticky red food Mother and Father like, and they lick it off and I drink the milk inside and we pass the milk box in a circle so we can all have a treat.

Mother and Father eat the box when it is empty, *"crunch-crunch,"* because it makes them happy and I am happy when they are. I tried to eat the paper box once, but it tasted bad and Mother and Father laughed and said maybe when I am older I can eat the grown-up food they eat.

Father was about to eat the paper box when his eyes got big and he showed it to Mother and she said a whispery thing *"pishha-pishha-pishha"* and they folded the box and put it between them.

I asked what was wrong…maybe the milk was rotten and would make them sick. But they said "No, No. Nothing is wrong, Little Round Head. You go to sleep now, and we will come sing you songs."

I went because I wanted to be good. I heard them tearing up the paper box and I was worried that they would be sick and I would be all alone.

When I went to sleep I dreamed about the Bad Mother and the Bad Father. They are ugly mean things like giant babies, without soft gray fur on them like Mother and Father have, without the fur that I will grow when I'm big. The Bad Mother and the Bad Father yell at me and keep me in an ugly thing like a cage with wood bars. The Bad Mother and Bad Father burn me with little white sticks that they put in their mouths and make on fire before they burn me with the orange parts.

I start crying because I am so sad and hurt so much. But Mother and Father kill the Bad Mother and the Bad Father and take me away home.

When I woke up I was still crying, and my real Mother and Father came and held me close and said, "Shh! Shh! It's only a bad dream, Little Round Head! It's only a bad dream!"

They let me sleep between them and they sang to me and I had dreams about a dark place with shiny black stone steps going down and down to a place where I could play all the time and get my own food like Father does from the hunts.

It is a nice dream, and the Bad Mother and the Bad Father are far, far away.

Today Mother and Father had to leave me all alone, and I tried to show them I was brave. They saw I was scared, and before they left they gave me the headbone that I had kissed and they told me I had to be brave and protect it. They made a little body for the head bone out of straw and skin scraps so it was a doll now, and they gave it to me as a present. I was happy and I held the doll close so it wouldn't be afraid and Mother and Father kissed and hugged me before they left.

I sang to my doll. I can't sing like Mother and Father. Sometimes the words come out right, but most times they don't.

When Mother and Father came back, they had cloth things that I wear with them. They tell me I'm getting big, and the cloth things that keep me warm are getting too small.

I say I want to have fur like them, and Mother and Father laugh and stroke the top of my head where I have the most fur and they say, "Little Round Head! You will be big enough soon!"

The cloth things are covered with the red wet food. Mother and Father put them in their mouths and suck out the red food, "*shluck! shluck! shluck!*" like how they sometimes suck food from the insides of bones. I take my old cloth things off and use parts to keep my doll warm. My doll is all bundled up to its little head bone.

When they are dry the new cloth things smell like Mother and Father's mouths, and when I wear them, it smells like I am being kissed and loved.

That is the warmest feeling of all.

Father said I could go with him for food, that I was big enough and brave enough to come.

He made me hang on tight to his back, where there is lots of hair and skin, and he carried me through the tunnels. Sometimes, there was water and Father splashed through it and I got wet.

Father caught two rats and "*rutch! rutch!*" he bit off their heads so we could eat them. But first he poured out the red food from where the rats' heads were onto his tongue, because he knows I don't like the red food yet. I tried once to bite off the head of a rat, but it bit me first and I cried and Mother grabbed the rat fast and smashed it against a wall and said words I didn't know at it and it burned.

So until I am bigger Mother and Father will bite off the heads.

Father carried me to a place with a wall and he shoved against it, "*thud! thud!*" and it was a door that opened and there was air like outside. Then I saw an outside place that was dark and the ground was wet and had big stones in rows like teeth coming out of it.

I stayed close to Father, because I was scared of the new place.

Father crawled behind the stone teeth things and I crawled behind him. Then he stopped and smelled, "*sniff! sniff!*" and we crawled to one of the stone teeth that looked bright and new and in front of the stone tooth was a long mound of dirt that smelled fresh and different from the rest of the ground.

Father shoved his arm into the dirt and made a hole. He put his nose in the hole and wriggled into the dirt and dirt got shoved up as Father dug in and I heard noises like wood breaking and then Father came up with food and he jumped and stepped on the mound to make it like it was before.

He gave me food to carry. We went a little way, then I looked back because I wanted to see how Father had made the mound like it was before and I saw that the ground with the stone teeth ended with a big metal gate with spikes on top and past that was lights and buildings and houses. I remembered being able to see a place like that through a square hole in the wall of the dream place where the Bad Mother and Bad Father live.

I didn't know places like that were real. And since the place was real, maybe so were the Bad Mother and Bad Father.

Father made a sound at me like a rat. He had gone far ahead of me. I hurried to catch up. We came to the door, and I saw that it was to a long white stone thing like a house that went into a hill. Father and I went inside and he pulled the door shut, and there were shelves near the door I didn't see before, and on the shelves were long wood boxes that were broken and inside were bits of cloth and skin and bones.

Father said, "You were very brave, Little Round Head. I want to give you something for being so very brave."

And Father put the food he was carrying on a shelf and picked up one of the long boxes and shook out the old rags and bone and skin and put the food inside it. Then he hunched down low for me to climb on his back.

When we got home we found Mother up high where the metal pipes are. When Father and I saw her there we all laughed because we knew she was scared and lonely and climbed up there so she can drop on things that come into our home and rip their backs out. Once she dropped on a thing that looked like the Bad Father except it had a yellow head bone that was metal with a light on the forehead. When Mother dropped on it, it screamed and the headbone fell off and the light made scary shadows on the wall while I hid. Later, I got the yellow head bone with the light so I could see in the tunnels better. The head bone was fun, but soon all the light got used up. I still keep it where I sleep, along with a belt the thing had that had lots of shiny metal things hanging off it that make a nice jangling sound when I shake it.

Mother dropped down and kissed us and cleaned us. Father put the long box up where I sleep and told me I could sleep in the box and not be cold from drafts at night. I got in the box and it smelled like the dry dusty food we get sometimes. It was warm and very soft because it had a special cloth in it. Father told me the special cloth is called "velvet" and he wanted me to sleep on something nice and there was even a fluffy thing where my head went.

Later, as Mother and Father clean themselves and bits of their fur come off on their tongues and hands, they put the fur in the box so I will be even warmer at night and the fur smells like them and I am happy and have nice dreams all the time.

Sometimes I wake up to find that Mother and Father have been kissing me while I am asleep and they put more fur in the box.

Mother sleeps and sleeps, and when she wakes up she doesn't move fast like when she is well.

I ask Father what is wrong, and Father says she is all right, and nothing bad will happen.

Father brings food like always, but he brings a little more for Mother. Father has to give her lots of milk and sometimes he saves the paper box and goes out and fills it with the red food. Mother wants to share the milk, but Father and me take only little sips so Mother will have more.

At night I go to sleep in my box full of warm fur and I cry. I have lots of dreams about the Bad Mother and Bad Father. They burn me with the white sticks and cut me with glass and hit me with belts.

I wake up from the dream lots of times and hear Mother breathing funny, like her chest is full of water.

I hold my doll close to try to make it feel safe, but it is too smart and knows that I am scared too.

Father took me to get food today.

I didn't want to go. Mother is too sick to go up the metal pipes to drop on bad things or go up there to hide.

But I went anyway, to carry more food back for Mother.

Father carried me along the tunnels, but we went a different way than before. Father whispered to me, "I want to show you something, Little Round Head." And then he turned to the wall of the tunnel and there were metal things sticking out that Father climbed up easy. When we went up top there was a metal circle thing that Father pushed, and "*shraaaang!!*" it moved and scraped against something.

There were outside smells.

Father climbed through where the metal thing was and I saw a strange, strange place. There was a big building made of blocks of red stones that went up and up. Way up top of the building were big tunnels and lots of smoke came out of them and went into the dark sky and funny smells and sounds came from the building. Sounds like "*rrrrrrrrr!*" and smells like the bad steams that come out from deep in the tunnels near home sometimes.

There were lights up high on green metal poles, but we were where it was dark and safe.

I held on to Father's back, and he crawled over piles of red stone blocks like the building was made of. There was a wooden box on one of the piles, and when we got to it Father took me off his back and whispered, "Look inside, Little Round Head!"

When I got close, I heard funny sounds, like rats but not as squeaky and mean.

Inside was an animal, with gray fur and whiskers and pointy ears and pretty green eyes that was laying on its side. Lots of little animals were pressed against its belly and they made "*mew! mew!*" noises. The big animal licked the little ones and I could tell it loved the little ones very much.

Father held me close, and even though we were far from home, I felt very safe.

Father said, up close so I could feel his nice warm breath, "Something like this will happen to your Mother, Little Round Head."

Mother's belly is getting big, and she is wanting more and more to eat that is wet with the red food. Father gets food for her all the time, and because he is away, we don't sing so much any more.

But I am happy. I bring Mother water and sometimes I catch a rat for her so she can bite its head off and get the red food inside. I rub her feet and her belly, and we clean the bugs off each other.

She kisses me and says, "Little Round Head! Little Round Head! How I love my Little Round head!"

Father spends lots of time rubbing her belly, only when he does it, he says special words, words like in the old songs and words that Mother said to make the rat that bit me burn. Sometimes when Father says the words, there are rumbling sounds and purple lights and cold winds come.

I sleep in my box and hold my doll close and wonder if I can hold the little one when it comes like I hold the doll.

I found the paper box Mother and Father hid from me. Just the one part they had torn off. It was up high, where it is drier and we keep special things to burn, like leaves that smell like the places where we get the food. I went up there to get leaves because I wanted to show my doll what the food places smell like. I was quiet because Mother was sleeping.

There was a picture on the box of a face that was my face. I know my face because I have seen it in a shiny glass thing that Father uses to make lots of light when we have fire and he makes shadow puppets on the wall that tell stories about the Old Days, and he and Mother sing the old songs in the old words.

I wonder why my face is on the paper box. I put it back, because Mother and Father put it there so I wouldn't see it and I didn't want them to think I was bad.

I go to my box full of good-smelling fur and I worry the Bad Mother and Bad Father can find me, because dreams are pictures, and if I can be inside a picture, then maybe they can get me.

I go to sleep and try to dream of the black stone steps that take me to the happy place.

Mother is hurting today, making "*arroooow! arroooow!*" sounds and she is biting a big piece of wood and it goes "*crack! crack!*" because her teeth are breaking it up.

Father is holding her and I am sad that she might die.

Mother is still hurting. I bring her water and she does not talk but she looks at me and I see in her eyes that she loves me.

Then she goes, "*arrrrrrrahhhhah!!!!!*" and her legs go wide and something comes out of her. It is a bag of wet skin and there is something inside. It moves like one of the little white fish we eat sometimes that live in the water down the far tunnels, but it is gray. I think I hear Mother and Father crying, but they are laughing. They are happy because of the bag of skin.

Mother bites open the bag and the little thing inside cries "*eeeeahhh!*" Mother licks it clean and eats the skin.

And I feel very sad.

The little one looks like Mother and Father.

It is not ugly like me.

It has fur, and its head is shaped long and right, not round like mine.

Mother and Father hold it close and they cry and laugh while the little thing goes "*eeeeahhh! eeeeah!!!*"

They say, "Look, Little Round Head! Look! You have someone to play with now!!!"

I try to be happy.

But in my box later I cry.

I don't want to be so ugly.

It has been summer and winter, now.

It is warm again and Little Velvet Ears can walk some.

That is the name of the little one. Mother and Father call him that because his ears are soft and furry and shaped right, not round and funny feeling like mine. Mother and Father touch their lips to the tips of his ears and say how soft they are and how good they smell. Sometimes, Mother and Father call me just "Round Head" now, because I'm not as little as the baby.

Father and I go for food all the time. Little Velvet Ears needs lots of food and Mother does not want to be away from him. Sometimes, Father and Mother chew the food up before they give it to Little Velvet Ears. Sometimes they bite the head off a rat and pour the red food into Little Velvet Ears' mouth and he laughs and giggles and makes funny "*squish, squish*" sounds because he likes the red food so much. It makes his pink tongue all red, and I wonder how he can eat the red food when he is so much littler than me and it is a grown-up food.

Little Velvet Ears gets food from Mother, too. She holds him close and he puts his mouth on her and he gets food that way. Father told me he gets milk that way, and I wonder how, because milk comes in paper boxes.

Little Velvet Ears can talk, some, too. He can even say words from the old songs that I can't say. He says them in baby talk, "*ghathoolo! ghathoolo!*" and he laughs and claps his little hands so the pads make soft noises. Mother and Father laugh, too, and say how clever he is.

I went deep in the tunnels where there is water to get white fish to eat. They have little red eyes that are sweet. I pretend when I eat the eyes that I am eating drops of the red food.

I put bits of food in the water that the white fish eat and when they are eating, my hands go "*splash!*" and I get the fish and their funny mouths open wide and I squeeze them, "*krutch!*" so they don't get away.

I was eating a fish when I heard a rat that sounded funny. I went where the sound was and saw a big rat in a nest made of leaves. It had little rats pressed against its belly and I thought of the animal Father showed me a long time ago in the box outside. The big rat was a mother rat and it made a noise at me, "*skreeah!*" The little rats were getting milk from the mother rat.

The little rats didn't have fur like the mother rat, they were all pink and ugly. Ugly even for rats.

That is how I am. All pink and without fur. The little rats had heads that weren't shaped like the mother rat's.

The little rats were so ugly I found a rock and smashed them. The mother rat tried to bite me, but I took the rock and crushed her head, so it was ugly and shaped wrong, like mine. There was red food all over the rock, red food that I couldn't eat. I got mad that I couldn't eat it, so I kept smashing the rock down on the mother rat and her babies.

After, I was breathing funny, "*hunnh! hunnh!*" and everything was all red. It was like a dream, and then when things weren't red any more, I was licking the red food off the rock. It was very, very good and I liked it lots and I was happy I was becoming more like Mother and Father.

But when I go to sleep I still think about the ugly, ugly pink rats without fur.

I had another dream about the Bad Mother and the Bad Father.

"You will grow up to be like us," they said. "You will not have nice gray fur and your head will be round and your ears will be wrong!"

And they laughed and laughed.

"You are not Little Round Head! You are a rat! You are like an ugly baby rat!"

I woke up crying, and Father came over to my box.

"Hush, Little Round Head! Don't cry!" he said and he touched my face. His hand pad was soft and smelled like wet dirt.

"Do you want to wake up Little Velvet Ears? You have to be brave and quiet for him. Bad dreams can't hurt you!"

Then he walked away back to sleep.

I was all alone in the dark, and thought about what the Bad Mother and Bad Father said.

Little Velvet Ears hurt me today.

Mother and Father had to go far down the tunnels, because it was a special day and they had to do special things in the place we get food from.

Mother wanted to stay with Little Velvet Ears. But Father said they had to go and that I was big and brave enough to take care of Little Velvet Ears.

Little Velvet Ears cried when Mother and Father were gone. I tried to hold him close, like how I hold my doll, but he kept crying and crying. I put him back on his little bed of cloth and I went to get my doll, because I wanted to share my doll with him because I thought it would make him not cry. But Little Velvet Ears jumped on my back, like he jumps on Mother's back, and tried to grab on.

His nails cut my back and I started crying, because I don't have nice loose skin and fur like Mother and Father have and I could feel the red wet going down my back and I tried not to hurt Little Velvet Ears because he is just a baby. I heard the cloth I wear go "*riiiiiipp!*"

Little Velvet Ears put his tongue on the bad cuts. He thought what came out of me was red food for him to eat and that made me hurt worse because red food that comes from rats is good to eat and I am like a big pink rat without fur.

Little Velvet Ears dropped off, and he cried too, because he fell hard on the floor. I ran to my box and hid.

Mother and Father came home and they were covered with red mud and dry skin and smelled like smoke. They saw Little Velvet Ears crying on the floor. Mother picked him up and she and Father came to my box and they looked like they were going to scold me. Then they saw the bad cuts on my back.

I told them what happened and Father picked me up and Mother started cleaning the cuts with her tongue. It felt nice, because she wasn't licking fast, like Little Velvet Ears did to lap up red food. Mother made little sad noises, "*huh! huh! huh!*" and Father sounded sad when he said, "Don't be mad at Little Velvet Ears! It's not his fault! He's just a little baby…"

There is hotness all over me, and I feel bad and sick.

Mother and Father are afraid I might die. Their eyes are all worried, and they keep licking my cuts clean. I am scared the Bad Mother and Bad Father will get me, because being dead is like being in a dream.

Father and Mother say some of the old words when they take care of me, and the big pipes glow all purple and green and red and cold and hot winds come.

Mother presses the cuts to get the sickness out. It smells bad. Then Mother and Father take leaves and mash them in hot water and put them on my back and I don't hurt so much.

Sometimes I wake up to see Mother and Father crying. They hold each other close and go "*huh! huh! huh!*"

I don't want to make them sad.

Mother and Father had to go away.

They had to get the leaves they put on my back, from a special place while the moon was a certain way. They have to go say special words over the leaves for them to make me better.

Before they left, they held Little Velvet Ears close to me in my box. They said he didn't mean to hurt me. But I turned away and said, "No! He wanted to, because he's bad!"

I said those bad things because I wanted him to feel bad. And I was sick and the hotness was burning me up.

When Mother and Father left to get the leaves, they put Little Velvet Ears in his nest and they were all quiet and sad when they went down the big pipe. I felt bad because I was being so mean, just like the Bad Mother and Bad Father who have no fur and have no goodness inside them.

This was when the bad things happened.

I fell asleep and kept waking up and I heard things that sounded like they were in dreams, but I woke up all the way and knew I really was hearing things from down deep in the pipe.

They were sounds like "*clank! clank!*" And voices saying words I didn't know, the kinds of words the Bad Mother and Bad Father use. It is bad when things in dreams become real.

I peeked over my box, then I went like a mouse that Father stares at to make it not move.

There were lights bouncing down the big pipe that leads to outside.

The lights were talking.

Then I saw under the lights two creatures like the one mother jumped on, with yellow head bones on the outside with the lights attached.

When they came into our home, Little Velvet Ears started crying, and they looked over where he was and they started yelling and I couldn't move because I was so scared. Little Velvet Ears was in the bad lights that came out of their heads and he covered his eyes because they were so bright. Then one of them that was yelling really loud took a big metal thing off its belt and hit and hit and hit and hit the baby over and over again until he was all red and mashed and then they ran away.

I climbed out of my box and the hotness was burning me up and there was wetness coming out of my skin and the crying was in my eyes so I couldn't see.

Little Velvet Ears didn't have a face anymore. It was all bashed in, but his chest still went up and down.

When I touched him, he fell over and there was one long last breath that fell out of the baby's mouth, "*skaaaaaaahgh!*" Then I knew the little one was dead and would never be with us anymore.

I screamed and ran down the tunnels, yelling for Mother and Father. I yelled and cried and yelled. I went "*splash! splash!*" through the water near where we get food. I ran to the door of the white place Father and I come out of, but I couldn't move the door. Then I ran down other tunnels.

I ran to the tunnel where Father showed me the little animal with the babies and went up the metal things to the round thing that went to the place with the red stone blocks. I felt sick and bad and redness was wet all on my back because the cuts got open again.

I pushed and pushed on the round metal thing and "*shrang!*" it slid open and I went out and ran yelling for Mother and Father, yelling for Mother and Father, yelling for Mother and Father.

But they didn't come.

Water was coming from the sky, soon.

I couldn't find the round metal thing I came up from.

Then I fell down near a door to the big building that made all the noises and put all the smoke in the sky.

Everything started to go all dark, and I thought I was starting to be dead. I wanted to be going dead.

Then the door opened and I screamed even louder for Mother and Father.

Because a big creature like the Bad Father came out of the door and looked at me like I was the scary thing. Like I was the awful Monster.

I ran, but I was too sick to run good and the Bad Father Thing grabbed me in its ugly hands and I started yelling "*Aahhhg! Aaaagh!*" The thing pulled me through the door and I tried harder to get away.

Then it hit me hard behind the ear and I went to a bad sleep.

Now I am in a bad place.

There are Bad Mothers and Bad Fathers everywhere.

They put tubes in my nose and fill the behind of my mouth with gooey food that is awful and stick metal things in me and they tie me with cloth strips to a big metal bed and make me sleep after sticking me with the metal things.

They are mean and awful, and they look like me.

Ugly, ugly monsters who keep me here far from Mother and Father, and no one gives me love or good food.

There are other little ones here. They look like me, but they are scared of me. They get to move around the big, big room we are kept in.

I will never see Mother or Father or Little Velvet Ears again.

Mother and Father will think I hurt Little Velvet Ears, because the thing the creatures used to kill him is like one of the metal things that hangs off the belt I keep by my box, that goes "*clanka, clanka*" when you shake it.

They will think I am Bad, like the Bad Mothers and Bad Fathers I look like.

The place is too bright and makes my eyes all hurting and the sun comes through a hole in the wall that has cage bars on it.

It is my bad dreams all come true.

Sometimes I dream Father is looking for me. There are green lights and cold winds, like when he says the special words. The lights and winds are looking for me and when I wake up, I think I see the lights fading and the winds stopping to move the air.

Other times I dream about the black stone steps going down, down, down to the nice place. I almost get to the bottom of the steps, and I can smell Mother and Father close, but before I can call them, I wake up in the bad place.

But one good thing could be happening.

On the front parts of my hands, there are little gray hairs growing.

Maybe I will grow up to be like Mother and Father anyway.

Then I will be big and strong. I will rip the cloth things that hold me down and break the cage bars and find Mother and Father. They will be happy to see me and love me and won't hurt me.

And we will come back and take all the sad little ones here away. We will take care of them and love them and not let Bad Mothers and Bad Fathers hurt them and make them grow up ugly.

We will give them red food and let them grow up strong and pretty, not like ugly pink rats.

And we will hurt the Bad Mothers and Bad Fathers if they stop us. We will hurt them bad.

A Bad Father comes with the tube to put food in my nose.

I say old words at him, and he hunches up like a rat smelling something bad.

The words are making him scared.

If I can say them right next time, I will make him burn.

Changeling

I felt myself blacken as if charred, felt my skin drink fireless smoke as I was stained with the echo of solidity. I remembered and re-lived another moment, one of freezing cold in the midst of a bright warm summer, a moment of my taking the fair color of frost amid green meadows and barrows as I was made pale as lime-bleached skin scant days before I'd first heard the sound of a man's eyes turning to wood.

And with that long-ago press of smooth wood against the soft cups of his sight, I had been freed.

I am not now free, any more than is the boy whose shade I reflect through his demonization, through the reverse-exorcism canticles that tend the seed of spite deep within him. The seed sprouts. I feel it. It earth-breathes despair the boy cannot grasp, but that the boy knows with the same intimacy that he knows his dreams. The boy does not feel the germ quiver to life…to *my* life…and the lives of my distant, more bodiless kin who sleep in his imagining.

I now know no meadows, no earthwork mounds heaped over chambers of rusting swords. This is a place and a time in which eyes are not turned to wood, but are turned to things like shining dark stones. There is no sound to accompany this changing of eyes to stone, for unlike the crack of rowan bursting thin socket-walls of skull, *this* change of eyes involves no alchemy of pain — it is merely the reflection of moving light that is pulled out of the air and forced to dance in a box with a face of curved glass. The glass face of the box gives the eyes of those who stare into it the same dead sheen I have seen in the eyes of blind grandmothers who crossed themselves feeling my nearness.

Invisible, I looked into stone-smooth eyes. I breathed without lungs a darkness like deep winter midnight behind the box that flickered the blue light of moving images no less alive than am I. Invisible, I swallowed the black of dead spectra while fear of persons and things dark-skinned worm-twitched in the minds of the boy's parents and envenomed the boy's mind and his image of himself. I felt myself stamped with fears I did not welcome, fears that would further color me and force upon me untouchable shape. I am clay molded by hands without nails, skin or nerves. I could be beautiful. I have been beautiful before, heralded by the crash of a snow-colored stag from out the brush and by the songs of birch to oak. But here, now, there is no desire nor need for me to be beautiful.

I felt kinship with the image moving within the glass face of the box. The image was flax-pulled from the ether by wire and metal that flowed with tamed and thunder-less lightning…just as I had been pulled from the air and given unfinished shape by this house of stifled, silenced anger. I am changed by this house, as a blown horn changes the air within it.

Later, as I was soured by the dreams of the child who slept above me, I wept a deaf nothingness from empty sockets of dust, knowing what I'd be made to feel and become.

The boy sweats poison, resting above me in a nest of blankets he twists about himself. His parents would welcome the hatchling of a cuckoo. They would embrace a twisted, stunted changeling, such as I had once been, running from the scalding of a font atop the backs of pews that were splintered by my hoofs. They desire a monster in lieu of their son, for such a monster would free them from knowing the child they have.

Longing for a monster, they craft one—and I am echo-crafted as well. Just as a smith would beat impurities from iron he shapes, so do they remove things they do not wish the boy to have, such qualities as they doubt exist in themselves, that they snuff to convince themselves of their worthlessness.

With morning, comes a new crafting.

"What is this?" asks the mother. Like the air above a bellows, the room shimmers in my eyeless sight as she speaks. She kicks with a soft-slippered foot a portrait of dust-grey strokes and red glowing eyes. It's a scrawl. A collision of bracken-angry lines. A portrait of me. The paper leaf-glides across a floor so smooth and clean as to seem rubbed with beeswax; it skids past where the boy lay on his belly next to a wall and comes to rest in my hovel that is the underneath of his bed.

The boy says nothing. I hear in his mind the belief that he speaks the word, "*Nothing.*" The belief churns the haze of the room. He draws a dragon on another piece of paper with a nub of green wax. There is no dust, here in my hovel. The picture of me, of the impressions of me that he has caught in moonlight, flutters from a slight draft that rides the smooth floor.

The boy's mother leaves. I hear her say what she does not speak. Her wish to truly say it makes the bellows-haze of the room flurry like wasps.

"*You're shit.*"

The boy presses harder with his stick of wax as his mother's thought grips the back of his neck.

There is pressure as I take the red eyes the boy has drawn, as I become a glamour just a bit more visible than I had been.

The boy feeds me poison in the night.

But only what poison he spits up.

The father sits before the box that sorcel-traps moving images. The boy is nervous as he sits beside the father, and wishes to be welcome, and to not be afraid. While fear murks with desire, I am summoned to stand behind the boy, pulled as if by a rope crafted of the twitching legs of wasps. The boy is aware of me, as some are aware of the coming of storms in their bones. I know this limbo. It is a home to me. It is the color of the boundary suspended between the earth and sky, where Beltane offerings killed by rope or fire are most treasured—where flesh burns best and where seed that would give me a woman's form of root-matter falls best. Time shifts, as if by a farewell, or by the start of a cloaked exile. The boy conjures, out of the need to be acknowledged, and by the fear that he *will* be acknowledged. The motes of my being respond to the boy's silent chant before this glowing altar.

Words of power and invocation filth the air, but they are not spoken by any who have breath or throat. The words are dream-syllables that accommodate the father's dread and desire. Though I know not what the words mean, they have the bile-flavor of *weregild*, of deep shadow forests forbidden to travelers and the desperate springtime lifting of flesh with a stone knife to ensure a bounty of crops. The words are pulled from the ether. The father takes the trance of their power, as if they are spoken by a hierophant before a bloody stone table. The bodiless voice carried from the box with the face of glass has the feel of greasy metal cooling.

youths…disturbances…wildings…

The words of power seize the mind of the father and wave-daub the mind of the boy. The un-present priest speaking the words is made of shifting light trapped within the box. He is a spell that itself casts a spell. He is less real than is the shifting light of heat and marsh-breath that births will-'o-wisps, though he is much more powerful in its capacity to bewitch and lead astray.

shooting…unrest…drug-related…

The phrases connecting the thrawn-words are nothing. They are like the chants that bridge the uttered Names of gods that are at once loved and dreaded; the bridging words serve only to pace out the invocations. The gorge of fear nourishes both father and son. The gorge of fear shores the walls, and makes this home a fortress of the imagination. It masques the walls in the guise of a haven safe from fell beings—beings who, in the minds of those who live here, carry only the *shape* of humanity. I had been once such a fell being of human shape in this very spot, which had been a wood-rimmed clearing scant years before the sundering of trees and the fever-swift building of houses. I had once been made a giant of a man, glimpsed. I had been the gleam of a hook where there had been a hand. I had been both the snapping of a twig and the imagined boot that snapped the twig. Fear and desire had danced in this spot before the coming of houses, though in a way much different from how they do now.

violence…urban…projects…

I am made more visible to the boy's storm-seeking nerves. I drizzle the blood in his spine cold. Were he to stand, his knees would be limp for reasons he could not guess. The father is made more uncomfortable by the boy's discomfort. He looks to his child, freshly in awe of the god-words of fear he has unknowingly worshipped. He hates the boy's lack of deformity. Hates the lack of wickedness in the boy that would exonerate him from the apostasy of despising his own issue. The father looks to the box's glass face, to the will-'o-wisp priest whose image gives way to images of shadow-people running on city streets. The father's own face would be reflected on the glass if he strained to see it, in the same way he would see the lack of monstrosity in his child if he chose to see it.

"Not my kid," he thinks for the pleasure of thinking it and the pleasure of controlling his reality by fiat. His discomfort abates, as if pressed under a poultice. And with that thought of the father's, the muscles of the boy's back clench as if a blade were drawn at his hind. It is the same tension I was aware of in a girl who long ago turned and searched for me beneath a great outcrop of rock without knowing why, but who knew that she would find me there swaddled in tresses of my own hair. The boy knows he is thought of by his father, and is in an ecstasy of hope for a kind word and of fear of punishment for an unspoken offense.

The father lets his hand drop to the back of the pillowed bench on which they sit, and does not know that the boy expects at once a pat upon the head or a pulling of his hair—both have been bestowed to the boy with equal suddenness. The father does not know why, but is pleased by the confusion he senses in the boy; hope and dread flavor the air in a way that allows me to taste my own ether-misted physicality.

The father himself becomes a hierophant, using words of power like those that have touched his mind. He gestures to the box, to the image of a city goblin led in shackles.

"You ever become a little white nigger like that, I'll kill you."

The father pats the boy's head, and the boy waits to feel fingers close and pull.

I darken. My red eyes take sclera of white.

In his ecstasy of acceptance and fear, the boy would see my shape if he turned his head.

The pictures tell a story in bright colors of god-like warriors and chieftains. The boy fixes upon one image that fascinates and terrifies him. He presses the image upon the paper with his gaze, and I am pinned beneath the boy in my hovel under his bed; his attentions and fears hold me fast, as would a needle driven through the back of a beetle. The boy has endured more this day. Conscripted by his mother to help make food, she reviled him for dropping eggs like those I would have once spoiled with an infusion of my essence to announce my coming with the retch-smell of sulfur. Still stinging from her reproach, in the night he now stares at the image of a monster, a beast-man, abominating it to feel superior to it while at the same time feeling kinship with it for being abominated.

The boy enters a new trance staring at the image, a new state of half-vision brought upon by half-wakefulness.

But later in darkness, the boy lies fully awake above me while he tries to sleep.

In darkness, in the deep night, he has made me densely formed enough with his trance for me to draw raspy breath that he barely hears. The branch-twig fingers of the claws he has given me can lightly click upon the floor.

I am the living *wyrd* he needs to despise. His eyes dry in the darkness, for he is too afraid to blink. He fears to whistle up the flame-less light he thinks may dispel me, believing I will seize his arm in the dry bark of my grasp as he reaches for the lamp. But I cannot seize him, so immobile am I made by his fear.

The boy's eyes are dry, and I speak to them.

I change the darkness; while I am so dense, it is my food. I fill the darkness with forms as I pluck shades from pitch and depths from moon-whispered greys. I force shapes and beasts and apparitions onto the smooth stones of his sight. Immobile, I feed on shadows. I must while so physical. And I exhaust him with fear. His racing mind finally sleeps, and I am free to wander the house that has snared me.

This home is orderly. Where there had been thicket and rim of moss-draped trees before, when I had been a hook-handed monster, there is now nothing for me to straighten in the night and so incur the thanks that would free me from this place. The tables and cutting boards are wiped with oil so fine, the wood beneath cannot ever breathe or rot. There is no winter fuel to stack. No wool to spin. No residue of the eggs broken at dusk lingers to give me a homunculus-like form that would drop to shapelessness with the crowing of the cock.

I stand above the mother as she sleeps, for she demands that I do. I become the intruder she fears. The Man With The Knife she welcomes to dread, so that she as a victim will be free of the sick burden of self-determination that she so resents. The father feels the house in his sleep more tangibly than he does the blankets he rests beneath. He feels himself shackled to his property; *it* owns *him*. His worries infuse the timbers. They vibrate and are strengthened with his sweat-slicked fear.

The boy had liked the screaming, and so I choke on remorse. Remorse is alien to me...thus I am more familiar with its cruelties than are those who are born with it. I have never welcomed it, any more than the boy would welcome the hand of another grafted to his wrist. I try to fathom remorse, to know it as would one for whom it is natural as skin. Thus am I hurt by it more.

The boy had liked the screaming; it walks his mind. And thus he presses regret out of himself. It flavors the poison that has flavored me these past six winters. The boy had liked the screaming, and the fur-warm twitching in his hands that became still.

I have lurked near boys like him, for whom the drowning of kittens had been a chore, and the screams a bother to be tolerated, like cuts inflicted by the baling of hay. I have stood behind such boys, who were infused with the smell of compost and rotting chaff. I have dried the milk in the udders of animals in their charge and made them fear for their blood in the night.

Remorse veins the air. I hate it. And in hating it, I feel remorse all the more strongly.

The boy has seen me, in the same way the farmer of long ago had seen me for an instant in glory upon the barrow I warded, in the second his eyes re-fleshed to smooth-grained rowan. The instant of the boy's blinding reveals me. The thunder of his skull shattering from scores of small stones thrown by a blast of charcoal and sulfur had been uglier than the sounds of wooden orbs pulled by the tongs of a blacksmith. The boy's eyes that had been made stone had been burst by stone.

The house, with the sundering of the boy's mind, has fully accepted the maledictions spoken to the boy over the passing years. They now invisibly wright the walls. They are the hated legacy of a hated place that holds the curse of a youth dying by his own violence within it.

The house is like the barrow. It is like the great stone I slept under by the roadside. Yet those places had been free to the air and sky. These invested walls hold me; they have been taught to grip fast the anxious worry that first snared me. They hold the boy who had found no release for his stifled remorse other than through thunder, fire and stones thrown through smooth and oiled pipes of metal. His remorse chokes me and thicket-traps me fast.

I am the conscripted mid-wife to the haunting of this place. The boy is that which haunts. He had seen me in the instant of his death. He is lonely and afraid of what I might be in the un-fleshed spaces of the place that had been home to him, and that shall be his home past death. His fear of me perpetuates the poison he had been fed; it no longer needs to be spoken. Yet despite his fear I cannot reach him. He is visible, yet untouchable as the grain of wood beneath beeswax.

We shall haunt this place separately until it falls.

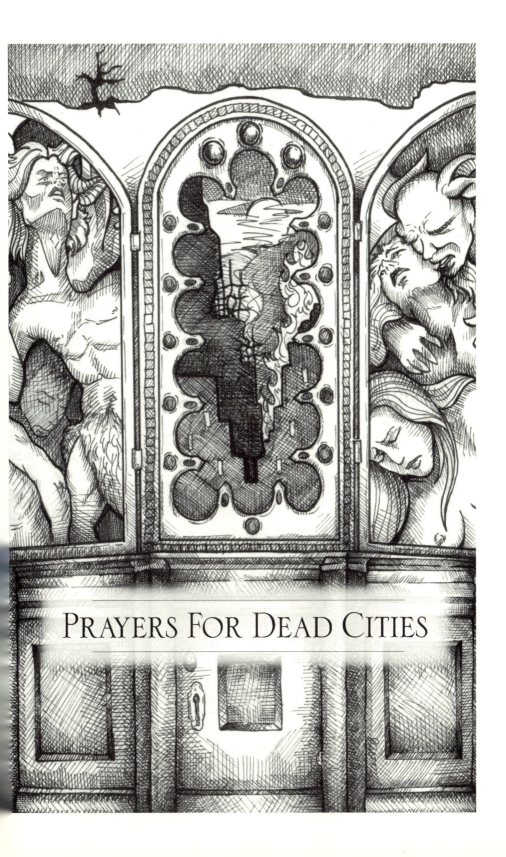

The Siege

I look at you and wonder if I love you.

We sit, and I see you. We sit, and can do nothing else. The light—the lovely light that entrances so many—touches you…mirages you…reveals the dusk of your brow and I realize for the first time how much we look alike. Handsome jaw. Handsome eyes.

"Is that why we first became lovers?" you say, speaking my thought. Speaking my *untrue* thought…pulling it from my mind with a sharp pain as if you had pulled a thorn. You know it to be an untrue thought. The pain you inflicted was an act of healing which will never form a scar.

I look at you, as I have without respite since last night, and am taken by your beauty. I wonder if to be so taken is a thing truly *felt*. What I feel that I might feel is a sadness unreleased, a sorrow held in a cold metal urn. I look at you, at the blood on you. It gives the smell of brass corroded by sweat. There is skin on my lips, and I would spit it away, if I could. But to do so would diminish my dignity. I can hold onto that—dignity. But not love? Not love for you or myself or anything? Together we shall avoid all things. We shall avoid our very selves if we can, split ourselves from ourselves and unknit the fabric of birth.

I would spit the skin away. Would you?

It was for dignity that we were born.

It was for lack of dignity that we died. I am aware of the phone beside you ceasing to ring. When had it started? We should answer no further calls. Perhaps one who finds us darling wishes us to come for gin and tonic (when had afternoon come?), for the boring spectacle of civility.

I shift my weight slightly, and hear a fragment of bone under my boot scrape the polished hardwood floor. Blood has leaked from my clothes, drunk up by the fine silk cushions of the sofa we restored. Darling of us, was it not?

The siege has ended.

And another has begun.

I remember what it was to cry. The lost faculty of tears pains me as would the itch of a limb long severed. If I try hard enough, I can remember what it was to dream. I wish I could again…both cry and dream. Were I able to dream, I could delude myself that we could wake from this. But mostly I wish to cry…for to release what I feel—what I convince myself I feel as an article of a heretical faith—would be a benediction.

"We can have no benediction," you say, "for what we lack so profoundly."

You are not welcome in my mind. Even in my emptiness, you are not welcome. But you are here, with me, in my mind. In my sight. I ache to ache for you. I ache to share myself with you as an act of volition.

I remember the snapping of my neck, do you? Is my memory part of that upon which you intrude? I remember the sound of cracking bone, the vibration of the break up to the base of my skull, bewilderment and the taste of the basement floor—concrete and mold. I remember your smothering the way I remember ever so vaguely what it was to dream.

I look at you, and remember love.

Can memory—a shared memory—of love be a kind of love?

When I saw you the first time, I knew who and what you were. When I saw you the first time, we, whose true aspects were then and ever shall be invisible, saw one another. We slipped into mutual visibility. Two pillars of refracted light, revealing configurations of dust motes. Seeing you seeing me had been a moment of completion. Completion is bittersweet. It is the fulfilling of a longing to which you have become accustomed. I welcomed you in my sight. You welcomed me in yours. It had been lonely, to be born of the dead, to have acquired a soul as a mushroom acquires the air from the forest floor, to not have a soul loomed into your mortality.

When I saw you the first time, I knew who and what I was. You defined me in your gaze.

History class—had that been irony or happenstance?

You stepped forward from out of the crowd…no…not from the crowd. But from the moving, featureless blur I had always seen the crowd to be, even when it had been comprised of my "friends." You stepped forward, the first face I had ever truly seen outside of a mirror. You stepped forward, a thing of solidity from out a bank of rain.

We knew each other.

Without a word—dead, yet able to breathe—we sat beside each other.

The rain of the others could have spilt rock, split the world; we took no notice.

We, splintered by murder—too old to be part of or fully with those who were so adolescently immortal—joined out of the churn of humanity. Our bonding was thing of heavy liquidity in the storm, of quicksilver droplets touching in rain.

The Siege

Of course we would meet in a History class. We are creatures of inevitability. Finality led to our first breaths in this life. History is the point where past and present meet, intertwine, interact. Flesh and memory join in History. We live for having been torn from our flesh. We said nothing, for we did not need to. As you sat in that plastic molded chair in the lecture hall, I had been relieved to hear your chair creak, relieved that you truly were a being of flesh, with the weight of mortality.

My return to flesh had been inevitable. For my father, while still a young man, had been unhappy because of the impolite dissolution of his affair with his secretary, and chose to deal with the end of that clichéd coupling by twisting my head almost completely around while I watched cartoons. He covered the tracks of his suburban murder by throwing me down the cellar stairs, and would tell himself later that I had driven him irrationally over the edge by incessantly pestering him for a popcicle… though in fact the offending popcicle…a strawberry confection that would be the last thing I would taste before my tongue lolled out to touch the cold cement on which I finally died…had been something already in my hand at the initial moment of my murder. But truly, he…with his new pot belly and just-softening muscles…had come home from the termination of his affair with the intent to kill me, with the intent to vent his flannel-suited anger by lynching me in his uncallused hands. I had been conceived that first innocent time as an act of coercion on the part of my hysteric, valium'ed mother. I was a desperate bargaining chip with which she could refuse him his desired divorce. No child, no chip. Later, better allimonied than she had expected and in her gin-and-pill induced bliss, she would at times not even remember my name.

You knew this, the circumstances of how I died…and drew a crude flight of stairs in your notebook while you should have been writing about Leonardo. You knew this, in the way all know the color of the ocean… even when we have never seen it.

You had been younger than I had been when you died, when your mother, desperate for the accolades and the attention of a tragedy, smothered you with a pillow and covered her crime by shoving a small plastic toy down your throat. She had not been insane, just bored. You had been another accouterment to her housewife existence. You, unlike a new 'fridge, had required more care than you had been worth. Dead, you were worth much more to her…a cross to bear. Dead, you had brought her a great crop of pity, on which she flourished much as a flower does in sunlight. Your mother's next child had been a girl, who for her own good had had the foresight and good sense to have been born autistic.

I knew this, and drew a crude pillow while I should have written about the Medici. I knew this, as you had known of my death.

No psychopomps had brought us back to this mortal coil, no spirit-animal had called us up from the earth.

Only Justice had brought us back. Justice…which may be older than God, for how else could He have judged Satan? Justice returned us from exile to flesh, to avenge ourselves on those who had razed our homelands of blood and bone, those who had rudely killed us in the summer, while the earth is easy upon the spade and funerals are not so uncomfortable. We had been denied the courtesy of burial while the world was not bright and warm.

We are the interruption of earthly creation.

Justice keeps those who murdered us alive, so that we may serve Justice by killing them. We, Second Born, were brought together by Justice. We, Second Born, knew each other, much as Jews in dull and primitive cultures know each other by a furtive glance. History is where the past and present speak and interact. We could have met no where else save in a History class. For others fleshed but only once, Exile from Eden is the Catastrophe to which they owe their bestowment of Original Sin. We are born of the first sin of the first sinners' progeny. It is a sin that is not ours. Can our flesh be ours?

If we had been brought back in any way to breathing life by agencies of this earth, it would have been by the random collision of genes instigated by both pairs of our respective second parents. Justice has its mercy…both couplings that produced us would have yielded stillborns if our vengeance-heavy souls had not been dropped into the womb-clothed blood clots out of which we grew.

My second parents never understood why they never connected with me as they had with my living siblings. You, an only child, as you had been at the time of your death, knew and still know the love of your second parents, though you have never been able to return the courtesy by loving them back.

Those who have besieged us no longer do so. Do I miss them? Do you? Their desirous gaze? Their imaged language?

I look at you. I look at your glance and I long to held by it. I long to be held by you. We no longer reflect each other in the polished stones of our eyes.

I am an absence in your glance. I hate to think…no…it is not thought…I hate to know that you are absent in mine.

"Where shall we go?" you say.

The Siege

We have met the inevitable. We have fulfilled it. Existence (*life?*) is a river full of currents and eddies. We have reached the inevitable end of our river. We followed it as one. Our journey became one journey on the afternoon we met, when we followed the immediate and facile path of living men who find each other.

"It wasn't facile," you say.

No. It wasn't.

"Then say it."

"It…wasn't facile."

A dorm room…walls of cinder block.

The first orgasm either of us had had—we shared it on a stiff unyielding mattress of which I had removed the pillows out of courtesy for you and your death.

The flow of our blood.

The flow of our breath.

The flow of concocted blood from our loins.

The still and rocky landscapes within us moving as would a draft.

Joined together in the larger flow of our lives, our shared inevitability bought us to this city where so many rivers meet the sea.

To our "friends"—our social peers we had to take up and keep on hand like tools in a drawer that are used once a year, yet are indispensable at that one time a year—we were "fashionably queer." To us, we were the only other members of our particular humanity. Around our island of each other was a poisoned silence, a waveless silver ocean that hurt to look upon.

We had encountered others like us as time went on and our horizons broadened. We met Sheila, the vapid princess who within her soul had been an aged homeless man beaten to death by a Legionnaire in Philadelphia. We shared the bland entertainments of youth with her. One day, we had been eating under a tree…three of the Second Born picnicking on a college campus as if they were happy youngsters with all their lives before them…two queens and a fag hag, with spirits older than their bodies.

There is a moment before a summer storm, when from out of all the green around you something is drawn out and dimmed.

Such a moment came under that cloudless sky.

Such a moment called Sheila, who glanced up from her student newspaper with a look like that of a fawn suddenly startled. For a moment, her face seemed reflected upon itself, as if she swam a still pond. She literally sniffed the air; we saw, from behind our eyes, the air acquire her.

"I have to go," she said.

We have not seen her since.

Though we had read in the Philadelphia newspapers of the suspected murder of a very old man—a veteran and a Legionnaire about to expire from lymphatic cancer—who had somehow been abducted from an ICU. Police were searching for the man, even though it was almost certain he had died within moments of being disconnected from his respirator.

We knew better.

Justice would keep him alive until its terrible will was done, until Sheila's will was done, Amen.

Inevitability had called Sheila away from our sweet picnic facade. She had broken from us as would a piece of ice from a larger floe.

"Where shall we go?" you say.

No such question had been asked before our arrival here.

Migration had brought us to this city…a faculty like that which calls birds had called us to meet the economic migration of our murderers. We knew we had to come here, with the finality and profundity of what had called Sheila to harvest her killer.

Our murderers—each of their own accord—had both come to this, "the Holy City", to retire. An unknowingly shared pilgrimage marking the fulfillment of two separate and distant suburban lives. Charleston, aged city, languid, rising in sea-level barely over a marsh, was the place our murderers had chosen to retire over Florida. Golf had been the deciding factor for both. A happy game to be played in sunshine despite at least one hip replacement between the two of them. Two people, two strangers, both marked by Cain, had both chosen to live their golden years in the same city. You and I, an echo of their crimes (*one* echo? can two sounds make the same echo?) went toward them. Their crimes called their echoes back.

Charleston is bright and warm…much like the days on which we had been buried. Noon here is a dream. Amid the steeples and streets, one can never truly wake.

Charleston is where many rivers meet. It is where they flow and intertwine and extinguish themselves in the sea. It is where land and sea suspend each other as marsh. We arrived posing as two respectable faggots drawn to the city for its great history, its great culture, its arts scene, its cheap antiques and charming bargains, its legacy of the dashing Rhett Butler, the city's most famous son…who never existed. What could such a pretty myth mean to us, jaded to existence twice?

Charleston is the confluence of many rivers, and what the rivers bear. Dreams and fictions cast into those rivers with the surrender of a coin to a fountain wash here. The place is composed of fictions that many have casually read and forgotten. They clog the air and the minds here as would silt.

"You must love it here!" said the real estate agent who showed us our house. Not an observation. A demand. A toll extorted.

"You must love it here!" said the furniture store proprietors.

"You must love it here!" Politely, we always said we did love it here. The demand, the statement, was an affirmation on the part of those who spoke it. To not agree would have been as rude as interrupting a prayer.

We did not come here to love the place as they did. How could we love the place, amid the screams?

"No, not the screams," you say.

No...not the screams. The screams that are not released, the screams that are held inside without respite among the dead. Even discorporate, the dead are denied the catharsis of a scream in Charleston.

"It's the quiet of the screams that deafens," you say.

The ghosts of Charleston are patient. So terribly patient. We... the dead...can see them. We...the avatars...can taste them. We cannot breathe, for Charleston is so thick with them. They are litter left by the inconsiderate. They are ignored, much as Charleston natives ignore visitors who do not fawn over the city as if it were a coddled trophy child. The solidity of their unreleased screams at times seems greater than that of the ancient brick.

It is the dead of Charleston who lay siege to us...desperate to have us see them. They hunger for our sight. They drink our gaze—clear mountain water amid lowland stagnance. The dead are creatures of dreams unseen in a city that never wakes. They are invisible as chime notes

Among the fleshless ghosts, we hunted our murderers. We did so as an act of will. Not in response to a profound call—as Sheila had responded to the call that drew her to her murderer's deathbed—for Justice is in part a creature of time. We know that, now. Justice is cause and effect. The fullness of effect is not always known before Justice is inflicted. We moved among the forested screams. The stone-still cries. We hunted our killers easily...the living eyes of Charleston are talked into blindness.

We stalked your mother to the beach. You knew where she would go. You knew where she would be. Standing on a pier the pilings of which touched the Gulf Stream, we looked down upon the stretch of cold sand you knew you mother would walk this mild winter day.

And for the first time in either of your lives, you were moved to tears.

Your mother led her autistic daughter along the surf. Gently. So lovingly. What had she become, this murderess, that she could love so tenderly? She still carried her cruelty…we saw it as a brimming urn she held by her heart. Yet she did not let it spill.

She who is your sister not by any flesh wore loose clothes that flapped in the wind. Fully grown, she still looked a child. Her hair flew in wild directions. Your mother carried a picnic basket, and your sister not of flesh bore fresh spills and stains on her shirt—traces of what the basket had held. The beach was empty. There were no accolades to be had. No pity to be bestowed by onlookers who admired your mother for her strength. Just a woman and her ruin of daughter.

You, unseen by her, gave her the pity for which you had been butchered.

I comforted you that night. I held you to my heart and stroked your hair. The comfort I gave you was too small a hill to rest upon, my body an inadequate homeland.

We hunted my father next, knowing we would not now kill him, but knowing we would have to know *why* we could not now kill him.

You gasped as you felt me feel a pang of love for the old man, as I saw the liver-spotted hands that had wrung my neck.

You exhaled softly what you had inhaled as a gasp as you felt me feel jealousy toward the young man who was now his son. Strapping. Beautiful. Glowing with health and vitality, the young man who in flesh would be my brother walked with my murdering father through the banal consumerist landscape of a shopping mall. He did not love his father. Filial hatred was etched into his face. Yet he walked with my father, who plainly loved him. Yet he walked with my father, who limped slightly due to his surgeried hip. Filial hatred was meshed with filial duty. You and I, knitted from behind time—who have never walked a visible path save for that which Justice had decreed—saw the injustice we would inflict if we killed my father now. To kill my father would destroy this boy…he would be the focus of an investigation that would ruin him, even if he were found innocent. To kill my father would kill part of him; to take away the object of his hatred and his sense of duty would flood him with an ambiguity of feelings he could not endure.

You comforted me that night by making love to me. You took away the pain of inaction by desiring me.

As best you could.

Justice would tell us when to strike.

And thus, besieged by the dead, we began our siege.

And thus we closed off ourselves from Charleston, living in it, participating in it, but always closing ourselves off from the place where the dead were so badly treated. Where ghosts were trinkets to lure tourists along with gewgaws made of sawgrass and plaster. We closed a siege wall around us, as we lay siege to our murderers, waiting, always waiting.

We waded into the confluence of Charleston. We waded into the silt of fictions and dreams and lies. We walked among the living and the ghosts.

The dead looked in our eyes and coveted.

Here, a woman in an ancient dress, her gullet full of holes. Her moonlight form rosaried with knots of the pain she had felt in life. She stood in the street, a thing of February forced to exist against a backdrop of May, forced into invisibility by the eyes of the city that had killed her for loving wrongly. We saw her on a bright corner, as a horse-drawn carriage freighted with tourists passed her.

We waded into Charleston's indifferent cruelty, "*You must love it here!*" punctuating our stay the way "*Amen!*" does a tent revival.

Commodities, we were invited by *nouveaux riche* Belles to behold and marvel at the purchases they had made with the money of husbands who saw them as trophies and incubators and little more. We, commodified as furniture queens, marveled.

Here, the mouth of a child gnawed away. The rats that had nested in her unfound body did not follow her in death, did not ghost themselves with her, though the violet she had died picking had. A man with a flayed back walked with her, a man who would have come back as an avatar to avenge himself if he had not died at the hands of so many who had been enraptured by the fiction of *Birth of a Nation*.

We, commodified as educated strangers who had come to Charleston and had learned the truth of how things really are (did we not answer in the affirmative to "*You must love it here?*"), agreed sagely with the city's fat white patriarchs, who would spout their provincial blather believing they could create informed opinions about anything, having seen nothing of the world save what they have seen through the fiction of tourism, the fiction of the dream of Charleston they take with them no matter where they go.

Here, a man composed of the sheen of tin. A thing of numb, uncaring fleshlessness, he walks the Battery, walks foolishly on the stagnant water of the harbor. He is a buffoon in death, as he had been in life. In life, he had been a happy figure, a person of frolicking dementia who ended the jolliness he provided by inconsiderately freezing to death one unseasonable evening. The sheen of his unliving flesh is as cold as the wind that had killed him. He sleeps his dead sleep at the very spot in the park where his body had first been flecked with dew.

We, commodified as faggots, fell in with the destitute and inwardly exiled gays of Charleston. We saw the broken down men of King street, coolies bitter that they have not married the Rhett Butler they had always believed they deserved. We saw the faggots from other places who come to Charleston to plunder fraudulent antiques much as Mr. Kurtz had come to the Congo to plunder ivory. We fell in also with the Charleston queer aristocracy, those who, less because of their sexuality than their caste perceptions, always went elsewhere to indulge their sexual proclivities. Some went to New York to screw young black men not as an expression of sexual taste or desire, but to express racial contempt, and contempt for the foreign culture of the North. Some went to Thailand to express their contempt for a culture older than theirs by fucking its youths. Some kept apartments under false names in San Francisco, simply because they could.

We became conscripted for the sake of Justice to save the life of one such Charleston scion, to keep his damp and earthen soul in his body. We interfered in his acquiring of AIDS by taking his attention away from a drag queen crack addict. We were compelled to interfere, saving the life of this respectable son of one of Charleston's finest families so he could be later punished by the as yet unborn avatars of those he had killed. He was marked…that we could see. His crimes could be read in his eyes. He was marked perhaps for fisting that boy to death in New York? Perhaps for that child whose kidney ruptured in Thailand? Maybe they both would be reborn to take him. Perhaps as twins.

As we led the scion away, we saw on the drag queen's face what she would become. We saw the mirrored unliving shadow of her that would move as a breeze—with the feminine grace she had in life always wanted—down the quaintly cobblestoned streets she worked.

Charleston is a mind set. Its crowded loneliness is an eyesore. We walk amongst its dead, those conscripted to invisibility, those whose screams are stifled by the apathy only the living could muster. Besieged, we waited. We could not breathe for the thickness of our fleshless siblings. Ghosts are born of guilt without catharsis. Without redemption. You cannot be rid of a ghost until you own the sin that has created it. To own a sin is to acknowledge History, and Charleston has none. History is where the past and present interact. There is no such interaction here. Charleston has no History…for though it loves its past, such love is nothing but antiquarianism. Such love objectifies. Such love is not, and can never be History. Justice is impossible in the drunken fog of such lack of History. Our fleshless siblings will never be free. The weight of the air is too heavy in Charleston. The cold places of the North—the dusty attics

The Siege

and the chilled cellars, the shadow eaves and October breaths—give expiation to ghosts. They provide a way home. Here, the weight of cast-off bourgeois dreams keeps ghosts earthbound. Slaves. The disenfranchised. The refugees who found refuge here only for their bodies, not their souls. The refuse of a brutal agrarian plutocracy based upon stolen labor. The foolish men who, having read the pretty fiction of *Ivanhoe*, had believed in the chivalry of agrarian plutocracy and who now cannot fathom why they did not die nobly, but died shitting themselves and screaming for their mothers.

Incontinent and bloody in their Grays, they are soldiers still of the siege. We would help them if we could. Yet how can you dig a grave for a body already buried in haze? They look and glisten in the moonlight. They hunger to be seen.

The city gets smaller as Justice makes us wait.

We go to our polite jobs as *Boys* such we are expected to. Yes, we are *Boys*. Queers are not full men…any challenge to patriarchal normalcy cannot be tolerated. Your female boss finds us "darling" and "clever."

Justice makes us wait.

Justice keeps us unseen for what we truly are.

Who, among the living, is invisible enough to truly see us?

The Call came in the depths of summer.

There is a peacefulness to butchery. Mining. Excavating. The path through flesh is a path of discovery.

We stood from our couches in our living room. The sound of the television passed to nothing; we were not truly watching it. We kept it on at night because the light of the screen reflected on the windows and blanked the faces of the dead who milled, who longed to be seen, who formed themselves out of ether not out of Will, but out of its terrible absence. Will is a thing for the living. Will is the ability to Sin, which we have not. Without Will (truly without Sin?), we stood and calmly took our quarry.

To have been near Sheila when she heeded her Call was to see—as you see in the moment before a summer storm—something drawn out of all the green around you.

We were that which is drawn out of the green. *We* were drawn out of where we were while still present.

"Where are we now? Where shall we go?"

There is a certainty a child knows with finality—that it must never touch fire.

We knew with the same certainty and finality that tonight was the night to avenge.

We harvested your mother, knowing her daughter was in the care of an aunt in a cooler place. The terrible heat was making the child mad. Dehydrated and sick, she had been packed off. To punish your killer tonight would not punish the autistic child she brought into this world.

We harvested my father, knowing his son was away hiking with friends. The closeness to his father in the heat was making him mad. He went to the mountains. To destroy my murderer tonight would not destroy his son. The boy could let go his filial hatred if he had an alibi not only for those who would investigate, but an alibi for himself…that he could not have saved the man were he with him the night he disappeared.

Out of politeness for my father, and consideration of his hip, we put him in the back seat of our car. Not in the trunk with your mother.

We, the unavenged dead, dug our graves in their flesh.

The marshes are tannic. The marshes crawl with life that is hungry. We buried our open-fleshed graves in the marshes.

I look at you, and wonder if I love you.

Dried blood on the lids of my eyes makes it hard to blink. My eyes hurt. The phone has stopped ringing again. When had dusk come?

There should be a difference in weight, for what we have lost.

There is skin upon my lip, and I would spit it away.

Yet we have been spat away this night, we have been left behind like skin.

Our souls, avenged…

ascended.

They cast us aside, we fleshy vessels. Justice was served by us — we things of marrow and blood and gristle are empty now. Our souls are free and we wish them back. We are uninhabitable, even by our selves.

Love.

How can we love while soulless?

I look at you, and wonder.

We are dead. Nothing is held by our gazes. No soul or spirit. The ghosts crave our glance no more than they would from corpses. They have ended the siege. As I saw them walking away, I realized that if I could still feel anything, I would miss them.

"Where shall we go?"

We have not even graves to crawl in to sleep. They have been dug into our murderers and given to the marsh.

You ask one last time.

We are in Charleston.

The Siege

We are dead.
We might was well stay.

Burden

With night, come the sounds.

You hear them as you walk beneath halogen street-lamps that give light the color of brandy, as October air touched with frost becomes warm, heavy as breath. Your step is muffled, as if you walk on a wool blanket. The sounds come, as they have come before, while dusk deepens and stars spread across the dull suburban sky, while lamplight and the flickering blue of TV screens fill the windows of the houses you pass.

Stiff leather creaks. Booted feet step. Chains hung from jackets clank. Keys dangling from out of pockets jangle.

You are alone, surrounded by sound.

Trying to walk away from it.

The summer-heat falls on your back, your neck and your hands, which a moment before tingled with cold. You smell the scents of The City you left long ago. The humid, dirty air. The musk of leather and the skin of the men who wear it. Cigarettes and a blend of after-shaves sweetened by sweat. Under the brandy-light you feel, more than see, stars eclipsed by grey city sky.

Darkness huddles the street. Night folds upon night before you. The suburban street fades as the stars have faded — the brandy-light is gone. The shadows breathe. They mill and they whisper. You walk among them. They have no form.

Out of the ebony nothingness, from behind the curtain of night, Tony steps before you, as if he has stepped from around the corner of a building that is not there.

You stop, held by Tony's stare. You knew he would come. But not as he has.

Tony is shrunken and ashen. No longer able to fill his leather jacket as he had in life. The weight of chains on the jacket make it hang slackly. Tight jeans that had once glorified his manhood sag loosely, as if worn by a boy who has yet to grow into them. Above his black T-shirt, his neck is thin as an old woman's. Tendons show through the skin of his throat. His face is gaunt—skull-like as a death camp survivor.

You see in Tony's eyes an awful, lonely fear, a pleading that fixes your sight and settles in an icy pool near your heart.

He steps toward you. You feel the shadows behind you become heavier, many eyes on your back. The sounds of chains and keys and boots and heavy belt buckles grow louder, closer…more distinct. The shadows breathe. They mill and they whisper.

Tony reaches for you; his ill-fitting jacket falls from his shoulder. Part of you insists that this cannot be.

His hand is on your shoulder, cold through your wool coat in the midst of this invading heat. The cold of his hand walks through your flesh to the cold in your heart. The air is warm in your lungs. Tony's lips move as a child's move while reading. No words come. There is only the chorus of metal and leather as the shadows behind you shuffle.

You hear his distant voice as the lights of a passing car burn Tony out of the night.

The crunch of tires smothers the sounds around you. The shadows at your back become wind. You feel living eyes upon you. Two children stare from the car's backseat window. As they pass, you realize you are cowering, your body hunched.

Stars fade into being. You feel them look down upon you, uncaring, as you straighten yourself.

Autumn wind comes, driving away the scents you have been breathing, replacing them with those of dead leaves, bitter smoke from fireplaces, the salt smell of the harbor.

Yet as you reach your apartment, you smell, just faintly, the scent of a leather jacket, of sweat tinged aftershave—as if you wear them yourself.

In darkness that is your own, sitting in a domicile that has never been a home to you, you think of Tony's eyes, how you would have longed for them to have held anger, accusation, the righteous fury of betrayal.

Not the awful desperation they did hold.

Dawn finds you awake, still sitting as birds begin to sing. You become aware, as you never have been before, of the beat of your heart and the flow of blood in your veins.

Veins bulge under the rubber tube around your arm.

The woman wears surgical gloves. She looks at your forearm, not your face, as she tells you, "You might want to look away if you're squeamish."

("*Bashful?*")

You don't look away as the needle goes in and blood arcs into the test tube. Someone once told you that blood is truly blue, and only turns red when exposed to air.

(*A clatter as jeans with a heavy belt buckle fall to the floor. "C'mon. Don't be shy."*)

The test tube fills. The blood looks black.

(*The Boy had been like Tony. A cocky, muscular, Italian kid who knew he was beautiful. You once knew the Boy's name, but you cannot, or choose not, to remember it now.*)

The woman whispers, "Okay," and pulls the needle out.

(*You had met The Boy in the park, which that night was so very much like the park in The City where men would walk together in pairs and threes to hidden places behind trees and bushes. Summer heat, summer sweat, summer air combining into an intoxicating liquor periodically spiked with amyl nitrate.*)

A warm red drop on your forearm, wiped away with cotton and cool alcohol. Rubber gloved hands apply a bandage.

(*You had felt a longing when you saw The Boy, beyond the sexual. You had wanted to be near The Boy so that you could say good-bye to Tony through him. For Tony had simply left…gone back to his family in Buffalo to die among people he could not stand to be near while in the prime of his life.*)

The woman labels the test tube with a number and puts it in a rack of others like it. She takes off her gloves and puts them in a red plastic container marked "BIOHAZARD."

(*At least you tell yourself that is why you let things go so fast with The Boy.*)

"We should have the results of your test in about six weeks," she says. A testimonial to the shittiness of this town, that all such blood work must be sent out-of-state in monthly batches.

(*Dangerously fast.*)

"And even if the initial results are positive, there is a possibility it could be a false positive."

(*Foolishly fast.*)

She hands you a slip of piss-yellow paper. It is a carbon copy of the label on your sample. "This is your test number. Call at the end of next month and give the receptionist the number. He'll tell you if the results are in, and you can come in for consultation."

(*Had you wanted this?*)

You walk the ugly green tiles of the Health Department toward the faint daylight at the end of the hall. You are nameless here, a number. It is for your own protection, to be nameless. Your anonymity is a shield. You leave the Health department through a soot-covered glass door.

(*Had you wanted to be reckless? Had you wanted this worry gnawing inside you?*)

The river, such as it is, flows by in an eroding canal of poured concrete. It is only a few feet deep, and you think of the college kid last year who had tried to commit suicide by jumping off the bridge you are now passing. He had landed in silt up to his knees, trapped, his upper chest and head above the water.

You hate this small and ugly city full of small and ugly-minded people. You hate the shitty suburb where your cheap apartment is. You came here to live this life because you were afraid to live a life that would kill you. You fled The City when you crossed off your fifth friend in as many weeks from your address book…when you looked through that cheap booklet of grey vinyl and saw listing after listing that you had blotted out with marker…when you realized that an inky smear in someone else's address book could be your only epitaph.

You fled, because you knew the temptation to continue the life The City offered you would be too great if you had stayed.

(*Was The Boy an atonement? A punishment you inflicted on yourself so you could make amends for the life and the people you abandoned?*)

Faceless pedestrians shuffle past.

Part of you is aroused by memories of The Boy. Even now, as your arm throbs where your blood has been drawn, you long for that moment when, for the first time in years, you had enjoyed sex free of the constraints of latex.

Part of you whispers that it is worth dying for such sex…that the enjoyment of such sex is part of your identity. You have a right to what you enjoy, no matter the consequences.

Later, in the indigo and umber of autumn twilight, you are frightened that you are capable of such thoughts.

With night, come the sounds.
Of chains, boots, keys and buckles.
You hear them in darkness.
You hear them in solitude.

Your radio, tuned to a banal talk show, fades to silence. Your drafty apartment becomes sweltering. Dusty air rising from the barely functional radiator is replaced by muggy summer air. You feel the calling of The City in your crotch. Just as long ago, in the life you abandoned, there had been the constant calling to the streets, to limbs and bodies, to thrusting hips and the taste of men.

Always, the calling.

You sit in darkness, trying to ignore the calling. Even as you remember, and as you feel again, what it had once done to you.

One late May, in your other life, you had worked in a bookstore near Columbia, taking second-hand text books from college brats eager to be rid of them. You felt the daylight fade, felt the coming of night like a rising fever. True summer had come early that year, announcing itself as an arousal spreading through you like the fire of cognac and the tingling thrill of poppers.

Working the late shift, which you had taken because it allowed you to sleep in, became intolerable.

A whiney Long Island girl, so much like your whiney sisters back home, demanded to know why she was not getting more money back for a book that was not on order for the next semester.

You stood from the counter and left, embracing the fever. Not caring that your fat and stupid boss saw you leave.

As you walked through the door, heat rose from your body to join the heat of the city. You felt yourself shimmer, felt the need to discharge the welcome fever with sex and the feel of hard-muscled flesh.

In the room you rented, you stripped off your ridiculous shirt with a collar, your narrow tie, your khakis. You clothed yourself in the identity you'd earned by coming to The City, pulling on the jeans and the black leather armor that kept at bay the life of sniveling mediocrity your parents had wanted you to embrace. Chains were your epaulets, a blue kerchief in your back pocket your standard.

You walked down the hall to Tony's room. You didn't knock—you never knocked.

Tony was lifting weights.

Sweat glistened on his body as he did military presses. He saw you in the mirror before him and smiled at your reflection, grunting as he pressed the barbell over his head.

He gave you that smart-assed Italian grin. Liking that you were watching, he did one more press, straining, the cords of his back and shoulders visible though his olive skin like cables.

He rested the barbell on his broad chest, then set it on the floor.

He walked toward you, and pulled you close.

With the door still open, with Tony's sweat-stained cut-offs filling the room with the musk of his crotch, the two of you fucked, not caring who passed in the hallway.

Afterward, you both went to the streets, to Washington Square, your steps falling in with the chimes of chains and the bass of heavy boot steps, to cruise for more bodies, more satisfaction.

The night made you both drunk.

Now, in this night.

Now, in the alone.

The sounds come, calling you to a night fifteen years gone in a City hundreds of miles away.

You feel the fever again. It pulls you to the window.

You pull the frayed curtains aside.

And see dead men cruising each other.

Two lines of men in jeans and leather jackets make an alley of themselves. Other men mill and pace within this alley. They are emaciated. Desiccated. Yet they move with swaggers, with cocky masculinity. One among them is not sick, but flushed with health. Glowing with sexuality and strength.

It is The Boy.

You grip the curtains. Your breath hits the glass, which is cold in the midst of this summer heat. The glass fogs over. You see The Boy through the glass as if the fog is not there. He grabs one of the walking dead men.

They embrace and kiss. The dead man's leather jacket falls to the ground as they grope each other.

You wipe away the fog.

And wipe away the alley of dead men that has imposed itself over the street outside your door. It vanishes behind the trail of your hand.

Where men walked, now leaves move in scuttling streams, driven by cold winds off the harbor.

You listen to your heart. Your pulse slows as you peer across the street to one of your neighbors' houses. Through the window of the other house, you see a flickering television screen that seems the size of a postage stamp from where you stand. Someone walks before the screen and stops. They turn and look at you, and with a start, you drop the curtain.

You turn and see Tony.

He is a deeper grey than the shadows of your bedroom. You see only yourself in the mirror behind Tony. He steps toward you and softly, lightly, grabs hold of your threadbare sweater.

"We needed you," he says in an intonation you feel as well as hear, fluttering against your face and throat like moth wings.

Before you can think or speak or move, he steps around you to the curtains at your back. You turn as he walks. The curtains wave as he passes through them without parting them.

Banal talk radio fills the air, drafts displace the false summer, and you realize how alone you have been these last fifteen years.

"I'm okay."

You tell yourself this as weeks go by, as you wait for your test results.

You have been tested before, and you had been okay then.

You had been nervous then, while you waited for your blood to be shipped to some lab in the Midwest, waiting for your anonymous number to return with news of whether you would live through next decade.

"I'm okay."

You say this out loud as you work your ridiculous job as the assistant administrator of a janitorial service, sending cleaning crews during the daylight hours to office buildings that have only a forty percent rate of occupancy. Graft runs this shitty small city, and kickbacks are plentiful as construction companies continue to build-up what is grandiosely called "the downtown district."

You sit at your desk between making calls, as dust settles in unused rooms for which you are responsible, yet will never see. You wonder what the crews think as they enter these offices, to clean only the detritus these useless buildings shed.

"I'm okay."

You work alone.

No one hears you mutter to yourself. Even the old and rickety building in which you work is mostly empty. It is lunch hour. No one walks the halls.

You think of when you got the results of your first test, how you were so nervous you vomited in the alley behind the Health Department. The health care official smiled and said, "You're negative, you're fine. Nothing to worry about."

"*Nothing to worry about.*" She had no idea.

You thought of the number of men you'd been with, the men you'd been with who had died, or were now dying, or who had disappeared, slinking away to die in home towns they had despised.

Since that day, you had practiced safe sex.

Except for that night with The Boy.

"I'm okay."

And in daylight, the sounds come to you.

You are alone in your office, hearing the clank of chains, the jangle of keys.

Your heart stops in your breast.

You tell yourself it is a janitor, a huge ring of keys to empty rooms in his hand. You tell yourself this, and you almost believe it.

Until Bobby steps into the doorway of your office.

He looks as he did in the beginning throes of his sickness, when you last saw him and pretended you did not know him. As you and Tony and your cruising buddies walked past him as he worked the corner of 53rd and 2nd, already a ghost of himself, already sick, one of the walking dead, peddling the poisoned fruit of his cock, ass, and mouth.

You walked past him, part of a living wall of leather, denim, and muscle as you and your buddies searched the city for one of the few bath houses not yet closed by the Health Department. You had all felt so lucky. So invincible. So immortal. Blissfully ignorant that some of those who were part of the living wall of denim and leather you moved within carried death inside them...that their hearts were busy pumping sickness through their bodies that would kill them, cell by cell.

Bobby worked his corner, skinny as a cur. You saw him, and you knew each other. You saw him, and you saw the fear and the shame in his eyes that he had been recognized.

Your friends all looked at him. These were the early days of the plague, when one could still take comfort in the lie that only the biggest sluts and the stupidest cruisers got infected. That only junkies got infected. That some form of Calvinist election was what doomed people on the scene. That only those stupid enough to fuck the Angel of Death would be taken.

You, yourself, had fucked Bobby.

Just eight months before.

Someone, to this day, you do not know who, snorted as you and the wall you were part of passed Bobby, going down to the subway that would take you toward St. Marks place. Then Tony spoke loudly enough for Bobby to hear...

"*Kid should be wearing a fucking executioner's hood.*"

Now Bobby stands before you. Sick. Shivering. Desperate. Junkie-pale in his leather and chains.

"I needed you, man," he says. He points to his sunken chest. "Even like *this*, I fucking needed you."

You stand, yet say nothing. You have no words.

Bobby turns on his heel and looks at you as if you are shit he has just stepped in. He walks down the hall, chains jangling fainter and fainter...

You walk to the door and see him at the end of the hall.

The Boy is waiting for him there. They lock arms and go down the rickety wooden stairway. As you enter the hall, the sounds of their footfalls on the steps and of Bobby's chains are gone.

You stumble back into your office and see the lights of your phone blinking, summoning you to send men to locked and empty rooms that will never be occupied.

You think of the rooms of The City now empty of the life you once led.

Weeks pass.

With the sounds and the visitations, the weeks pass.

Sick and dying men litter your home, incontinent in their denim and leather. Each night, at three, you see Tony die. He quivers in what looks like nightmare-laden sleep, quivers in a way that makes you think of a cat you saw die in the road when you were small.

"We needed you."

The words become a chant.

Echoing through your mind, your world. You do not escape the words. At work, you cannot function. The sounds of chains in the hall become a cacophony. You take sick leave. You do not know, do not care, who has replaced you at your desk.

You walk through leaves that crunch underfoot, over soil hardened with frost, surrounded by the step of boots on concrete. You sit watching a silent television as buckles and keys clatter around you with the constancy of waves breaking on a beach.

"We needed you."

The words become the fabric of night.

Lack of sleep makes you nearly mad. You think of killing The Boy. You think of tracking him down like some righteous movie hero and beating answers from him that will explain everything that is happening to you, that will provide you with a way to exorcise this torment. A few hours respite from the sounds restores enough balance for you to realize how absurd these thoughts are. No easy answers will come to you.

Yet you look for The Boy anyway, to find what answers you can.

In the grey of November daylight, when all this shitty town seems the color of smoke, you go to the park where you met The Boy. No one is there. It is too cold and windy. You find nothing there but litter and whispering dead leaves. You go to a bar a few blocks away, a crappy little blue-collar place that specializes in serving the disowned faggot offspring of this dying industrial town.

A kid named Alan is at the bar, smoking expensive clove cigarettes. He is a watcher, not a cruiser. He has listened to you intently as you told him stories about The City back in the days when the idea of men fucking each other while wearing rubbers was the most absurd thing imaginable. Alan listened to you intently as you told him about the occasional bout of gonorrhea or syphilis you got when you were his age, and how a trip or two to the free clinic made these bouts less bothersome than a cold.

Alan is a sensitive kid, a poor-little-rich-boy romantic with big brown eyes like a deer. You do not like him. But you like how he listens to you very much. He broke up with his long-time lover in a series of annoyingly public incidents, and is now a barfly and a gossip, sitting here for days, watching other lives as he convinces himself of the tragic nature of his own.

You ask Alan about The Boy.

Alan thinks a moment, absently peeling the label off his bottle of beer with his thumb.

"Yeah. I know who you mean. He left town," he says with a shrug.

"When?"

"Couple weeks ago."

"What's his name?"

Alan frowns, now looking intently at the work his thumb is doing.

"Frank, I think."

Frank. The name rings true.

"Where'd he go?"

"Back to Cranston."

"He's from there?"

"Yeah."

Alan, young enough to be your kid, does not know what this means. Alan, who had been five years old when you were seeing your friends crawl back to their home towns to die, cannot see that Frank went back to Cranston as the first step to his grave. Alan is from this city. He has never gone away to another place, never been more than fifteen miles from where you sit right now. He does not know what it means when a fag returns to his home town.

Now Alan looks at you.

"Why are you looking for him?"

He cocks his head slightly, fixing his big brown eyes on you, giving you what he must think passes for a meaningful look. He knows that you know he has been dumped. He thinks you are asking about someone you are stuck on. Now, in his stupid Pollyanna world view, two lonely people have the chance to not be lonely anymore.

In another life, you would have fucked the little brown-eyed dreamer and dumped him to teach him a lesson. For the sport of it.

You leave the bar, feeling his gaze on your back like fleas crawling on your skin.

In the grey daylight, you walk into a congregation of dead men. They have been waiting for you, expecting you after they have given you this respite. You realize they have left you alone long enough for you to discover what you have about The Boy. Now you must rejoin them, to take up your burden once again.

You stifle your sadness and your fear as they shuffle in a bank of fog-colored bodies around you. They say nothing, but the sounds of their chains and keys is a layered chorus of heavy chimes around you. Tony is beside you, his mouth quivering, not trying to speak, not trying to whisper. His lips tremble out of some spastic disintegration of the nerves of his face.

Out of the corner of your eye, you see among the dead men a living face, keeping pace with you. You look to your left and see The Boy.

He smiles as you walk unthinking, within a bank of men made of fog. You know then that the young man named Frank was just a mask that this being has worn, just a mask that it wears now, for you. You know that you have seen him many times before, with many different faces. You have seen him walk away with your friends into shadowplaces, where he quietly slipped a drop of the shadows themselves into the streams of their blood. He is the darkness of the heavy ink you have used to blot out your friends' names from your address book, the hopelessness that called your friends back to their broken homes. He has walked behind you for fifteen years. Now he walks beside you, as you once again walk beside Tony.

"Hey, man!"

You turn to see Alan, trotting to catch up with you. The dead around you stop and huddle behind you like an army waiting at your command. The thing that wears Frank's face stands beside you, your lieutenant.

"What the fuck was that shit about?" he asks, now standing before you. "Giving me that fucking look and sticking me with paying for your beer? What's *up* with you?"

Alan is performing the classic role of the "don't-fuck-with-me" faggot. You have seen it many times before and performed it before much better, yourself. Though you had the bulk and the strength to back it up. Alan scowls at you. He is so young. So transparent. You know his type better than he knows himself.

He is doing this in the hope it will lead to a confession on your part about being hung up on Frank. That this bold and macho performance will lead to romance between you both. You hear dead voices murmur behind you, as you once heard voices murmur whenever a queen laid down a particularly vicious line of dish.

You look at Alan, and he steps back. There is a look in his eyes like that of an animal frozen before an oncoming car.

You feel the shadow that wears Frank's face slip its arm around your shoulder.

Alan walks back another step.

"Sorry, man."

He does not see them.

Of this, you are sure.

But he does feel them, as surely as he feels the bite of the November air around you.

He walks back to the bar as you walk within your own Purgatory.

With night, comes silence.
With night, you are no longer among the dead.
You no longer hear their words.
The silence fills everything.
You cannot sleep.
When the morning comes, you will know.
When the morning comes, the wait will be over.
In darkness, without the accusing company of phantoms, you have never felt more alone.

Monday morning, in late November.
The hallways of the Health Department are full.
People walk with brisk steps, carrying mugs of coffee, newspapers, clipboards, briefcases.

You wait outside the office where the woman drew your blood. There are at least fifteen men there with you. A batch of test results have come back over the weekend. No one makes eye contact. The fear of revealing an inner stigma through one's gaze is too strong. The possibility of any man in the room being condemned is too great. The possibility of death knowing you through the eyes of a man it has claimed is too great.

The men around you are called into the office one at a time by a gesture.

The door opens. The woman summons you.

She is pleasant and reserved as she asks for your number, which you provide by handing her the ugly slip of paper she handed you six weeks ago.

She checks the computer readout before her, with its long chains of numbers that you cannot fathom.

She looks at you. You see what is in her eyes, and you know she has never gotten used to bestowing this news.

Even as she tells you of the possibility of a false positive and the need of a further test, you know your life will be over, soon.

You walk past the river among the dead.

They have rejoined you.

They say nothing, yet you feel their anger.

You feel summer heat press around you as you shuffle past the living. The first snow of the year falls around you.

It is summer.

It is The City.

But you feel neither the summer or The City, as you are clothed in an eternal day of autumn grey.

Full of anger, full of need, you part the curtain of night to accuse Alan of shirking his burden to remember you.

Two For Marian

...And the Damage Done

I see them, and they know I see them. That is why they want to break me: because I see. The theater of stealth they enact is just that—theater... designed to exhaust me, so that I forfeit my vision. I should stand from the cigarette-scarred table, walk away from their performance. But my friend is dying, and I'd sooner die than leave her.

Marie smiles at me with lips turning the color of lead. She sips coffee with a mouth that should soon go into rictus, and I ache to kiss her mouth and say a true good-bye.

"So, I'm doing better," she says. That she means it twists a flat blade in my heart. She runs her thumb along her cup while her eyes film, as if skins peeled from eggshells are pressed upon her irises. She has always met my eyes with her stone-deep gaze, and that is one reason I've always loved her. I should take the hand that has left her cup and now rests on the table beside a profession of love knife-etched into the wood years ago. But I'm afraid of what I'd feel under her skin, that the feeling would brim my vision, that I would flinch at the touch of loose skin sliding over bone. *They* who press their sight on me like sweat-slick fingertips would know that such vulnerability would clench my spine and make themselves yet more visible to me. My hand is bound to where it rests, as I am bound to this city of my hijacked birth.

Instead of taking her hand, I meet Marie's eyes, now gone the white-blue of watered milk. I smile back. The skin of her shoulders, of which she has always been vain, is as-yet unblemished, still snow-smooth and firm. Her tattoos seem transparent as stained glass. Both her hands, which have cupped my face while I grieved, now rest on the table. I hate that I have pinched out, even partly, the light that had come from her smile. Once, while awaiting a bus across from her apartment, I saw Marie's sister walk to the building's front door with the grace that only one who has studied dance as a child has and press the ringer. Marie leaned out her window and waved before buzzing in her sister. From above, Marie's smile had banished the gloom that clung to that shitty place more surely than did the dying paint on the chipped brick buildings. Her light challenged the sky, and, as if in shame, the sky rallied and for a few heartbeats seemed able to house choirs of seraphim, to become a sky like that over Sinai in a Bible painting.

I take her hands and redeem what I can of her light. *They* lean out of the faceless banks of the innocent, forcing themselves into my vision the way that stones in spring press themselves out of thawing soil; a remembered pain runs under my jaw from ear to ear and over my brow, and I feel the parting of skin that is not mine being cut like kid leather.

I should leave this city. But I am tied here by the only relation I have on this Earth, who despite the womb we shared is not, nor will ever be, a relation of blood.

One of *them* filths the space I share with my friend, setting down his newspaper and grinning as if Marie and I are lovers through whom he lives vicariously. In a more civilized time, one who lived in a port city such as I would have never encountered those to whom he is joined, for they would have been far-flung sailors afraid to drown. They who watch, and who do nothing else, are not sailors who dread scalding brine in their lungs; they bear the corruption unique to those whose hands will never know a callus.

I *see*. I do not *hear*. Such deafness can be a mercy. For the creak of the brittle leather that Marie's hands feel like would be much more than I could bear. "Do you remember…" I say. "Do you remember how cold it was, the last time we held hands?"

"It was freezing," she says, and I reach as would a drowning man for the sensations of that fog-chilled San Francisco night. Her death-gloved hands grip mine tighter. "Why?"

"It was kind of nice," I say. "I liked holding your hands, then. Staying warm, the way we did, even though your Granny brought down on us the wrath of the PC police down on us."

"It was nice." She smiles a bit wider, showing the capped tooth that crystal meth had cracked, and turns her filmed eyes, now flecked with dust, upward an instant as she touches the January night that we, in the corner of a bar near the Bay, had huddled as if it were a quilt beneath the heirloom that was her grandmother's fur coat as if it were a quilt. The bar had no heat, and in back, near the old rotary pay phone, you could see your breath in air touched with sea smoke. Less well than my breath, I could see the beautiful array of ha'penny nails, less solid than sunblindness, that would one day protrude from the bar's blackened timbers. Under the fur coat, against the rich, silk lining, Marie and I held hands as we pressed our temples together. I could smell the sandalwood-like conditioner she used, and the ugly ghost of rubbing alcohol in the left sleeve of the coat.

The mercy of that memory, of blood flowing to our fingers, of silk and the warmth of that unethical yet wonderfully thick coat, dispels the feeling of her unliving skin against mine. Her hands dawn with smoothness. I feel the flecks of paint beaded on her nails. She never scrubs off the flecks or dissolves them with thinner, always wanting to leave a reminder of the pallets she uses. Marie senses an echo of what I sense. Gooseflesh dews her skin, giving new texture to the indigo fan of peacock feathers painted into the milk of her right shoulder and to the cloud-whiskered face of Old Man East Wind tattooed on her left shoulder.

Despite the chill that writes itself on her skin and the tomb-color of her lips, her inner light that I had partly snuffed is re-kindled, and it feels again as if angels might grace the sky. And sitting behind Marie, one of *them*, in a taunt, removes a pair of shades from his jacket and puts them on. He then raises the ever-present newspaper to his face, and, as always, it is turned to tight columns of stock listings in print so fine as to make the paper seem a field of grey.

Later, in the sun, I kiss Marie and say only half my good-bye. "Farewell" is a word that bleeds from two wounds. She can't know what I see. I bleed alone. I can't change what will come. I have tried to help others less dear to me. But the lessons of inevitability that most learn from a play about a Scottish king, I have learned through sifting the ash of failure.

"You'll come to the showing?" she asks, running her hand from my shoulder to my wrist. "I'd really like you to be there. I'll be pretty scared."

"I'll be there," I say, and deny myself the luxury of letting my knees fall from under me, the luxury of screaming my grief at the mockingly bright sky knowing that she will not be at the showing. Her bus charges around the corner a few blocks distant. She must meet it at the stop. I embrace her. We are in a neighborhood in which Spanish mingles with English. I whisper as a prayer by her ear what in Spanish is most often mere phrase: "*Go with God.*"

She walks away, the circle of her twenty-nine years closing, her white skin graced by the sunlight that cloaks itself across her shoulders, that makes the peacock feathers and the face of the East Wind translucent in her flesh, that dances radiance off of the fog-dense glass syringe embedded in her arm below tightly knotted rubber tubing. Whimpers rise behind my throat as I watch her meet her bus, as I know with the certainty of each breath I draw that I will miss her each moment of each day for the rest of my life…as I know that in death, she will never be far from me, that she will loiter and brush against me in the way half-remembered dreams do upon my waking. One of *them* stands at the bus stop that Marie has marked with her absence, and pantomimes the pressing of a syringe into the crook of his left arm.

It took me days to remember there are such things as barbers. Drunk with grief, I walk into the shop and into the past that pools there like blood under a bruise.

I sit in the cracked leather chair as the old man sets a hot towel on my face. I will not go to Marie's showing, that has since its announcement become her wake, looking like the drunkard she saved me from becoming.

"Ever since the AIDS came," the barber says, as he had the first time I had come here and the day after that, "the Health Department makes us wear doctors' gloves." He scrapes my face with a latex-sheathed hand that, in the corner of my sight, is free of the glove and of liver spots. I breathe slowly as the razor touches my skin where a blade less fine and wielded in a drug-addled grip had made its enduring mark on me. The past displaces the present in my awareness as a stone displaces water in a dish. Behind me, in the mirror, men the color of twilight sit in suits with broad lapels and wait for their turns in the chair that had come and gone decades ago. They are like the men who had courted my mother, who told her they could give her "a better life" and lift her to respectability. I smell colognes no longer manufactured, and the ghost-scent of saddle soap. The cracked leather at my back feels whole and smooth.

As the barber finishes the task I cannot do myself, he pulls away the bib and fully leans me forward in the chair. "How's it look?" he asks, as I see what I can of myself in the mirror and as the glimpses and scents of the past wink out.

"Great," I say…though the truth would be, "*I don't know.*" I'm thankful that I do not breathe, in the way that I just breathed the air of the past, the smooth featureless suffocation reflected back at me.

On the street where the barbershop rots, a wind comes off the Bay, cold. It touches the rawness of my freshly shaved face, and all of me feels the need to tremble.

"*You're greedy. And selfish. Because you're not whole.*"

Imagine the beast that hid under your bed, the branch-clawed thing that cast moon-shadows on your window stepping from childhood fear and walking beside you on a street littered with the wrappers of takeout meals.

I look to the man walking beside me, to one of *them* who have hounded me since childhood. He draws my attention with the same revulsion and fascination a hornet does when it lands on my arm. I see the *both* of him; the man's younger self walks like a grey shadow within the man's present self. Like all of *them*, the one who accosts me is a pale, slovenly old shit, paunchy from knowing the world from what he can grasp and consume. The man reeks of his own past.

"*And you're cruel*," he adds. I see past his worn denim jacket, his dashiki straining to cover his gut, and his kinte headwear and glimpse the young man he had been when this city and what he understood to be the world had been indisputably his. I taste his hatred of me mingled with his stink.

The man's shadowy, younger self wears a fringed jacket of suede and a wide-brimmed hat. It looks as if the man's older self has eaten his younger self, as if his own youth were yet another thing to be taken in to nourish him. A rose-colored newspaper is tucked under the man's arm; his younger self carries the *Berkeley Barb* same way.

In the late afternoon, I step into twilight, into the dusk that made up the flesh of the men I glimpsed from the past. It is the dusk in which I am deaf—the wordless non-present in which past and future blur and bleed. I find safety there, as the old bastard spews forth his prattle. I walk miles to where I will take the bus that will bring me to the Waterfront where Marie's showing and remembrance will be. In my chosen deafness, the words of the man's present self, designed to erode my will, are dim as words heard through a thick stone wall; the words of his past self are purely silent. I don't know why he…why *they*…now forsake their program of stealth and city-hidden harassment.

In a twilight I have made, I walk, with a monster from my childhood shuffling beside me, until Civic Center, the rotten heart of this city to which I am shackled, looms ahead. The knotted trees before City Hall take afternoon shadows, and the row of portable toilets for the city's human detritus are packed close like a sea-wall containing the destitute who mill in the park nearby. The man beside me, who has spoken to me, his quarry, is too winded from walking to say anything. I step from my twilight. I see his goal ahead, the bus stop that is my destination, and the collision of fury and dread that has no name in any language I know cracks frost along my spine. At the bus stop is what looks like the mass of grey necrotic tissue I once pressed out of my wrist into a basin of scalding salt water when, uninsured, I had been bitten by a brown recluse spider. The mass waves as did the tendrils of dead flesh that had been part of me.

The mass is many of *them*, expectant and hungry as they await me at the stop. Their ghost-fleshed, younger selves that had first hunted me when I was a child mill within their softer, older bodies. In their translucency, their younger selves overlap. It is as if the film that infection coats on the lenses of my eyes has been given the form of living people.

They await me. Knowing this is the way I have chosen to go to the Waterfront. Knowing that this is the way I have chosen to honor my friend whom they knew, from the diluted sight they have stolen from me, would die. They wish to ambush me in a group...the way they used to while I still drank to the excess to which they drove me.

I turn and cross against the light, ducking SUVs and mini-vans. The faces of children in one vehicle look away from the DVD they watch in the back seat to gaze at the man inches away from their careening window.

Once across, I look back to the crowd of stalkers. Their ghost-bodies seem agitated, like river grass whipped in a current.

I walk quickly along alleys, ways impassable to cars and cabs in which they may try to follow. I take steep hills, knowing that they would not follow or keep up.

Alone, at the top of a hill, I let out my rage that they would so trespass on my pilgrimage to Marie's wake. She stirs again within me; the part of her that loiters in my heart and brushes against my thoughts has been soiled by *their* proximity. I lean against a wall of cinderblock and, swearing, strike it with my palm as would one frenzied by angel dust.

The gallery had been many things. All it had been over the years puts pressure on my forehead, the weight of its past packs around me like the underneath of snow. The buzzing energy of the shouts of children, though not the sounds, echoes from when the place had been an unlicensed play-school. I bow my head from the pressure as I enter and lift my gaze slowly...

And I drink what had been Marie. The taste is like the scent of a stem of rosemary drying. The feel is as soft on my skin as lake water in the summer. Few of those here mourn Marie, and I'm thankful for their hypocrisy—I could not have withstood a room full of people wounded by the loss of Marie while I was touched by her art, and while they were so touched. I said I lifted my gaze to her art; that is only partly true. For to lift your gaze to her art is to be lifted *by* your gaze; it is for your vision to be drawn in the same way her deep brown eyes trapped your gaze, welcomely, whenever she spoke to you. The angels summoned to the sky above Marie's light seemed to grace what she had crafted with her sight and her hands. To walk into the space where her art is hung is like walking into her arms, the very arms into which she pressed the numbness and death that she had first melted in a spoon, the very arms which, holding you, would let you know the grief and love she wore as a raiment upon her soul.

A few patrons look my way, as if they know me. None is one of *them*. It is as if I am expected, though why, I cannot guess. Yet a few among the few who look at me do so the way that *they* do—as if I am their property that has rudely not acknowledged their ownership of me. I look away from them, and suddenly feel as if the earth rises to meet me. As if I have been taken by a swoon and fall to the floor of a red-sanded desert.

"I'm glad you came," says a soft voice as a hand is placed on my shoulder, as I remember such a touch from all the times Marie had so greeted me. I turn and see a mask of Marie, fleeting, as if I have stared at a black and white photo of her and suddenly looked to an expanse of pure white. The mask fades and a face like Marie's lingers in flesh where the mask had been.

Nell looks much like her sister, and what is more wounding to me, she smells like Marie, if such a family likeness is possible. She is the ground—the earth that supports—beneath the radiant sky that had been Marie. Nell's eyes are blue, the near opposite of the warm brown of Marie's eyes, yet just as deep and arresting. I place the hand I abraded on cinderblock over the hand she has placed on my shoulder, and see under the sleeve of her blouse the raised, worm-colored scars along her forearm that are there, or that will be there one day. Where Marie has used a needle, Nell has used, or will use, the teeth of a broken bottle.

"Marie said she wanted you here. For this." She swallows after speaking the last two words, as if to take them back.

"I had to come, and I wanted to."

"Could you…could I ask you come with me?" She takes my chaffed hand and leads me past the deep forests Marie had painted half from the banks of brush and trees in Golden Gate Park and half from her imagination, past the seascapes Marie had done of an ocean she had never seen but had read about, past the small cottage in Berkeley she had painted that she had transplanted to a hillock like one in a work by Cezanne. Nell walks ahead of me with near-unreal gracefulness that shames me in a way that I cannot name. There is a memory that stirs warmly inside me, and I realize that Nell leads me the way Marie led me to the corner of that freezing bar in January.

Nell stops us before the far wall of the space, near windows that look out on the Bay.

"Can you tell me who they are?" she asks, gesturing to Marie's portraits.

Empathy is what scholars say is the investment of oneself into a painting. It is an incomplete notion, for a painting can intrude upon *you* and your perceptions. Looking at the canvas that Marie painted, looking at how Marie had forced her own compassionate and loving sight to *stay* within the textures and strokes she crafted, I *felt* all that is, that was, that had been, Janet intrude upon me. Marie had painted Janet reading a book in the Park. The curling flames of Janet's rich, thick hair were draped over one hand. So perfect were the textures, one could see the motion of Janet's fingers twisting a lock as she read.

"Do you know her?" asks Nell.

"It's…she's…Janet. Marie and I knew her years ago. She disappeared." I stumble for the words. "Could you ask the curator, or whoever is handling the sales, not to put this one in the catalog. Or on-line? And maybe leave the work untitled?"

"Marie arranged for all that weeks ago," says Nell. Her words are clipped, not out of anger at my request, but out of discomfort for speaking of Marie in the so recent past.

"*Of course she did, of course she would,*" I say. Or think I say.

So frightened, so sleep-deprived had Janet been before she fled town and her stalking ex-husband, Marie and I had heard her scream when a lock of her hair, flowing around her like red-brown smoke, had been caught in a low-hanging branch one windy day.

"Marie said that she…*Janet*, you said? That she probably wanted to stay disappeared."

Nell next walks me to a portrait of Tom, whom Marie had painted in warm earth-tones. In his portrait, Tom smokes while hunched over his coffee. Marie had caught the happy semi-grin that Tom wore whenever he lit up, knowing that he had successfully displaced his need for coke to the less lethal need for cigarettes and caffeine. Tom had disappeared as well, either to leave the city and its temptations or to be consumed by those temptations elsewhere, with no witnesses to his defeat by that which steady smoking and coffee had held at bay.

"'Tom,'" says Nell after I have named him. "I met him, I think. I just couldn't remember his name."

We next stand before a portrait of Paul, whom Marie and I had met while he wore a cast, as he was recovering from the spite of a girlfriend who had smashed a jar of pennies onto his hand. Marie had painted Paul with his guitar on his lap—his face set as he worked the hand-exerciser that might one day give him back his music. The play of light on Paul's face is like that of a Hopper; the look in his eyes is one of pain and hope.

I tell Nell Paul's name and his story, though I do not know if he has ever learned to play again.

I feel my pulse throb in my neck as I speak to Nell, as I realize that Marie's art has become more beautiful with her death. While she lived, it was timid of her light, even though what makes it beautiful is the investment of her light.

Nell thanks me by offering me a plastic cup of jug wine from the crumb-ridden caterer's table. I decline, and she seems to nod, as if remembering. By the table, on a small podium, is a photo album of Marie's unfinished works. The cityscape view out of Marie's living room window floats like some half-realized dream in the album behind a clear plastic sheet protector. The album feels as if something close to me might sleep among Marie's other half-finished dreams and visions. If it is the face of another dead or lost friend, I can't bear to look at it.

Nell's glance falls to the album, to the cityscape that had filled the window beneath which Marie had died.

"Do you still have a key to Marie's place?" she asks.

"No," I say, giving Nell insight into my relationship with Marie of which she may not have been aware.

Nell looks down to the scavenged table, as if embarrassed by the question and my answer. She reaches for her purse and opens it.

They are coming. I feel them. Their approach is like the spread of wasp venom under newly stung skin. They have known my destination. They approach *en masse*, to re-attempt the ambush they had intended for the bus stop. Because of their numbers, they feel close. Closer even than does Nell standing before me. I should flee to the anonymity of my apartment, to the safety of its smallness and the invisibility of its single window that faces a brick wall.

Yet there is a safety in this moment I feel as Nell reaches into her purse and pulls forth a key ring. They will not come, I know, until this safe moment is over. Nell removes a key from where it dangles next to a shiny, newly-cut one just like it and hands it to me. I feel the residue on it of the grief and the anger she felt when the clerk at the coroner's office handed it to her. The key scalds my hand, and I feel as if my palm might blister where she has placed it.

"I don't know how long I'll be here," says Nell. "Can you meet me at Marie's sometime after ten? There are things…" her throat constricts, as does mine while I meet her eyes. "There are things Marie said she wanted you to have if anything happened to her."

Nell is furious; there is terrible beauty to rage on the face of one as graceful as she, even when such rage is hidden. Loss masks itself beneath her skin. She wishes to make her rage known, rage born of the sight of Marie's face, haloed by the glow of a metal slab, the face I had seen moving with the simulacra of life when Marie and I had spoken our maimed farewell.

"I can meet you there. After ten," I say, putting the key in my pocket.

"I have to play hostess. Please excuse me."

She gives me her hand, now slick with cold sweat. I have upset her, or she has upset herself. This moment and its safety dissolves around us. "Thank you for coming," she says.

I leave the showing. I walk past the colors and the palettes I recognize from the flecks on Marie's nails, from the smears on the overalls she wore while working, from the reeking drop-cloths that she piled in the corner of her kitchen. I take the back stairwell where the caterers loiter, feeling *them* come closer. At street level, I see *them* coming—a few cluster near rusted cars and vans parked in the Waterfront lot.

They will position themselves throughout the neighborhood. They will hunt me in bars and coffee shops, and coordinate themselves through their cell phones and voicemails and text messages. I do not fathom this breaking of their theater of stealth, and though I know going to Marie's home will savage my heart, I am thankful to have a place to go besides my home, which will be watched closely tonight.

Nell waits in the hallway outside Marie's apartment, tapping cigarette ash into a beer can. The sleeves of her blouse are rolled up, revealing smooth skin etched with as-yet-unbroken blue veins.

She smiles as I walk up the hallway, as I smile politely and smother down my horror at what she will do.

She drops her cigarette hissing into the can. She stands and again fixes me with her blue eyes. I hide what I see of her future, what I see of her choices and how they will write themselves deeply in her flesh. For the second time tonight, she says, "I'm glad you came."

There is no graceful reply to what she has said, so I say next to nothing: "Have you been here long?"

"About an hour. I couldn't stand being at the showing after a while. A lot of the so-called patrons were just vultures."

I smell *them* on her as she says "*vultures*". They have been close to her, soiling the space of Marie's art, her empathy, and her mourning.

"Is there anything I can do? To help settle…things?"

...And the Damage Done

"No. Not now. I just want you have what Marie wanted you to have. I need to see something *done*. I want to have some closure, tonight."

She opens the door and the residual smells of Marie—the lingering scent of the expensive lotion she always used out of vanity for her skin, and also the scent of the sandalwood conditioner she said always made her feel calm—choke me with memory.

We enter. On the couch before us is an amorphous mass, the color and texture of which is immediate in the tactile memory of my hands.

"I couldn't figure out why she wanted you to have this ratty thing," Nell says, picking up her grandmother's fur coat. Trying a feeble joke, she says, "You're not going to wear it, are you?"

"No," I say, and the word is more coughed than spoken. I can't bear the thought of touching the coat, even as Nell holds it to me. Nell, with her otherworldly grace, steps toward me and I nearly step back. She hands it to me and I feel I could tear it as if it were paper. The sensation, the remembered feeling of holding Marie's hand under the silk lining, trembles in my blood.

"We…had…with the coat…" Nell eyes never leave mine. I see in her the frailty behind her strength that will lead her to run broken glass along her wrist. I want to reach through the time separating us from that moment and snatch away the bottle before it can rip her.

"You don't have to tell me," she says, and takes back the coat. She rests it on the chair that Marie and I had salvaged when the college kids down the street had moved and had dumped it on the curbside. Nell walks to the battered desk where Marie's ancient and paint-smeared laptop sits. Nell picks up a stack of disks and hands them to me. Some bear multi-colored thumb and fingerprints in oil-based paint.

"Marie didn't want you to know how she worked. She was almost kind of…superstitious about it. She said you always figured things out with just a few hints. She called you 'Sherlock', sometimes. As a joke. Behind your back. She didn't want you to know that she took digital snaps of people when they weren't looking. She hated doing portraits from sittings. She didn't want you to know, because then you'd be self-conscious around her and her portrait of you would come out wrong."

I hold the disks as if fanning cards. Nell says, "These are the shots she took of everyone she did portraits of. I think they're all your friends. And hers. She said you had a real big heart. That you're sentimental. I think she wanted to print them out for you, but she never got around to it." Nell shrugs. "I'd do it, but I don't know how to work her printer, and I can't find the manual to save my life."

"I don't own a computer," I blurt, looking at the discs. More in control, I say, "But I can take them to a print shop, I think." I run my thumb along the oil-based mark of Marie's thumb on a disc of bright orange, remembering the feel of the flecks she preserved on her nails.

"Marie said you were a real techno-phobe," she says with a half-smile. "There's another thing. I don't know if you'll want it. She never really said that she wanted you to have it, but I think you should at least see it." Nell leads me to the gutted walk-in closet that is—that *had been*—Marie's studio. We tip the electric fans in the doorway that had been her ventilation system to one side. A *person* awaits me in there. I feel his presence, almost in the way I feel the presence in this city of the one relation in this world that is *of me*, yet not truly of my blood…despite the blood we shared.

On the easel Marie's uncle had made from scrap wood is an unfinished canvas, a photo of which must have called to me from the album of incomplete works at the showing. The face of the man in the half-done portrait is the face I have not seen for days in the mirror. I recognize myself in the way that I had recognized Janet and Tom and Paul, refracted through Marie's eyes, illuminated by her light.

"She couldn't finish it," says Nell. "She kept trying to catch you in just the right moment, to take a digital snap that'd be just right. She took a lot of snaps of you while you weren't looking. She said it was easy, because you were always distracted. But she could never find a way to complete you. Do you want it? The art dealer wasn't sure he could sell it, because it's the only unfinished portrait. Will you take it?"

"I don't know."

I lean out the closet doorway, almost knocking over one of the fans. I grip the glass doorknob; it creaks. I let go, and am next aware that Nell's hands are strong. They are like the hands of a nurse used to heaving the sick and the dying from bed to gurney. Her strong hands lift me to my feet and guide me to the sofa. Discreetly, she leaves me to sob there, laid out as I sense that she has repeatedly sobbed in the same spot while she deals with her sister's unfinished affairs…her unfinished life.

After a period of time I can't measure, after I have sat up, she walks to the sofa and says, "It's okay." She gestures to her own dry eyes, "I have nothing left. If you can still cry, I kind of envy it. If you still got grief to let go, let it go." She pulls matches from her purse set on the floor by the sofa and lights a candle that rests in a holder by Marie's laptop. "It's okay," she says, then shuts off the lights, leaving me in dim comfort. After a moment, I hear the refrigerator door opening and the cracking of a beer can in the kitchen. Nell returns, holding the can in one hand and a bottle of non-alcoholic beer in the other. "You don't drink, right?" she asks.

"No," I say, as I sit up a little straighter.

With her strong hands, she twists off the bottle cap, which seems to fly off. There's hardly any sound as the cap is released, so fast does she remove it. I take the beer and sip. It's flat, but very cold. I only realize it is flat as I take a second sip. I look to the amber glow of the candle. I drink again, and I *know*. I know that this is the candle Marie used to melt the smack that killed her. Time slows, and I feel what I at first think is the ghost of the numbness Marie felt as she began to die. In the flame, in the flow of wax, I see who sold her the smack and why, and I realize I am partly culpable in her murder, that I led her killers to her. I realize, without the use of my sight, that *they* who have tampered with what Marie pushed into her veins have tampered with what I have taken past my lips. I look to Nell and stand. I won't make it to the door. Dumbly, moving like the drunk I once was, I turn to the window, the very window that Marie looked out to greet her sister below, the very window from which I had seen Marie's light shine forth. I see in reality the unfinished cityscape Marie had painted, thinking I might open the window and cry out to someone who might care.

In the dim-lit glass, my reflection changes. The smooth expanse that has covered my face fades and my features return to my sight for the first time in days. In my sight, *I* have disfigured myself in the mirror before, knowing of ugliness in my future I could not bear to see. Yet the new, smooth and featureless face, that I now realize was not new at all, was no mere self-disfigurement, but *portent*...inevitability. A future I no longer see, because it is a future that is now arriving.

I turn back to Nell and speak meaningless syllables as the doped beer she has been given to offer me falls to the floor on which Marie died. My sight fades and returns. Nell stands in the doorway, cradling the phone in her hand. As I black out, I see that *they*, in their past and present split selves, will soon come through the door to claim their prize.

The fur coat is on me, draped like a quilt. Nell does not know that the people she helps, the people who have hunted me, have killed her sister with uncut dope...much stronger than anything Marie, or any user in this city, could withstand.

The place I've been taken to, the place I have been returned to across the gulf of my life, reeks of stale curry and incense. My life away from this spot, to *them*, has been mere *caesura*. The *caesura* now ends. I am on the floor. Nell holds my cinderblock-skinned hand under the coat and through the reek of the place, I smell that she has anointed herself with the lotion and the conditioner her sister had used. Against my will, the sensation of the coat and the scents that Nell wears summon the memory of Marie that is more than memory, that I realize has been haunting me with greater force than any mere memory possibly could. *They* mill about, their grotesque treads making the floorboards creak as they light candles around the room.

What Nell had been given to slip me in the beer still addles my brain, though not nearly as much as does the sudden full and terrible restoration of my sight. So blind I have been, I did not know that I was blinded. I could not see my own future. I could not see this trap, because the mere envisioning of it in a future relative to the present I have just quit had snuffed my sight to the future I could have otherwise seen. Inevitability… the lesson of the Scottish king.

I am prone on the very spot where I was born. It is the very spot that has tied me to this city full of the desperate and the wounded—this city full of those incomplete souls whom I could not leave once I knew them and loved them as my kind. I could not leave this city, even after I had left *them* who have lived in this house as a commune for decades, who have been held together as a clan by their quest to reclaim me…the lump of flesh that came stifled and silent into their world, and that now draws shallow breaths upon the very spot where it had nearly suffocated at birth, the very spot on which I had been born sheathed in skin that is not my own.

Nell sees me draw breath like a grounded fish, sees me trying to speak and to warn and to plead. There is pity in her eyes, and beyond her eyes, which in this candlelight seem as brown as those of her sister, there is the terrible beauty of rage. The rage half-expresses itself in the play of candle-shadows on her face. The shadows are like a portrait of her splintered fury and sorrow. Her pitying face is silent. The amber glow makes this un-speaking face look like that of a North German Madonna. The anger-shadows scream, distorted as a face painted by Munch. They bellow and they wail. And dimly, as if from underwater, I hear the amber-shadows speak what the pitying face of Nell does not. *Deafness* and all its mercy partly fall away.

I try to squeeze Nell's hand, to let her feel just slightly what I feel, the way her sister always could. My grip is weak; my hand has less strength than does a dying kitten.

The man who had accosted me on the street looms between Nell and me. He grunts as he leans his saggy bulk forward and runs his acrid, food-greased hand over my face. Up close, I see that he has the ugly ogre's teeth of one who has sucked his thumb into late childhood.

"It's good you got a shave this afternoon," he says smiling, as his younger self smiles with teeth less yellow, that are lit by the sunlight that had once streamed through the window behind Nell that is now painted black. "We don't want to damage anything important," he says.

"*They said you knew what Marie would do...*" It is Nell's fury that speaks. The words are nearly muffled, but are so loud to the faculty through which I have never truly heard before, it tears at my mind. I long for the sweet deafness I am losing.

"You brought this on yourself," says the man, happy now that I must hear his prattle. "Not sharing has made you incomplete. It made you cling to incomplete people that you used to feel complete. You're wounded. That's why you use the wounded. It's time to heal. Time to grow." Two layers of ogre's teeth speak at once, out of sync, looking as if they will crack against each other.

"*And you didn't stop her, you shit!*" Nell screams at me without breath, with the airlessness I will soon know.

The man's two faces are joined by a third. The space where his two faces now squat takes a face from the past, spectral—that of the untrained, self-appointed midwife who cut the bloody tether between my mother and me, when the commune this place had been had taken in my mother during the ninth month of her carrying me. And after the self-appointed midwife had cut the tether, she had raised the steak knife to my throat and face and peeled away my bloodless relation, the amnionic skin that through the ages has been a blessing to others.

"*They told me,*" bellows the shadow of Nell as her nails cut my already skinned palm. "*They told me you could see her ghost if you wanted to. You could let me say good-bye to her, but that you wouldn't!*"

The silence of the pitying face of Nell gives greater volume to the part of her that so wordlessly shouts. That of Marie which has haunted me stirs. It hears its sister's voice. It cries out in my mind, and I wish to comfort it.

More of *them* stand around me, looking down. *They* from whom my mother fled. *They* who have harassed me from the moment *they* were aware of my still living in this city and of my inability to leave. *They* who have harassed me from the moment they were able to in part steal my sight, just enough to know what I saw while they hunted me. *They* who could partly steal my sight through that which they have owned over these many years, through that which that had once belonged to me before I had owned anything on this Earth.

"*You owe me. You owe Marie. You owe us our good-bye.*"

Against my will, the memory of holding Marie's hand, the scents of her hair and skin as worn by her sister, pulls Marie close. I call her as would a medium, as would a spiritualist. She is caught here in this place. The trace of Marie that has haunted me has been caught here, *trapped* in the home of those who murdered her, bound by the needle that killed her, that hangs from the ceiling above me like a reliquary on black thread spun from strands of hair stolen from her brush. The dangling syringe glints as it did in the sun, when I saw it as a phantom buried in Marie's arm. It is now not lit by the sun, but by an imprisoned light that should no longer be in this shitty world.

I speak the words, "*They* killed her," yet make a sound no more understandable than a death rattle.

The *Jar* is brought forth…the vessel I have always been aware of, because of its decades-long housing of part of my awareness. That of me that *they* have owned is passed from one hand to another in a circle around me. I do not know with which sight I see the caul I was born with floating in its preserving brine. I do not know if it in true physicality swims in the brine, languidly flapping as would a manta ray.

"It told us of its loss," says the man who followed me. "What it lost was *you*."

And I know what *they* have always believed to be true is now true enough for *them* to make real: that I was not born with the caul that gave me sight—the caul was born with me. They have prayed and hungered this into reality.

Free of the Jar, it lives in their hands as *they* pass it wetly to each other, as *they* invest themselves with that which *they* once thought could grant them cosmic insight of what will come, but which *they* only desire now in order to accrue material wealth. It is returned to my face, dropped like a shroud after it has been pulled into the shape of one. The last breath my lungs draw becomes a still pocket in my chest.

The mercy of deafness, the mercy of muted hearing, is fully stripped away. I hear the cacophonic indifference of the universe. Marie's trapped ghost speaks through my smothered mouth. The taut skin makes sounds as would the buzzing of fly wings. Nell pulls away her hand and slashes my palm with her nails. She is screaming as I fall into Marie's sky, full of cruel seraphim and their awful songs.

Exit Wound

Though I know he hates when I watch, each time my eyes drink the glory of him taking the gun to his mouth, it excites me.

What contrition do I owe, if he does not fully close the door of his studio?

And though it excites me, I also know the betraying thump of remorse to see him committed to anything I am not. His attention on anything but me severs me from myself. The weakness in my knees and the glutted emptiness in my loins are born of famishment for his gaze.

The shot that flies apart his head flies apart my heart. In that smothered limbo, my consciousness burns as would shadow-eternal flesh in sunlight.

I share the music of the red fog in which he drifts, his song of self-killing from which he wakes to begin his Art while the thunder-shot he limits through his Will lingers in my hearing.

Thus, do I share his Art. But never completely. His creativity defines my heart. It is right that I shatter for it, that I die during his hymns to immortality. I leave him to his Work as he replaces the gun, still oozing blue smoke, on the table before him; I leave him to the earth-marrow pigments and scabbing shade-forms he has freed.

And afterward—when he has done taking brushes crafted of his own hair and bone to what the shot has thrown of him to the canvas, and he has patched the hole made by the bullet as it passed through the canvas—it excites me again to come to him…to taste gun-oil on his lips and powder-burns upon the back of his scalp and to kiss coagulate paint from his fingers.

Often, in the studio perfumed with cordite, I reach down to find his Art has given him release. I touch him as if *I* have brought him release, and claim by proxy the beauty of his Work. To taste the gun-oil distilled through his blood into the saltiness of his release is to hold his Art upon my tongue and take it as Communion.

It is only after I have given him chilled fruit and mineral water to cleanse his palate that I dare a horizon-glance upon his work. *My* cleansing comes as I am burned by the russet fires the bullet has cast as layered vistas upon his canvas…the passions of his vision risen as living earth-tones. At times, the exhaltation from the back of his head strikes the canvas so that, with a few brush strokes, working this day's red vibrancies into yesterday's browns, he creates swirling infinities that breathe, as if the paint still pulsed as it had within his body.

November dawn-fire dims to ash all that surrounds it. The white of the studio walls becomes smoke-stained and sad beside his Art. It scalds my eyes.

"It's beautiful," I *wish* to say. I'd not let my words sully air through which his vision has just warmly flown, even if I *could* free my voice from the snare my throat becomes before his Work. The canvas is a well of genius. Images overlap, at varying depths.

Here—painted upon rough fabric and branded on the rough gel of my eyes, the oft-painted "house of the suicide" is reclaimed by my lover's light. Here—the folded, churning clouds of trite dusks over the Hudson are infused with the depths of desert canyon walls. Here—a lily in a French garden flowers the colors of both new and old scars, floating on a pond of iron-rust. Here—cloaked like the images hidden within the game-pictures children love, a Starry Night made a Starry Twilight… with a firmament of red-crystal flecks.

Life and movement, granted by his drying blood. The blood of his life, the blood of his Art. The skill of his long and nimble fingers summon Truth. Patches of singed hair give texture to waving copper grass. Bits of teeth are pebbled to fairy-land cobblestones. A spiral of skin dances with cochlea. A scrap of eye, the pupil and iris, had, on one marvelous day, struck the far right corner of the canvas, so that the painting became a kind of mirror (so he explained), able to gaze back at the viewer with the reflexivity unique to great Art.

While he sips mineral water and tastes fruit, I clear the art books that have offended him as I would dirty dishes…the collections of images done by mediocrities whose work has been lauded as masterpieces over the ages…images my lover salvages, then unfetters with his vision and Will. Fools would call my lover's Work "pastiche"—the taking of images into himself, so he can re-use them his own way; I rightly call it "redemption."

It is my art to serve him and his Art.

As he showers the powder and flecks of himself from his hair, I clean his brushes and his gun. I then go to work…and so ensure him the solitude that gives the world such Beauty, even though the world is not yet ready to see it.

He met me on his porch.

The porch was *his*, though others eddied there as they fumbled with keys to mailboxes and to the converted house's front door of molded wood and fine leaded glass.

He parted my loneliness and asked, "Do you wish to be sired?"

His first words to me, swimming stars in my awareness, burning through years of smothered want. I'd made coming to Berkeley my pilgrimage to find myself...that my *self* could find me seemed too impossible to hope for.

Desire for him rewrote me. His question pushed all I'd been before coming to Berkeley into dream. My history, my life, became soft-edged and distanced-fogged. I was afraid.

A patch of sunlight had drawn me to his porch—I'd found it an attractive place to read of those dark angels for whom the sun is destructive. The light of this moment scattered the ash of what I'd been as would wind. I held up the book, invoking a barrier of the mundane (despite the profound truths the book itself held), so he and I could chat as if we'd met in a café, speaking in hushed, awed tones of the passions within the book. Muddy flirtation, to candle-dim the incendiary terror of that moment, to hold on to the dust-cool world in which I'd lived, because leaving it seemed too frightening.

"We won't talk about the book," he said, blocking my parry, sitting next to me. "And we won't talk about the movie. *Do you wish to be sired*? Do you wish to take the Gift of my blood..."

'...*into* your blood?' would have been a more complete asking of his question. More complete, yet less True. The Beauty of the thought lay in *my* completing it...and thus allowing my mind to touch his as our bodies would touch while he sired me.

I drew a breath to speak my Completion when the rough tread of one of his neighbors intruded. The thud of work boots approached the door of molded wood behind us. I glanced over my shoulder. A brutish head was framed in the leaded glass.

I dropped my worn paperback shield as the door scraped open and I muttered, "I should go." I walked away as the oafish neighbor clodded onto the porch. He who would become my lover smiled as I fled to a familiar landscape of want.

"You know where to find me," he said. As I backed away, his neighbor gave him the quizzical look the ignorant so often throw at artists.

I waded into Berkeley, my Promised Land whose Promise I'd forsaken. I let Berkeley huddle me as a vixen would her cub. Berkeley's hills and her trees were diamond-sharp in my sight, now that my past had become so dream-diluted. The foundations of my existence seemed no stronger than the floss of long-dead spiders.

Berkeley carried me till evening, when I'd next meet *him* in a way that could not be called Fate, as "Fate" implies a thing from which one can charade an escape. I found myself at a reception honoring an artist whose work honored his own caricature. I understand that, now. I'd then been impressed by all art, no matter how facile.

I wasn't "drawn" to that small gallery. I felt as if I'd refracted there, an illusion suddenly visible to my own perceptions.

Yet once in the gallery, I *was* drawn to a group of beautiful men who stood about, talking. I was drawn by their looks, the musk of their bodies and the scented oils they dabbed. I was drawn by the confidence they exuded and the sweet smoke of clove cigarettes woven into the clothes they wore, by the knowledge that these were men who could *create*...who could give the gift of what they saw with their hearts to the entire world.

I stood within ear-shot of them, wanting to be desired by at least one of them. To be wanted so would be a trinket to replace the life-treasure I'd lost that afternoon.

A lovely man, ashen-skinned, with green eyes, spoke to a man with golden hair. "You're obliged to keep a journal," he said, "for the sake of those who will study your work. Your life is your art."

The golden-haired man said, "No! I'll not make the study of me or my work less of a challenge for anyone. Even *myself*. My work is my journal."

The other men listened with the solemnity of oaks. The looks that they breeze-cast to one another were a web of intensity in which I longed to be entangled. I wanted to be taken into that emotional matrix that has existed among artists and their lovers throughout history, and that has defined subsequent eras of creative thought.

I stepped toward that grove of men and felt something unfold behind me. If was as if a rose the size of a cloak had unfurled. My imagination told me such a miracle had transpired, yet when I turned, I saw a miracle of another sort.

He whom I knew would become my soul-mate stood before canvases that suddenly seemed drab. No great rose had unfurled. Just his hand, extended. To me.

"Your red hair was how I found you," he said as we walked to his home. "Your red hair and your green eyes. They're a beacon. *You* called me. I answered. Now things must be finished." His hand gripped mine tighter. "Now you must be finished."

To be finished...

...a prize much greater than what I'd just sought within the web of artists I'd left behind. An eternal moment of fulfillment, like the interrupted moment in which I had, in my mind, finished his question to me: "...*into my blood*?"

Completion.

"I..."

"Don't say anything," he said. "Don't say a word."

We took the steps to his porch. The paperback I had no recollection of dropping was left there like a small altar. It filled me with something like nostalgia. I'd spent many hours holding it as a totem. Yet when had I first opened it? Did it have the smell of a new book, or the musk of a used one? I reached through the dream-floss of my memory just as my hand was let go. My companion snatched up the book. He flipped through it. Smiled.

Then molded wood was pressed against my spine. The small spaces in the leaded glass caught the hairs on the back of my head as he followed the fluid motion of seizing me and pressing me against the front door with the cupping of his mouth over mine, with the rubbing of the back of his hand that held the book against crotch.

His beautiful face came back into the focus; the rapture that had blurred him had also made the trees on the halogen-lit street a backdrop of velvet-green.

"Seized first..." he said.

He shook me in reply to my silence. The hand that held the book pressed harder against my crotch.

"Seized first..."

"...then...sired."

An instant of *Completion* that brought stem-drops of pre-ejaculate from me.

His apartment was home. The jumble of canvases was welcome in my sight as would be the faces of family. Each canvas was blank. I loved them for what I knew they would wear, and the depths they'd acquire.

"Do you *see*?" he asked.

"Yes."

"I need you to see more."

He showed me the studio that been a kitchenette before he had sheathed the space in rubber foam and clear plastic. The Great Canvas, for I knew what it was despite the tarp draped over it, leaned against a far corner. Like a magician producing a card by sleight of hand, he drew forth a postcard promoting the reception we'd left. The card reproduced a painting I'd seen at the reception: a lifeless portrait of a lifeless face. It had no character, for the subject had no character—I suspected it to be a self-portrait.

He hung a blank canvas behind a small paint-smeared table and chair. Rough, scarred, and much-spackled plaster marked the wall. "Leave," he said. "You'll know when to come back in."

I stood outside the French doors separating the studio from the living room. Foam obscured the windowlettes of the doors, yet spaces allowed me to peer through—as must have been his intent. The man with whom I wished to spend my redefined life came to the table with a tray holding his gun and brushes. He seated himself and placed the postcard before him. The sight of his raising the gun to his mouth was as agonizingly slow in my suddenly brimming sight as would be the sight of him driving nails through his own flesh.

My vision ripped with the ripping of his skull.

I hung in the eye of the sun, unblinking in the forever of the shot.

A lifetime of dawns erupted behind my sight.

Then the grain of the wood floor onto which I'd collapsed filled my vision.

Consciousness was a sodden burden I did not want.

I stood from the fallen bundle I'd become, opened the French doors.

Through the blue veil of smoke, I saw the beatitude of him standing from the table, rising as red and rose-pink matter slowed its cascade upon the canvas.

Within the viscous, blossomed smear, the face of the portrait scabbed itself into visibility. No longer a self-portrait, it was now made valid by a true artist having seen it and transposed his pure sensibility upon it. The image on the postcard was reborn, re-visualized to be what it *should* have always been. I came to myself as I saw in the crimson portrait's eyes a new profundity.

The portrait's eyes were now those of the man who would make me his lover this night. I would be granted an infusion of the same spirit through his blood. The immortality of great Art would be attainable for me through the angel-destructive taking of his spirit.

"We'll burn this canvas in the morning. I'll not dirty my brushes with it. But I needed you to see."

"I'm glad I saw." My words were church-whispered soft.

He smiled, "I'm glad you're brave enough to be glad. But *this* is not my Art," he said, hefting the canvas off the wall. "I'd not summon you to my life if it were. You're worthier than that." He dropped the canvas by a pile of rubbish near what had been a wooden ice box, then crossed the studio to where the tarped canvas leaned. "*This* is my Work," he said, pulling away the tarp.

Masterpieces as collage, *Completed*. Transposed, dragonfly-wing translucent. Works that had been wrongly called "Great Works" were made valid by their being re-written and re-painted through my mentor's perceptions and blood.

His vision and his courage recast Renaissance Madonnas and cubist landscapes. Still-lifes and portraits were fully realized and improved by his giving himself to their redemption. The images shifted and blazed in front of each other, as if each session's work had been done on panes of air-thin glass.

He offered me this Beauty. He offered to let me take it within me—*my* Completion, like that which he'd given to the "great works" the world had mis-guidedly thought to be already timeless and eternal.

Blood is his Art. And his Art is his Gift.

What matter that the body may be too fragile to endure the immortality the Gift offers? What matter the eventual loss of life to become as eternal as his Art? His Art sustains him. It resurrects him each day as he lifts Art from the dust in which it had been buried.

That night, for the first time, I knew pleasure unmitigated by latex. He bestowed the Gift of his Blood and Art to me. Sired, Complete, I woke the next morning knowing I'd found a Homeland nourished by the rivers that flowed within my lover. I left his bed to find my Sire placing my battered book on his shelf, next to other books by the same prophetess who had germinated in me the desire I'd just known fulfilled. He slid the book in a space on the crowded shelf, as if he'd just taken it from there.

"Your first item moved in," he said.

We laughed. Embraced. Made love and re-quickened my blood with his blood. My veins felt cut into my flesh, etched as are the depth-giving grooves my lover makes on his canvas with trowels fashioned from shards of his own jaw.

It happened on Monday morning. A bourgeois joke. Fodder for greeting cards and coffee mug slogans to amuse those whom my lover's Work was destined to elevate. The banality of the moment when disaster chose to strike pained him the most, at times. I shared his anguish that Mediocrity had dealt him such humiliation.

As always, on that Monday—my furtive glance and the single shot. The shattering red fog and the willow-tree spray of blood and bone and flesh. Then, in the world-stunned silence, the rustle of his brush-strokes as he redeemed an image of Redemption as painted by a medieval primitive.

I waited, while he worked, in a place where time seemed to sleep. Then I heard the distinct click of him setting down his brush crafted from a splinter of his femur. I took fruit and mineral water from the mini-fridge in the living room—a gesture that served Art more than did entire lifetimes nominally dedicated to Art—and heard the rare treasure of him calling me by name.

I went through the French doors, and glanced upon Beauty—the new layer added this day to the Work. It was the image of a dying knight carried to Heaven by the reputed mother of Christ. My lover had dared the ancient fresco to magnificence, finding a way for it to truthfully catch the fires of Heaven that it had before lyingly portrayed.

He stared at the canvas as I placed the tray on the book of medieval art I'd freed from the library.

"I can't find it," he said.

I looked. The kit with which he patched the canvas sat by his brushes and gun. A lesser lover of a lesser man would have said, "*It's right there.*"

Yet I failed him in another way by saying nothing.

"Look...at...the...*Work*," he said.

My eye was drawn to the scrap of eye in the painting's far corner. His martyred iris still reflected his soul.

"*Look...*" he said.

I ran my eye over museums-worth of sublimnity.

And realized with a shock...

...no patch today.

I turned. His patching kit was unopened in its ribboned box, as I'd placed it for him.

"I can't find the *bullet*," he said.

Together, we ran our fingers over the wall, to see if the bullet was embedded in the plaster beside the canvas, in wood or a metal stud behind the plaster. The abattoir-perfume of the canvas made me giddy as I stood closer to it than I ever had. Yet still I kept my focus to his task.

As one, we both looked to the floor.

And I felt a burning migraine-like pain as he lowered his head...a sharp, weighty pressure atop the loam of my brain.

The pain I felt was an echo, reaching me from his blood. The cry I let out was a leakage of the cry he held tight in his throat.

The sudden pain that subsided in me endured in him as it made twisted branches of his body. His knees fell from under him and he held his head in his blood-caked hands.

"It's still inside me."

The days that followed still shame me.

I was jealous of the bullet.

Jealous of his obsessive thinking of it, of the constant circular caresses he made on his scalp as it gnawed at him from within. I hungered for the caresses he no longer gave me.

The bullet sported in the paradise *of his mind*. An unthinking bit of stone had through accident attained the beatification for which I prayed. Yes, it hurt his thoughts—yet it was closer to him than I was…entangled in the lattice of his genius. It was an unborn half-self to him: what I longed to be, above and beyond the conjoining of blood we shared.

And through that which is and ever shall be his Gift to me, I felt the bullet change his blood. Since he had Sired me, my own blood had the sweetness of honeyed milk in my veins. Now, that was tainted with metallic hurt, a sour buzzing eroded from the stone lodged in his mind. Lead infused my vision. At times, all Berkeley itself became tinted with greyish cobalt in my sight.

My lover's Work dried on the canvas—it took an opacity that dimmed its layers. Though still beautiful, since it failed to be renewed each morning, the Work lost vividness—rearing suns aligned in harmony became as one sun.

And I lost something as well, no longer replenished by the exquisite spirit he granted me each time our love-making re-enacted the moment of his Siring me. Even with the taint of the bullet in him, I hungered for such renewal.

Yet my needs were unimportant. My lover was not painting. Art was not being redeemed. That to which I'd dedicated all I ever could be was suffered into stasis. I was cut off from my own life—a bluefly tapping against the window of where I as a person should live. To re-enter, I tried to awaken his passion…for his Art, and for me.

I brought him new books of art to look on and redeem.

The person I *had* been might not have suffered the wound of my lover leaping from the couch and flinging into my face the damp, oil-and-blood-stained cloth that had been on his brow. The person I *had* been might have said what he said to me: "Why are you hurting me like this?"

He grabbed the books and flung them to the floor. His teeth ground like a handful of pebbles. "You're happy," he said. "You're fine. I gave you all I can of me. You have parts of me I can't touch anymore. And you resort to cheap taunts?"

"I want you to work."

His voice became like that of a sick child. "That's very funny, coming from you."

"Your work is important to me."

"So, I should work?" Again, his voice was child-like, like that of a boy sorry he has broken the favorite plaything of another.

"Yes."

"You'd just love that wouldn't you? If another shot got stuck? Why not let me have two hot little pebbles in my head? You'd like that, wouldn't you? To be the strong one? You jealous..."

He held his head, sat upon sofa. "...jealous little shit," he finished. He glared at me. "'*Two hot little pebbles*'. That's not very good, is it? Certainly not worthy of *you*." He stood, walked shakily to the bookshelf and pulled from behind a row of novels the rolls of vellum-like paper on which I'd begun this account. He held them to me. "*You're* the artist now? You're trying to write like the 'poetess'?"

"I'm...trying...to document what you do."

"I gave you *this*." He shook the papers that I'd made into scrolls, so they'd have the solemnity they deserved. "I *gave* you your words. But you can't use them to describe what I do. I gave you all I'd learned from 'your' precious 'poetess', because you're that important to me."

"You're everything to me..."

"Then why do you bring me art to look at? You taunt me with a need to create that I can't fulfill?" He looked down upon the art books I'd freed for him...looked down upon the images only half-finished by Cézanne the way a starving man would a full and steaming plate. The images seemed to hunger for my lover as well...desiring his vision and blood to dream them into wholeness.

He dropped the scrolls and fell to his knees, touching the books. He sobbed the way I had when he re-wrote my blood. I tried to hold him, to help him to the couch.

He pushed me away, then pressed his hands against the back of his head.

"You're worse than the fucking bullet."

I returned to work. I rode the train from Berkeley to my empty job, which seemed all the more hollow now it had no purpose than to support our basic living. The drudgery I endured had once served the redemption of Art. Now it served the mere paying of rent. I sat surrounded by drones never touched by the sublime as I have been. I looked to the empty faces my lover's Work would have touched with fire. I pitied them. They were not ready to receive the Work that would free them from their prisons, that would bring *to them* the higher plane for which they were too afraid to reach.

And I pitied myself. I was suddenly in fact that which I had mimicked.

I tried to read a newspaper. The words blurred to a wall of grey. Yet as I tried to read, the roar of the train…

…took a solidity…

…that stood upon the loam of my brain. The sound of the train became the buzzing of the bullet in my lover's mind; it compressed itself into an impacted tooth of metal in my thoughts.

Sublimation…the passing of a thing from one state to another. Isn't that what my lover's blood does? What Art itself does? The pain at the back of my head was the call of my body for the bullet—just as the dull eyes of those around me was the call for the semblance of life my lover's Art would bring. The bullet's sound, its sourness, its pain, infused me through my lover's blood. Could it not crystallize into me? Could it not flow as solution to me and metastasize in my mind? Drawn as gold was once belived to be from base lead?

Thus, could my lover be freed to create his Art?

I changed platforms at the next stop, and returned home to realize I'd no idea we owned so many mirrors.

That was the thought that jangled in my shattering mind as I arrived to tragedy and desecration.

My lover had taken the mirrors from the bedroom, from the medicine chest, from the hall, even a shaving mirror I'd forgotten we owned, and placed them on easels of varying height so he could see reflections of reflections of his newly-shaven head as he brought the electric hand-saw I used to make his canvas frames to the base of his skull.

The buzzing in my mind externalized itself; it left me to become the light-strobing buzz of the hand-saw as it lay jammed with a thumb-sized shard of skull. In that strobing light, my lover writhed, unable to raise his hands to the shark-bite wound he had inflicted upon himself and gouge the hated nugget from his mind.

I knelt to him, held him as the Madonna held her Son in the *pieta* my lover had once amber-trapped in his blood.

Spray had geysered the studio that was no longer a studio, now that my lover's blood and tissue had haphazardly smeared the Work. His palsied hand, unlike the sure hand that brought the gun to the loving smooth roof of his mouth, had plashed gaudy rain upon the canvas. The translucent layers had blended into each other, had made the Work appear nothing more than cloth dropped on the floor of a slaughterhouse.

I unplugged the saw. The lights above stopped strobing. The buzzing fell silent. I replaced the shard of skull from where it had been torn.

"Don't speak," I said. "Don't say a word."

In that place where time held itself hostage to our plight, I knew what martyrdom he wished.

A woman screamed upon seeing us, apparitions smeared with what she could only know as "blood". Yet it was also our Gift—our shared legacy. I'd not let anyone steal or sully it.

It was wasteful to spill our Gift upon the train platform. My lover, his head bandaged with duct-tape and dishtowels, paid the mid-morning commuters no heed as we shoved past them. All we could focus on was the oblivion promised him upon the track down which eighty tons of careening metal rushed.

I stood to his back as he dove before the train as if into pure and cleansing waters.

I knew joy, and release, as my lover was pulped to moist, red clay... as he found the sublimation that would free him. No one could steal his Gift, now that the Art it allowed him to create had been taken from him. No lesser talent would ever desecrate or appropriate his blood for their own re-visualizations. He'd not become paint for lesser talents, not while his flesh and blood and marrow were dispersed so thinly. I smiled to know he was free.

And I split along that smile, casting my blood upon the wind-swift metal canvas of the train. I shattered along my skeleton as the *first* flesh from which my lover had crafted me burst upon the track. My dissolution had none of my lover's fire, had none of the profundity of his Art.

Exit Wound

I hoped to ascend, to find myself in the sublime heaven my lover had painted with that Gift from which I'd been conjured.

But I found myself earthbound by a small metal nugget with the weight of a thousand suns. I…my lover's least creation…reached to him through the liquidity that joined us, through the blood-spirit-thought that defines our Gift and that now forms my words.

We cooled together, two careless smears, blended as are cheap pigments by the hoses of those who washed us away.

For Marian Anderson (1968-2001)—neighbor and friend during the dark years. You left us to endure darker years without you.

Winter Tales

Winter Requiem

David watched a red streak of November sunset turn to a bloody serpent hung in the darkening sky.

He knew, sitting in the wine-colored dusk beneath the eaves of a great oak, that the vision was a phantom conjured by the seeping toxins in his blood. He chose not to dispel the vision by blinking or glancing away. It didn't threaten him as did most others; it was not vivid nor clear enough to possibly be real. It had the quality of art. He found comfort in the serpent's rich color, its slow smoke-like undulations.

After a long moment, the serpent became still, and slowly lost its shape to become again a burning cloud in the west.

When dusk gave way to moonlight, and the scent of autumn's dead leaves meshed with that of smoke from fireplaces miles distant, and the sound of the brook that ran through the grove of oaks to the south became sharper with the cold night air, David stood and leaned on the branch he used as a walking staff. In his youth, not so very long ago, he'd secretly called this hill "Weathertop," and carried a staff as a prop when he imagined himself a peer of Gandalf. Now he needed a staff to negotiate the terrain; the illness that had turned his blood to slow poison had also given him gout.

He hobbled down the hill toward the house where he'd grown up, past fields he'd once run and played in, now brown from the withering touch of Fall. When he reached the yard he was sweating with exertion, despite the night air. Drowsy greyness filled the corners of his sight, as if another phantom would accost his senses. At the door, he stood a moment, and breathed deeply until the greyness passed.

When he entered, he saw his work, the sheets of music he'd been composing, crumpled and torn and strewn about the living room. The piano bench had been toppled and shoved to a far corner, the piano itself dented and banged, its rich wood splintered and scuffed from the blows of the poker that lay upon it. A bottle of ink had been thrown against the far wall, leaving a blue smeary blossom upon the white paint and shards of glass upon the wood floor.

David stood aghast. For how long he didn't know. The clatter of his staff as it toppled from his hand brought him out of his shock.

He limped to the center of the room, turned in circles, filled with panic, filled with fear, filled with rage. He was about to phone the police when an ugly thought struck him, making him flush, making his knees weak.

He searched the house for signs of break-in. Who would break into a house in the middle of the woods? No forced windows, no broken glass, no splintered wood on the doors.

David went to the ruined living room and sat, feeling his heart thud in his chest.

He could have done this, himself. Made drunk by the disease that was killing him. Enraged that the degradation of his mind would not allow him to compose a legacy of music before his body destroyed itself. He had been frustrated, angry for most of the day, unable to focus on his work or to experimentally play musical phrases.

He had no memory of what he'd done before he'd left the house...no memory of actually leaving. He could only recall a need to be outside, to feel wind and see the sky before he could resume composing.

He could have done this.

Not wanting to cry, feeling lancing pain in his gouty joints as he knelt, David gathered the sheets off the floor, unrumpled them, and placed them on the mantel. He righted the piano bench, and took the poker away from the scarred piano. He cleaned and tidied the room, but left the stain upon the wall, not wanting to make it worse by trying to wash it off.

Afterward, he put on his favorite recording of Mozart's "Requiem" and pressed a razor against the blue veins of his forearm.

The hunt was on.

His pursuers mocked him by signaling the chase with horns.

The deposed commander of twenty-nine scattered legions ran through living muck that screamed and writhed under his monstrous footfall, then crossed a swampy river as a horse would ford churning waters, his head and neck craning and bobbing with the strokes of his shoulders and arms.

As he surged through the stagnant channel, a new crash of horns came like a storm wind across the wailing marsh. He stopped swimming and listened, looking back the way he'd come for his pursuers. Through the thick, perpetual fog of that starless, sunless place, he saw signal fires flash atop a watchtower on the shore he had just left.

Ahead, he saw answering fires atop the ramparts of the city of burning red iron on the shore before him.

He wanted to bellow his rage, scream his fury, but he dared not give away his location. Then he thought to make his position known in a manner that could save him.

He sounded the filthy, brackish water, warm as fresh blood yet laced with Death's cold touch, and pulled from the corrupted slime at the bottom something ruined: something that had been breathing muck for the long centuries since it had breathed air.

He broke the surface, and held aloft by one hand the screaming ghost he had pulled from below, hiding most of his own bulk under the water, yet keeping his gaze above the surface…watching through the low mist with the careful expectation of a predator.

The debased soul, able at last to shriek the agony it had felt since it had dropped to this spiritual vomitorium, summoned the river's guardian. Fast as an arrow freed from a bowstring, the guardian's skiff skimmed the water. The twisted grey creature on board smiled gleefully, eyes alight with the color of ice as he poised his oar like a weapon at the screaming soul's breast.

"You are *mine*!" said the guardian.

The hunted prince lashed-out from the water, hurling the ruined soul aside. He crashed his head and his single, spiraling horn against the skiff's prow, then gripped the prow in his claws. The guardian shrieked, raised his oar overhead, was about to bring it down on the prince's claws when the prince hissed, "I'll sink you!"

The boatman froze, eyes burning with cold fire, teeth clenched.

"I'll sink you!" said the prince. "All your little charges will be on you, biting, gnashing and clawing. They'll rise up for you from below, and the ones from the shallows will be on you like the water itself."

Again, the crash of horns came, this time from the shore, so close it made the air shudder. The twisted boatman smiled and set down his oar.

"There's no room in *this* ark for you, either."

The prince growled, then splintered the prow's lip, rocked the skiff to and fro.

The boatman stepped toward the prow, leaned forward to the prince's equine face, and spoke calmly. "The boat cannot hold your royal weight. Were you to come aboard, it would sink beneath you as if you stood on a floating leaf. Rage away, *Regulus*. Rage away."

The prince lunged and gripped the boatman's corded throat in one claw. The skiff tilted forward with his bulk, pressed into his belly, and began to fill with the river's broth-thick water.

The prince spoke in an intonation he had used in cold defiance against the Archangels: "Enough theater. Take me to the safe shore."

He released the boatman's throat, slid back into the water. Without a word, the boatman piloted the skiff along the shores of the city of burning red iron; the prince hidden, clinging to the skiff's underside. In the shallows, far from the city's ramparts and gate, the prince let go the skiff and waded ashore through water choked with rotted souls, slick as stalks of decayed kelp.

Standing upon the bank, he pried several of these gurgling souls from his limbs, his chest, back and genitals. They were too corrupted to scream as his claws tore them.

Soon he was running again, the hoof beats of creatures both two- and four-legged thundering behind him.

The razor broke David's skin as the voices of the chorus gave earthly expression to the sound of Heaven.

Blood ran down David's wrist, baptizing his hand in red warmth, when he stopped the razor's path through his flesh.

"*If I survive this, I won't be able to play,*" he thought. His riot of emotions fell quiet; grief and anger and despair calmed within him like a breaking tempest. "*The tendons will be cut, then I'll have nothing left. Nothing. Not able to play or compose. Or I'll be put in a ward somewhere, not allowed anything as sharp as a pen to compose with on scrap paper…*"

Leaning over the deep kitchen basin, watching red drops make sudden blossom on the white porcelain, he knew he would not survive the opening of his veins. No one knew where he was. No one would look for him. No ambulance could reach him in time if he phoned, bleeding, for help.

His own sister didn't know what continent he was on. He was hiding from people who would want to hospitalize him, who would keep him bedridden in the name of caring for him, who would not allow him to exhaust himself while composing his legacy, while he gave meaning to his last months in this world.

And if he died now, there would be no meaning to his life. Nothing left behind. A few minor compositions already performed that his teachers and a few critics had said showed the potential for greatness. But nothing of lasting value. Nothing that would endure as a testament to the sacrifices his parents had made for him and his music.

He, and his music, would not survive this.

He set down the razor and inspected the wound.

It was minor. No vein had been opened. He flexed his fingers. No tendon had been cut. He washed the wound under warm water, and watched currents of red flow within the stream of water.

"*If only I could clean my blood. Wash out the enzymes my liver is leaking into it. I wouldn't be in this fog. My music wouldn't be hidden away in my head, all nestled in cotton wool. I'm drowning in my own mind.*"

A thought struck him as he watched bloody water swirl down the drain and the "Requiem" played itself out. David took a wine glass from the cabinet beside the sink and let his blood flow into it, making a fist around a dish towel as he did so.

He made a tight bandage around his forearm with gauze, and carried the glass to the living room. He took from the shelves there the books bound in dusty leather that had belonged to his mother, and that he could not bear to sell to collectors after she had died. He took from the mantel the large clay bowl his mother had had made at great expense by an artisan who lived near Jerusalem. Dust covered the vermilion lines of concentric lettering inside the bowl: lettering in Hebrew and Aramaic and other languages David did not know.

David wiped away the dust and set the bowl in the center of the room. His joints felt full of sand as he kneeled over the books and began to read.

The prince ran through a forest of those who had, in life, made a gibbet of their existences, and had ripped their souls from out of their bodies so that they dropped here and germinated to twisted, black trees. Knotted branches inlaid with tendons and veins quivered with unreleased suffering. Blood spurted from the branches that he broke as he ran, and the blood wept, vibrating softly as if each drop were a tiny throat pressed upon his skin.

The prince stopped, listened for his enemies. He did not hear them above the steady cries that hung thick in the forest's air. Harpies, perched in the upper branches, pecked at the trees, taking communion in small bites from the ruined souls, from their unreal flesh transubstantiated to twisted wood. The wounds the harpies caused gave ruby outlets to the pain of the suicides; their droppings, in turn, nourished the soil that fed the souls that had been so wretchedly starved in life.

The sounds of the forest were calming. They reminded the prince of the dark places where the newly-dead congregated, wandering like sleepwalkers, bewildered, whimpering because of the sudden loss of their bodies. In happier days, the prince would often run through this limbo, scooping up souls like bundles of wood to give as playthings to his followers.

The prince crouched low and rested, thinking of new strategies, new allies to find, new armies to rally, once he escaped the toadies of those who had deposed him.

His punishments, his vengeance, would be hailed as atrocities, legendary in their cruelty even in Hell. He would make of his enemies living standards, erect cathedrals to his own honor from their bones. He would create orchestrations of suffering that would make his enemies envy the damned they'd once had charge over.

But first he had to escape those who craved his blood and coveted his horn: the blessed mark of his power he wore upon his brow.

The cries from the trees closest to him quieted. The trail of lamentation from the scarlet path he'd beaten fell into the regular rhythms of the forest.

The prince absently etched his mark upon the trunk of a tree as he thought, making the soul inside cry softly in a tune he found soothing as he pressed his claws into the bark, nimbly as a violinist fingers the neck of his instrument. Perhaps he should enlist aid from the Master of Fraud, sound a clarion call while riding on his back as they flew in a gyre to the deepest part of the writhing abyss. If he could double back, the keeper of Hell's gate would allow him to weave sundering music from the suspirations of the newly-dead that would…

A sound came from the way the prince had come, like a great wave crashing, the fabric of thunder meshed with the sound of a raging sea. And beneath those sounds came a brutal melange of suffering: the screams of thousands as a horde of what the prince knew to be his enemies crashed through the wood. The prince stood, and climbed the sobbing tree he had been scarring with the speed of a hunting cat.

In the distance, through the gloom, he saw hundreds of points of light spread out in a line just within the edge of the wood—the flames of torches held by those who hunted him, darting, curving in a wide ribbon among the bleeding trunks. Some points of light were too fast, too agile to be from torches; they were the burning faces of yith hounds, black hunting bitches maddened with the need to rend and tear and wound and…

The prince dropped to the ground. But did not run. He was a strategist. A tactician. Nothing he did now could be without thought. He could not afford the luxury of blind flight. He stifled the sound of his pursuers in his ears, reached out with his senses for *anything* in the ether that could help him. There was something. Something informed so slightly by the aura of this eternal place of suicide that, at any other time, he would not dare pursue it and face the oblivion of the journey to Materiality.

But now he had no choice. Now he answered the far call from one who hung near the spiritual death that fed this wood.

At the trunk of the tree he had climbed, he kneeled like one about to take communion and forced his hands into his mark, pulling open within it a portal made by the dim invocation of his name. The blood of the tree screamed as loudly as the sound of the hunters behind him.

And in the void, he waited for the remote chance that the calling of his name would carry him to a place closer to the Heaven that had expelled him.

"There are no such things as demons, Mother."
His mother had smiled when David had said those words to her.
"Then you don't believe in angels, either?"
"No. I don't. There's only us, Mother."
His mother had touched his face, then. Caressed his cheek as she said, *"When you're older, you'll see how little you know about the world. How much of it is a mystery. Then you'll come to treasure the mystery."*

David had not believed her. For, at that point, belief in magic and hidden things was behind him. *Once*, before, he had believed in unknowable powers that were partly revealed in the myths, epics and folklore he'd read so as a boy. When he was young, he had known in his heart the *sidhe* lived in the woods nearby, that the War of the Ring had truly been waged, and that somewhere in the world, a dragon still lived.

But he had set those beliefs aside.

His mother had been partly right; David had come to treasure mysteries as he grew older. Not the mysteries of the world, or the wide, ethereal universe that she held dear. What he had come to treasure were the mysteries of the *mind*, the forces within that his mother had freed with her incantations and formulas to attain what she needed and desired.

Once, when the family had needed money, Mother had burned a dollar bill in a ritual, "giving it back to the Universe." Within the week,

Father had a new job. It was a wonderful thing. But no real magic was involved. The ritual had simply forced his parents to focus on Father's job search with renewed intensity.

And now David, on his aching knees with his mother's books before him, hoped to tap his own mind. To use ritual to lift the hateful fog his disease had imposed on his thoughts and creativity, and so liberate his music.

David read aloud the Latin incantations of the books, and also the Hebrew his mother had phonetically scribbled on sheets of yellow legal pad and inserted within the pages. Toward the end of his ritual, David took the wine glass that held his blood and poured a few drops in the center of the bowl, so they were surrounded by the concentric lines of script.

Then he turned the bowl over, and read a final Hebrew incantation.

And something quietly opened inside David's mind. A flowering of images and sensations unfurling like a white rose. A vista of alabaster filled his sight, and a sound, distant as the step of a ghost, grew louder and more tangible in his ears.

It was the sound of snow.

A memory rose like mist from the shadows of his childhood…a memory of lying with closed eyes on the white blanket of a winter field. Even the wind had been silent. In that unreal, timeless quiet, deeper than any he'd known even while in dreamless sleep, he had heard the breath of the sky itself, the whisper of the dome of grey clouds above.

He had heard the voice of each crystalline feather of snow as it fell, as it alighted upon the earth, upon his lashes and face. He had heard the snow's delicate poetry, but could not fathom its language, the key to the beautiful things it spoke. The language was more than one of sound; it was a language of sensation that touched him as the morning of the year's first frost touched him, telling him of its presence the instant before he woke and opened his eyes.

He had wanted to know each secret thing the snow spoke. But after what seemed a very long time, he realized the snow's words and poems would stay secret to him. He'd opened his eyes, and the dull winter sunshine behind the clouds seemed blinding. He'd heard then the thunder of his breath, the roar of his own heartbeat. He'd stood to wend his way home, and saw that the new snow had covered his track to where he'd laid himself down.

Each step he had taken marred the perfect, pure field, imprinting it with the mark of his passing, had drowned the voice of the falling snow with the ugly crush of his footfall.

It was the sound of snow... David remembered the sound, and remembered the person he had been when he had heard it: the boy who knew and believed in mysteries and magic hidden everywhere around him. The sound of snow, how it had touched him so deeply with a beauty he could not understand, was what he needed to give musical expression. This was the essence of what he had to compose, yet he had not been able to name it before. This was his trophy, his prize seized from the distant, shadowy part of his mind. Now he could touch this memory, hold it close and nurture it...set it to music to share it with others and grant it new life.

David wept, softly. With relief and joy and with pain. For the memory had been pulled from his deepest sense of self, drawn forcibly to the forepart of his mind.

The vista of whiteness filling his vision faded. The floor of the living room, the inverted bowl, became visible, but still shrouded, as if David were looking through gauze.

Yet the sound of snow maintained.

And became louder.

David wiped his eyes, listened like an animal hearing the tread of a hunter. A cold touch ran up his back, over his arms, across his chest.

Strands of mist, like wisps of white hair, streamed from beneath the bowl, flowing into a smoky pool by the hearth.

The wine glass vibrated, as if a tuning fork had been touched to it. David's blood, its redness muted from the gauze, shook within, concentric ripples washing to the sides. The vibration of the glass, the movement of the blood, had a rhythm, a pattern. David knew the rhythm, felt it inside himself.

He leaned forward, looked into the glass.

The rhythm was that of David's breath...as if the blood were still within his veins, pulsing with the other rhythms of his body. The blood had a voice.

The sound of snow spoke from David's blood.

Winter filled David's body, coursed in a February wind through his torso, his limbs, filling each capillary, collecting in an icy fist in his heart.

He screamed. And the blood in the glass screamed with him; the sound of snow bellowed from the glass, reverberating through the room like the ring of a cathedral bell. The sound endured past David's scream. He tried to stand and run into the cold November night. But the rotting joints of his legs gave way under him. He could not rise from his knees.

More mist flowed from under the bowl. The pool of white smoke by the hearth now looked solid through David's shrouded vision. A hump formed within the pool, as if it were a sheet and a man stood up from a crouch beneath it. The floorboards by the fireplace creaked loudly, as if suddenly taking on a heavy weight.

The sound of snow was snuffed. The gauze before David's eyes fell away; all within his vision shifted to clarity the way midnight shadows shift with the light of the moon.

And a hunched abomination stood before David.

"Yes?" it said.

With that one word, the veil of sanity in David's world was torn away.

"*I'm hallucinating*," David thought. "*Be rational. This is nothing. This is a dream. This is a ghost. It comes from the sickness.*"

The thing rose to its full height, towering above him. Fine mist came off its heavily muscled body, off its chiseled legs, its arms, off the torso that looked as if it had been sculpted in marble. Up to its neck, its skin was white as bone. Coarse hair with the sheen of sea-foam grew over the throat and the bestial head was at once like that of a horse, and that of a deer and of a goat. A mane of human-like hair fell in foppish bangs around the great spiraling horn that grew from its brow and that glowed like mother of pearl in candlelight..

"*It's not real. It can't be. It's a demon from one of Mother's books. A demon. You saw it's picture and you…*"

The monstrosity fixed David with eyes violet as the cusp of a January dawn. Again, it spoke.

"Yes?"

The square animal mouth moved, making human speech that didn't vibrate as sound in the air but *occurred* in David's mind, like a premonition given grammar and cogent thought. David tried to speak. His jaw trembled, as if from cold, and the beast cocked its long, equine head, as a man would cock his head trying to hear a faint sound, never taking its gaze from David's.

David clenched his trembling jaw, forced his gaze to the floor and then forced words from his lips.

"You're not real. I don't believe in you."

He looked up, hoping, *knowing*, his words had banished the thing, driven it away with the other phantoms his sickness created. That this creature would…

David was again held by the violet gaze.

"But *I* believe in *you*."

Winter Requiem

David fought the urge to drown in the morning sky those eyes held and made himself speak.

"You don't exist."

"Oh, but I do."

"I didn't call you. I didn't summon you. You're nothing. I'm dreaming you."

The demon, glanced away, freeing David from its opiate stare. Then it leaned forward. Its horn lowered like a pike before David's face; it reached down with its great lion-clawed hand and lifted the bowl from the floor as David would lift a teacup from a shelf. It turned the bowl over in its palm, then pointed with a claw of its free hand to the red inscriptions inside.

"You did call me. And politely, I came. If you look closely here, you will see my name. You invoked it. Of course, if you look closely, you will also find the name of a very splendid Nazarene carpenter. I'm afraid *He's* too busy knocking together cabinets and tables for his dear Tyrant of a Father to answer your call. I, however, am free this evening, and so accept your invitation."

"I...revoke my invitation."

"After I have come all this way? Why? Have I been rude? Of course I have. I have come empty-handed. Let me give you a gift."

It brought its horn down on David's shoulder, as if the horn were a sword and the creature were knighting him. David was seized by cramps. His every muscle clenched, every tendon pulled tight. Still on his knees, he fell backward, paralyzed on the floor.

The thing stood above him, its horn almost touching the ceiling. "There. Now I am a decent guest. But I'm sure there are other exchanges to be made between us. By the way, does this go here?"

The thing held out the bowl to David, then turned partly to place it on the mantel. "Ah! You compose!" it said as it set down the bowl. It picked up the rumpled sheets and read. "Oh, this is splendid! You have a rare gift. I am a patron of composers. But you must have known that when you called me. Yes, I'm sure we can make an arrangement."

And David, gripped by nightmare paralysis, could not scream when he saw upon the thing's back another atrocity that sent his mind reeling, that had him uttering silent prayers for the first time in many godless years.

The thing turned its back away and faced David. It stepped forward, looked down at him and said: "I have helped composers for many years. I have stood invisible at the side of great *maestros*, guiding their batons. I have stood in cold, dusty garrets and revealed my secrets to composers whom you venerate. I have bestowed hidden musical voices to great cities.

Woven melodies from their footsteps and from the clatter of wheels on their cobblestones, melodies that have touched the entire world. I would be happy to help you with *this*." It held David's rumpled compositions out to him, then it made a bow, like a courtier. "We must be introduced. I am Amduscias." The demon stood upright. "I am pleased to…"

The thing that had clung to the demon's back fell wetly to the floor. David tried to look away as the spectral grey body of a young woman, torn in half, glistening translucently as frost, reached out to him on the floor. Her eyes held the pleading desperation of a drowning person as she tried to crawl toward him. She mouthed words, but all David heard were choking sounds.

The thing that called itself "Amduscias" snatched the torn woman from the floor by her hair. "I've tracked mud into your home," it said. "Forgive me." The woman continued her wordless pleading; David could see the transparent organs of her opened torso as she raised her arms over her head, trying to free herself from the demon's claws.

Buzzing greyness filled the edges of David's vision. He embraced the coming hallucination, the seizing of his mind by familiar sickness so it would blot out what he saw now. The light in the room changed, became dappled, like afternoon light in a deep forest.

"Let me present to you an offer," said the demon. "You said that I don't exist. I won't argue with you in your home. That would be impolite, and I have made one *faux pas* too many as your guest tonight."

It held the mauled ghost aloft, almost to the level of its head. In the dappled light of David's hallucination, Amduscias looked like a poacher holding his catch in a wooded glen. The demon's animal face gave the woman a sickeningly human look of contempt. Then it looked back to David.

"Since I do not exist, I am a product of your mind. Therefore, if you were to *allow* me to possess you, no harm could come of it. I would be one part of your mind returning home. A part of your mind you've lost touch with, that otherwise would help you create sweet music such as this." The claw that did not hold the woman held forward David's compositions, the sheets small as those from a notepad in the huge palm. "Allow me to demonstrate my musical ability."

It drew the sheets over its heart, and the room filled with snatches of music. David's music. The bars, the sketches, the phrases he'd been working on performed faultlessly by invisible musicians. The air shimmered as if from the heat of a fire. The dappled forest-light glinted as if the very leaves above shook with the music's resonance.

Then the music stopped in a heartbeat.

"Think what I could do *in your mind*. Think what I could liberate within you if you willingly took me back to your mind. You needn't answer now. I know that you can't. You will feel like a new man in the morning. In the meantime, I must find a way to make this little river leech pay for coming to your home uninvited."

It shook the woman as a sadistic child would shake a cat held by the scruff of the neck. Bits of cloudy, dust-colored flesh dropped to the floor.

The demon came down to one knee. "There must be blood here somewhere, for you to have called me. If it's fresh, I can make a gift of her. A little aid to help with your composing. Ah! just so."

It set David's sheets down and lifted the wine glass. The dappled light grew dimmer as the demon held the glass to its eye. "I'll do what I am able with this. But watch! Watch what is possible when two agents meet to create something new and wonderful. Watch what could happen if you and I were to join."

It set the woman like a broken doll on its knee, and with one claw forced her mouth open. It poured the blood from the glass down the woman's throat.

David watched the blood flow through her like streams of red candle wax. Her flesh shrank, took on the texture of a wet scab. Then the demon began sculpting her, molding her as if she were red clay. "She will be of great use to you. For how long I can't say. We'll make the best of…"

Welcome hallucination suffocated David's senses, eclipsed the violation of sanity before him. He floated, as if the floor were water. The room warped as if it were an image painted on a flapping sheet. David could move. He felt his body as a weight he knew only from its sudden absence. He walked, and despite his weightlessness, the ground gave way under him like loose sand. He followed a red snake that floated in his vision like noon sun streaming through his eyelids. It took him to a place he knew was safe.

Dreams moved like föhn winds through the ether, carrying seeds of madness and obsession in the night the way summer winds carry milkweed strands over green meadows.

The whisper of damnation touched sleeping minds, and people dreamed of a magnificent white beast, the embodiment of purity and strength of redemption. They coursed the beast, running joyously with neighbors and lovers and friends through dark woods until they caught the animal, felled it, and were made clean, whole and redeemed by its blood, and by the power of its glowing, divine horn.

Morning brought to them a heavy sadness, and a vague memory of salvation and innocence they had lost.

David woke to the smell of urine.

He was curled in a fetal ball in the house's entryway, beneath the line of hooks that had once held his family's winter coats, but now looked so barren with only his coat hanging on one of them. The smell came from him, from his jeans. He was relieved, in a way he could not fully understand, that he didn't care.

David stood, went out to the yard, and crawled on his belly through dead November leaves, smelling, tasting, feeling them, rubbing them on his face, drinking in the sanity they represented, their naturalness. He sobbed. Whimpered. Then turned over on his back and looked at the glory, the sanity, the God-decreed *order* of an autumn morning sky.

"I'm losing my mind," he thought. "*I'm going crazy. Demented. My blood's rotting my brain. Beethoven must have felt like this, going deaf. Losing his music bit by bit. But he had his sanity. He didn't face this. I don't have much time.*"

He stood and looked down at himself.

"*God. What am I becoming?*"

He thought of the homeless men he'd seen in so many cities, suffering from AIDS dementia and from hepatic conditions like his own, because they had destroyed their livers with drink. They stank of piss. They were dirty. They were covered with leaves from the parks they slept in.

He went in the house to wash. To work. To escape the meaningless, brutal fate of mumbling, premature senility that awaited him.

Amduscias the Prince settled in a wooded hill that overlooked the home of the little conjurer who had called him. The place was special to the conjurer; he could smell the man's spirit invested among the oaks.

His pursuers could not reach him here, in the Living World. Not unless they were called. But they *would* find him, eventually, and continue their chase as avatars moving through the bodies of others, unless he found safe harbor within a willing human soul.

The little conjurer had a ripe soul. Fragrant. Full of vibrancy and poetic insight. The prince could use it as a shield and as a weapon, create within it a fortified tower from which he could attack. He would cleave to and cleave through the man's soul, make it a source of *elán* to face those who hunted him and crush them for their arrogance in taking arms against him. He would descend upon them as the Great Archangel who routed him and his followers had descended, just before The Expulsion.

It was a simple matter of time before the little conjurer capitulated, before he invited the prince to transmigrate into the chamber of his soul where his music was born, into the realm of his spirit where the prince would have complete dominion. Forced possession would shatter his soul, make it useless.

Soon the sickness of the conjurer, or the desperation it inspired, would vaporize the rich metal of his will. All just a matter of time.

Rather than stay idle as he waited, the prince summoned a cruel and early spring to the wood, calling forth new buds from the dead trees and drawing new shoots from the hard soil. From another grove of oaks to the south, he summoned the welcoming and comforting sounds of a brook. He waited for migrating birds to come settle here, unable to resist the new and vibrant green of the wood and the stolen music of the brook, unable to leave a place they would know as their journey's end.

And in the coming nights, he'd take great pleasure watching them freeze to death.

David's fountain pen glided over the staff paper.

The requiem's first movement would be carried by the piano, creating a foundation for the sound of snow translated as music. Wagner's *Das Rheingold* was his model; he would invoke sky and snow as acoustic collage the way Wagner had invoked the slow, deep power of a river. The piano would build a layer of sound echoing the heartbeat and breath of the person hearing the snow. Slow heartbeat, quiet breath…

David had found the pen on the living room floor, beside a stack of freshly transcribed notations: copies of the sheets he had destroyed.

…breath that is soon joined with the breath of the sky, articulated by a French horn…

Several steps away, he'd found a moist, thick bloodstain.

…and the breath of the sky would fall in harmony with the steady notes of a flute…

The bloodstain had the vague outline of a small human body.
("She'll be of great use to you.")
...and the flute would change, creating a counterpoint to the piano and the French horn...
("A little aid to help with your composing.")
...a counterpoint that would parallel the opening of the senses of the person hearing the snow...
David undid his stiff, brown bandage, to see if his cut could have produced enough blood to make a stain that size.
("Watch what is possible when two agents meet to create something new and wonderful.")
...and then soft notes of a guitar would paint the movement of snowflakes falling through still air...
The wound was closed.
("Let me give you a gift.")
...soon joined by another guitar to suggest layers of snow...
And the joints of David's legs no longer ached.
("You will feel like a new man in the morning.")
David's hand jerked; the nub of the pen cut through the staff paper.
"It didn't happen," he said out loud. He paced as dusk filled the room, made arguments to himself that what he had experienced was delirium. When he had convinced himself, he sat down to work again.
But could not focus.
The feelings of guilt and unfulfilled obligation were too great for him to bear. He went to the trash and fished out the soaked, bloody rags with which he'd cleaned away the stain. He buried them in the yard, straining with the shovel to break the hard soil.
The pleading eyes of the torn woman stayed with him though, well into the night.

A mother looks at her beautiful child, and wonders how she could ever be worthy to care for her.

A man laments the death of his sister ten years before, bemoaning the injustice that she had died in the car wreck that had spared him.

Despair and a sense of worthlessness spread like contagion. All who live within ten miles of the hilly grove resurrected by the prince feel it ... some fleetingly, some for long, heavy hours.

A farmer feels an accusing guilt for killing a fox that had been preying on his chickens; the farmer's son wishes he'd never been born, and had become such a burden to his parents. The boy's mother hates herself for placing her father in a nursing home.

Whisperings are carried to the shadow regions of their minds by creatures of a deeper shadow than they could ever know. And with these whisperings come a hint of redemption, pulled from the rich landscapes hidden within their minds. Landscapes they have known in dreams, or glimpsed with the mind's eye in stories they'd been told when they had been very small.

A hunger, a great famine for salvation moves over the countryside on unseeable wings.

As evening comes, the people have quick, flashing dreams as they close their eyes. Dreams of glimpsing a creature white as bright noonday snow, with a horn glowing like a beacon toward deliverance and the resurrection of their tarnished souls.

The hunger for salvation becomes a hunger for a hunt.

Amduscias walked among the trees.

Perhaps he should shove the little conjurer's soul into one of these oaks, when he was done with it. Give it a home like the one it would have had if the conjurer had taken a few steps closer toward the bloody wood where the prince had heard his call. He'd use the spent soul as a conduit, a portal to this wood whenever he had need to escape the Abyss.

Something came to the prince on the air.

He walked to the edge of the wood and looked down at the conjurer's home. He smelled in the ether the process of sickness, the touch of madness. The prince's host from the night before was having another of his episodes.

Splendid.

He could never resist a dramatic entrance.

The prince crouched down and waited for an opportune moment to invade David's weakened mind, and so hopefully invade his soul.

David fought the coming delirium with his music.

As the room spun, as sickness and drunkenness and nausea turned the room the color of jaundiced skin and melted sharp angles to arcs and curves, he stumbled to the piano and grabbed hold of the day's composition. He focused on the staff paper and read his music, *heard* his music. Grasped at the tranquillity, peace and beauty of the sound of snow.

And the music surrounded him, filled him with joy and a sense of being healed. His requiem held him in a comforting embrace and flooded his reeling senses.

The piano notes moved within his breast, his heart. The French horns called him to the sky. The movement unfolded…and his awareness unfolded as flutes joined the horns and then broke away from them.

Suddenly, David could see clearly.

His eyes showed him the hall of the great Regio Theater of Parma: the place of his dreams. Where he had always hoped to have his music performed. He knew his vision showed him a lie. But he treasured the lie. For though he was hallucinating, *he was still himself*. Not transformed to a maddened, bestial state.

The hall was empty, but his music resounded through the place, among the Baroque circular tiers of the box seats that reached the painted ceiling high above. He walked the center aisle toward the orchestra pit, his music held before him like an icon.

And now the first guitar came in …weaving a swaying tapestry of notes like a soft flurry. The second guitar joined the other and…

The music stopped.

David had reached the end of what he had composed …not halfway through the first movement. He stood, terrified that without his music, the delirium would sweep him away to a place of demons and torment.

Yet he was still in the opera house of Parma, not ten yards from the orchestra pit.

"Bravo!"

David spun around.

And saw the towering abomination he knew as Amduscias walk the aisle toward him. It walked erect, with a shocking grace that belied the monstrosity of its form. Its grace offended David. Revolted him.

"Bravo! You are touched with magnificence. I see in you the fire that has burned within the Greats! I *hear* it. I see it in your heart and your passion. And I treasure your greatness as no other can."

The demon stood only a few paces from David.

It turned its animal head about, looking, seeing, with human intelligence.

"I know this place," it said. "Is this the hall of your secret wishes? The temple of your artistic desire? I should have guessed. There is a flair to your work unsuited for the halls of Vienna and Paris."

It looked at him and pulled its animal mouth into a smile.

David looked away. Then spoke in a steady, even tone.

"I banish you. I cast you out."

"Do you?"

He looked back to the demon.

"Our Father, who art in Heaven, hallowed be Thy name…"

The demon cocked his head, as if David spoke a foreign tongue and it were trying to understand.

"Thy kingdom come, Thy will be done…"

"On Earth as it is Heaven!!" said the demon. "But this is not Earth, and it is not Heaven. This is yourself. This is your dream, though you dream of a real place I know well."

It turned its gaze to the stage behind David. "Here, I once infused genius into a rather tired production of one of Verdi's operas. I whispered a jealousy into a diva's ear here, that drove her to betray a friend and so become the greatest voice of her day. This is a *wonderful* hall, with wonderful acoustics."

The monster threw its head back and sang with many voices snatches of an "*Ave*" with impossible pitch and clarity, as if an angelic choir found outlet in its throat.

David dropped his music, pressed his hands over his ears to shut out the blasphemy. But the demon's lilting voices still rang in his mind.

Then suddenly it stopped singing.

David slowly dropped his hands from his ears.

"Forgive me," it said. "I simply can't resist songs of innocence."

"What do you want of me?"

"I want what you want. I want to be returned to you. I want to help you with your great work."

"You can't have my soul."

"Why not? You share your soul through your music. Let me return to your mind. Let me free what's inside your soul so it can touch the souls of others. So your music can be shared with the world."

"And what do you gain from this?"

"Joined with you, I'd be a heavenly creature again. I would be pure and splendid. Able to sleep again on the laps of maidens and heal the sick. Able to resurrect kings and foretell the birth of prophets." It raised its powerful arms and turned joyfully. "You would not wish to deny me salvation, would you? I have healed you, have I not? At least partly? Imagine what I could do within you, what healing powers I could liberate. I might be able to save your life."

"You don't exist."

The demon growled, looked at David as it had looked at the torn woman that had writhed at its feet.

It strode toward David, made a slow fist with its clawed hand before his face.

"Then what have you to lose?"

David stepped backward, slowly, toward the pit.

"What you have to gain."

The demon reached for his throat.

But the beast looked up, startled, as a sound reverberated through the hall. Then it turned and was gone, parting the substance of the hall as if it walked through a sheet of rain. The sound came again, closer this time.

The hall dissolved in a wave, became a dizzy landscape of swirls like the grain of wood as David realized he had heard the sound of hunting horns.

They each wandered the countryside, wordless, in the night. Sadness, emptiness, despair drew them out of their homes. As they met one another on the road, in the woods and in the fields, they silently joined and wandered together. One came to walk with two. Two with five. Five with seven. Twelve with twenty.

Until at last, near midnight, more than forty people stood milling in the darkened wood. A calling touched each of them, and all of them as one turned toward a hill crowned with a grove of oaks that was touched by the setting moon.

Salvation awaited them there.

No longer themselves, filled with and guided by denizens of a world no living person has seen, they ran toward the hill and toward the sacred beast of their dreams whose blood and horn could save them.

The hunt was on.

The prince, Amduscias, pulled himself from the conjurer's mind, stood, and looked down from the hill he had claimed for himself.

Scrambling up the hill from the west were the human puppets of his pursuers. He could see pressed around their fleshy bodies the shadowy forms of those who had hunted him across vistas of damnation.

The sound of horns crashed through the ether.
And Amduscias ran, the thunder of many footfalls behind him.

David stumbled as the swirls faded and became the solid contours of the scarred piano. Hazily, he picked up his sheets of music from the floor. He thought absently that he should try to play part of the piece, now. Get his mind working on the fine points so he could focus and…

The entryway door burst open.

Amduscias forced his towering bulk through.

David bellowed, picked up the piano bench and hurled it at the monster.

"ENOUGH! GOD-DAMN YOU! *ENOUGH*! I BANISH YOU! I EXILE YOU! YOU'RE NOTHING! YOU'RE…"

David was seized in the thing's claws, lifted, pressed against the cold plaster of the wall, just above the ink stain. The spiraling lance on the demon's brow hovered inches from his breast.

"Enough theater!" it said. "Do you hear them? Listen! They'll be at the door. The barrier I evoked will not hold them. They are my enemies. They will destroy us both unless you admit me to your soul. I can't ward them off without you."

"No."

The demon pulled him from the wall and smashed him against it.

"You don't know what's at stake!"

"*This isn't real*! You don't…"

There was a crash in the entryway, and David saw, over the demon's shoulder, his neighbors, people from town, old teachers and classmates press into the room.

For an instant, David thought he was saved.

The monster that held him in its claws looked toward the people piling into the room, then back at David.

Rage burned like diamond-fire in those violet eyes.

It bellowed and pulled David onto its horn.

David screamed, back arched, arms flailing at his sides. He felt the horn pass through his flesh, his lung, his heart, his back. A fire coursed through him. He began to die as the horn that was killing him cleansed his blood.

His mind was freed from the sickness as his lungs filled with blood. He tried to cry out to the people below.

The demon's claws gripped David, its voice echoed in his mind.
"Give me your soul! You will live! We will live!"
The people in the room snarled like dogs and leapt upon the demon, rending and biting and tearing.

David fought the demon, joined to it by its horn, its mind groping, lunging, trying to cleave to his soul as its horn had cleaved through his flesh. The horn kept him in his body. His soul did not rise. He felt his being change as he and his enemy fell to the floor under the crush of bodies.

"Yes! Give me your soul! I can spare you this!"
Hands were upon David, pulling, ripping.

The demon pressed into David's spirit through his sundered heart, through the strength of its will and David's longing for the agony to end.

David felt the atrocity of the thing's mind within his own mind. With his last act of will as his body tore, David reached out with his soul, pleading for salvation. Before his dimming eyes, he saw the red serpent—the guardian of change and benevolent passage. David embraced it with his spirit as his arms were pulled from him.

Between life and death, David joined with the demon. The serpent moved through him, and he knew it was a thing of his own creation, part of his own mind given form, his own strength given tangible shape.

He put the demon down as his existence ended. The serpent's red glow burned away what he had been, cleansing the demon's contamination of his spirit.

In an unnamable limbo, he knew the quiet of snowfall…and the dead ethereal form of his enemy.

He made them both his own as he heard the cries of tortured living souls around him.

🦉 🦉 🦉

A November sunrise, burning with secret fire and the rich amber of autumnal light, touched the faces of more than forty people as they drifted across the countryside, covered with blood, covered with flesh, covered with scraps of skin and torn clothing.

And as the songs of larks echo across a wooded valley at dawn, so did their screams, cries, and sobs reverberate among the fields. Some of the wanderers fell to their knees, some tore their hair, some curled into fetal balls upon the cold, hard ground.

Their souls had been mauled, made sick and withered by the things that had possessed them and filled them with a passionate, blind lust for blood.

Blood of their prey that was absorbed through them, that gave rebirth and empowerment to the demons inside them…as had the horn that crumbled to dust in their hands while they groped and clawed and worried at it.

Grey clouds drifted from the west, towering in the sky like cliffs of granite, dimming the sun's light. The cold, bitter rains brought by the clouds drove the people home like slow-moving animals. The anointment of the rain did not wash away the filth that clung to their spirits.

What happened among them was kept secret, in the way witch hunts and midnight lynchings are. The house where the torn flesh of their prey lay piled thick on the floor was burned several nights later, as was part of the fields around it.

The fire's glow brought a false dawn to the moonless sky; the clouds of smoke carried with them the ghostly scent of sulfur and rot, of burned hair and sickness.

A spiritual plague hung like choking fog over the countryside. A plague that would have warped and killed the soul of all whom it touched.

Had it not been for the visitation in dreams of a magnificent snow-white beast that came to each of them, that touched their hearts and souls with the healing light of its horn at the moment when the burning clouds of sunset had hung upon them a great serpent the rich color of cinnabar.

The beast came to them atop a hill crowned with a grove of oaks that was held by the eternal rebirth of spring. The coming of the creature was heralded by music. Sweet music, reminiscent of the sound of snow falling on quiet winter fields, of the breath of the sky, and the voice of each crystalline feather as it alights upon the earth.

Shibboleth

A mirror of steel is oddly silent.

There's a depth to your reflection missing in polished metal…the impossibility of an echo. You can speak your thoughts in silvered glass and know that you're heard.

The last dressing room I shared with Justine had steel mirrors, made of bulkheads from a dead country's navy. It was part of the glut of such steel that flooded markets while warships loaded with corpses were scuttled as tomb-reefs that pressed pearls of eyes, coral of bones. Steel desks, benches and chairs crowded out wood furnishings…the grain of which was scarred by winters made harsh by ash-clouds of the dead and by the rings of trees that marked not just years, but tons of human soot held in the sky. Justine and I had sat beside each other, applying our make-up in the steel's gaze, dumb as we harlequinned ourselves with the simple lines we'd devised for our *Cymbeline*. We were startled by our not speaking to each other's reflection as we usually did, when streaming chatter replaced the dream cycles lost over days of rough travel. Our gazes twined in the mirror, and as one, laughing, we touched the unwhispering steel as if to shake it from its deafness.

Alone, farther from Justine than I've ever been and standing more than a year from when our gazes could next touch, I now looked at myself in a steel mirror and heard its silence in a new way, with the hum of flooring against my naked feet as I shifted and bobbed, trying without knowing why to mime the tilt and roll that the train I rode would have if it moved on metal rails on solid ground. If I pushed the mirror from its silence, I'd feel the roar of the train's engine, conducted by porcelain walls at a frequency that, if it I could hear it in the anemic air, might sicken me with vertigo. The steel was treated to not fog, and the steam I breathed in that coffin-space that doubled as basin and shower held an emptiness compounded by the steam's inability to clear the allergy-like congestion behind my eyes, or ease the swelling in my face that made me look like a mountaineer healing after a brutal climb. The steam looked like what folktales say a sleeping dragon's breath is like in a vale, hanging as threads far thicker than it could at sea-level, in droplets too large for the pull of an earthly ground to allow.

Steam can be silent, just as it can speak. In a free zone of Palestine, my oldest friend Jim and I had breathed the steam of a bathhouse that had been in operation eight hundred years. The bathhouse stood, and might stand eight centuries more, near a graveyard of the land that had drunk nations of blood since Caleb had first stepped there. The proprietor had let his hens peck among the sun-cracked stones, so that even the boiled eggs he offered as a parting courtesy were flecked with death. The herb-scented steam of that place, which once held the breath of Crusaders, had felt heavy and *present* in our lungs. Ripe with the taste of the past…as the quarantine baths Jim and I had shared during the Dying couldn't be. Those baths burned with tinctures that left us unable to stand the touch of the softest towels and with fumes that scalded our lungs. Jim lived the past, breathed the past. And now, as he chipped the bones of giants from the Gobi and tasted the dust of dead strata, he was less remote from home than I was…because he was camped near trade routes and would be able to post letters. When I return home, I'll taste the same dust, drifting from creases in the letters he'll have sent while I was gone.

 Breathing out steam born of water so young it had been drunk or passed by none of God's creatures but Man, I stood before my mute double and worked foam from fine glycerin soap that had been liquefied and re-poured around a magnetized disc in case the train's turbines stopped spinning and made the soap drift as lazily as the bubbles it made. I lathered my swollen face, and knew the steam I breathed wasn't silent because it misted from distilled water. Such steam could yield hymns from all it touched—as the perfume my mother pressed from sheets in the violet of winter afternoons, and as the mist that combed a fresh-turned-soil scent from the dust of centuries-old dressing rooms…a scent joined in my mind with the flurry of costumes being pressed, the flinging open of make-up kits and the whir of hand-held sewing machines. The steam I now breathed smelled only of the tungsten coils that heated it and the plastic pipes that carried it. My lungs full of the steam's absence, I placed the soap unmoving on the steel mirror, raised the glass shard I'd brought from my compartment and ran it up against my throat.

 "*Is this a weapon?*" the Customs Official had asked when he'd lifted the shard from my effects. Though I said it wasn't, the shard *was* a weapon… the same way soldiers' camouflage is. On the day I'd first pushed a shard like this along my throat and jawline, while I traveled another outland for Justine's sake closer to our home but much crueler, I'd faced soldiers in brown and green camouflage milling in snow, ready to kill me. Theirs, though deadly, was a *theater* of authority; it was made a performance by their being distracted by religious theater they listened to on the phones they pressed under the helmets, that they commented about to each other through tactical headsets, even though they stood close enough to speak normally. They had poor costumes for their play. They lacked the winter fatigues that would have bent light around them as they hid on the embankments of the highway choked with stripped and derelict cars that Allen and I walked to get home. Such gear would short the electronics that let the soldiers be audiences of the drama that so enthralled them, that made their daywatch a mummery that would have killed Allen and me in front of an unseen audience with one lone member…a being I'd later learn was himself fleshless, and less visible than these soldiers would be if outfitted in stealth gear.

The few soldiers who didn't have phones pressed to their ears smoked contraband—slouching, undisciplined as the deserters I'd seen as a boy looting warehouses and hospitals. They milled at the roadblock with the foot-to-foot hopping that told me they'd sooner shoot Allen and me and pack our stripped bodies with thermite than scrawl form entries accounting for our deaths. No more would be left of us than fragments like the furnace-cracked teeth I picked from the tread of my boot after walking access roads near factories. Not even a smear of ink on government foolscap would be our epitaph. No Boston Police were at the roadblock. No Stateies, private military or CDC personnel…a cold, sea-water dread pissed into my guts as I wished to God for the presence of those from whom I'd hidden as a boy, who'd often deserted to form kidnap gangs that preyed on families desperate to reclaim their few scattered members.

The soldiers seemed to be waiting the half hour until dark before taking to the embankments—when those not enthralled by serial dramas would use nightscopes to shoot travelers with Godlike impunity, mimicking their own cruel, arbitrary God…whom they resented for not lifting them in the promised Rapture, leaving them in an emptied world with no warrior Christ under Whose flag they could butcher. My life and Allen's had been spared for the moment by the oversight of a quartermaster too busy commandeering quicklime to properly camouflage these irregulars pulled from the staffs of rust-sealed prisons and the sheriff's departments of counties that now only existed on roach-spotted maps. To this day, I can't stand the grind of sled runners on pavement—the memory of that sound while waiting to feel bullets shatter my ribs is too strong, as is my memory of the fear that I'd not be dead when hooks would bite around my collar bones and drag me to a pit greased with the jellied gasoline that had once been a weapon of war, but that was now a tool of "civic hygiene."

I skimmed the shard from jaw to cheek, over the swelling in my face where blood and lymph pooled that would have, at home, settled near my ankles. My face had been wolf-gaunt when I'd had to first learn its contours under the kiss of glass on my skin, in a room thick with toxic smoke, with food long rotted to clay and the smells of wine, beer and liquor that had evaporated in their glasses, leaving concentric rings of mold.

    The steam of *that* moment—maybe an hour before I'd faced the soldiers—had reeked with the newly woken musk of decay and mildew… even though the plastic-tinged water that had made the steam then had been pure enough to drink. I myself had reeked like a thing dead on a summer road, from a week of back-crooking labor in a hinterland that consumed itself. Knowing I'd face men eager to kill me, I'd pressed broken glass to my face in a room so cold, the mist beading on the windows froze into stars like those etched in Polish crystal. My hands shook from hunger as the glass skated where blood pulses closest to the skin. Allen, casting aside the urgency of just a heartbeat before—an urgency that felt as if it stood breathing by our shoulders as a third person next to us— grinned after my first stroke didn't add the steam of my split jugular to that which froze on the windows. I grinned back, drunk with a euphoria I never want to know again.

    "*Did you know that we're cool?*" he asked, making a gallows joke of a phrase we'd used to make light of toil and filth. With that joke, he rewrote the moment when he'd first asked the question into a halcyon time of a few days before, when we'd had the luxuries of a fireplace and a roof over our heads, and had felt able to handle any danger with two guns and three rounds between us.

    When he'd first asked *"Did you know that we're cool?"* it was with staccato anger accenting each syllable. It was the same anger that had scarred his voice when we were ten, and he'd asked an older boy who'd invaded the isolation ward we shared with Justine and Jim why he'd punched him…as if the boy had hit someone else that Allen wanted to defend.

    "What do you mean, 'cool'?" I'd asked, turning in my sleeping bag that smelled achingly of Justine's hair and feeling the wadded bills in my pocket we'd banished ourselves from the city to earn.

    Allen lifted the book he'd been reading by the light of the portable lamp fueled by what we stole off the nearby traffic grid and by the firelight fueled by woodscraps and books we'd found in the house we squatted. Hunger punched our insides as we lingered in the ugly twilight between having too much empty pain in our guts to sleep and the moment we'd be too spent not to sleep. At dawn we might buy food from half-empty farm trucks heading to the freight wagons that were light enough to be pulled over the ice by horse teams. Or we could earn mouthfuls in lieu of pay by unloading the trucks. If we didn't eat tomorrow, we'd become too hungry to feel hungry, and then we'd be too weak to work. Our boots dried on the hearth, sweating the manger-stink of the greasy, near-useless waterproofing we'd slathered on them. Our wool socks hissed on the grate, wafting the sourness of lanolin and the compost-musk of our feet.

By the amber light of the fire and the lamp, I saw that the book cover depicted young people—boy-men such as we, standing in god-like defiance atop a mound of rubble and curled metal in the square of a ruined city. The mound was both like and unlike the mound near the Center where Justine and I had met Allen when, before he lived there with us, he'd thieved into our ward for the fun of it—*like* and *unlike*…the way a storybook castle is like and unlike a real castle. The boy-men on the cover gripped ornately useless firearms and had musical instruments strapped to their backs like broadswords…lords of a fanciful desolation. Looking at them, I tasted the same contempt I do when I face the soft-bellied smugness of a man who lives off of women.

"People wanted this," he said, deadening the anger in his voice with that profoundly adult authority he could conjure, and of which I'd always been jealous. Allen was himself like a boy whisked from a storybook: bright and wise enough to not talk like a boy. He spoke as if he'd already been a parent--as if telling young people how things were had been something he'd done since he first learned to speak. Despite the acting and the elocution I'd studied, I couldn't project the sureness he could… even when I played a young, wise boy such as Allen was, who told a sad tale of sprites and goblins to enthrall his mother, too terrible even for the crickets to hear. Around Allen, I had the same uncertainty I did when I forgot lines in rehearsal. I never felt alone with him, never felt without at least another pair of eyes on us. With a finger the nail of which was flecked with plum-colored blisters, Allen pointed to the pile of rubble on the cover, the thing of a bygone era's playground-dreams that we'd known as a place to avoid the bite of sick rats.

I groped in my kit, felt for the stick of licorice root wrapped in plastic that smelled like the dried spit that clings to the toys of small children. I thought a moment before using the splintered licorice root to dig the day's rot from my teeth. My mouth was slick and foul, but the resin of the licorice would make my guts bend even more for real food. Out of boredom, not hygiene, I chewed the end of the root I'd frayed with my teeth to pick away the smears of the ptomaine-foul meal of canned pork and crackers we'd choked down eight hours before, having passed on a flank too grey and stinking to have not come from a sick mule. I wondered how badly my gums would bleed should they again feel the bristles of a toothbrush.

"Who wanted what?" I asked, with a small fear that I wouldn't fully grasp what he'd say with his grave boy-from-a-storybook authority.

"People who lived in this house," he said. "People from Before. They *wanted* what we deal with. I think they thought it'd be fun. Like school letting out for the whole world."

I considered what he said, digging plaque from the back of my mouth and fearing that the soreness behind my molars heralded wisdom teeth I couldn't afford to have cut from my jaw, and that I might instead have to hire a blacksmith or iceman to pull my back teeth to prevent infection. I realized I envied another skill of Allen's—the ability to think of Before as a time like any other, and not an ideal that we only knew through dim childhood memory and the burning of its remnants to keep warm.

"Let me see it," I said. He tossed me the book. The pages smelled of the naked pine shelving that had kept it from turning to mulch…the shelving that we saved for the hearth should the boxes of old files, bank statements, letters and utility bills run out.

The book cover was in the garish melding of the photographic and the painted favored by publishers when my father had been young. I knew the style from the crates of books from his boyhood we'd packed for library donation before we made our exodus from the dying fringes to the center of town. The youths on the cover had the vapid idealized beauty from a time when surgery and hospital space could be spendthrift'ed on the sculpting of faces and the reshaping of flesh. (True, those who lived on the outlying estates made quilts of their flesh, yet for this they used private surgeons, whom they treated a bit better than cooks and stable boys: court jesters with scalpels and needles full of lotus to soothe their masters' anguish of being cosseted.) The beauty of the youths was the inverse of the beauty of the faces on old coins and medallions. The youths were posed in a stance of triumph that echoed the propaganda of dead tyrannies; the only triumph I'd known amid such rubble had been when all of us from the wards had marched with borrowed shovels to stove the rats that fled the piles we'd drenched with fuel and set alight.

"I'd like to give it to them. Right in their faces," Allen said, as if he held his staccato anger in check for the sake of one of those teacup-fragile kids born after the Dying.

"What?"

"The shit we eat that they thought'd be so cool."

Looking back, I know why Allen and Jim never got along; Allen punched through the past that Jim so treasured.

I wish I'd torn off and saved the book cover and shown it to others from the neighborhood and the ward, even though it affected me in a way that made me feel as if I'd already shared it with one or two others. Instead, I threw the book on the fire, along with scores of books like it that had belonged to the last owners of this house now deeded to the squirrels that scurried in the upper floors. If we were better trappers, at least one squirrel would now be turning on a makeshift spit, dripping fat. We didn't dare talk about this; if we did, our hunger would make us stupid enough to try to flush and catch a squirrel in the dark, rotting upper storeys. Instead, Allen and I read aloud a few pages from each of the books before conscripting them to the drying of our socks; in draping whimsy over the days Allen and I endured, all the books voiced an ulcerating need to forsake, in the name of edgy "authenticity," comforts for which Allen and I would have given much…had we anything to give. I put away the blood-spotted licorice root, and was about to say something—probably about girls we knew—when Allen's stomach growled, loud as the grunt of a small dog, through his wool sweaters and the thickness of his duct-tape-patched sleeping bag.

"I guess this means we're cool," he said. And in our giddy hunger, the crack seemed worthy of the laughter we gave it.

Our breakfast was coffee stirred from crystals and melted snow in our electric pot. Rust from the pot made my tongue rough and dry for hours. We trudged along the highway that took us away from Boston, the choking city where there was no work, and few goods anyone could afford in the markets. No checks had come from my father, nor had any mail from past the Rockies reached anyone I knew for a month, fueling rumors of closed airports and cut lines of communication, though wire reports still came from past Denver. Even if checks from my father had gotten through, it was doubtful that banks would convert them to cash we could use. Friends who'd returned from trading had told us that Manhattan was worse off, and Providence had closed all points of entry. Boston starved—as it had previous winters, yet those lean and brutal times had ended after a few weeks…broken by the coming of vegetables and citrus from ports as far away as South Africa, and by the sing-songs of butchers walking the streets with their obsidian knives, offering to slaughter and dress backyard livestock in exchange for a few dollars or a shank. Fresh pork, stringy old geese, oranges, rosen kale, and greens tough as parchment even after being boiled in vinegar had ended those famines before winter stores became too meager and bodies became too ruined to fight infection. This year Boston had felt dangerous as a mastiff gone feral. Each piss-reeking corner was heavy with violence—the maybe-innocent shuffle of footsteps behind you became threatening as the sound of a mercyheart drawn from its sheath. Hunger, and the rat-gnawing worry that the rough times might not end, made walking from one house to another feel the same as did drifting into a provincial bar and knowing that you are the only unarmed man there.

Before I'd taken to the road with Allen—with our sled weighted with the gear we'd need to husk work outside the city, helping farmers and scavengers clear what had been suburban lawns for spring plowing—Justine's Aunt Louise (whom I've called *my* aunt, but only, it seemed, as a gift granted by Justine) had taken my face in her cool, dry hands. "Child" was the one word she said, as if to acknowledge I was a child no longer. "Child"...a *word*? Or a *name* she gave me, to carry as a shield, or an inner-lamp to fill the dark places I'd travel? In Florence, I met a man who'd been named "Fool" by his grandmother, so that he, the youngest of his family, would find fortune when at fourteen he'd struck out on his own. Is "Child" a name, a title, I still bear in the folds of all that I am?

Justine had leaned on the railing of our porch as Allen, pulling the sled a half-block down the street, offered us the gift of a good-bye alone. We stood among blood-rubies flecked on snow—with the disappearance of scraps and cat food, Crispin had foraged for mice and had scattered the innards he couldn't eat in front of the window we left cracked open for him. With so little fuel that winter, no soot dusted the snow. Tiny red spleens gleamed against untainted whiteness. "Come back to me," she whispered, close to the nape of my neck, as she had the times before when I'd left to search for food and money during times less dire.

"I promise."

"Don't promise, *do it.*" She gripped my coat by the lapels, and, unmoving, we stepped into one of the timeless moments we shared, when the span of a heartbeat seemed the whole of an evening. The feel, not the sound, of aged seams tearing brought us out of that moment, as her grasp inflicted the first of what would be many small rips in the coat we'd pulled from the charity bin two winters before.

"I'll come back to you," I vowed to her and to the God who in His mercy had brought us together. I held her and breathed the new scents her skin bloomed now that she was becoming a woman, scents I could only taste for what they were now that I was becoming a man. I lifted her palm and kissed it. We looked at our hands as lovers would at a rose the perfume of which they've just shared. My hands were corpsewhite, flecked with dried skin, cracked from the winds that had scoured them as I did what work I could find that winter. Justine's hands weren't as dry as mine...she hoarded near-empty bottles of lotions she scavenged for the small vanity she had for her skin. Our hands seemed two types of earth intertwined, like those near riverbeds when rich silt is left behind by spring floods. Her sister Janice's tread on the snowy porch behind us didn't pull us from the moment. Janice forsook her good-bye to me so Justine and I could whisper our farewell. Janice's silence was a presence— it touched her sister as only a bond of blood can allow. Through Justine, it touched me as well...the way that beauty can touch the face of a blind man.

I'll always ache that I didn't say a true good-bye to Janice as I felt her watching us, the same way you can feel when someone you love watches you sleep. The neglect I showed her when she'd given Justine and me a quiet time of farewell is one of the small crimes that doesn't mark my soul, but stains its core. Sins of inaction leave the deepest scars, because the keen of *nothingness* never dulls. With the warmth of Justine's cheek on my neck, I was aware of my memory cupping the tableau in which we stood, aware of those whom we loved looking away. And I was aware of the unseeing gaze of her father's telescope above us, a dented thing pulled from a university dump, in the far window to my right. On our narrow street, the telescope had only a sliver of sky to search. Knowing now that its gaze has since been further clouded by the sky-borne ash of the daughter of the man who owned it is a thorn in my heart. Not saying good-bye to Janice that day—as opposed to the day that I last saw her, when the smoke of her rushed cremation and of all the others who died that day painted the dusk with the colors we would wear to mourn her— is a very small sin. Yet it is a sin that has been rewritten within me, the way a simple cell can be rewritten as cancer. That moment of good-bye with Justine was the last moment that I had, without reservation, liked myself. To have shared that moment with Janice as well would maybe atone for what I'd become before I returned, when I'd begin a walk toward a loss that through frostbite might leave my body as lame as my soul.

I began the trek away from what and who I'd been at that moment of good-bye—marking distance in spirit, not miles—when Allen and I left the house in which we'd read the books that had painted our lives and times with the paschal-egg colors of Romantic fantasy.

We waylaid farmers and bargemen uninterested in selling us goods for which they'd get much better prices in the city, and who had no work for two boys sallow with malnutrition. It was past noon before we earned salted fish that we hoped came from waters not too near treatment plants, and winter apples soft and almost brown that had the mustiness of a root cellar clinging to them. Late afternoon, we earned a single potato. By night, we squatted another house marked with door scratchings that told us there was a working fireplace within. A cache of old phone books, the only paper left in the house, and the pine shelving from the last house we'd squatted (which we'd chopped and stacked on our sled) fueled our fire that night. We wrapped the potato in already twice-used foil and placed it in the fire. When we'd eaten it, we used the ugly paste boiled out of marshmallow root to pack our guts with the illusion of a full meal. I fell away from my own unfed sides, a hollow man, of whom famine was making a wilderness in which I'd wander and die.

Allen pulled stalks of willow wand from his pack; boiled into tea, they'd stave off fever. "Should we?" he asked. And if I weren't so cold and tired, I would have found small joy that the boy who seemed ever-wise was now asking me what was wise.

"Shouldn't risk it," I said, thinking of the rot willow wand had caused within kids who'd drunk it while malnourished…we'd filled our bellies with a lying food that, even as it bloated us, would let us starve if we ate it too long.

"We're still going to risk fever."

"Maybe we need to risk fever," I said. In my mind, I tasted the death-stink of a girl named Susan in our ward whose liver had dissolved because of willow wand she drank during the mild famine of three winters before. Her body pooled ammonia. She convulsed so violently, the nurses restrained her with belts and strapped a helmet to her. I saw the fountain-marks on the walls by her bed, like those on stable walls when a steer's throat has been slit, after she'd gouted blood from her nose and mouth during the fit that had killed her. Jeremy, her friend, had no Dusk Colors with which to mourn her the day she was buried. As if lifting the sins of his fathers, he took up the Before mourning color of black, which made him look paler than he truly was. In my memory, the kicked-dog hurt in his eyes will always be joined with the poisoned breath that infused the ward long after Susan had been lifted away and her mattress burned.

I know Allen and I spoke of other things after he put away the willow wand. What they were is muffled by the hunger I knew as I was transfixed by my hands. I'd last truly seen them while saying goodbye to Justine. They were forms unknown to me, grafted to my arms. The veins at the backs of my hands stood out as they never had before. I'd once read in a rotting book with no cover that it's when these veins stand out that you've truly become a man. Yet did they stand out because I was no longer a boy, or because famine had burned away tissue that had been between the veins and skin? What man would I be? Could I be a strong, decent man if my adulthood was midwifed by starvation? How would the man I'd be unfold himself, should I meet him on the road?

I hope the young man whom we did meet the next day still lives…that in this world made so brutally small, I can find him and make amends…

both with him, and the self I lost in meeting him. I hope my hunger during our meeting was an alien thing, a possessing spirit, like those I've seen blamed for the fits of epileptics in the outlands near Chicago. Allen had his own specter to carry, woven into his flesh. By shirking that burden, he too changed. I choose not to endure the thought that maybe he changed because his burden had shirked him.

    When we met the young man, our feet were lead-heavy and numb, our hands throbbed in our wool gloves. The rot of our skin slicked oily on our clothes. It had been afternoon before we found work, heaving salvaged pipe and wire onto the cart of a scrap dealer who paid us in bills so old and greasy they smelled of the horses that pulled his cart and looked as if they'd melt if we balled them in our naked hands…a thing we'd not do, for our palms were crisscrossed from handling the copper razor-strands of cable that had once streamed data to houses now infested with creatures that dulled their teeth on wire insulation. Our work gloves, good for pulling bramble, were too thin to turn frayed metal threads. We thought to buy a pot recast from melted cables from the merchant but didn't, knowing that the desire to own the pot was born of our hunger to imagine food in it.

    The later opening of our jackets was motivated by the same stupid and hunger-driven desire. In twilight the color of boiling sap, Allen and I, our hands too raw and swollen for us to work the next day, fumbled with hook-eyes and let the sick breeze out of the west make wings of our coats, and so made the wind our accomplice. We had to give our hands a day to scab. This was our unspoken motive for what we committed. The young man pulled a child's wagon, the carboy of telltale orange in the wagon visible from tens of yards away. In light narrow as an old woman's breath, the silver wedding ring he wore, unscuffed and still bright, sponged up the yellow dusk. That he was desperate enough to take to the road alone, was stupid enough to travel with such a precious thing on his finger, and didn't put a tarp over the carboy told Allen and me more about him than we should have known. I often think of his wedding ring, and the young woman who wore…or still wears…the ring's mate. I've prayed that he—just a few summers older than I—returned to her a victim of no greater crime than what Allen and I inflicted on him. I've prayed that the wedding ring didn't find its way, black with grease, tossed among the buckets of wedding rings saved so that their inscriptions could identify the cremated dead who'd owned them. I have prayed he went home after meeting us, and that brigands didn't cut his ring from the cooling body that would feed the whelps of foxes in their winter lairs.

We stopped him, letting him see our guns, letting him see that we could take what we wanted, even though he had the hands of a farrier and was broad-shouldered as a miner. The fear on him was like a thing seen in deep winter morning—a rock or tree that is as much shadow as substance. We "bought" the carboy of treated nitric acid from him for far less than it was worth, as the one thing on his wagon full of cheaply made tools that could find him any work. Whether Allen and I would have taken the carboy if he had not "sold" it to us is a thing I'll never consider. Had we not been starved and filthy, had we not been cold and afraid of being unfit to work because of our savaged hands, had we been the decent boys we'd been before that moment…we would have shared our heavy-duty wood bore in exchange for use of the acid and sought work *with* him, this fool who had no bore, only a chrome-forged pick that would bend against frozen soil.

I've stood on the porches of houses in fields when summer storms have arced like waves over the horizon. I've felt the air drawn out of those houses as thunder crashed nearby; it has touched my shoulders like a cloak before moving past me and away. Something that had been part of me flowed over my shoulders and away from me in the same way…my decency? Or my perception of a decency I never truly had? The shame, I knew, came from within and without, as if draped on me by one who was saddened by my apostasy, but who didn't understand it well enough to judge.

In another house, heated by the fire of newspapers bundled for recycling the year I was born, Allen and I peeled off the linings of our soft woolen gloves, gaping apart cuts that had scabbed to the fabric. Our lacerated canvas work gloves stood blood-hardened near the fire…like mandrake roots made into Hands of Glory in the witches' shops that linger in the rotted neighborhoods of university towns. Allen's whimper as skin came off with his glove lining was like the cry I've heard a mute girl make while she dreamed.

"Guess this was a cool thing we did, huh?" I said. Together, we let out sounds at once like grunts and laughs, as we waited for the sweet cicley root and aspen bark we'd use as poultices to boil in our rusty electric pot. In silence, we avoided adding to our guilt by making excuses for our crime.

Shame of what we'd done roared like the noise of water in my thoughts the next day, as we came upon one long-term squatter after another clearing what had been suburban yards for planting. The long-termers were easy to mark along the roadway, given away by the unseasoned cordwood of newly felled trees piled so the long-termers could cart it away to sell.

Two clever boys we seemed, to be able to drill deep into new stumps that would take horses and tractors hours to clear, and to pour nitric acid infused with accelerants into the borings, so the partly dissolved wood itself became the explosive that would blast the stumps out of the ground. We'd detonate the stumps with wires strung to an old tractor battery, or we'd make a punk out of rags sopped with clay dug from under bramble that had been hedges. What punishment we saved our hands fell on our backs, as splinters hit us like small hatchets; our coats were no protection, for we had to take them off to run from the stumps while the punks burned more quickly than we'd have liked.

We worked, it seemed, as quickly as the punks burned, lest the blasts lure other traveling workers, who'd try to rob us of the carboy that we had ourselves robbed.

We stayed that night in a house the yard of which we'd cleared. By the warmth of the electric heater we ran off the grid, we salved our hands with cheap amber disinfectant we'd gotten from a long-termer and dared count our bills for the first time. Some bills were near worthless as bavin-coins, and would have to be exchanged at the bank or through black marketeers for fresh currency. Others were printed in the blue ink that marked them as worth exactly their dollar amount in gold on any given day in any district on the continent. Yet others were so mulchy and porous, they sponged the orange tinctures from our fingertips. We'd each earned enough to pay rent on a large house for three months. We divided the bills, and, knowing what anguish cheap gun oil full of impurities would leak into our hands, we cleaned our weapons anyway, to make sure our three rounds would truly matter, should they need to.

The next day, we found a truck on the road, the rusted contents of which, had we found them in the ground, would have prompted us to dig deeper for the bones of dragons. No scrap hunters had gutted the swords, fit to kill ogres in fables, and the suits of mail, fit for exiled princes, that rotted in the truck. Maybe scavengers--finding a cache like those mentioned by the old professors and teachers who wandered to people's homes in these parts and told a night's worth of stories in exchange for a meal and a bath--felt they shouldn't loot a tomb that might have a curse protecting it.

The swords were of good steel, not like the lightweight swords I'd helped propmasters make. The chainmail, grimed with blood-smelling corrosion, was as heavy as five of the coats of costume mail I'd worn that were made of thick yarn hardened with grey paint. Lances and what had been saddles of fine leather were now mold-eaten as the boots we still found on unburied corpses.

"It's for a play," Allen said. And as I *felt* more than knew that he was wrong, I was sickened by something. In my hollow guts, the sickness had a weight. The time I knew as "Before" had a Before. I could see that while a wise boy like Allen couldn't. I remembered when I was small, banners advertising fairs that recreated the past without the unpleasantries of war, famine, plague…the hardships that made the art of the past passionate and enduring. Though it seemed that plague had risen up to brigand this fair, so that the owners of this truck would abandon it and hide until a burnthrough could occur. That they never reclaimed the truck told me the past had claimed its due from them.

I lifted a sword the way Arthur would lift it from the Stone and Before burned my palm, as the damp leather braided at the pommel seeped rot into my wounded hand. I—newly born a thief whom those of Before might see as a highwayman of the romantic past, and who walked the tomorrow they thought would be a holiday—couldn't stand holding the weapon they'd have me bear. I dropped the sword. "No. It's just another thing that was supposed to be cool," I said, pleased to say something dramatic and final, to eclipse the wise boy Allen could be while he faced the past. Allen was quiet. I felt as if what I'd said had been heard by someone who wished to speak, but couldn't. We left the past's dream of the further past to corrode in the snow.

That night, in the final house we'd squat, I saw my face for the first time in days. There was no connection to the grid to link our heater. We didn't light a fire, so the smoke wouldn't attract the desperate fools who took to the road to find work and food only now, weeks into the famine. We'd be prime victims to rob and kill, with the small fortune we carried. Our foot-and-sled tracks in the snow leading to the front door were betrayal enough, without smoke to promise our killers a warm night's sleep by our looted bodies. I shuffled to the first floor bathroom of the house, to piss in the sink rather than face the cold outside. The bathroom had the unique stink of raccoon shit, but no shaggy forms ducked from the beam of my flashlight. Even in a room rank with the dung of scavengers, the stink of my own crotch was offensive to me…as was the spoiled beef smell of my steaming piss, rich with the proteins my body had taken from itself and now sluiced as waste. With my flashlight set in a mounted toothbrush holder, I saw myself lit from below in what my old acting mentor Frank had called "Shylock lighting"…transformed into a caricature of the Dirty Jew. I looked like a villain in the illustrations of the misspelled tracts that hayseeds leave stacked in train stations to extend their ministries while they traveled.

My eyes in the mirror were unliving as a doll's and underneath had the blotches that, as make-up, I'd applied to play characters who were aged, dying or dead. My beard, such as a boy could raise, looked like mange on cheeks so hollow they made my jaw seem long as a wolf's. My hair hung lank as the bloody locks I wore while playing Banquo's ghost in the days when a foodstuff like corn syrup could be wasted as stage blood. I raised disinfectant-stained fingers to my face, touched whiskers that had the same frayed tips that a sickly girl's hair takes when it grows too long. I twisted a few. They snapped like the strands of spun sugar that clung to Aunt Louise's wooden spoon when she made sea foam candy.

I looked at the monster I was. Then lifted the flashlight and lit myself from above and the side, changing my image to one like the portrait of a sixteenth-century saint, giving humanity to myself through the airy nothing that made me seem a lunatic, a lover and poet as I moved the light like a will-'o-wisp around my face. I left the dung-thick room and soaked rags with bleach I found in the kitchen, then stepped on the rags, cleaning my boots of any trace of the pathogen in raccoon shit that rots the brain of a healthy man to dementia in a matter of days.

I wished to go home, but I knew I never could again. Not truly. Not as the thief I'd become. *Home* would never accept me, because I, re-born a thug, could never again fully accept it. Yet Justine needed me to return, whatever was left of me that was worth her love. The bills I carried were her sliver of hope, and I'd never cheat her of hope, or make her hope in vain.

"We need to go back," I told Allen as we "ate" cold, snot-like marshmallow root we'd boiled that afternoon.

In a dream-state of hunger that I could feel in the stoop of his shoulders, Allen lurched around the living room where we camped, scraping his spoon against the tin plate as he paced, as if trying to summon true and plentiful food through the sound of it being casually eaten. He stopped in the lantern light dim enough not to be noticeable from the road, looking at once-white carpets, at the tracks left by the distinct bootprints of the containment suits that CFDC teams used to wear as Before fevered into the Dying. The leaking bodies dragged out by those crews had left smears on the carpets like the brush strokes of an abstract artist.

"We need to go back," I said again.

"We strong enough?"

"There's going to be even less food on the road. The farmers'll hoard what they got. More people are looking for work. I think we're too weak to do more work. What we got left, we need to get back."

"See how we feel in the morning."

"Could you work a whole fucking day tomorrow?"
"We got to eat before we go back."
"Nothing's out here."
"We might be too weak to make it home."

I was stiff with the poisons leaked by my body's feeding on itself; when I blinked, it felt like my eyelids scraped sand. Tomorrow, we'd have the final burst of energy that famine brings, or we'd begin the half-senile walk toward organ failure. Either way, I didn't have the strength to talk further with Allen. I fell asleep to the scrape of his spoon across an empty plate, the noise of a conjurer without even a lump of lead to transform.

I dreamt of the smoke that bore my mother to the sky, of the colors I saw paint the sunset of the day she bride-stepped to the clouds. So near to death, I dreamt that my mind rose as did smoke, straining the silver thread that joins it to my body. In the dream, I heard my father's tread behind me, and waited for him to say, as he had said in fact, how the colors of that twilight suited my mother. His silence startled me. I turned and saw my mother, wearing the colors of her own mourning, gold and vermilion, looking at the sunset that would be her only grave.

I began to hate Allen then, as he woke me before my mother could speak, sitting up and gasping…the way I'd once woken gasping when Crispin had pressed against my nose and mouth for the warmth of my breath. A third being stood in the room with us, a person-shaped collage of shadow and dust that unwound as does a small whirlwind in a cross-current. Afraid that I was so unafraid, I looked to Allen, who, still sitting up, breathed as does a mouse dying in a trap. The cataract of moonlight that dropped from the windows painted his breath, which misted in an almost still cloud near his lips, as if his newly lost soul lingered on the step of what had been its home.

"We've got to go back," he said in sudden dawnlight. How dawn came in a turn of heartbeats, I can't know. Logic would say that I fell back asleep, and Allen woke me. Yet there can be no logic when your mind is gutted by hunger, and I have known logic to sow ugly lies. Dawn came, and she came boldly, from behind the tattered curtains. My senses burned in her lavender-grey fire.

As we dragged our sled over the carpet smeared by lymph that seeped from the family that had laid the carpet down, I felt the echoed ghost of the third person who'd stood over our sleeping bags, the dust-angel who'd watched over our sleep as neither sentry nor foe. I looked over my shoulder at where the ghost had stood, and the ghost refracted into greater solidity over the span of the deep breath I took--gaining shape as does an audience the instant house lights come up--only to fall back into greater nothingness as my eyes widened to see it. The *feel* of the ghost stepped into me, as if filling the void left by the person I'd been before taking to the road. Had I been stronger, such a violation would have felt unreal. In my unreal hunger, I felt the ghost with the same patient dread one feels standing under a dead oak on a winter's night. That dread seemed to leave the house with us, following as would a guilty thought…walking, perhaps, as it had since I'd left Justine in the hallowed space that Janice had touched while her sister and I said goodbye. What followed us was *hurt*, and feral. It lurked on the periphery of our senses in a way that made me think of the street kids who used to stand at the gates of our wards and cut themselves down to the muscle with smashed bottles, so they'd be let in as emergency cases and so gain a meal and a night of peace in a true bed.

Miles down the road…how many I can't say, but we'd made good distance, because we were close to the old toll stations on the border of town…we smelled smoke rich with the scent of roasting meat. We coursed the scent as would hounds, hoping to trade or buy food, knowing that no one who didn't have food to share would light a fire so near the road, *telling* ourselves this was the case, not wanting to admit we were being stupid—maddened by the promise of meat—approaching somebody with food and fuel that he may not want to share or trade, and who might be too eager to defend what he had. The carboy held enough dregs to trade for a meal, giving a patina of sense to our dash to the smell of cooking flesh.

By dying embers in a yard, we found rabbit pelts curing above the reach of wild dogs atop what had been a children's swing set. Within the embers, we found rabbit bones we snatched up and sucked the marrow out of. On the rim of the fire were orange peels we devoured; the smears of rabbit grease on the peels left by the man who'd eaten the orange were savory as a banquet on our brittle, coated tongues. On a peel was an import sticker bearing the name of a grove near Cape Town. Allen and I looked at the pelts, to see if any meat or fat could be gnawed from the skins. Our host made himself known then, with the slow, deliberate cocking of his rifle from the window behind us. We walked away slowly, following our own sled tracks.

The earth-heavy *dread* of a bullet is a mark on your back, on the coin-sized spot that waits for the impact of what you'll only feel as a tackle. The mark presses into you as you hold your shoulders low, not daring to show your worry, lest it encourage the one in whose sights you walk to squeeze the trigger and punch apart your spine and lungs. The dread forced breath out of us even as we reached the road again, out of range of even the most high-powered rifle.

Adrenaline and food scraps are a cruel mix while you starve. There is a sadism to being partly fed, regaining only enough strength to fully feel how hungry you are, losing the numbness that is the one meager gift of malnutrition. We could feel, with the new volume of our famine-thinned blood, with the rush of receding adrenaline, the rotten wood in the joints of our feet, the cramping poisons in our calves that meant the scarring of muscle. We could feel—with the new flow of nourishment to our brains—how invasive and sick was the way that "we" were feeling. Old grandmothers preach that familiarity breeds contempt. What *I* felt was past all contempt for the "we" that Allen and I were…who felt together, who saw together, who spoke together, who shared the convulsions of our folding bellies. It was hunger, not fellowship, that made Allen and I the "we" that we'd become. Famine had scoured away the walls of "self" that had separated us. Allen and I had been sharing our thoughts, our discomforts and our desires because *we* were too physically weak not to. It's a sharing without language, without the mortar of syntax and words: a pre-literate, pre-verbal bleeding of what's within, like the sadness you feel as your own when you see it in the eyes of a dog trained to guide the blind.

And I realized that the "we" that Allen and I were was a "we" of more than two persons. "We" were also the ghost that followed us…that *had been* following us…the living, guilty thought whose tread was distinct, even as it filled our footprints behind us the way the absence of the newly dead fills a sickroom.

Allen felt my realization…and in my awareness of his feeling what I'd realized, we reaffirmed the "*we*" that we had been. *He'd known* of our follower with a surety I didn't have until now. It dawned on me that since leaving home, I'd been dimly aware of our follower the same way a child who has only seen pictures in fairy books would know a sylph were he to see it, a thing the unreality of which had yet to be tested…like the unreality of a fox the child has only seen painted in rich watercolor reds and browns staring up at a crow it will outwit.

Our follower wasn't welcome, not by me, who found him lurking in my thoughts as I would a bilge-damp stowaway. He followed out of hunger, a scavenger tracking sick animals, even though he had no flesh to nourish.

Allen's shoulders rose as he pulled the sled. I waited until we'd walked another mile, and his shoulders had dropped, to ask what he knew about our follower, even though I knew he'd lie…

...when again the smell of smoke stained with meat wafted on the road, pressing our skulls, bringing gorge to our throats and the danger we'd vomit the precious scraps we'd wolfed. The smell was a flood-crash of memory that struck us with the feeling we all know when we talk to old friends in dreams, and only remember as they walk away that they're dead. Had the wind blown another way, Allen and I would now only walk the dreams of friends who'd known us while we lived. We fled the road and the memory the scent brought the same way we had, as small boys, run from what such poisoned air had carried as *sound*: the music of people driven mad by panic and grief, made with the clatter of scrap metal and the blowing of horns made of bones pulled from slaughterhouses and the heaps behind triage centers. The memory of lunatic marches followed us, the way those processions had years ago coursed people and animals that they tore and held aloft as standards, still bleeding and thrashing on pikes, under banks of crematoria smoke.

Allen and I hid the sled behind a rusted van, too panicked to care that our tracks made hiding it futile. We climbed an embankment, our minds packed with ghosts of spinning deathdancers. Our footing on snow and mud, we clung to the barrier rail of what had been a playschool, almost level with snow-buried yard-toys humped like fresh graves, cursing the tracks we left, yet knowing we had to take high ground. We reached a tree that jutted out of the embankment, gaining footing on the barrier rail to climb it in our snow-slick boots. We reached a stout branch, gripping another branch above us for balance with our scabbed hands. We saw along the road for miles...and so saw our city dying. Greasy smoke rose like funneling leaf-swarms from what had been factories: the fruits of hunger and weakened immune systems. Perhaps a death-gift from ships that had brought plague along with crops from the southern hemisphere. We clung to the tree, watching as if from a masthead scores of people drowning on land. *Burnthrough*...when sickness devours the flesh that fuels it, until no more kindling that has loved and mourned and suffered and walked in God's image remains for it to burn, and the husks of those who have been scalded by fever and suffocated by the water of their own lungs must themselves be made ash in furnaces.

The smoke was beautiful the way that only things that herald death can be, haloed by swirls of crows we were thankful we couldn't hear. The smoke loreleï'ed us to sleep, even as it caked our throats with tomb soot. In sleep, there'd be no hunger. No cold. The smoke of our sleep would paint the sunsets of latitudes to which we couldn't fly over the span of a single day. We couldn't know whose bodies danced as ash within that smoke, who among those we loved now found homelands in the sky.

In sleep, we could join them. In sleep we'd be warmed by the hearth of dusk....

A sound like a child in pain pulled me from the trance to which the smoke had lulled me. Had I been stronger, alert, I could have better caught Allen as he tried to catch the bird's nest we'd dislodged. He gripped the higher branch with one hand as I gripped his collar to steady him. I read in his face, as a feeling through my skin, his need to have saved something fragile. We looked at the smashed nest below, and tasted the fragility of our own lives.

Quarantine would be enforced by those with the authority to do so and by panicked homeowners with rifles. After sunset, the city would be shut down. Guns on the roofs and streets. Anyone found on the roads without permits or proof of residency in the hinterlands would be herded, thrown into holding pens to control the spread of sickness, where we'd be certain to contract sickness in our weakened states. We didn't dare sleep without a fire tonight, yet any squat with a working chimney would be raided or burned or held by squatters better armed and stronger than we; any fire lit outdoors would be shot at from a safe distance. There might be aerial monitoring. And it was too cold to find adequate shelter in one of the rotting houses, little more than lean-tos, far from the roads that were still traveled. Martial law, and vigilante law, could already be enforced in the city to which we had to return tonight, before weakness, starvation and cold killed us while we waited for quarantine to end. I'd read stories about long-ago travelers on roads stalked by the blood-drinking dead, and the dread those travelers felt as they saw the day end. I knew such dread, looking at the long shadows before us as the sun stepped west, and knowing this was likely the last day I'd see.

But I'd not give Justine false reason to hope. Even as a footpad with a shit-smeared soul, having exiled myself from my better self, I'd never betray her. I had no right to the luxury of dying out here, with the money that'd be the salvation of Justine and the others I loved. I hadn't earned the privilege of sleep, even in death.

There's a fire that's snuffed in the plumage of a game bird that's been shot; it dies before the bird itself does, even while the blood around the quarrel in the bird's chest is still warm enough to nurture hatchlings. I saw an ember of such a light return to Allen's eyes, and felt a flush return behind my own eyes. It was like the feeling that pushes into a limb when a tourniquet is cut. All wish to live. Yet to wish is not to *will*. A wish is not a choice that pulls your sinews tight, that wakes the blood in your marrow.

"The Club," I said softly, as if I spoke with a candle flame before my lips I didn't want to make flutter, as if I honored in near-silent *kaddish* the thing I'd just killed. Becuase the decision to live is a kind of death; it's the stone-knife sacrifice of the part of you that'd be happy to die. To rest. I gave that part of me what it longed for. It was the Isaac within me to whom I showed no mercy, though since that moment, I've felt a trace of Isaac's brother in my heart: the wanderer, the ever-homeless exile.

"The Club," I said again, for Allen's sake and my own. No prayer of mourning can be uttered just once, nor can any cantrap for strength. In a way that could happen at no other time and in no other place, Allen understood what I meant. I saw in his rekindled eyes the mirrored understanding that we should make pilgrimage to a site of atrocity while we dreaded snipers' bullets, to a place that was a witch's lair of candybread stabbed into reality…so that once there, we could make changelings of ourselves.

To walk to The Club was to live a life sustained not by breath and heartbeats but by ruin such as I'd tasted once before, when, with numb hands, I'd clung to the vents of an ice-caked subway car, balancing on the rear coupling as tunnel walls screamed past, proving my manhood to boys who were not my friends…and whom I despised in the way we all hate those to whom we feel the need to prove ourselves. Gripping that train, my knuckles about to shatter, the rumble of wheels punching through my boots into my knees and hips, I was then further from death than I was walking through the fallows of ruined houses and looted businesses toward the The Club--the hulk that had been the tinderbox of an isolated, virulent burnthrough that littered the surrounding parking ground with victims killed by wind-like fever and the bullets of panicked sheriffs. I was nearer, because I now waded into the dreamworld that borders death as if into a riptide.

The concrete plain around The Club for the stowage of vehicles was cracked as the mosaic of a child's puzzle. It was visible under the waist-high, sword-sharp canopy of lethal plants above the lot that kept snow off the fractures. The blood of a man walking through and cut by that canopy of leaves would fall to the mosaic in snowy wet clumps with his strides. Jumbled bones lay framed by broken windshields…blackened by the fumes of rotting upholstery like scraps in a roasting pan. Other cars, their roofs made smooth-edged by snow, were nests to feral things that had found the marrow of human femurs sweet, and still other vehicles bore the neat bullet holes that kept their would-be drivers forever behind steerage wheels. I don't know if this harrowed place had called to the razor-leafed bramble that grew out of the pavement. I can't know, anymore than I can palm the smoke of my thoughts, if the bramble knew the dreams of those who still lived nearby, and so answered the enticement to root among the vehicles as it would around a spell-trapped castle. Maybe the bramble—which I've seen grow wild around rust-vacant military bases where it had been planted in lieu of barbed wire—had been seeded like hydra's teeth around the club as a forbidding. What might have been the last minutes we'd know still warm in our bodies were lost hacking bramble to the club door through which we'd have to pass, and there take the elf-glamour that might let us live past moonrise.

A shoe…

The first solid thing I saw in the unbreathing dusk of that crypt. The shoe was alien--finery from Before made with tight factory seams, not stitched by a cobbler. It was of a kind worn in the stead of foot-binding, that women stilted on while dancing, while trudging stairs, while walking the smooth sidewalks without *pavés* that had been the skin of the city before the concrete flagging had been wrenched up for foundations and breakwaters. The angle of the shoe in the dust evoked the snapping of an ankle. My eyes trespassed on the burial mound of a dead kingdom, a sin that in other eras would have them bewitched to wooden orbs by barrow wraiths. Allen and I stepped into folklore, walking past the shoe that lent a seed of truth to the stories we'd heard about what kinds of detritus of Before had been left here when the place was shut down. We entered a legend, to find treasures in the ruin that might save us.

Panic leaves strokes distinct as smears of bloody lymph on carpet. Meals, left when I'd been a child and had seen grainy footage of this place besieged by gunfire, lay finished at the bar by rats and fungi, reduced to dust-furred shapes beside cutlery rusted to abstractions. Coats were draped over chairs, some made of quilted down like the sleeping bags Allen and I carried. They were chewed, most of the feathers inside taken away to make nests for the animals that thumped near the ceiling at our coming. There was no smell of death here, because not even death walks a place so forsaken, and the smell of death is still a smell of nature. This place stank of an emptiness that didn't oppress our breath, but pulled it out of us.

A woodsman without his tools can't know who he is. I've seen them wander into town…their hands dead at their sides for want of an axe or saw. Allen and I, in this death-forsaken place, didn't know who we were without the sled of tools we'd left outside the sword-bramble, didn't know who we were without the gear that defined the world we knew. Even our thresher's knives had become dream-things, dulled by our hacking the bramble and dripping a thick sap like the blood of a thing killed by a

Shibboleth

warrior saint. Not knowing ourselves, intruded upon by each other, poisoned by crematoria fumes the Furies would savor as wine, followed by an un-bodied thing in a place that worried our hearts the way incubi and infant-handed *maras* worry the backs of sleepers, we were in a Hell like that of the peoples who'd been old before the Greeks had been young.

We risked a fire in the great steel sink of the kitchen, risked the poison smoke of varnished wood cracked from gnawed chairs that rose to the high ceiling as if in a curing house. We made a cauldron of a soup pot, pouring spring water from age-brittle plastic bottles to cast a transformative spell on ourselves. The dishtowels we soaked with liquor turned grey-black and reeking from the filth we scraped off our goosefleshed skin. I sweated in the cold as I saw steam cake the windows, and in my malnourished state, the sweat that ran to my mouth was salt-less as rain. The beer and gum-thick dishsoap we worked into our hair foamed slick as grease pools near rendering plants. Our newly scrubbed skin had the look and scent of the laudanum addicts who sprawl in the shallow hallway graves where they let go the fruit-sweet musk of their last breaths.

Colognes and hand soap from the washroom nearly completed the guise we needed to take: that of wealthy boys indulging in the sin of the rich who make a game of poverty. The sin that lets debutantes play at being whores, knowing they can cast off that life while the disowned girls of port cities can't. That lets students make a hobby of addiction and the Japanese tea-ceremony of melting smack and shooting up, knowing they can take cures in Lucerne clinics, their track marks closing near the platinum bands of watches custom-made in Geneva. The sin that lets boys whose nascent beards are shaved in bed by servants frolic in the shitholes in which boys like Allen and me toiled, that makes a sport of what we do to survive…that lets these lads boast while being seen by the right people lunching with the right heiresses in the right clubs.

To perform such a masque—that of boys who masqued themselves as what Allen and I really were—we'd have to scrape off the mange-whiskers we'd grown, the beards frayed by starvation and worry, that marked us as two who could be easily killed and forgotten. We'd packed no razors, why should we? Cooking oil and dishsoap made our lather…warm water from the pot took a rust tinge from our flayed palms as we wet our faces. As I'd seen done by vagabonds who rode freight rails from city to city, I smashed a bottle that had held a sugar drink and tested the keen of the longest, sturdiest shard. With hands that felt gloved within their new scars, I raised the shard to my throat. When the ugly scrape of the first stroke fell quiet and even the crack of the fire was mute, Allen grinned and asked me, the universe, and maybe even God, should He have bothered to look down, "Did you know that we're cool?"

A prop dagger, sharpened, can stab a man through the heart, then be put in its scrap-leather sheath and be a prop again. Allen and I were costumed, wearing what had been sweaters of spun glass that hadn't rotted over the years they'd been left draped over chairs. We packed wet cooking salt on our boots, so they'd be stained as if by road salt, making us look like we'd walked streets populated enough to have been plowed and salted, and not the roads of the decaying outlands. Our "make up" of freshly shaved skin howled in the brittle air as we walked the path we'd cut through the bramble that smelled of citric extract and the tannic vinegar used to clean head wounds. We were keened props, things of reality pretending to be false. We felt sheltered by our deception, as if we held a lock of the Elf-Queen's hair that would turn a sniper's bullets to frost. Like Orfeo or Lot, we knew not to glance back at the place we'd quit.

The *we* that Allen and I had become let our thoughts be non-verbal, let us speak in near-grunts as we hiked to the checkpoint that would grant us passage into the city. Our approach was a dumbshow, done for groundlings whose displeasure would leave exit wounds. As we reached the wall of ill-shod soldiers milling in front of what had been a tollbooth, Allen muttered to himself, and the mutterings we'd shared and understood became gibberish to me. I was suddenly afraid to be so alone in my own mind, unable to be aware of the third being I'd felt trail us. I realized that I'd welcome awareness of that specter…who else but the dead could bear witness to my death?

Some of the soldiers, as they weighed life and death under a forest of smoke columns swaying in the east, couldn't be bothered to close their phones while they listened to the Evangelical plays broadcast at that hour. Allen, I realized, wasn't muttering, but *praying*. He, a Catholic, walked beside a Jew along a corridor of wrecks towards death as if in some Romantic Era parable, whisper-praying as did the Hasidim who'd taken me in after the first Center to which I'd been sent was burned down. I wished to pray, but couldn't while walking that frozen path, while the river that had been the lifeblood of my home became that of Babylon. I felt overwhelmed by Allen's faith, a *converso* for the span of those heartbeats as the storm of my soul was billowed under by the storm of his soul…

…and which I knew was too strong to be his alone.

Amid the noise in my mind, like the memory of the plague-mad revelers' music, I felt a wish to kill the soldier who walked up to question us in the filthy air. Behind him, commandeered backhoes widened the pit in which he'd gladly burn us. I hoped the wish was a goblin-thought.

Something nurtured by the memories of the music made by rioters maddened as if by Hearn's horn. Maybe it was Allen's blasphemy that put me in such a Godless mindset, because as we'd entered the checkpoint I'd heard Allen tell the God to whom he muttered to *hush*, as if he spoke to a noisy pup he trained.

There was a rawness in the soldier's voice. It filled me with a dread like that of falling in a dream. Because although he wielded deadly force, he himself was not deadly—he was far worse. I've known deadly men. They've never frightened me the way this man did. True deadliness is patient, like a predator waiting in reeds by a stream. It's a decision to be lethal that's never impulsive and that can be countered like a chess move, by the recognition of that willingness to kill. Men who aren't deadly are wielded *by* the power they think they wield. And they're jealous of that power…knowing it can abandon them like the wives they beat into fidelity. Anger shakes in the eyes of a man who's not deadly while he holds a gun, palpable as the misogyny in the eyes of those who first "become men" as clients of whores.

I've since learned that to look at an enemy is to look at yourself. But then, as a boy, I didn't know why I looked to see if the soldier had the scars that would tell me if he'd had the kitchen table surgery that would have torn the corners of his mouth while a butcher-priest cut the wisdom teeth out of his jaw amid prayers shouted in ecstatic tongues. I wondered, as he looked at Allen and me, if he'd had the other surgeries that would have removed his appendix, tailbone, and one rib to rewrite his body in accordance with Scripture, erasing the lies that Satan had written into his flesh the same way the Deceiver had hidden fossils under the skin of the Earth.

I know *now* that I looked at him so because I was aware in a deep, wordless way that if he knew I was a Jew, he'd search my brow for traces of horns.

The man's hand shook as he questioned us in his lazy-tongued dialect, under a bank of meat hooks hung on the chain link fence like wash drying, by rusted barrels of thickened fuel that with their patches of red, waxy polymer looked like an art installation made of junkyard salvage. The Church Militia patch on his shoulder, stitched over the flag there as if to cover something shameful, told me he was used to the spirit of God working and flowing through him the same way as did lethal power, moving him to do things for which he'd have to take no personal responsibility—from dervish-running in circles at revivals to proselytizing strangers to shooting a man. I didn't shake. Because that would loosen the mask I wore of the specter he'd been raised to fear: that of the shape-shifting Jew who passed for "normal."

I stood before him, to his eye with the complexion of a saint and the condition of a devil. I was the fiend that boys such as he had been told would carry him off in a sack if they were bad. I addressed him as if he were a recalcitrant Gabbo, acting impatient and weary and invigorated beside my friend as if we were on our way home from a day of shovelboard and bear baiting, speaking to him as if he didn't grip a weapon, but loitered expecting an undeserved tip. We were each other's monster. To me, he was the villain, descendant of the shiftless *villein* of old dramas. I feared him because what I'd seen of his kind stranded at docks and rail yards, who cursed the Sodom in which they were marooned and that I called "home"…when the Sodom they endured was what they brought in their hearts along with their scar-widened grins, as they awaited passage to the countries that let them pursue the Hammite slave trade they claimed as their lost heritage. I know now that by looking for traces of crude stitch-work at the corners of his mouth, I wished to put a mask on him out of anger for the mask I'd been coerced to put on…that made me the embodiment of the mask-wearing fiend he dreaded.

The living mind can stand only so close to death and remember its face. Death is eternal, an infinity of mirrors with no object of focus. It's indifferent to time, and while we breathe, we can't grasp an unchanging end. That's why drowning men spin into a pit of memory as they die, awaiting the heaviness of the sea in their lungs. That's why sailors, knowing such a crush of memory might await them, always carry the horizon's span in their eyes, even when inland. Death smothered my memory of passing that checkpoint. Yet in that darkness, I know I felt the being to whom Allen had prayed and knew him not to be God, even though he touched me as would God, granting me some small peace in my terror. It was a peace I felt he granted Allen out of a kind of love I'll never know.

I slumped like an old man as we walked away from the barbed wire gate bordering the converted tollbooth, our masque (our farce?) ending as we crossed into the Commonwealth of Boston, out of the jurisdiction of the soldiers. Allen looked about to fall in the snow like a drunk whom the cold would either sober up, or numb to sleep and let him freeze to death. We became the starved and desperate boys we were, home in our dying city as smoke stained skies the color of bile, too tired to flinch as shots rang out from the checkpoint; the people behind us on the road must have been worse actors than we. They'd burn in the failure of their performances, executed by men enraptured by phone plays about their promised Rapture while they sent strangers to the Heaven they'd have to earn, and not be lifted to.

As we parted, Allen had the expression of a diver looking at water from a height he'd never attempted before. The "*we*" that we'd been was dying. Through that death, I knew whatever pained and frightened him waited for him at home. Years later, with my lover Cynthia in her studio redolent with paints, clays and exotic yarns, I felt pain behind my eyes and heart the moment she set down her brushes after doing my portrait, when she severed the connection we'd shared while I sat in active stillness and as she pressed her will onto a blank canvas. Looking away from her was like tearing stitches in my mind. That pain echoed the pain of leaving Allen, as our famine-sharing of our selves rended. Torn from him, I could see, but not understand, the grief that waited for him, the grief that made me hate myself for hating this boy who in his desperation had clung to my mind the way a drowning man would cling to driftwood.

There was another sadness standing at that corner with us, besides that which nearly bent Allen double. The being that had walked with us faded from our senses as its sadness grew. It billowed to nothing the same way our breaths did, lifted by the cold air. And for the first time in my life I knew that I'd stood beside a ghost of someone newly dead, who'd just recently let go his last breath and his soul with it. Allen looked to the plumed sky, and I knew the colors of that twilight would be the colors he'd wear in mourning.

I didn't see that sunset.

Pulling the sled, I came to Aunt Louise's home. Crispin was the only one to greet me, leaving the blood-jeweled snow on the porch where he crunched mouse bones to wrap himself around my legs. A note from Justine and Janice, written in the shorthand of the wards, told me that everyone in our household had gone to gather fuel from the abandoned lawns near the fallen overpasses, where no snipers or home-defenders would be. I fell into my bed still in my coat, and knew from the stray hairs on and the scent embedded in the pillow that Justine had slept there while I was gone.

I woke to the smell of smoke, *pure* smoke from a woodfire, not poisoned by fumes of human blood, hair and fat. The bills that had been in my pocket were gone, and I felt panic at what I might have done while Justine or Janice pulled the money from my coat as I slept gripping my gun beneath my pillow.

A plate on my nightstand dusted with soda cracker crumbs told me I'd woken and eaten. I had no memory of it. I touched a dim awareness

I'd had…of being comforted by the sounds of sniper fire, that in my half-dreaming mind sounded like the fall of smiths' hammers in a stable.

The silence told me I was alone (without even Crispin for company, since he'd have cried from the hallway at my stirring). I stripped and walked to where the fire I smelled burned in the yard. The insulated gloves and tongs I used to lift flagstones from the coals and drop them hissing into our cedar tub were stained from the times we'd used them for cooking shanks in the pits we'd dug in the summer. While the stones warmed the water, I scrubbed with snow, burnishing myself with the flush of a healthy man; the snow was clean…too close to the factories that were now crematoria to be stained by human soot, the way a man standing right under a fountain might not be hit by the spray. I washed in heat and cold until I felt faint, dried myself with a towel warmed by the fire.

Duck eggs, bought from a vendor or stolen from the nest, waited for me in the kitchen…along with a loaf of Justine's bread, oven-warm in the center, and mare's milk poured through pine branches and left by the stove to set. I'd slept long enough for the food to be bought on the black market the morning after my return, long enough for someone in this house to brave snipers near the center of town and return with food and fuel for the tub and stove, long enough for Justine's bread to rise and be baked and for the milk to turn to a rich qvark.

No longer feral for being washed and fed, I wondered if Justine could still love me even as I heard her tread behind me, and felt the placing of her cool hand on the still bath-warm skin at the base of my neck. She took me in her arms as I rose, and as I crossed the threshold of her gaze into the one home I've ever known, I knew that she knew that I'd wounded my soul. And that she forgave me for marring something she loved.

I didn't cry with her as we lay in bed. Crying is a flowing outward. I folded inward. Justine let me fall…and so pulled me from my hurt. Scarred, but healed. I knew I could come home, because the best part of me had never left. Justine and I rebuilt the quiet inner spaces that Allen and I had razed while we starved.

When next I shaved, I used the shard I kept wrapped in my pocket as a talisman, so I'd never forget what I'd survived. I barely nicked myself; more blood flowed from me because of the new toothbrush I found in the bathroom, which scrubbed red yolk from my gums in a way that made me look like a dying man spitting the milk of his ulcer. No razor has touched my face since.

My face smooth and resting on Justine's breast, I asked her what had been the colors of the sunset the night I'd returned. She stroked my hair in rhythm with her speech.

"Burgundy…and a kind of ivory. There was green, too. The kind you see in marble, sometimes."

I love her deeply for never asking me why I needed to know.

A mirror of steel is oddly silent….

Yet what of a mirror that's fallen mute? What's the nature of that quiet, that shocks you to deafness? Is it the void of a retreating echo? The quiet after a gunshot? Is the silence odd because it's really your twin who's now dumb, the self that you can't hear, yet with whom you speak in the language that's too fragile to bear the weight of uttered words?

I never spoke to Allen again. After what we'd shared, I couldn't, any more than nerves can speak to a severed limb. I waited to know what happened to Allen, and to me, while we roamed in exile. Spring came, as did barges heavy with crops from upriver and seafaring ships that didn't bring new plague strains along with cargoes of fruit and grain. The Charles spoke as its frozen sheets cracked and icebreakers made paths for flatboats that brought livestock to the Magazine Beach slaughterhouses. Among the stalls of the open-air Cambridgeport bookmarket, I saw a boy whom I knew to be Allen's cousin, who wore colors of mourning that were burgundy and ivory…and the kind of green that hides in marble, sometimes. I led him away from the beehive hum of writers and poets reciting their works to potential readers to a spot by the shore, where the most distracting sound was the blows of rivermen cutting blocks of the Charles to cart to icehouses in midtown and to fish markets by the harbor. Under the buds of a willow tree, he told me that I'd had by proxy a brother whom I'd never meet, even though I knew his face, and his spirit, with an intimacy I'd shared with very few very.

I've played in comedies about twins as separated as two drops in the ocean who seek each other, and who are reunited. I've made burlesque of mistaken identity and farce of confusion. I know now that it's a great loss that there are no tragedies or mourning plays about twins. No farce can speak of the language that is rejoined when two who've shared a womb meet again. The language of twins is urgent as the language of your heartbeat. Words are the lies we place between a thing and what it is, like when we say that *lightning* is *flashing*, even though we know lightning can't exist without a flash…any more than you can exist without that which is reflected in burnished metal. Maybe this realization, not a sword, killed the Gorgon.

Allen had been cut from himself, as cruelly as language cuts lightning from its flash. I was scarred the moment that he was cut, burdened with a *wyrd* that was as inescapable as the birthmark of a seer. Allen's twin brother had been born simple, choked into that state by the birthcord of his brother. He could speak with Allen as he could with no one else, his speech as limited as that of the street kids who lurked on the peripheries of the wards who'd cut themselves to be let in and treated, the kids who were raised feral, who didn't fall to that state, but were stunted to it, cut off from human voices and human touch…so much so, it was rumored that some had been raised by dogs.

Allen and his brother shared language the same way they'd shared womb's blood, and so had bled into each other. I, sharing a crucible far crueler, had bled into Allen. His brother…frightened…dying of fever, and maybe not knowing what dying truly was, reached out to Allen, through whom I'd felt Death as it took Allen's brother, my twin, whose name I'll never speak, because I'd "heard" his name through the language that is felt, not spoken. Through the silent language of steel mirrors. By touching that dying boy I'd felt the soul of one who was becoming a ghost, the presence of a shade-not-yet-dead who'd followed Allen and me into the dead lands we walked so the ones we loved could live. The boy had died in delirium, between two worlds, between dreams and waking. From there, he'd called to his brother and summoned me into a dusk the mere sight of which changed my sight, the way that vision of our world as seen through a birth caul changes the sight of a child born with one draped on his face.

A mirror of steel is silent, as are the ghosts I still feel each day as I walk streets that plague has emptied. Ghosts, like reflections in steel, have only the voices we give them, even though what they speak is theirs alone.

I look at myself in a mirror of steel, newly shorn by a glass blade, unable to bear the vertigo inspired by the too-slow, counter-clock swirl of stubble and glycerin foam down the drain that will remake stubble, dead skin and foam into food that I will not eat. I pushed the basin flush with the wall, then activated the spray of water that streamed too thinly and slowly to truly be called a shower.

The droplets fell so that I saw through them as if through tears wrung by gusts of bitter cold. The ceramic walls of the train could never know the voices of ghosts such as I'd been taught to hear by Allen's brother. No ghost's voice could be heard over the train's engines and the spin of its turbines that kept my feet too lightly pressed to the floor. No ghost could ever walk from such dim shadows as those cast by artificial light, amid hallways and corners that even while they were constructed never touched sunlight.

Washed for the first time after half a year of sleep, I walked back to my compartment and spoke a *kaddish* into those voiceless spaces for the brother I'd lost and whom I'd never know, and through whom I'd tasted the bread and the prayer of his deathbed Communion.

In these voiceless spaces, what voice have you, that we may speak in this way? What prayers in what language shall we offer as mirrors silent to each other?

Afterword

Irwin Shaw, a member of what we've dubbed "the Greatest Generation", even though not so long ago as a Boomer-dominated culture we vilified and ridiculed that generation as a kind of two-headed monster in the form of Peter Boyle in *Joe* and Archie Bunker, wrote how he and his stories are products of their times (...the Depression, WWII, the rebirth of Europe, McCarthyism, Kennedy, Vietnam...). I'm not a product of my times. I'm a carrier of them. My times, those of my friends and my work don't end. They go into remission. In my boring middle-class neighborhood of Buffalo, New York in the early 1970s, it seemed a really good idea to get home from school one day by cutting through neighbors' yards because there were rumors of an impending race riot, and the prospect of taking a stray "Kent State" bullet and dying like a lung-shot deer in my GrrAnimals-like polyester finery and Keds didn't seem that much fun. This was the same school, PS 22 on Huntington Avenue, where as a kindergartener, I'd played "House" with an Asian girl, Lani Wong, and we used a Black doll as our baby, not knowing in 1970 the extent we were realizing the Dream of a certain Reverend who took a slug through the neck on the balcony of the Lorraine Motel in Memphis 20 or so months before.

That fever returned when I was an apartment building manager in a crack neighborhood in Oakland—reading Jack London's *People of the Abyss* and sitting in a chair that had been re-upholstered with a bed sheet by one my tenants before she'd abandoned it upon moving out around the time someone torched a drug dealer's car under her window—when the Rodney King riots broke out. I'd been thinking of going to see a band I liked in San Francisco that night when the radio said that the Bay Bridge and Market Street were shut down. Unlike what had happened when the legacy of a different King had defined how we all got along, there'd be no neighbors' yards for me cut through to duck the violence.

If what Henry Miller said is true, that all a writer "succeeds in doing is to inoculate the world with a virus of his disillusionment", then these stories hold strains from the Plague Years. In the interest of medical disclosure, and to steal from William S. Burroughs when he wrote about "a frozen moment when everyone sees what is on the end of every fork", here's what's on the tip of the vaccination needle pressing into your skin.

"Displacement"

I wrote the first version of this in the early '90s. The original back-of-the-junkmail-envelope note read: "guy with cancer kills knowing he'll get chair but killing makes him better". Thought I'd write it as a 10-page Henry Slesar riff and send it to *Hitchcock's* or *Ellery Queen*. Then I read Michael Crichton's autobiography/memoir *Travels*, in which Crichton describes a bug-fuck-crystal-rubbing New Age ritual he undertook to rid himself of a child-shaped agency that was the vessel of his rage and that clung to him like a psychic lamprey. Yep…when you think of hard-science advocate Little Mikey Crichton on CNN telling you that Global Warming is as about real as Santa, keep in mind this was a guy who participated in rituals like that, who claimed to have Uri Geller'ed spoons with his mind, and who said he'd had a meaningful, tear-streaked psychic dialogue with a cactus. Groovy. Crichton's rage-child nudged my idea about the killer cancer guy into what I'd read about *egrigors* and *tulpas*—externalized thought-forms that act independently of those who create them.

I wrote this while my friends and I dealt with AIDS, crack, yuppie trickle-down oppression, and street-corner death threats being no more uncommon an urban occurrence than stepping in dog shit all while stepping in human shit was even more common than that. I showed it to my neighbor Cori Crooks, who's now an accomplished feminist writer and who was at the time roommates with Amber Tamblyn's sister (really!) and it freaked her out good. This made me happy.

I was getting nice feedback from editors for this piece when *Se7en* came out, and I said, "I'll *never* place this!" *Se7en* was just too good, and screenwriter Andrew Kevin Walker developed too many of the same themes too goddamn well. I figured Walker, a guy my age, was stepping in the same shit on different streets and came up with a similar idea. But over the years *Se7en* so completely re-wrote the mythology of the "killer with a purpose" (without *Se7en*, there'd be no *CSI, Cold Case, Millennium, Taking Lives*…) that with tweaking, I could incorporate that new mythology. Hell, I felt obliged to incorporate that mythology.

This story, about payback, itself settles a score. A character I renamed Keene gets bumped off in this work. A guy named Michael Marano dies horribly in Brian Keene's *The Rising*. Coincidence? You be the judge.

"Little Round Head"

I sorta don't want to say much about this one, as a lot of people who have read it have come away with wildly different understandings of it. I don't mean different understandings of abstract things like themes and symbolism. I mean, totally different ideas of the story's time, setting and background that are so off from what I'd imagined, it makes my frontal lobes spin. I don't want to sound like some patchouli-soaked, espresso-sipping jerk in a frayed sweater doing the "mysterious artist" schtick, but I think this one's a Rorschach test. I left a lot of it ambiguous—even the gender of the narrator, if you squint right—and if I say, "Hey! This is how I wrote it and here's what it's about!" I'll limit how people read it, and maybe it's the story's flexibility that makes some people like it. Only one person who's talked to me about "Little Round Head" read it the way I wrote it, and that's Brett Alexander Savory.

I'll just say that John Gardner's *Grendel* taught me an important lesson: when in doubt, tell the story from the monster's point of view. It's just hard to figure out who's the monster, sometimes.

"Changeling"

Speaking of Brett, and monsters, he tapped me to contribute to a charity anthology entitled *Last Pentacle of the Sun: Stories in Support of the West Memphis Three,* which he edited with M.W. Anderson. "The West Memphis Three" refers to Damien Echols, Jessie Misskelley and Jason Baldwin, kids from the Robin Hood Hills area near West Memphis, Arkansas who, if you see Joe Berlinger and Bruce Sinofsky's documentaries *Paradise Lost: The Child Murders at Robin Hood Hills* and *Paradise Lost 2: Revelations,* seem to have been railroaded in a fit of "Satanic Panic" onto Death Row for the 1993 murder of three little kids just because they themselves were "weird" teens who dressed in black and liked Stephen King and Metallica. You can read up on the ugliness at www.wm3.org. These kids were made into monsters, because others required them to be monstrous. To be "other." Teratogenisis is an anxious husbandry, a need to grow strange and ugly fruit in other people's souls in order to convince ourselves that what grows in our hearts is godly and wholesome. In the case of making kids into monsters, you're swapping out a child for something warped—a changeling. It's not always wicked fairies that do the swapping.

Mary Shelly kinda got it wrong. We don't make monsters that *are* monsters with their first breath. You don't need atomic fallout or genetic engineering to make a monster. Malignant narcissism and a bit of contempt do the job just fine. Unca Friedrich might have been off too, when he said, "He who fights with monsters might take care lest he thereby become a monster". To *really* become a monster, all you have to do make someone else a monster.

"Burden"

The chronology of "Burden" makes no sense, if you think about it. The guy the story is about couldn't be the age he is, with the past he has, in the era when HIV tests still took weeks to process. Oh, well.

I saw a documentary about the early years of AIDS, and I remember those days when AIDS was a weird and nightmarish rumor whispered out of Manhattan. "Gay *cancer?* You can't...*catch*...cancer, can you?" The documentary crew interviewed a guy who was the last man standing among all his friends, and he said that every time a friend dies, a library burns, and that when he dies, there will be no one around to remember him. I thought about my friends who'd been devoured by the virus and said to the TV: "What about *your* obligation to remember *them?*"

"The Siege"

Charleston shrouds herself in her own ghost. My friend, Charleston writer Harlan Greene, has described the town as being like Norma Desmond, dressed in her former glory and angry that time has had the hubris to pass her by. A city that wears her ghost might draw ghosts to her who are still living, even while so much of the town's tourist trade exploits her haunted past. It's a weird town to live in, and this story grew out of my culture shock when I first moved there. My mother claims that when she was pregnant with me, she toured the plantation where *Hush… Hush, Sweet Charlotte* was filmed, so maybe I was imprinted with to be wigged out by that kind of vibe *in utero*. The kernel of this story is something I was thinking of writing as a novel—but a whole book with protagonists who have lost their souls might be a little…I dunno…soulless?

"...And The Damage Done" & "Exit Wound"

When you write about someone who has died, you're appropriating that death, which is a trespass. Maybe mourning is itself a trespass. But I do grieve for my friend Marian, and everyone who knew her I'm sure still grieves. She was born in 1968 on the Friday the 13th that the Beatles recorded "Sexy Sadie" and "Yer Blues" and Soviet tanks rumbled toward Prague. She died on a Sunday in 2001, while the steel at Ground Zero still burned. As a homeless and formally homeless teen, she was the subject of two short documentaries: "Sadobabies" and "The Loser's Club" by Nancy Kalow. And she's the subject of a full-length documentary in the works, *Last Fast Ride: The Life, Loves and Death of a Punk Goddess* by Lilly Scourtis.

Marian lived down the street from me in Oakland, and she used to cat-sit for me when I was out of town. Part of "The Loser's Club" was filmed in Marian's apartment, and in one shot you can see my old building through her window. It's weird to see a room you know artfully framed, even through the "true and non-fictional" medium of documentary filmmaking. I used to hang out with Marian in front of that window, talking about music and horror...written, filmed, and lived. Talking to Marian was a terrible and wonderful gift, because she never broke eye contact. When you talked to her, only a small bit of what she said was spoken. Most of her voice was in her gaze.

This was in the days that she was the lead singer for the now-legendary punk band, The Insaints, with Daniel DeLeon of Rezurex and The Deep Eynde on guitar. The art of the documentarian's eye intrudes on my memory of Marian's apartment and that window. The posters on her wall. The dolls she had everywhere. Her LPs, the sleeves of which were used as scratching posts by her cats. The way light hit the place in the afternoon and how that light touched her eyes and changed how she spoke with them. Which makes me wonder, what about my eye as a writer? Is that gaze an intrusion? How about your eye as a reader?

I don't know if I have the right to mourn Marian, to intrude on her death by writing about her. We had a really shitty falling out, and if I wouldn't have been welcome in her home while she lived, why would I be welcome into the situation of her death, and drag you with me?

But the dead intrude on us, too. When a friend dies of an overdose, it throws a shade over places you've walked. Under that shade, landscapes take textures, detail, an awful richness that has always been around you, but that you've never seen. Drugs are so all-pervasive, you can't see them until your experience of them is immediate. Poe...Baudelaire...Bukowski…Hunter S. Thompson…Cheever…the specter of drugs haunts all their work, and in the vein-blue dusk of a friend's overdose, their writings change…to the point that re-reading them seems like reading new works. The weight of drugs and how they thieve people from us is something you don't feel until you've lost someone to them. The voice of drugs is something you don't hear in music except in the shadow of that loss. So many songs of addiction and loss changed after Marian died. Songs like "Suicide Child," "I Don't Want To live This Life," "This City of Vice" cause me physical pain, a folding behind my throat and ribs. The intrusion of Marian's death has rewritten them.

In writing these stories, I hope I haven't stirred her ashes. That I haven't rifled her memory. Yet it's a thing I couldn't not do, because of how she has re-written me.

"Winter Requiem"

This was my first fiction sale, solicited by Janet Berliner for an anthology themed around unicorns and immortality. I bled it out during one of the worst times of my life. My best friend, Lee Marshal, was dying of AIDS. Family members were being sliced, sutured, gutted like fish on operating tables. Someone I loved teetered on the verge of madness and suicide, while her supposed "best friend" couldn't be bothered to hear her pain, 'cuz she was…like…being such a *downer*, y'know? I tried to get from Oakland to where Lee was on his deathbed in Buffalo by cashing in all my frequent flyer miles, but a fuck up at the airline delayed my departure a few days, and Lee died while I was in the air, just hours from landing. There were more deaths, more illnesses, not to mention the loving company of my dear old friend emotional cruelty, to the point that acquaintances stopped me on the street to ask if I was OK. All during this, Janet guided me through rewrites and went to bat with the powers that be to keep me in the anthology. I'll always be indebted to her for that.

This version is not the one that finally appeared in the anthology. It's the penultimate, longer draft that was serialized by Seth Lindberg on Gothic.Net a few years after the anthology came out to coincide with the release of the paperback edition of my first book, *Dawn Song*. "Winter Requiem" has the same backdrop of "The War in Hell" as *Dawn Song*, and in this version there's more of that background on display.

"Shibboleth"

A lot of this is taken from my reading of history, especially about 14th century Europe. One of the main inspirations was Hans Koningsberger's *A Walk With Love and Death*, about a poor student and his noble girlfriend wandering the smoldering shit-heap of France in 1358, during the *Jacquerie* uprising. I'm not convinced those swell gems from 1358, epidemic, class warfare, starvation, aren't milling offstage, waiting for their cue to visit us again. I feel the need to say up front that this isn't a joke, seeing as my hometown of Buffalo is so often the brunt of jokes, but…watching a major city contract, wither and fall to ruin is humbling. There was a point in the Dark Ages when Rome shrank back to the 7 villages atop the 7 Hills it had been originally, and when I read about that, I thought of how when I was kid, older kids would go to the abandoned train station downtown to make out. When what had been the hub of transport for a major industrial center gets used as a lover's lane, it makes you think about the future *and* the past, and what kind of Shibboleth we'll have to speak to slip past those cruel and monolithic sentries.

Acknowledgements

I'd like to thank my wife Nancy for the gift of her love. The late William C. Nenno for allowing me to be his son. Dietmar Dath for reminding me there's a point to staying in the game. Devin Grant, Derek Judson and Nancy Santos for the times in the trenches. Gabrielle Faust for being a friend and for the beauty of her artwork. Monica Sullivan and Steve Rubenstein for giving me a break in 1990. Larry Queen for crash pads and talks about art. Brett Savory for edits and Hannah Wolf Bowen for slogging through the slush with me. Cori Crooks and Ed Brubaker for memories of the Oakland years. Kamela Dolinova for wonderful breakfasts and saving me from a really crappy job. Alison Novak for being a loving friend, *Buffy* sing-a-longs and loaning me comic books. Geoffrey H. Goodwin and Nick Mamatas for taking me along to The City of Eternal Darkness, among other things. Lisa Morton for locking horns and throwing down. Larry Creesey for long nights of beer and horror talk. Janna Silverstein for throwing me tethers of hope, now and then. Staci Layne Wilson for junket tips. Rin and the Metal Monday crowd for getting me to sing. Michael Rowe, Nancy Holder and Nancy Kilpatrick for tapping me on the shoulder. Seth Lindberg and Mehitobel Wilson for the 56.6 K baud days. My colleagues at Grub Street and my "Page-Turner" students for helping me remember stuff I forgot I knew.